The Heat of Desire

"Once the fire is lit, the temperature will rise quickly." He glanced at her. "But I don't know if it will rise high enough."

"It will," Gwen said quietly. "I will see to it."

"With magic."

"Aye."

"What will you do?"

"I...I will need to touch ye."

He sent her a slow smile. "I've no objection to that." The heat in his eyes matched that in the furnace. His voice was pitched low. "Where?"

She ignored the fluttering in her stomach. Harder to ignore was the memory of Marcus standing half naked in the woods, of touching him intimately. She placed her hand on his shoulder and felt the muscle leap.

He was remembering, too.

She drew a breath and considered her next step. She had thought long and hard about the spells and methods she would employ to enchant the sword Marcus created. "I...I will send my magic through ye, as ye work the bellows." She took a steadying breath. "Aye. Let us begin."

Other *Love Spell* books by Joy Nash:

IMMORTALS: THE AWAKENING
THE GRAIL KING
CELTIC FIRE

JOY NASH

Deep Magic

LOVE SPELL NEW YORK CITY

To Jim, my one true hero—
there's so much of you in Marcus

LOVE SPELL®

January 2008

Published by

Dorchester Publishing Co., Inc.
200 Madison Avenue
New York, NY 10016

ISBN 10: 0-505-52716-2
ISBN 13: 978-0-505-52716-5

The name "Love Spell" and its logo are trademarks of Dorchester Publishing Co., Inc.

Printed in the United States of America.

10 9 8 7 6 5 4 3 2 1

Visit us on the web at www.dorchesterpub.com.

Deep Magic

Chapter One

AD 132

A wolf could go where a woman could not.

Gwendolyn padded through night-shrouded mountains, her tracks disappearing like whispers of forgotten breath. Newly budded branches, colorless under the spring moon, sighed in her wake. Human thoughts tumbled behind gray lupine eyes. She risked much, venturing this close to the cavern where she'd once been a prisoner of Deep Magic. The heart-wrenching despair of that time clung to her paws like refuse from a dung heap.

The teasing scent of a hare wafted on the thin breeze. Her wolf's heart battered her ribs, urging her to the hunt. Panic flashed. The part of her mind that clung to humanity recoiled. She did not dare sink so far into the wolf's instincts, for fear of not finding her way out again.

Bounding up a rock-scrabbled path, she put temptation behind her. Dawn was not far off. She could not afford any distractions.

Her destination came into view. Lupine ears flattened. Delicate nostrils flared, plucking the odor of man from the mix of scents in the air. It was but a single Legionary, leaning on his spear, but like rats, more of his kind lurked nearby. Torchlight glinted on his armor, a harsh note in the dark melody of wilderness.

The man guarded an encampment the Roman army had recently constructed on a bluff overlooking the swamps surrounding Avalon. Gwen crept as close as she dared to the edge of the camp's encircling ditch. The excavated turf had been piled high and topped with wooden stakes to form a tight palisade around rows of tents. The structure had an air of permanence Gwen did not like.

She'd been watching the camp since the first day the soldiers had arrived, a moon ago. At least thirty men, far too many for comfort. Avalon had fewer than twenty Druids—and that was if one included the children. If soldiers discovered the illegal settlement, retribution would be swift and horrible.

So far, the Romans had not ventured into the swamps. Their days were spent exploring the warren of caves and abandoned mines below their camp. This did not reassure Gwen in the least. The soldiers could only be looking for silver. If they found it—and Gwen knew it was there—they would never leave.

Cyric, of course, had set powerful spells to hide the Druid mine. And Gwen knew her grandfather's Light was more than enough to deter a hundred inquisitive soldiers. But she could not seem to quench the acid panic that ate at her gut whenever she imagined the Romans somehow stumbling past his illusions. She wanted to add a spell of Deep Magic to Cyric's protections. But there was no sense in even suggesting such a thing.

2

Cyric forbade Deep Magic.

The fur on her neck bristled. Still crouching, she hid herself more fully behind an unruly clump of moor grass. A faint, rhythmic vibration shook the ground beneath her paws. A horseman, traveling toward the camp. A moment later, the sentry heard the traveler's approach. He unsheathed his sword and peered up the muddy track.

A huge black warhorse cantered into view. Gwen blinked. Dark light—deep blue eclipsed by fathomless black—surrounded the rider's helmeted head and armored shoulders. But surely, the aura was a trick of the moonlight. She rubbed a paw over her eyes. The light remained, streaming in black sparks along the newcomer's billowing red army cape. Her stomach lurched. She'd encountered magic of that color before. The Dark spell that had trapped her had carried that same blue-black aura.

"Who goes there?"

The man reined in his mount with a negligent motion. "Titus Opimius Strabo. At ease, soldier."

Gwen felt the guard's astonishment. His sword dropped; his spine snapped into a rigid line. "Legate Strabo! We had no advance word of your arrival." He shot a glance down the path in the direction from which Strabo had ridden. "Your escort . . ."

"No escort. I travel alone."

"But sir, is that wise? There could be brigands about. *Brittunculi*—"

Strabo swung from his saddle, his booted feet striking the ground with a thud. He was a tall man, much taller than the sentry. When he spoke, his voice held a knife's edge of menace.

"You doubt my ability to best a barbarian, soldier?"

The smaller man backed up a pace, hastily sheathing his weapon. "No, sir. Of course not. My apologies, sir."

Strabo advanced toward the man. The shimmering aura trailed his movement. Gwen could not tear her eyes from it. Magic was rare among Romans, yet this man's magic surrounded him with a halo of Dark Magic no Druid dedicated to the Light possessed.

Deep Magic, bound by Darkness. A chill chased along her spine. Her tail lowered. Who was this soldier? Why was he here? His aura was strong, and unrestrained by Light. If his Deep Magic pierced Cyric's wards, it would mean disaster for Avalon.

Strabo's gaze swept the camp perimeter, lingering uncannily on Gwen's clump of grass. She went still as death. A Word sprung to mind. A *not-there* spell seeped into the space between them.

He looked away. She exhaled.

"Have you seen movement in the past hour, soldier?"

"Movement? No, sir. The night has been quiet."

Strabo stared out over the swamp to the mist beyond. "I'm in pursuit of a Celt male. A traveling minstrel."

Every muscle in Gwen's body went rigid. *Rhys.*

"He entered the swamp just below this camp. Within sight of your post."

The sentry shifted on his feet. "I saw nothing, sir."

"Difficult to see anything with eyes closed, I'll wager. Ten lashes for your slothfulness, soldier. Inform your centurion in the morning."

"Yes, sir," the man all but choked out.

Strabo eyed the man, frowning. "I'll give you another chance to be useful. Is there a barbarian settlement nearby?"

"No, sir. There's the odd band of brigands, but permanent settlements were cleared from this area decades ago."

"Then where, I ask you, might the minstrel have gone?"

"I'm sure I don't know, sir."

Strabo gave a derisive snort. "Of course you d—"

He stopped abruptly, pivoting, his gaze once again veering to Gwen's clump of moor grass. The night sky was retreating before a pink glow. The dawn wind shifted. Strabo's warhorse, which had been tearing at a clump of mud-spattered turf, lifted its head, nostrils flaring. It tossed its head and pawed the ground.

At Strabo's sharp order, the sentry caught the animal's reins. Strabo himself did not look away from Gwen's hiding place. A heartbeat passed . . . two, three . . .

The Roman's Dark aura deepened. Swirled. Sparked. The display was plain to Gwen's eyes, though the mundane-witted sentry, occupied with soothing Strabo's mount, took no notice.

Deep Magic sought her with tendrils of Darkness. Gwen gathered her Light and bolstered her protection. Her magic was strong, almost as strong as Cyric's. It would hold. It had to.

Look away. There's nothing here.

But Strabo did not look away. He paced to the edge of the camp's encircling ditch, his gaze narrowing dangerously. Gwen shrank back, paws slipping on the mud.

"*Lupus.*"

The sentry's head jerked. "A wolf, sir? Where?"

"There. Behind that clump of grass."

"I don't see it, sir."

"Nevertheless, it is there."

Strabo snatched the sentry's spear, his eyes burning

with a predator's fire Gwen understood only too well. But when the weapon flew, she was already gone.

Gwen's paws scrabbled for purchase on the muddy slope, her heart pummeling her ribs. The startled shout of the sentry scattered into the wind behind her. Strabo had seen through her illusion. He'd trailed Rhys from Isca. Why? Had her brother known he was being followed? Thank the Great Mother he'd disappeared into the mist before this Roman sorcerer caught him.

She bolted deeper into the hills, praying she could reach her secret sanctuary undetected. She circled it once, scouting behind to be sure she'd outrun any pursuit. Slipping under the outcrop of rock and into the narrow crevice, she turned to keep the dawn light in view as her pulse slowed and her wits calmed.

She crouched, silent, her ears slanted forward. *Nothing.* A sniff of the air revealed only the scent of spring. Mud and moss. A young clump of goosefoot.

She nosed to the cave's entrance and peered down the slope into the deserted ravine. The sky was awash with color; the sun would soon break over the ridge. Another slice of panic cut, one that had nothing to do with Roman soldiers. If she were missing from the village at dawn, she would suffer Cyric's disapproval. And Rhys, if he were on Avalon, was surely looking for her. He would not be pleased to find her gone—again. And if he guessed what she'd been doing . . .

Gwen's guilt, never far from the surface, rose. She scuttled backward into the shadow of the cave until her tail struck stone. She wished Ardra were beside her; the she-wolf never failed to calm her. But Ardra had given birth to six mewling cubs just the night before. Gwen's companion wouldn't run in the far hills for some weeks yet.

She drew a centering breath and summoned the Words to mind. Words of Light to chase the Deep Magic of the wolf into the recesses of her consciousness.

The wolf refused to go.

Nauseating terror bled through Gwen's veins. A year had passed since the time she's spent trapped as a wolf, but the effects had not faded. If anything, they'd grown worse. Her mastery of her Deep Magic had slipped dangerously. She could not always control the wolf's emergence, and that was bad enough. But her greater fear was that the time would come when she could no longer banish it.

With desperate effort, she quieted her terror. The Words rang again in her mind, like bells inside her skull. They were sounds in the language of the ancients who had raised the mysterious sacred stones across Britain. Words of Light, taught to her by Cyric. But Cyric did not know of the wolf—the spell she'd crafted to banish it was her own. A chain for the beast's Deep Magic. So far, it had not broken.

After a fierce hesitation, the wolf inside her bowed before the Light. Relief flooded Gwen's veins, even as the change ripped through her body. Her lungs constricted, her guts twisted. Bone, muscle, and sinew burned. With a shudder, she surrendered.

The agony tore at her with wolf's teeth. Clamping her jaws shut, she willed herself not to cry out. There were spells she could use to mute the pain, spells she had crafted for others, but she did not use them for herself. She deserved the pain. She was weak. Too weak. She could not resist the lure of the magic Cyric had forbidden her.

Searing heat spread, melting her bones. Her limbs stretched; her body elongated. Her face contorted, skull and skin shifting. If she could hover above her own body, what would the change look like? Horrible, surely. Evil. A perversion of nature. Anyone watching would surely avert his eyes.

But Marcus Aquila had not.

The thought shone like a beacon in her mind as fur smoothed into skin. Flesh tingled. The worst of the pain passed, lingering only as an uncomfortable vibration in her bones, a dim buzzing in her ears. Gwen lay on the damp earth, panting, too tired even to curl in upon her naked human body.

Marcus Aquila had seen the change, and he had not looked away.

She closed her eyes. The heat blossoming in her cheeks had nothing to do with magic. A man's face appeared in her mind—familiar, because even though she'd only seen him once, he'd lived in her dreams ever since. He was exotic and beautiful, with eyes and hair the color of freshly tilled earth. His golden skin was so unlike the ruddy complexions of the men who lived on Avalon. His clear brow, firm jaw, and straight nose were engraved upon her memory.

Marcus Aquila, a Roman, was—improbably so—her brother's closest friend. When Gwen had been trapped in darkness, Marcus had been the only man Rhys had trusted to help free her. As such, Marcus was the only person apart from her twin brother who knew the secret of the wolf.

But only Marcus had seen her change.

While Rhys had worked feverishly to dismantle their cousin's Dark spell, Marcus had entered the twisted bowels of the cavern. The wolf had wanted to kill him. If Gwen hadn't been wounded, weak to the point of exhaustion, Marcus Aquila would now be dead.

She'd collapsed and he'd scooped her into his arms. His touch, surprisingly, had comforted the wolf. Just when she thought her humanity had completely vanished, Marcus had called her back. He'd watched as she'd reclaimed her woman's body. His woolen shirt had been rough against her bare skin, his breath warm on her temple. Some unfathomable emotion flickered in his eyes. His arms flexed around her, his muscles banding like iron. Vaguely, she remembered emerging from the cave. But afterward . . .

Days later, when she woke from her fevered sleep, Marcus had been gone.

Now, she pushed herself upright, trying to shake off the memories. Like burrs, they clung to her soul. Her chest felt strange, as if the past bound her ribs too tightly for breath. There was no use dwelling on such things, no use allowing her thoughts to drift so often to Marcus Aquila. He was Roman, and had no magic. Gwen was Druid, chosen to be the next Guardian of Avalon. They were as far apart as the earth and the moon.

Woodenly, she groped for her tunic, slipped on her shoes. She lifted her mother's pendant from its niche, and placed it around her neck. The silver was old and powerful, imbued with the protection of the Light. The wolf did not like it. The triple spiral of the Great Mother rested in the center of the pattern. A four-armed circle woven with vines encircled it. Gwen passed her hand over the pendant's face, straining to feel a spark of its Light. She could not. This was the price her treacherous Deep Magic demanded. Her powers were gone; they would not return before sunset.

A basket lay nearby, half-filled with the herbs she'd gathered as an excuse for crossing the swamps. She grasped the handle and eased into the burgeoning daylight. Fortunately, not a soul was in sight. Out of habit, she cast out her senses, searching for hidden dangers. She came up against a wall of deadness before she remembered her power was gone. The sun hadn't yet appeared over the high ridge of hills. Perhaps, if she hurried, she could reach Avalon before Mared awakened. She was in no mood to endure the old healer's scolding.

She hurried downhill, intent on reaching the cove where she'd left her raft. It was cloaked in illusion—she hoped it would not take long to find. In the aftermath of shifting, she was as much at the mercy of her own spells as a stranger.

She skidded down the steep slope to the muddy shore bordering the swamp, searching the bank for nonmagical landmarks. A clump of willows, an oak sapling. The lair of a fox. A large hazel shrub stood between her and the raft's mooring place. As she rounded the newly budded branches, she swallowed a cry of shock.

Strabo stood examining her raft.

He'd removed his helmet. His complexion was swarthy; his black hair was clipped short in the Roman style. Mud spattered his muscular legs, and his boots had sunk into the silt at the edge of the swamp. He was not a young man, but far from softened by age. His body looked as if it were hewn from rock.

With her magic muted, Gwen couldn't see his aura. Often, she could anticipate a person's magical intent by noting subtle changes in the color encircling head and shoulders. To be deprived of this talent now, when she desperately needed it, was like walking with her eyes covered.

She started to ease away. The Roman's head came around sharply, his heavy brows slanting downward as he focused on the hazel shrub. Great Mother, what should she do? Run? Remain motionless and hope that by some miracle she escaped his notice? She couldn't fight him, not without her magic.

Flat, dark eyes locked with hers. His eyes widened slightly. His lips parted, revealing even, white teeth. For several long heartbeats, time was suspended. Then he lifted one hand, with fingers spread. The gesture seemed almost like an entreaty. Or preparation for a spell.

Gwen's wits abruptly returned. She turned and fled, scrabbling up the steep trail with all the desperation of a hunted beast. Deprived of her own magic, her only hope of escape was to reach the shelter of Avalon's mists before Strabo's spell caught her.

Basket thudding against her thigh, she swerved onto the trail that afforded the thickest cover. It skirted the swamp, disappearing into a heavy fog. No ordinary morning mist, but part of the spells of protection Cyric had woven around Avalon. She prayed her grandfather's magic would hold.

The mist closed about her like a mother's arms. She ran until a stabbing pain in her side forced her to draw up short. Another mooring place was just ahead; the Druids maintained several such hidden refuges. If Gwen's luck held, a raft would be waiting. But she couldn't risk leading her pursuer to Avalon.

Dropping into a crouch behind a curtain of willow fronds, she strained her ears for the Roman's footsteps. She let out a long sigh when she heard nothing. Had she eluded him, then, even without magic?

She waited, barely breathing. The birds that had been startled by her passing renewed their morning songs. Even then, she remained motionless a while longer, until she was sure the threat of discovery had passed. Finally, she took a deep breath and rose, murmuring a prayer of thanks to the Great Mother. She made her way through the thick mist to the dock, where two blessed rafts bobbed gently against a mooring post.

"Gwen?"

She shut her eyes and halted, expelling the air from her lungs in one sharp breath. Goddess, not *Trevor*. Not *now*. Not when her magic was gone and her mundane senses overwhelmed.

"Gwen? Is that ye?"

What was Trevor doing on this side of the swamps so early in the morning? Belatedly, Gwen realized her haphazard flight had taken her to the edge of his carefully hidden barley field. One of the rafts was Trevor's; he always kept his craft in this mooring place while he tended Avalon's crop.

His firm footsteps came up behind her. Constructing a smile on her lips, she turned, her fingers clutching the handle of her basket far tighter than necessary. Trevor was a large man, tall and thick with muscle. Rhys had encountered him on the far northern isles of Caledonia last summer, and had brought him to Avalon at the first frost. Eleri and Siane called him handsome, and even Dera, who was handfasted with Howell and should not notice such things, smiled widely when Trevor came near. Gwen supposed the man *was* striking. His eyes were a piercing blue. His waist-length blond hair was bound so tightly in its queue she wondered if his scalp ached. His beard and moustache were braided in the northern style, and he wore a silver torc at his neck, the adornment of a chieftain or king. But he spoke so little, as if words were jewels and he a poor man.

"I sought ye afore dawn." Trevor's northern burr held

no hint of anger. But then, of course, it wouldn't. Trevor never lost his temper. Never.

"Did ye?"

"Ye were gone."

"I left early to search for bindweed. 'Tis more potent, ye know, if gathered under the moon, with the flowers open."

"Ye shouldna be here alone."

"Ye are alone," Gwen observed.

Trevor sighed, rubbed the back of his neck, then seemed at a loss as to where to place his hand. Finally, he anchored it on his hip. The pose gave him the look of a disapproving husband. Gwen's irritation grew, though she knew he'd done nothing to provoke it.

"Cyric forbade your wanderings," he said at last.

"Cyric need not know."

"Ah, Gwen."

The two words communicated a wealth of frustration and reproach. Sudden guilt swamped her. She *had* promised Cyric she would stay on the isle. It was a promise that had proven impossible to keep. She could not risk shifting into wolf form in the middle of the village common!

"I . . . I had trouble sleeping." That, at least, was not a lie. Since her captivity, she'd not slept through a single night.

"Ye could finish Eleri's pendant. Rhys brought her to us two moons past."

"I cannot do that at night. It would disturb the village."

" 'Tis dangerous, Gwen, wandering outside the mist. What if ye cross paths with a soldier from the Roman camp?"

Trevor had no idea his fear had already come to pass. She didn't wish him to guess, so she forced a laugh. "The

Romans bundle themselves tight in their camp after dark. Their sentries are blinded by their own torches."

Trevor laid a hand on Gwen's arm. The unwelcome touch jolted her to the core. "Your safety is important to Avalon. After we are handfasted and the babes come, this need to roam will pass."

Gwen forced a swallow down a throat suddenly thick with dismay. Trevor might be dull, but he was a good man, loyal and steady. His magic was of the earth, pure and strong. Under his influence, living things thrived—plants, animals, children. She should be glad he wanted her as his wife.

Cyric had asked for the union. And in truth, Gwen liked Trevor. Or at least she had before Cyric announced his wish they should handfast. She knew little about Trevor's past in the northland, for he did not speak of it, and Rhys would not elaborate. She suspected he'd endured much, for his eyes held shadows. But he was not ruled by them. Unlike Gwen, Trevor had banished his demons. His hand on her arm grew unbearably heavy.

"Do not fear for me." Her tone was deliberately willful. A man like Trevor did not want a willful wife. "I go where I will. No plodding Roman will catch me, I assure ye."

She'd thought to annoy him with her defiance; her words summoned an opposite effect. His blue eyes darkened; he leaned close, his palm traveling up her arm to her shoulder. "Ye dinna need to be so strong, lass. Nay with me."

Sincere affection thickened his accent. For a brief moment, Gwen imagined coupling with him. She'd never lain with a man, but she knew enough of the way between a man and a woman to picture the deed. He would be gentle.

Marcus Aquila would not be gentle.

Great Mother, where had *that* thought come from?

Trevor's fingertip drew circles on Gwen's nape. Her stomach turned to cold lead. Even so, she might have forced herself to smile up at him, if not for her secret. Trevor knew nothing of the wolf; if he did, he would not want her.

"Gwen, I know ye dinna feel for me as I do for ye, but . . ."

She shifted her basket to her other arm, dislodging Trevor's hand without seeming—she hoped—too blunt about it. She made a show of squinting at the dawn.

"The sun rises swiftly. Mared will worry when she wakes and I am not there."

Trevor sighed and stepped back. "I'll take ye home, then."

"Nay. Finish your work in the field. I do not need ye."

" 'Tis my duty to protect ye."

"Nay, Trevor, 'tis not. I—"

"Cyric wants us to wed."

Gwen bit her lower lip. "Aye, I know that well enough. But Trevor . . . do ye not want a marriage born of love?"

"I *do* love ye."

It wasn't what she'd meant, and Trevor knew it. The man might not be garrulous, but he was no fool.

"I would not make ye happy," she said gently.

"Let me be judge of that." When she didn't reply, he plowed on. "Cyric grows frail. I know the duty of taking on the role of Guardian when he passes weighs heavily on your spirit. I would help ye with that burden if ye would but let me."

"Trevor, can ye nay see that—"

The screech of a merlin interrupted her words. The bird flew low out of the mist, narrowly missing Trevor's head.

A genuine smile sprang to Gwen's lips. "Hefin!"

She extended her arm; the merlin alighted. The bird ruffled its wings and cocked its head, blinking. Hefin was Rhys's companion, as Ardra was Gwen's. Her twin could not be far.

"Is my brother in the village?" Gwen asked Trevor.

"Aye, he arrived before dawn," Trevor said, clearly not pleased to have Gwen's attention turn from talk of handfasting. "He wasna happy to find ye gone."

"I imagine he was not." Gwen sighed and turned her attention back to Hefin. The bird was one of the few animals, other than Ardra, that did not cower in fear of the wolf. The small falcon shared a magical bond with Gwen's twin, but with her magic dimmed, she couldn't feel it.

Gwen looked at Trevor. "I would seek my brother alone. Would ye excuse me?"

Trevor's disappointment was clear, but Gwen knew he lacked the self-conceit for protest. She felt his gaze on her as she climbed aboard one of the rafts. Hefin took wing when she lifted the long pole laid crosswise atop the craft.

Trevor's outline faded as the mist closed about her. She felt a twinge of guilt at treating him so poorly, but her regret was small compared to her relief at leaving him behind. She inhaled, filling her lungs deeply with damp, fragrant air. Thank the Great Mother, she was free of the man, if only for a while.

It was hard to breathe in the face of such unfaltering decency.

Chapter Two

"Marcus, why *do* you stare so at that wolf?"

Marcus Ulpius Aquila started at his half sister's exclamation. The silver wolf figurine slipped though his fingers and fell to the scarred surface of his worktable with a thud.

He swung his head toward the door with a scowl. He hadn't even heard her enter the smithy. "By Pollux, Bree. Must you sneak about so? You're disturbing my work."

Breena snorted and tossed her head. She'd made a valiant attempt to tame her wild russet locks, but the ladylike coils she'd pinned at her nape were already beginning to unravel. Marcus couldn't suppress a chuckle. Having passed her fourteenth year, his little sister thought she was a woman.

"You're hardly working. The furnace is cold."

Marching past him, she peered around the wooden screen that shielded a rumpled bed from the rest of the room. It was the only soft place in a building constructed of stone, slate, and heavy timber. "You slept here again last night, didn't you? You *know* Mother hates it when you don't sleep in the main house. And she's so fretful about everything these days."

That was certainly true. His stepmother was with child, more than halfway through her term. The pregnancy had been a shock, both because of Rhiannon's age—forty—and the fact that she hadn't carried babes easily, even when young. Breena had been the only child she'd managed to carry to birth, a month too soon, at that. Three other babes had not survived past their quickening.

"I wasn't sleeping." At least, not more than an hour or two. Whenever he closed his eyes, he saw the wolf. "I was drawing. I didn't want to disturb the household by coming to bed."

Breena eyed the fallen figurine. "What is it about this wolf, Marcus? Every time I come out here, you have it in your hand."

"It's nothing," Marcus mumbled, scooping up the wolf and setting it on the shelf with its companions. Making animal figurines out of scraps of silver, iron, and bronze left over from more functional items was a hobby of sorts, begun when Breena was young and Marcus was just discovering his passion for working metal. He'd made most of the figures for her.

Except for the wolf. He'd fashioned that piece last spring, upon his return from Avalon.

"What are you doing here, anyway?" The words came out sharper than he'd intended. His habitual good humor was in short supply this morning.

But Breena had never been one to take quick offense. Her smile was suspiciously sly as she held up a covered redware bowl he had not noticed earlier. "I brought you this."

He eyed the offering with grave mistrust. He'd heard

the gate bell ring, but hadn't thought much of it at the time. "*Please* do not tell me that's another of Lavina's cream puddings."

Breena set the bowl on his worktable. "Aye, brother, it is. With honeyed figs this time." She gazed at Marcus thoughtfully. "Do you think perhaps she wants a portly husband?"

Marcus swore under his breath. "Is she still here? Is Mother demanding I greet her?" Rhiannon never allowed him the luxury of avoiding a female visitor.

"Luckily for you, Father took Mother to town to visit Morwenna and her new babe. They were gone when Lavina arrived. I told her you'd gone to town as well, but I'm not sure she believed me—she gave a *very* hard look across the yard to the forge. If there'd been smoke curling over the roof, she would have marched out here to investigate."

Marcus rose abruptly. "Why can't the woman understand I don't wish to marry her?"

"Perhaps because you haven't told her?" Breena suggested with characteristic sarcasm. "Really, Marcus, even I had begun to think you were considering the idea. You're never anything other than friendly to her."

"What else am I to be? Rude? It's not as if I dislike her. It's just that I don't wish to marry her. She looks at me as though I were her next meal."

Breena burst out laughing. "Oh, come now, Marcus, don't pretend to be the shy virgin lad. You know what to do with a woman." Her tone turned a shade darker. "You and Rhys certainly spend enough time at that broth—"

"Stop," Marcus interrupted, holding up a hand, as if such a gesture could halt one of Breena's tirades. "Stop talking now, Bree. I will *not* discuss brothels with you."

He frowned. "In any case, one has nothing to do with the other. Brothels are entertainment; marriage is . . . not. Getting married would change my life."

"For the better, in my opinion. Ever since Clara chose Owein over you, you've barely glanced at a respectable woman."

Marcus was silent. True, Clara Sempronia had declined his offer of marriage in favor of a Druid hand-fasting with Rhiannon's younger brother, Owein. Breena had latched onto the idea that Marcus was still brooding over the rejection, and Marcus hadn't denied it. But the truth was, he hardly thought of Clara these days. An entirely different woman filled his mind.

He turned away. "I'm not interested in marrying. At least," he amended, "not right now."

"Lavina is pretty, and kind, and intelligent. You could do far worse." She stuck a finger in the bowl and brought a dollop of cream to her lips. "And you must admit, she makes a lovely pudding."

"Once she realizes I'm not going to marry her, she's liable to leave out the figs in favor of belladonna," Marcus grumbled.

Breena laughed and pushed the bowl toward him. Marcus ignored it. He watched as his sister crouched to retrieve several balled-up sheets of papyrus he'd thrown on the floor.

"Leave those," Marcus told her.

She only shook her head as she gathered the trash and pitched it into a barrel he'd reserved for that purpose. "Really, Marcus, the pig barn is neater. How can you think while surrounded by such clutter?"

"I *like* clutter. Neatness stifles my imagination."

"I suppose you must be right, since you seem to thrive amidst chaos."

"Just as you thrive in Father's library."

She crawled under the worktable for another crumpled drawing. When she resurfaced, Marcus snatched it out of her hand and tossed it in the air. Breena jumped to catch it, but missed. The wad landed on the ground and bounced under the worktable, coming to rest very close to its original position.

"See? That drawing knows where it belongs, even if you don't."

Breena laughed then, and he laughed with her. The vast difference in their preferences for neatness was a long-running joke between them.

Still smiling, she settled herself on Marcus's stool and smoothed her skirt over her knees. Pulling an uncrumpled sheet of papyrus across the table, she bent her head to examine it.

Marcus gave a sigh of mock exasperation. "Don't you have work to do?"

"Of course. We live on a farm. I always have work to do."

"Then go do it."

"In time, brother, in time." Leaning close, she peered at the drawing of a sword and its accompanying notations. "What's this? A new commission?"

"No."

"Then what?"

Marcus shrugged. "It's just an idea."

Breena's eyes lit up. She loved his "ideas."

"Tell me," she demanded in the imperious tone she'd perfected when she was five years old.

He chuckled. "It's a new type of sword, Bug."

She shot him a dark look but didn't comment on his use of her childhood nickname. "But it's so oddly proportioned! The blade is too long."

"It's not a *gladius*. Or a Celt sword."

She looked up, interest kindling in her eyes. "Then what, exactly, is it?"

"A new design. My own." Her enthusiasm sparked his. He reached for a second and third sketch and arranged them on either side of the first. "This is a *gladius,*" he said, pointing to the drawing on the left. "It's short, light, and easily maneuvered. The Celts prefer a longer blade." He tapped the drawing on the right. "But with length comes increased weight, making the weapon harder to control."

"But your new sword is even longer!"

"Yes, but it's thinner as well. That will make it easier to handle. It will have the reach of a Celt sword, but weigh no more than a Roman sword."

Breena's brow furrowed as she compared the three designs. Marcus watched her with true affection. His half sister was no typical girl. Her interests were not anything one might describe as womanly. She could read and write both Latin and Greek. When she wanted entertainment, she did not shop for imported silks and shoes. She studied Aristotle and Euclid.

"It won't work," she declared after a moment. "The slender blade won't be able to counter the strike of a heavier blade. It will break."

Trust Breena to focus on the heart of the matter. "It won't," he told her. "Not if I succeed in smelting bright iron."

Breena's blue eyes fixed on him. "Bright iron? I've never heard of it."

"It's the latest talk at the blacksmith's *collegio.* A very hot furnace produces a stronger, brighter iron. The new metal is properly named *chalybs,* after an iron-working tribe in Anatolia."

"If this *chalybs* is so wonderful, why aren't all swords made of it?"

"It's extremely difficult to smelt. The heat that's needed is incredible, and must be sustained for hours."

"Ah," Breena said, reaching for yet another drawing. "Now I understand what this is."

She smoothed the wrinkled page, which bore a diagram of a furnace. She squinted, trying to read the notations Marcus had scrawled in heavy, messy letters.

"Will building a deep furnace chamber within the existing chamber and increasing airflow truly produce enough heat for your purpose?"

Marcus grimaced. "I'm not entirely sure. A higher quality of charcoal will also help, I expect. I mean to explore all possibilities."

Breena grinned, showing the gap between her front teeth. "You'll do it, Marcus. I cannot remember one of your designs that didn't come to life." Her gaze drifted to the shelf above the worktable. "But that silver wolf you're always playing with is more alive than anything you've ever made. Look at its face! It almost seems human."

Marcus closed his eyes, his throat suddenly tight. The wolf *was* human. Memories, more than a year old but still as vivid as yesterday, flashed behind his eyelids. He was back in the dank, dripping cave, the dying light of his torch illuminating feral gray eyes.

The she-wolf snarled and leapt. But weak as it was, the attack fell short. The animal collapsed at Marcus's feet. Battling every sane instinct he possessed, he bent and gathered it in his arms. The beast shuddered, sending vibrations up his arms. And then it began to change . . .

Until the wolf's fur smoothed into a woman's damp

and feverish skin, Marcus hadn't fully grasped the depth of the magic he held in his arms. Rhys called it Deep Magic. It was the raw power of the gods, a primal force that existed independently of any human notion of good and evil, Light and Darkness. It was a primitive and dangerous force. Unpredictable. So much so that Cyric, Rhys's grandfather, had forbidden the Druids of Avalon from calling it.

Deep Magic. The refuge of the truly desperate, and the truly depraved.

Which was Gwendolyn?

The transformation he'd witnessed had been a perversion of nature. Why, then, had it aroused him so? What did it imply about his character that now, more than a year later, he still woke in the dead of night with his cock stiff and his stones aching for . . . *her*. For her magic.

". . . do you think, Marcus?"

With a start, he realized he'd completely missed whatever question Breena had asked. "What?"

She gave a huff of exasperation. "See what I mean? You were gone again. Whenever you look at that wolf—"

"I'm listening now."

She glanced at him and frowned, then looked away. Her earlier good humor had fled. Marcus's attention was drawn to the circles under her eyes, more visible now that she was silent. Her freckles stood out starkly against too-pale skin. She hadn't been sleeping. His heart sank. With Breena, that meant only one thing.

Her hand crept to her throat, fingering the silver pendant that hung there. It was a Druid charm, one that Rhys had given her. Marcus knew Gwendolyn had made it.

"I need to talk to you about Avalon," she said.

"Breena, no. We've talked about it enough already."

"But . . . Rhys says I must go. And I would go, if not for the babe . . ."

"Mother needs you here."

"I know. I would not leave her, not now."

"Even afterward," Marcus said. "Avalon is no place for you."

"But Rhys said—"

"It's a primitive place, Bree. Do you really want to live in a hut of mud and straw? With nothing but a meager peat fire and a dirt floor? There will be no plaster, no tiles, no soft beds. No wine, no wheat bread. You can forget hot baths." He paused, catching her gaze fully. "And if all that isn't enough, consider this: no *library*."

He felt a grim satisfaction when this last pronouncement caused Breena to wince. Truly, he couldn't imagine his sister without her nose in a scroll or codex.

"And another thing," he continued ruthlessly, "the settlement on Avalon is illegal. *Druidry* is illegal. What if the Second Legion were to discover the existence of a secret clan of Druids? Every man, woman, and child would be put to the sword."

"That will never happen. Rhys says Cyric has hidden the isle within magical mists."

"Yet another reason to stay away. Who knows what dangerous spells the Druids have conjured?"

"None!" Breena stood so abruptly her stool tipped over and clattered to the stone floor before Marcus could catch it. "Rhys says the Druids of Avalon practice only the Light!"

Marcus retrieved the stool and set it upright with a deliberate thud. "Except that a little more than a year ago, Rhys's own cousin called up the darkest form of Deep Magic, and nearly killed Clara and Owein. And

Rhys himself"—Marcus flattened his hand on top of the stool—"Rhys is no stranger to Deep Magic. You know that as well as I do."

"But that was only one time! Rhys said—"

"Enough," Marcus ground out. "I am sick to death of hearing what Rhys said."

Breena stared at him, stricken.

"I'm sorry," he said gruffly, shame flooding through him. "I shouldn't lose my temper. Not with you, at any rate."

A moment passed before his sister responded. When she did, her voice was quiet, but calm. "Rhys is your closest friend, Marcus." She paused. "And I . . . I care for him."

"Jupiter's throne, Bree! The man is nearly twice your age. He thinks of you as a sister—nothing more. Don't shame yourself by chasing him to Avalon."

Breena flushed bright red, but her voice remained steady. "I'll not be chasing Rhys if I go to Avalon. He's hardly ever there, anyway."

"Then why go? There's nothing for you there but danger."

She walked to the furnace and stared at the cold coals. The sense he'd done something wrong niggled at the back of Marcus's mind. He pushed it away. He wanted only happiness for Breena. He was sure she would not be happy on Avalon.

"I . . . may not have any choice but to go, Marcus."

He swore softly. Breena had the Sight, as did her uncle, Owein. But it had been half a year since a vision of the future had come to her. Marcus had hoped the curse had deserted her. "The dreams have returned, haven't they?"

"One dream. I started having it again about a month ago."

"A *month?* And you didn't tell anyone?"

"It doesn't come every night. But when it does . . ." She gripped her pendant so tightly, he thought the chain might break.

Anguish dimmed her bright eyes. Marcus drew her into a firm hug, one arm encircling her shoulders. But Breena did not turn and cling to him, trembling, the way she had when she was small and suffering some hurt. She stiffened and twisted her fingers together.

Marcus sighed. His Bug was nearly a woman now. She eased out of his embrace and he let her go.

He did not ask her what she'd Seen in her dream. He knew she wouldn't tell him. But whatever it was, it upset her deeply.

"You haven't told Mother?"

"No! The babe . . ."

"Of course, you're right. It would distress her greatly." He paused. "Is the pain very bad?"

"The worst it's ever been. My skull feels as though it will split in two. I . . . I prepared a draught of valerian and willow bark. It helped. But Marcus, I can't bear it much longer. Not alone." She paused. "I told Rhys when he was here."

Marcus tensed. Rhys had left just a few days earlier. He'd said nothing to Marcus about Breena's visions. But then, he wouldn't. "What did he tell you?"

"He wanted to take me with him to Avalon. He told me his sister has crafted a spell that's helped Owein ease the pain of his visions. She could help me, too, he thought. But . . . I told him I couldn't leave Mother. Not until the babe comes."

Marcus made an effort to keep his voice steady. "Breena, listen to me. There must be some other way. Some other remedy than traveling into the wild to live with Druids."

A tear traced a path down her cheek. "Why do you hate Avalon so? It must be more than the magic. Mother casts healing spells often enough."

"Mother's magic is herbcraft. Any Roman or Greek physician might employ it. Druid magic is far more dangerous. It's a power best avoided."

"You only say that because of our uncle. The one who died before I was born."

"Father's brother was murdered by a Druid, his soul imprisoned by a dark spell. Father nearly met the same fate." And Marcus, ten years old and cowering in the mud, had watched Lucius battle for his life. The events of that night had haunted him for years afterward.

"The Druids of Avalon are not like that," Breena said. "They practice only the Light."

"You're exceedingly naive if you believe such a thing. Where power is possible, someone always seeks it out."

"But you must trust Rhys! He's your best friend."

"Friend or no, Rhys hid his powers from me for years. Would he have done that if he were completely innocent?"

"He had no choice! He knows how much you distrust magic."

"That's no excuse for his deception."

"Perhaps not," Breena allowed. "But I know he regrets not taking you into his confidence sooner."

"It wouldn't have changed my mistrust of magic. Forget Avalon, Bree. Please."

"Sometimes I wish I could," she said, her voice betraying a tremor. "But Marcus, you don't understand. These visions—if they get any worse, they'll break me to pieces. If there's a chance Gwendolyn can help me, I have to go to her."

A wolf's eyes flashed in Marcus's mind. *Gwendolyn.* What kind of aid would such a woman offer his innocent sister?

"What is she like?" Breena asked.

Marcus blinked away his thoughts. "What? Who?"

Breena exhaled. "Gwendolyn. Were we not just talking of her?"

"Oh. Yes. We were." He groped for something to tell her. He'd never spoken to Breena, or to anyone else, of the wolf. "I have no idea what she's like."

"Marcus, how can you say that? You saved her life!"

"I say it very easily. She was unconscious. I left Avalon before she woke."

"She's fair-haired, like Rhys, isn't she?"

Marcus sighed. "Yes. They look very much alike."

"She's his twin." Breena was silent for a moment; then her eyes widened. "Do you think she can shift, like—"

"By Pollux, Bree!" Marcus's palm slapped the worktable, nearly upsetting the cream pudding. "*This* is why you need to stay away from Avalon. Deep Magic is far too tempting. Even Rhys succumbed to it. By Jupiter, the man was a *merlin!* A bird! He flew over our heads."

"But afterward—"

"Yes, *afterward,* Rhys admitted he should not have gone against his grandfather's teachings. *Afterward,* he vowed never again to call the Deep Magic. But will he be able to keep his word? I highly doubt it."

Breena crossed her arms over her chest. "Surely Rhys's actions were not so evil. He had to reach Clara quickly, or people would have died! The good he achieved justified his action."

"That's precisely the kind of logic that can get you killed."

Breena threw up her hands. "By the Great Mother, Marcus, there's no reasoning with you." Her gaze lit on the redware bowl. "Fine thanks I get for sending Lavina away. Next time she comes around with a pudding, I'll escort her to your door!"

She whirled about and stomped out of the smithy. Marcus winced as the door slammed. That was Breena—generally even tempered, but capable of erupting when pushed too far. Marcus should know— he shared the same traits. With a worried sigh, he turned back to his worktable. Something had to be done about Breena's visions, especially if they were getting worse.

But what? Last summer, Rhiannon brewed potion after potion, but nothing had helped the pain that accompanied Breena's Sight. The family had breathed a sigh of relief when, three months later, the nightmares abruptly ceased. Now they were back.

Rhys insisted Avalon was the only solution. The sacred isle, he claimed, would temper Breena's gift. But Rhys had made no mention to Marcus about Gwen's spells. The only information that Rhys had imparted about his twin on this visit was that she was soon to be handfasted to a Druid Rhys had brought from Caledonia last summer. The revelation had churned in Marcus's gut like rancid meat.

And yet, he couldn't help gazing at the silver wolf. He reached for it again, balancing the figurine on his palm. The beast's eyes challenged him. He stroked the silver fur, lust coiling and uncoiling in his belly. The sharp, sweet arousal cut like a finely honed blade.

What was Gwendolyn like? Marcus did not know. And likely, he never would.

Chapter Three

Gwen found Rhys on the shore near Avalon's dock. Hefin was already perched on a branch overhead. Gwen thrust her pole through the murky water and pushed her raft closer to shore, thinking her twin did not appear the least bit angry with her. Yet.

He stood with one shoulder propped against the trunk of a great oak, watching her approach. His rangy body exuded a careless grace. His white-blond hair was clipped short, and his beard was no more than three days' worth of stubble. Both features were oddities among Celtic men. For the first time, it occurred to Gwen to wonder if Rhys actually preferred shorn locks and a bare chin, or whether he'd adopted Roman grooming customs in an effort to move more easily in that world. It bothered her that she did not know.

Their eyes met briefly as her raft touched shore. A sense of joy at his homecoming flooded her. She always felt more complete when Rhys was home. They'd shared a mother's womb, had entered the world together. Rhys had been first. Gwen had emerged gripping his heel.

Looking into Rhys's gray eyes was like gazing at her own in a clear pool of water. They were very similar physically—male and female images of the same person. Their hair was unusually fair, and they were both slender and tall, though it had been years since Gwen had been able to claim superiority in the latter trait. Aye, on the surface, she and Rhys were much alike.

Inside, another tale unfolded. Inside, Rhys was so much *more* than Gwen. More loyal, more thoughtful, more truthful. Rhys did not disobey Cyric's commands— even the ones he did not agree with. He accepted his duty with grace and humility.

Gwen did not.

To be fair, Cyric's orders had been no easier on Rhys than they had been on Gwen, though it had taken Gwen years to realize it. Why had their grandfather seen fit to assign his grandchildren tasks that went against their natures? Rhys, who would have thrived on Avalon, had been ordered to travel in the outer world, seeking Celts touched by magic—children, especially, for their Light was not yet polluted by Darkness. Gwen, who longed to roam, was told her duty lay on the sacred isle, teaching the initiates Rhys brought home.

For many years, their differing paths had torn a deep rift between them. Through their adolescent years, they'd barely spoken. But last winter, when Cyric had been struck down by a Dark spell, and all of Avalon believed Gwen guilty, Rhys alone had believed in her innocence. He and Marcus Aquila had saved her life. And learned her secret.

Rhys met Gwen at the dock, taking her pole as she looped the raft's rope around the mooring post.

"Well met, sister."

She smiled. "Well met, Rhys."

He grinned down at her, pulling her into a brief embrace. "It's good to be home."

"It's good to have ye here." She settled her basket on her arm. "Ye've come from Isca?"

His brows arched. "Are ye a Seer now as well as a spellcrafter?"

"Nay." She gnawed her bottom lip, wondering how to broach the subject of the Roman officer who had trailed him from the fortress city. She did not want to announce the fact she'd been snooping about the Roman camp. Rhys would be livid, especially if he realized she'd done her spying as a wolf. She was loath to lose the good feelings between them so quickly.

She cast about for a safer topic. "Did ye . . . did ye stay at the Aquila farm?" *Perhaps not so safe, after all.*

"Aye. I sought Lucius Aquila's permission to bring his daughter to Avalon."

"Is he still unwilling?"

"Nay. But Rhiannon is with child, halfway through her term, and Breena will not leave until her mother is delivered safely." He made a gesture of frustration. "Breena should have come to Avalon last year. Her magic is far too powerful to be left untrained."

"She is young yet, nay? No doubt her parents do not want to part with her so soon."

"She's no younger than I was when Cyric sent me away. Her visions cause her to suffer greatly. The dreams had ceased for a time, but now they have returned, though she would not tell me much. But they are more troubling, I think, than before. She needs your help, Gwen. She needs to be here."

An uneasy note had crept into his voice. Any discussion concerning Breena seemed to strike a raw chord within Rhys. But the lass was so young! Gwen's curiosity burned, but her brother's eyes had already shuttered, and she knew she would not succeed in prying any more information from him. At least not about Breena. But about Breena's half brother . . .

She affected a casual tone. "How does Marcus Aquila fare?"

Rhys shot her an inscrutable look. For a moment, she thought he wouldn't answer. "Marcus is well," he said at last.

"His work prospers?"

"Aye, I think so. His skill as a bladesmith is well known in Isca. His swords and daggers are as beautiful as they are well crafted." He gave a small shake of his head. "But I do not know if Marcus will achieve his latest goal. He means to smelt a metal he calls bright iron."

"And ye think he will not succeed? Why? What is this bright iron?" Gwen worked only in silver, a softer and more delicate metal than iron. She knew little of blacksmithing.

" 'Tis a rare, shining metal, born of the hottest furnace. 'Tis very difficult to smelt. Few smiths can smelt enough to make up an entire blade. But Marcus swears he will do it."

"Then perhaps he will," Gwen murmured. She paused. A moment later, goaded by some urge she did not want to examine too closely, she asked. "Does he remain unmarried?"

"Aye, he does."

A fierce elation tightened her chest. The emotion must have shown on her face, because Rhys's gaze narrowed on her. "Why do ye ask, Gwen?"

She did not dare look at him. "He is your friend."

"He'll never return to Avalon."

"I know that." She studied the weave of her basket. "I only wish I might have given him my thanks last year . . . when . . ."

"Gwen. Look at me."

She did, reluctantly, lamenting the fact that Rhys was so much taller than she.

"Marcus helped save your life. That's a debt that can never be repaid, but it's *my* debt, Gwen. Not yours. Put him out of your mind. Completely."

She felt an urge to cry, which was absurd. "That seems callous."

"'Tis not. Marcus is Roman. He distrusts magic. A Druid spell killed his uncle and nearly destroyed his father. Then I wronged him by keeping my own powers secret. Our friendship has suffered because of it." He paced a few steps away, then turned back to face her. "Marcus does not trust Cyric's purpose and vision for the sacred isle. He would prefer the Druids of Avalon disband."

"Are ye saying Marcus Aquila would betray Avalon to the Second Legion? I cannot believe it!"

"Nay, not that. But Marcus does not believe the Druids of Avalon can practice Light without turning to Deep Magic."

Gwen drew a breath. "Have ye ever considered, Rhys, that he may be right?"

There was a brief, deafening silence in which Rhys went very still. His gaze sharpened. "What do ye mean by that?"

Gwen swallowed, but didn't answer.

Rhys stepped closer and pitched his voice low, though there was no one nearby to hear. "Ye've called the wolf. Again."

The quiet statement vibrated with frustration. She searched his eyes, but for what, she wasn't certain. She'd long suspected Rhys had the same talent that she did—she had even suggested as much to him, more than once. But even if Rhys *were* able to take animal form, he wouldn't dare go against Cyric's orders to shun Deep Magic. Her dutiful brother practiced only the Light.

The elation Gwen had felt at Rhys's arrival evaporated. She sighed. It was always like this. Rhys returned home after one of his long absences and Gwen greeted him joyfully, his familiar presence reminding her they were two halves of one whole. Then, invariably, she remembered which of them was the better half.

"Tell me truly, Gwen. Did ye call the wolf while I was gone?"

She bit her lip hard enough to draw blood. "Promise ye'll not tell Cyric."

"Ah, Gwen . . ."

" 'Tis nay my fault! I cannot always control when and where the wolf will appear."

"I wonder if ye try to control it at all."

The accusation was like a fist to her gut. "Ye only say that because ye have no idea what it is like."

A shadow passed over Rhys's expression. His gaze dropped. For a long moment he was silent, the corners of his mouth turned down. Deciding what he would tell Cyric, no doubt.

Gwen's stomach churned. He could not tell their grandfather about the wolf! He could *not*. And yet, if

Rhys decided that he must, there would be nothing she could do to stop him.

When he looked back at her at last, she nearly sagged with relief. There was no anger, no censure, in his eyes at all.

"I understand your struggle," he said quietly. "Deep Magic seduces. But Gwen, ye must find a way to resist it! Ye know Cyric's teaching. The more often ye call the Deep Magic, the stronger its hold on ye. Soon there will be no controlling it at all."

"I'm well aware of that." *More than ye know.*

Rhys's expression was pained. "The past year has been difficult for ye, ever since . . ." He trailed off, not wanting to speak of her time in the cave any more than she wanted to hear of it. "Gwen, have ye ever considered that perhaps it does not have to be so hard? That ye need not face what happened alone? A husband—"

"Rhys—"

"Nay," he said, halting her protest with a raised hand. "Hear me out. Trevor is a good man. Loyal and strong in the Light. And he . . . has endured his own pain. Ye could confide in him about the wolf. About the time ye spent trapped by Blodwen's spell . . ."

Gwen met Rhys's eyes, then looked away. The pity there was more than she could bear.

He touched her shoulder. "I'm sorry I did not find ye sooner. If I had, ye might not be so unhappy now."

"How could ye have known what was happening? Ye spend so little time on Avalon."

"I . . . I wish it were otherwise."

Gwen knew that was as much of an admission of dissatisfaction with Cyric's commands as Rhys was ever likely to admit. A sigh escaped her lips. Did he have to be so . . . accepting? So *good?* She resisted an urge to fling her basket into the swamp.

"Why has Cyric required this of us, Rhys? Why did he choose me as the next Guardian when 'tis clear ye are the better choice?"

"I do not believe that. Cyric chose rightly. Your power has always been greater than mine. Once the effect of Blodwen's Dark spell recedes fully, ye will see the truth of that."

"And what if the Darkness never fades? What then?"

"Cyric says . . ."

"Cyric does not know about the wolf! What would our grandfather say if he knew there were times when I would rather rip the hair from my scalp—nay, the flesh from my bones!—rather than deny the beast inside? Would he name me Guardian of Avalon if he knew I cannot deny the call of Deep Magic?"

Rhys was silent for moment. "I do not know," he said at last.

Gwen clutched her basket to her chest. "The clan would prefer ye to be Guardian after Cyric. And ye want that, too. Ye belong on Avalon, Rhys. Not wandering the Roman world like a beggar."

The truth of her words was reflected in Rhys's eyes. Her twin longed for Avalon as much as she longed to escape it. But she knew he would never voice that yearning.

"It does no good to rail against one's duty. I follow the path Cyric has set. Ye must do the same."

"And if I cannot?"

"Ye must. Ye are a Daughter of the Lady, Gwen. Her line must continue."

"Clara is a Daughter as well. Her babe will be born soon."

"Mared predicts a lad, not a lass."

"Perhaps Mared is wrong. In any case, Clara and Owein are rarely apart. No doubt Clara's belly will be round again before this babe is weaned."

"It will be a year or more before that comes to pass. All the better if ye marry and bear a Daughter before then."

"What good are any number of Daughters if the Romans discover Avalon? Did Trevor tell ye? Legionaries set up camp in the hills a moon past. They are looking for silver. If they find it . . ."

"They will not. Cyric's illusions veil the Druid mine."

"Aye, but what will happen when Cyric passes and the protection of Avalon falls to me?"

"Your spells will protect Avalon as securely as Cyric's."

"And if they do not? If a power stronger than mine assaults the sacred isle, we will be revealed."

"Ye belittle your power. Ye will not fail."

"I am not so certain." She drew a breath. "Rhys, did ye know ye were followed here from Isca?"

"That cannot be. There was no one else on the road."

Dread tightened Gwen's gut. "Ye felt nothing? Nothing at all?"

"What is this about, Gwen?"

"There's. . . . a Roman soldier. An officer. He trailed ye from Isca, but lost ye in the mists."

"Nay. I am sure I was alone."

"I saw him, Rhys! He arrived at the Roman camp not two hours past. I heard him tell the sentry at the gate he'd lost the trail of a fair-haired minstrel."

"Ye *heard* him? Ye were that close?"

"Aye."

"But how . . ." He broke off as understanding dawned in his eyes. "Ye called the wolf. To spy on the camp."

She lifted her chin. "We need to know everything we can learn about that Roman camp. As a wolf, I was able to get closer than any human might have. The soldier who arrived from Isca knows there's a Celt settlement nearby. He *followed* ye here, Rhys. He may even know ye are a Druid. He is looking for Avalon."

"Let him look. He will not find us. No soldier can see through the mist."

"This man is no ordinary Legionary. He's a sorcerer. His Deep Magic is bound to Darkness. He looked right through my protections."

"He saw the wolf?"

Gwen nodded.

Rhys swore. The sound startled Gwen—her brother so seldom uttered profanity. "By the Great Mother, Gwen, what were ye thinking? Ye are lucky your hide isn't draped across an army tent!" His gray eyes sparked with rare fury. "Ye are too important to risk yourself so. I cannot believe ye would put yourself— and Avalon—in such danger."

"Do ye nay understand, Rhys? Avalon is already in danger. How did this sorcerer learn of us? How did he know ye would lead him here? If he is bent on finding Avalon, Cyric's mist may not be enough to turn him away."

She watched him consider her words, frowning. "I'll assemble the Elders. Cyric, Mared, and Padrig will guide us."

Mared and Padrig were fools, in Gwen's estimation. And Cyric would never consider utilizing any magic other than the Light. "The Elders are too blind to see what is true! To fight Deep Magic, we must call Deep Magic."

"Cyric will not allow it. Ye know that as well as I."

"Cyric," Gwen said slowly, "does not need to know."

Rhys regarded her with something akin to horror. "Ye cannot mean to defy our grandfather, Gwen."

"I do. I must. Rhys, have ye seen Cyric since your return?"

"Nay. He's asleep yet. Padrig bade me wait until he woke."

"He's much weaker than when ye last saw him. I do not think he will survive to see another spring." She paused and drew a deep breath. "If I'm to be Guardian after he is gone, than ye must trust me to do what I believe is best for Avalon."

"Ye made a vow," Rhys replied harshly, "to walk only in Light. Ye cannot abandon that promise."

"And if the Light is not enough to save us?"

"Who is this Roman who has ye so frightened? Did ye hear his name while ye were spying?"

"I . . . think so." She closed her eyes and sorted through the wolf's memories. "It was something like . . . Stratus? Nay." She dug deeper. "Strabo. That was it."

"Strabo?" Rhys seemed stunned. "Are ye sure?"

"Aye. Do ye know him?"

"I know of him. Everyone does. Legate Titus Strabo is the new commander of the Second Legion's garrison at Isca. He arrived at the fortress last autumn, direct from a posting in Egypt."

"Egypt?" The exotic word felt strange on Gwen's tongue.

"A desert land far to the south, ancient and timeless. Their Old Ones raised great temples of stone to their gods, as ours did."

"A land of Deep Magic, then."

Rhys met her gaze. "Aye."

"Then we have much to fear, brother."

* * *

Late that night, the wolf within Gwen woke, and began to howl.

The vibration whispered in Gwen's mind, too faint for human ears. The sound was alluring. Seductive.

She thrashed, throwing off a blanket that had become unbearably heavy. Behind her eyelids, she saw a flash of greenery. Felt the dew, damp on her paws. The rich smell of blood told her prey was near. A deer. Wounded. Weak. The wolf leapt. For one exhilarating moment, it hung between the earth and sky. Then its claws snagged on flesh, its teeth sank deep . . .

Gwen came awake with a jolt so hard it took her breath. Her heart slammed against her ribs; the taste of copper fouled her mouth. *Blood.*

She put her fingers to her face and realized the blood was her own. She'd bitten her lip while caught in the nightmare.

A sob welled up in her throat, but she did not allow it to escape. Her body was on the verge of shattering into a thousand fragments. If the tears came, she would be lost. Calling all her strength, she willed them gone.

Had Mared heard her cry? She peered across the dimly lit roundhouse. No, the old healer was snoring peacefully. Gwen thanked the Great Mother for that small favor.

A charcoal slice of night showed through the half-open door; Gwen doubted much time had passed since she'd fallen into her fitful slumber. Sweat stung her skin, making her thin wool tunic cling uncomfortably to her breasts and thighs. She wanted it off. Needed to be naked.

Now.

The wolf called again, its howl shrieking through her skull. She started to rise, to give it what it wanted. Then, with a groan, she checked herself. Sinking back down on her pallet, she buried her face in her hands.

She could not live like this.

Perhaps Rhys was right. Perhaps she did not resist the call of Deep Magic as strongly as she should. Her human will was stronger than the wolf's instinct. It should prevail.

The wolf's howl came again.

She squeezed her eyelids closed. With all her will, all her magic—all that she *was*—she summoned her link to the Light. The sacred Words sprang to mind. Her spell was potent. Even whispered, she felt the sharp edge of its power on her lips. The wolf howled in protest. Writhed and whimpered, like a beast in a cage. Her heart twisted at its plight, but, recalling Rhys's words and the vow she'd made to Cyric, she held fast.

Deep Magic seeped away. The wolf retreated. Gwen breathed a prayer. Rhys and Cyric were right. The Light *was* enough.

The inner battle left her exhausted. Her eyelids seemed weighted by stones. They closed as a dark, heavy sleep descended.

She stood on Avalon's shore, gazing across the swamp. A black pall hung over the flat water, like a storm descended from the sky. As Gwen watched, the Dark mass contracted, expanded, and contracted again, as if drawing breath. A searing wind swept toward her, bringing the hot stench of burning flesh.

The white mists of Avalon wavered.

Where was Cyric? He was Guardian of Avalon; it was his task to hold the mists. The power resided in Cyric's family line; of all the Druids on Avalon, only Gwen and Rhys could hold the spell in Cyric's absence. Gwen spoke the Words, seeking to bolster her grandfather's spell. Her effort did nothing. The mists were thinning. Fading.

The Dark cloud drifted toward the island. At the same time, Gwen became aware of a white nimbus beside her. She turned to see a woman. Her features were brilliant; her robe dazzling, as if she were clothed with the sun. In her hand was a sword. Its blade shone like polished silver.

"My Lady," Gwen breathed.

The woman inclined her head. "Daughter." She held the sword aloft, its blade shimmering white and blue.

The power in the Lady's blade sang. It was magic, but more—it seemed to possess a life and soul of its own. Gwen's lips parted. Never had she beheld such unfathomable, dangerous power. Deep Magic, certainly. But not Deep Magic alone. Deep Magic bound to Light.

A tingling sensation ran up Gwen's arm. In the next instant, the Lady was gone, and her sword was in Gwen's hand. The dark cloud advanced, the blackness folding in upon itself until it took the shape of an otherworldly creature. Short, squat legs, ending in hideous curved claws, supported a thick torso covered with black scales. Great batlike wings unfurled from its back.

The beast's mouth opened, emitting a blast of dark fire. Gwen leaped backward, pointing the Lady's blade at her foe. Light shot out, striking the beast's chest. The creature was far from cowed. Rearing up on its hind legs, it gathered its might for a second time.

Gwen willed the sword's magic to life.

Light and Darkness collided.

* * *

She woke with a gasp, loud buzzing in her ears. The stench of burning flesh lingered in her nostrils. The wolf was howling, its call gripping her like panic. This time, no spell would deny it. She crept to the door, pausing only once when Mared wheezed in her sleep. An instant later, Gwen stepped into the night, shivering as cool air met damp skin.

The wolf would not wait long—already she felt it tearing at her bones and muscles. There was no time to cross the swamps. Once clear of the village, Gwen bolted to a hollow hidden by a screen of willows.

Ardra greeted her with a weak thump of her tail. One of the she-wolf's pups, a bold male, climbed atop its littermates in an effort to reach a swollen teat. But Gwen had no time to greet her companion. Deep Magic was upon her.

She all but ripped off her tunic in her haste to be free. Her precious pendant fell roughly atop crumpled wool. She crouched, naked, arms wrapped around her legs, her forehead pressed to her knees. *Cyric. Rhys. Please forgive me.*

Her heartbeat measured the passing moments as she fought back tears of shame. Then, in the hazy half-light of her magic, her guilt fell away.

Freedom—exhilarating, liberating freedom—burst upon her in dizzying glory. Shame had no place in a wolf's mind. There was no room for duty, no path for regret. Deep Magic was the power of the gods; it did not recognize such human trivialities.

A sensual thrill, both anguish and bliss, flooded her body. Triumph and pain ripped her bones and muscles. Her skull squeezed. Shards of agony scraped across her face. Chin and lips elongated; skin furred. A tail sprouted. Legs narrowed, fingers and toes curved into claws. She dropped to all fours, acutely conscious of the banquet of smells beckoning from across the swamp. Plunging into the water, she paddled toward freedom.

It was only later, when the wolf was gone and Gwen lay huddled and shaking on her pallet, that she remembered the Lady, and the Dark beast, and the shining sword that had held Avalon's enemy at bay.

Chapter Four

$\mathcal{A}$ jangling bell pierced the turbulent heat.

Marcus bolted upright, gasping for breath. His heart was pounding, his shirt drenched with sweat. His phallus hard as an iron bar. Where was she?

He came more fully awake. Gradually, he understood he was alone in his bed, but the image of the woman did not clear from his mind. If he closed his eyes, he could see her stretched out like a goddess, white-blond hair cascading over smooth, naked shoulders. But she was not here.

The last remnants of his dream scattered like hard grains of wheat spilled on a clay-tiled floor. Marcus shook his head, trying to settle some sense back into his skull. Just a dream. The inferior mattress on his bed in the smithy was not conducive to deep slumber. He should have a new one made.

But he doubted it would make a difference. He'd slept little in the past week—almost every moment had been spent in his smithy, pursuing what had begun to look like a fool's task. He'd built the new furnace chamber, shoveled in great heaps of unadulterated charcoal, added the purest iron ore. He'd set two boys on the new, larger, bellows, instructing them to keep the air flowing over the coals.

The heat had been tremendous. But each attempt to smelt the bright iron called *chalybs* had failed. He'd fallen asleep wondering what technique was left to try. Surely he'd missed something.

The gate bell rang again, insistent. Marcus blinked. So that had not been part of his dream. Frowning, he disentangled himself from his blanket and rose to peer out the smithy door. It was not yet dawn; no light shone in the windows of the main house. The bark of a dog sounded from the servants' cottages beyond the orchard and kitchen gardens, but he could see no movement near the stables near the front gate. Was Linus deaf? More likely the stable master was visiting the latrine.

Nighttime visitors to the farm were rare. Was some neighbor in urgent need of Rhiannon's healing skills? Marcus stripped off his wet shirt and grabbed a clean one. Lifting the gate key from its hook by the door, he started across the yard, peering ahead.

The night air was cool, but the clear sky carried the promise of a warm spring day. His boots crunched on the crushed-stone path as he strode past Rhiannon's budding roses. A vague, hooded shadow was visible beyond the main gate's iron bars. Was it his imagination, or did the figure stiffen as he drew near?

"Who's there?" The question was sharper than he'd intended.

"Many apologies for ringing so early, but I have traveled far to reach ye."

Marcus hesitated. He'd called out in Latin, but the

visitor's reply had come in Celtic—in a lilting, feminine tone. The sound was a soft melody, like petals on fragrant dew.

"Who's there?" he asked again, more softly, in Celtic this time. He spoke the language as well as any native.

The hood fell back. The woman's features were fine, her gray eyes clear. Moonlight gleamed on her white-blond hair.

Marcus could do nothing but stare.

It was not possible. It could not be *her*.

He opened his mouth, closed it, opened it again. Ran a hand over his hair, then clenched his fist and let it drop to his side. His heart seemed to have taken up residence in his throat. He could not force a single word around it.

"I am—"

"I know who you are," he managed.

Their eyes met. Hers were the color of the mist in the valley, the shadowed veil that hid so many of Britain's secrets. Marcus, with his pure Roman blood, could never hope to uncover all the mysteries of his adopted home. No matter. There were many Celt secrets he did not wish to know.

"Gwendolyn." Her name felt strange on his tongue. "Is something wrong? Is it Rhys? Has he been hurt—"

"Nay," she replied quickly. "My brother is well."

"Did he travel with you?" The question was inane— there was no one with her. But why would she travel from Avalon alone?

"Rhys is in Avalon. He . . . he advised me to seek ye."

"He did?" Marcus couldn't keep the note of disbelief from his voice.

Gwen flushed and looked away. "Aye. He . . ." Her voice trailed off, her attention darting past him toward the stuccoed villa. When she looked back at him, a half smile was playing about her lips.

"Marcus Aquila," she said softly.

He started at the sound of his name. "Yes?"

She gestured toward the iron bars that separated them. "Do ye intend to open the gates?"

Marcus stared blankly at the key in his hand. Then he looked up and grimaced. "Of course. Just a minute."

He fitted the key in the lock, the temperature of his skin notching upward as the action brought to mind a more sensual deed. Avoiding Gwen's gaze, he swung the gate open and stood aside. She brushed by him, almost touching. His lower body clenched.

He relocked the gate and led the way to the main house, his skin tingling at her nearness. He was intensely aware of her every step, her every breath. Her wild, earthy scent. *Gods.*

He cleared his throat, intending to speak, but could think of absolutely nothing to say. Why in Hades didn't she fill the silence? In his experience, most women were happy to do just that. But Gwendolyn, it seemed, was not most women.

He dared a sideways glance. Now that the sky was beginning to lighten, he could see the lines of stress around her mouth and the dark smudges under her eyes. Her cloak was but a thin scrap of wool against the night's chill.

She carried no satchel or bundle, a detail Marcus thought odd. On foot, Avalon was a hard two days' journey from Isca. No woman traveled so far with nothing but the clothes on her back.

But a wolf? A wolf might travel with nothing.

He drew a sharp breath. Gwen glanced in his direction. Their eyes met before he could look away; he had the sensation that the world around him was collapsing. A jolt of pure lust shot through him.

"I . . . is something wrong?" she asked.

"No," Marcus muttered, reaching for a lifeline in the form of the farmhouse door. He yanked it open and held it for her. "You're welcome here, of course. I only wonder why you have come. I can't believe this is a casual visit."

When she did not reply, he did not press her. She hesitated, then entered the house. He escorted her along the entry gallery, past the altar to the household gods and the formal Roman-style receiving and dining chambers his family rarely used. They stepped into the hearth room, where Rhiannon, a habitually early riser, was already stirring the coals under her cauldron, one arm curved protectively under her burgeoning belly. She looked up as he entered. Her amber eyes alighted on Gwen, widened, then moved to Marcus in silent question. He shrugged a reply.

Gwen's brows rose as she took in the circular room's curved walls, the center hearth, and the high, peaked ceiling. Herbs hung from iron hooks; open shelves held a jumble of pottery, cups, and glassware. A long table flanked with chairs occupied one side of the room. A large loom bearing a colorful, half-woven blanket stood on the other.

"Why, 'tis like a Celt roundhouse," Gwen said.

Rhiannon came forward. "Aye, so it is. My husband was gracious enough to build this room at my request." She smiled. "After I told him I wouldna eat lying on a bed, as many Romans do. This hearth room is much like the home of my childhood."

"Except that the walls are brick and plaster, not mud and straw," Marcus commented, striving to keep his tone light. He and his father often teased Rhiannon about how accustomed she'd become to the comfortable aspects of Roman life. "The floor is tiled, with heated air flowing beneath it. Smoke doesn't collect under the roof, but is funneled outside. Not to mention that clean water, and a hot bath, are only a few steps away."

Rhiannon laughed easily. "Aye, I've found Roman cleverness has its purposes. My husband and stepson do not let me forget it." She reached out and took both Gwen's hands in her own. "Ye can only be Rhys's sister. Ye favor him most strongly."

"Aye. I am Gwendolyn." She inclined her head. "I'm honored to meet ye, Lady. I've . . . I've never met a queen."

Marcus shifted, uncomfortable with this reminder of his stepmother's heritage. If Rome hadn't conquered Britain, Rhiannon would be a powerful ruler, not the wife of a retired Legionary soldier-turned-farmer.

"A queen is but a woman," Rhiannon said lightly, taking Gwen's arm and drawing her toward the table. "And as any woman might, I welcome ye to my home. Sit, for ye look weary. I'll make ye a warm draught. Marcus, remember your manners and take Gwen's cloak."

Gwen shrugged the thin woolen garment from her shoulders. Marcus, glad to have a task to distract him, took it. He still could not believe she was here. Did Gwen's sudden appearance have something to do with Breena? Maybe Rhys *had* sent her. Maybe he believed Gwen would succeed in bringing Breena to Avalon, when he had not.

If so, Rhys was destined to be disappointed. Marcus moved to the hearth and dumped a shovelful of coals under Rhiannon's cauldron. No woman, no matter how beautiful, how desirable, how powerful, would make Marcus believe his sister should live a primitive life with a band of outlawed Druids.

As if summoned by Marcus's dark thoughts, Breena appeared in the doorway, followed closely by Lucius. Aiden, the old Celt who was the father of Owein's first wife, hobbled in close behind.

Breena's eyes went as round as two platters when she saw Gwen. "I thought I heard the gate bell ring."

"I did as well," declared Aiden, "but I ne'er dreamed our visitor would be so comely." He gave Gwen a broad wink. The old man's walking stick clicked on the tile as he made his way to the table. He managed a bow before lowering himself into a chair at Gwen's side.

"Ye must be Aiden," she said with a smile. "Owein has spoken of ye. As has Rhys."

Aiden looked Gwen over with unabashed curiosity. "Well, lass, your brother speaks precious little of ye."

Gwen's smile faltered.

"Gwendolyn is Rhys's twin," Rhiannon told Lucius in Latin. Marcus's father was less comfortable speaking Celtic than his children were.

Lucius nodded. "Welcome," he said in heavily accented Celtic. "What brings you to Isca? I was given to believe that Rhys was the only Druid who traveled outside Avalon."

Gwen cleared her throat. "Aye, that is usually true," she told Lucius. In very passable Latin.

Marcus regarded her with some surprise. Rhys's Latin was flawless, of course, but Marcus hadn't expected Gwen to speak it.

"I come regarding a matter of great urgency."

"If this urgent matter concerns Breena," Marcus muttered, "you've wasted your time."

Gwen frowned. "Breena?"

"Have you come here thinking you'll be more successful than Rhys in convincing us to send her to Avalon?"

"Ah. 'Tis true enough that Rhys and Cyric believe Breena must be trained in Avalon."

"And ye, Gwen? What do ye believe?" Rhiannon handed Gwen a cup of a fragrant herbal potion. Marcus knew Rhiannon did not want Breena to leave home any more than he did. But Breena's visions troubled Rhiannon deeply.

Gwen's gaze traveled from Rhiannon to Lucius, and from there to Breena. Marcus's blood boiled. What right did this Druidess have to appear uninvited in his home and . . .

"I believe Cyric and Rhys see only one path, when in truth there are many. They do not believe one can reach the Light unaided."

"And you believe the same," Marcus said.

She shifted her gaze to him, her gray eyes shadowed. "Nay. I cannot say that I do. I believe there are many paths to the Light, though perhaps more paths that lead into Darkness. Certainly there's an advantage in learning from others. But some who are touched by magic must travel alone."

The unexpected declaration took Marcus aback. So Gwen hadn't come to plead Rhys's case. Twin vertical lines had appeared between her brows. He was struck by an urge to smooth them away with his thumb.

Their gazes collided once more. "Whatever Breena's path," she said slowly, "I would not advise her to travel to Avalon now. Legionaries have set up camp in the hills across the swamp. They are searching for silver, in Avalon's mine."

Rhiannon gave a cry of dismay, while Lucius swore softly. "Rhys told us nothing of this."

"My brother only learned of it after he left ye."

Marcus advanced from his position by the door. "Thank Jupiter we didn't send Breena with him."

Rhiannon looked ill. "But what of Owein and Clara, and all the others?"

"Surely Cyric's mists will protect the isle," Lucius said.

"So far they have, but my grandfather's health is failing."

"If that's so," Marcus interjected, "why aren't you at his bedside? Aren't you his successor?"

Gwen's hand trembled as she placed her cup on the table. "I would not have come here if the need were not great. There's a sorcerer in the Roman camp. The man is not looking for silver, but for Avalon."

"The army is harboring a sorcerer?" Lucius asked sharply.

"Aye. He is their leader. His name is Strabo."

"Titus Strabo? The Second Legion's new legate? Why, that's impossible!" Marcus couldn't contain his astonishment. He'd seen Strabo many times, even met him once. The man struck him as solid and unimaginative. He was certainly not Marcus's idea of a sorcerer.

"I assure ye, 'tis true," Gwen said. "Strabo followed Rhys from Isca. He suspects my brother is not the simple minstrel he pretends to be. He knows our settlement is near. I've felt his magic, probing the mist." She met Marcus's gaze. "If he should find us, the Druids will have only two choices. Fight, or flee."

"Flee, then," Marcus said. "Better yet, disperse."

"To scatter would weaken our power!"

Marcus placed both hands on the table and leaned toward her. "Exactly."

For a long moment, silence hung in the air between them.

"Marcus—" Rhiannon began.

He straightened. "It would be for the best, Mother. Avalon cannot hide forever. With so much power concentrated in one place, it will grow beyond any man's control. The Druids of Avalon profess to follow only the Light, but for how much longer? How long before they delve into Deep Magic?"

Gwen made no reply.

"I don't understand why you've come here, of all places," Marcus went on. "What can any of us do if the Second Legion forces the Druids to abandon Avalon?"

Gwen rose and faced him. She was tall, Marcus realized with a start—not as tall as Rhys, but very nearly of a height with Marcus. Her chin lifted and her shoulders went back, as if her spine were made of *chalybs*.

"The Druids of Avalon will not flee. We will not grovel before the Roman army or before any Dark sorcerer. I will see my own death before I allow the sacred isle to be defiled."

"And yet you left it," Marcus challenged. "Why?"

She turned her palms upward. "I came to ye, Marcus Aquila. I need your help to stand against Avalon's enemies."

Marcus regarded her with patent disbelief. "You think I will help you battle the Second Legion? *And* a sorcerer? You must be insane!"

A feral light sprang into her eyes. *The wolf.* For an instant, he saw the beast clearly there, within her. In the same instant, sudden, irrational lust surged hotly in his loins.

Gods.

"I've not lost my wits," she declared hotly. "I've come

to ye, Marcus Aquila, because ye have the skills I seek. I need a sword."

"A sword?" Marcus said the word as if it were a syllable in Greek—a language he hated with a rare passion. He shook his head. "I don't understand. You wish to . . . what? Offer me a commission?"

Gwen's eyes did not stray from his face. "Aye. A commission."

"Then I trust you've brought coin." He knew she had not. She'd carried nothing.

"Marcus," Rhiannon chided. "Must you be so blunt? Gwen is Rhys's sister. Almost family."

"Even so, my skills do not come cheaply."

Gwen did not blink. "I did not bring coin, no. But I can promise you a portion of Druid silver."

"Can you?" His tone was blunt. Beside him, Breena sucked in a breath. It was unlike Marcus to be intentionally rude, but standing so close to the woman who had been his private erotic fantasy for more than a year was driving him stark raving mad.

"Avalon will pay whatever price you name," Gwen said.

"You cannot want a common sword," he said tightly. "Do you mean for me to forge a weapon of magic?"

"Aye, Marcus. I do."

Marcus was well aware that every eye in the room was fixed on him. It was no secret he hated magic. His immediate instinct was to spit out a refusal, and yet, he hesitated.

His gaze flicked to Breena, then back to Gwen. "I'll need to know more before I agree to anything. We'll speak of it in the smithy. Later." *Alone,* he added silently.

Gwen hesitated, then nodded. "All right."

From the corner of his eye, Marcus saw Lucius and Rhiannon exchange a glance. A moment of awkward silence ensued, until Rhiannon broke it. "Ye must be hungry after your journey, Gwen."

"A little."

Breena sprang into motion. "I'll see to the food."

"Nay," Gwen said, half rising. "Do not trouble yourself—" But Breena had already left for the kitchen.

" 'Tis no trouble," Rhiannon told her. "Alma—that's our cook—will not have today's bread ready yet, but there will be one of yesterday's loaves and some meat left from last night's supper. Sit, Gwen, and finish your draught."

Gwen sat, though she looked ill at ease. Marcus guessed she was unused to being waited upon. Life on Avalon was primitive. Not for the first time, he wondered how Clara was dealing with it. Did she regret the loss of the luxuries she'd known in Isca? He thought not. Clara and Owein shared a rare love. Lovers were blind to inconvenience.

Lucius took a seat at the table with Gwen and Aiden, awaiting Breena's return from the kitchen. Rhiannon poured mugs of *cervesia* for all but Lucius, who had never developed a taste for the Celt barley beer. He received a cup of wine instead.

Aiden wasted no time in plying Gwen with questions. "Now then, lass. Rhys told us Clara's babe is very close to coming. I trust your healer is competent."

"Oh, aye," Gwen replied. "Ye must not worry about that. Mared's healing skills are vast."

"And Owein?" Rhiannon asked, taking an empty chair. "How does he fare? I canna believe my brother will soon be a father."

"He will be a fine one," Gwen replied. "He hovers

over Clara so closely, she barely has space to draw breath." Rhiannon laughed and asked more avid questions. Marcus knew she regretted not being able to travel to Avalon for the birth.

Breena returned from the kitchen with a tray of bread and cheese, followed by Alma, who carried a platter of cold mutton. Marcus was not hungry. He retreated from the table to stand with his back to the wall, sipping his beer. Breena took an empty seat across from Gwen. His sister's gaze clung to their visitor as if she were a goddess come to life.

Marcus scowled. It was bad enough Breena looked at Rhys that way. She didn't need another Druid to idolize.

Rhiannon turned and frowned at him. He recognized his stepmother's expression for what it was—a summons to the table. With a sigh, he took the last empty seat, next to Lucius, and accepted a plate of food he did not want.

"What do you make of the army sending an expedition to the Mendips?" he asked his father in an undertone. "Those mines were abandoned years ago."

"And yet the existence of Avalon's mine proves that silver can still be found, if one is willing to dig deep enough. An unscrupulous legate could skim a fine profit off the top before the army records the weight of the metal extracted."

Marcus frowned down at his mug. "If the army finds silver, they'll build a permanent fort. Avalon will be even more vulnerable. The Druids will have no choice but to flee."

"Perhaps," Lucius allowed. His gaze drifted to Gwen. "What do you make of her coming here?"

Marcus's eyes cut to Gwen. She was relating a humorous story about Clara's adjustment to life in Avalon.

"Certainly, she wishes to protect her home," Marcus said in answer to his father's question. "But she is not being entirely truthful." He paused. "She told me Rhys sent her here."

"You do not believe that."

"I think it highly unlikely, especially as she has not come for Breena. If I were given to gambling, I'd wager half the farm that Rhys has no idea where Gwen is. And the other half that Rhys would be furious if he knew." And what of Gwen's betrothed? Marcus mused silently. Did the man know his intended's whereabouts?

"Why would she go behind Rhys's back, do you think, seeking a magic sword?" Lucius said.

"I don't know," Marcus replied grimly. "But I mean to find out."

An hour later, Gwen's lithe form moved through the smithy door and into Marcus's private sanctuary. The place was ruined for him now. It was a testament to the potency of his unabated lust that he did not care. How many times had he dreamed of her here? More than he could count. She approached the sturdy oaken worktable. He'd once fantasized about taking her on that table. Now she paused just in front of the place where he'd imagined her sitting, naked, with legs spread wide in welcome, and touched the blade of a just-completed dagger.

He let out a slow, painful breath.

"It's beautiful," she said in Celtic, trailing a finger along the edge of the dagger's blade.

He reached out and caught her wrist. "Have a care. I just honed that last night. It's very sharp."

She started, staring down at their joined hands. Despite her height, her hand was much smaller than his. Her fingers and palms were callused from years of hard work. He drew his thumb across the base of her fingers.

Her head came up; her eyes were wide. She took her hand from his grip with an embarrassed laugh. "I will endeavor to be more careful." He watched as she put some distance between them, first inspecting the furnace, then studying a rack that held daggers and swords in varying stages of completion. When she peered around the wooden screen that hid his rumpled bed, color rose in her cheeks. But she did not, Marcus noted with interest, immediately turn away.

Was she a virgin? She was betrothed. Her intended must not be much of a man, to let her travel alone to Isca. Had she already lain with her Caledonian? It was entirely possible; she was no girl, after all. She was near the same age as Marcus—twenty-five. She should have wed years ago.

He cleared his throat. Gwen, who was still staring at his bed, spun about. The flush on her cheeks was a becoming pink.

"I sleep here sometimes, when I'm working on a difficult piece," Marcus offered.

"Ah. Ye must love your work, then."

"I do. I was ten years old when my father retired from the army and purchased this farm. I spent all my spare time here in the smithy, watching the old smith. There was something about working iron that fascinated me. Father, of course, was appalled when I declared I wanted to learn the craft."

"But why?"

"Patrician Romans do not, as a rule, become crafts-men."

"I do not understand. Why not?"

"It's beneath us," he said wryly. "We patricians own land, and serve as military officers and civil magis-trates. We don't engage in mercantile trade. But I hated politics and war, and loved the forge, so I was deter-mined to become a smith. If we lived in Rome, it would have been impossible. Even here on the fron-tier, I'm ridiculed. The patricians in Isca think I am mad." He smiled. "But somehow, that does not stop them from offering me commissions."

"Because your swords are so beautiful."

"Any fool can make a beautiful sword. No, they seek me out because my blades are strong. They won't bend or shatter."

"Why is that?"

"A smith is like a cook. His ingredients must be pure and his methods precise. The iron cannot be inferior, and it must be forged at the right temperature. If it's not worked long enough, the blade will be too soft. It won't hold an edge, and can bend in battle. But if it's worked too long, after a time its strength fades. An overworked blade is brittle, in danger of breaking. It's a smith's task to strike the right balance."

"And ye have found this balance." She crossed to the forge and peered into the furnace. "Your furnace is very large. I use only a small fire when working silver."

"I work in silver and bronze on occasion," he said, indicating his own clay crucible on a stone ledge nearby. "Soft metals such as silver melt at lower tem-peratures. With iron, a large chamber is needed to ac-commodate enough fuel to sustain a high heat."

"It must be a very hot fire indeed, judging from the mountain of charcoal ye have piled outside your smithy."

She eyed the separate chamber he'd lined with new brick. It was not yet as black with soot as the rest of the furnace. The floor in front of it was littered with rejected half-hammered blooms of newly smelted iron. "This section is new?"

"Yes. It's the reason there's so much charcoal outside. I'm trying to smelt a newer, stronger type of iron."

"Bright iron, ye mean."

He blinked. "You've heard of it?"

She glanced at him over her shoulder. "Rhys told me of it, only a few days ago. Have ye met with success?"

"Some."

"But not as much as ye want."

"No," he admitted, then frowned. "But I didn't bring you here to discuss innovations in smithing. I need some answers. The truth, this time. Rhys doesn't know you are here, does he?"

Gwen's brows rose. The half smile was back, playing on her lips. "Whatever sort of man ye are, Marcus Aquila, ye are not an unintelligent one."

He did not acknowledge her compliment, if indeed it was one. He was too arrested by the clear gray of her eyes, made even more compelling by the tilt of her chin and the regal set of her shoulders. Her clothes were at odds with her bearing. Her tunic was old, almost threadbare. The slight swell of her small breasts barely filled the thin wool. She was tall and thin—most men would say too thin. Marcus had never understood the Roman obsession with small, curvaceous women. He much preferred Gwen's sleek, willowy form.

Reluctantly, he tore his gaze from her body and returned it to her face, flushing when he read the frank knowledge of his appraisal in her eyes. But she didn't mention his rudeness. Instead, she answered his question.

"Ye have the right of it. Rhys does not know where I am."

"No doubt he's worried about you."

"And angry at me besides. Neither emotion, I fear, is anything new."

Marcus filed that information away. "I suppose that means he also doesn't know about this sword you wish me to make."

"Nay. He does not."

He paced to his anvil. "A magical sword. Tell me, exactly how am I to provide you with that? And why?"

She turned away, studying his rack of tools. Half of them were missing, scattered about the smithy. She hefted a wooden mallet that he seldom used, testing its weight. "How else might a small band of Druids face the threat of a Dark sorcerer, except with magic?"

"You speak of Legate Strabo. I've met the man. He is not at all magical."

"Forgive me for speaking plainly, but ye are hardly an expert in matters of magic. Rhys hid his power from ye for years."

Marcus felt his face heat as his old anger flared. He did not like remembering what a fool he'd been. "Let's not mince words, then. Tell me everything. Describe this sword you wish me to forge, what magic you mean to bind to it, and, most importantly, why Rhys and Cyric disapprove."

" 'Tis not so much a matter of disapproval," Gwen said quickly. " 'Tis only that if I'd told Rhys of my plans, he would have insisted I bring the matter before the Elders. Mared, Avalon's healer, and Padrig, my uncle, would never support any plan I put forth."

"Why not?"

Gwen grimaced. "They do not trust me."

"And why is that?"

She weighed the mallet first in one hand, then in the other, as if weighing the possible answers she could give. He wondered how much of what she told him was the truth.

"Cyric has chosen me to be Guardian after his passing," she said finally. "But Mared does not believe I have the constancy for the role. She and Padrig believe the role of Guardian should pass to Rhys. Indeed . . ." Her voice faltered. "Even I believe it."

The self-doubt that flitted across her face made something in Marcus's chest catch. "Rhys doesn't believe that, I'm sure. He's told me your magic is stronger than his."

"That may be true," she said, "or not. Rhys does not embrace his full power."

"How can you say that? The man can change into a bird! If there's a power beyond that, I don't want to know about it."

The mallet slipped through Gwen's fingers and fell to the floor with a thud. She gripped the upper bar of the tool rack. "*What* did ye say?"

Marcus regarded her with some amazement. "You didn't know?"

"Did he . . . did he tell ye he could shift?"

"Hardly. Breena and I saw him change quite by accident. It was in the wood behind the barley fields, last year, when you were . . . in danger. Rhys flew from Avalon to Isca as a merlin, searching for Clara."

"After I begged him to try to shift," Gwen whispered.

"He did it. But he never told me. He only warned me . . ." Her expression hardened.

"Warned you about what?"

She shook her head, her brow creasing. Her upper teeth caught her bottom lip and she bit down on the tender skin, hard.

Marcus's groin tightened. Hastily, he looked away.

Bending, Gwen retrieved the dropped mallet and replaced it on the rack. She let out a slow, tightly controlled breath as she exchanged it for a smaller iron hammer.

"Were ye disgusted? When ye saw the change?" Her tone was carefully bland. Marcus did not miss the raw pain beneath. She was not, he thought, speaking of Rhys.

"No," he said, because it was the truth. He'd been shocked when Gwen had shifted in his arms. And yes, terrified—at least for an instant, before he'd become unbearably aroused. But disgusted? He almost laughed. No, not disgusted.

But he could hardly tell Gwen that just the memory of watching her shift from wolf to woman left his cock hard and his stones aching. She bit her lip again. Lust struck like hammer against anvil. His body vibrated with the sheer force of it.

She met his gaze. His throat tightened as her pupils went dark, the gray circle of her iris thinning to a slender ring. The gray was lightest near her pupils, and deepened to charcoal at the outer ring.

The hot thread of emotions drew taut between them. Her fingers twisted together. She felt the attraction between them, as he did. He was sure of it. Gods help him.

For a long moment, they just stared at each other. His brain had gone blank. He didn't dare touch her, but he didn't—*couldn't*—hide his desire for her. Her eyes flicked downward, then widened. He could tell she thought she should look away. But she didn't.

A sense of unreality settled around him. He wanted her. What was he thinking? This was no tavern girl, no marriageable neighbor. She was Rhys's *sister*. Promised to another man. A Druidess. A shape-shifter. A *wolf*.

None of it mattered. He wanted her, with a lust so fierce it sucked the air from his lungs.

She finally snatched her gaze from his body, her breathing rapid and shallow. Taking a step backward, she looked about—most likely for anything other than his . . . *regard* for her, he thought wryly. And so it was with a sense of burgeoning inevitability that he watched her become aware of the high shelf above his worktable. Her gaze touched on each animal figurine in turn, until it came to rest on the wolf.

"What—" She swallowed visibly. As if in a trance, she took the few steps needed to bring her within reach of the display. She surprised him by touching not the wolf, but a fat sheep.

"What charming figures. Did ye make them?"

"Yes."

"They seem so . . . frivolous. So unlike ye."

He grimaced. "Am I so deadly dull, then?"

"Nay! I did not mean it that way. I only meant it seems odd that a man who forges weapons also crafts such whimsical ornaments."

"I started when Breena was small, when the old smith was still alive. I made most of these figures for her."

Gwen's gaze darted to the wolf.

"But not all." Deliberately, he reached past her and picked it up. "This one, I made for myself."

She bit her lip again. He nearly groaned out loud. "Is . . . is it . . . me?" she asked.

"It might be. Then again, it could be my ancestors' *lare.*"

"I do not know that word."

"The *lares* are Roman guardian spirits. My full name is Marcus Ulpius Aquila. In Rome, the second of a man's three names comes to him from his ancestors. Mine is especially ancient. Ulpius. In the oldest language of Latium, it means wolf."

"The *wolf* is the guardian of your clan?" Her shock was palpable.

"Yes." Marcus ran his thumb over the curve of the silver wolf's back, then set the figure on the worktable between a sheet of papyrus and an open wax tablet. "But you're right—I would be lying if I said I was thinking of my forefathers when I fashioned this figurine. I thought only of you. As I have every night since I carried you out of that cave."

Distress flashed in her eyes. Distress, and something more. His body tightened. He felt a predator's energy gather inside him, as if the spirit of the wolf his forefathers had worshipped had come to life in his belly.

"I have thought of ye as well," she said in a rush. "I've long wanted to thank ye for saving me. When I woke from Blodwen's spell, ye seemed like a dream scattered by the dawn."

"No. No dream."

"I also wondered . . . what was it like for ye, watching me change? Ye are the only one who has ever seen it. I cannot help thinking it was horrible."

"I won't insult you by pretending it wasn't a shock. But horrible? No. That's not the word I would use."

Her laugh was bitter. "What, then? Repulsive? Perverted? An abomination?"

He caught her arm and waited until she looked at him. "It was none of those things." His voice sounded raw to his own ears. "Startling, yes, even though Rhys had told me you were trapped in the form of a wolf."

His gaze drifted to her lower lip, red and a little swollen where she'd bitten it. *Gods.* Her eyes were so innocent, so uncertain. And he was so hard. How could she not know how her nearness affected him?

His fingers pressed more deeply into her upper arm. He had to be hurting her, but she didn't try to pull away. "The experience was far from repulsive, I assure you."

The doubt and shame didn't leave her eyes. He was gripped by a visceral need to banish it. And so he lowered his head, intending to kiss her, just to prove his words were true.

He moved swiftly, sensing that if she guessed what he planned, she'd push him away. When his lips met hers, she stiffened in surprise, drinking in his breath with a soft gasp. On the next heartbeat, her body went soft.

Marcus's head spun, as if he'd drunk a pitcher of unwatered wine, too quickly. He watched as if outside himself as his lips brushed over hers. Fire burned in his veins; a savageness almost wholly unknown to him screamed at him to take her, mark her as *his,* whether she was willing to accept such intimacy or not. But violence was not his way. In truth, he abhorred it. His muscles went rigid as he fought to stay in control. She belonged to another man—he shouldn't even have touched her. But now that he had, he couldn't bring himself to let her go.

He kissed her again, suckling and nipping her lower lip. She tasted of wild things—heather and honey, and the wind on the moor. He cupped her cheek; he marveled at the softness of her skin under his callused fingers. His tongue teased the ragged terrain of her lower lip. He ran a hand over her hair, wishing fervently it weren't bound in a braid. He wanted it loose and flowing.

She trembled under his touch. Not from fear. Or anger. He was certain of that much, at least. The knowledge emboldened him. He pushed aside all thoughts of her betrothed. If the man hadn't been able to keep her by his side, he did not deserve her.

He pressed his thumb to her chin, parting her lips so he could slip inside the slick hot mystery that was her mouth. She made a sound in the back of her throat as his tongue touched hers. Not a protest. Not exactly, anyway.

She tensed, her palm flattening against his chest. He thought she would push him away—he'd even begun to withdraw. Then her fingers fisted in the loose fabric of his shirt. A small, helpless moan sounded in the back of her throat.

He resisted the fierce urge to press her against the edge of the worktable and grind his lower body into the soft cradle of her thighs. Instead, he held himself still while she hesitantly returned his kisses. They were sweetly innocent gems, uncertain and untutored. Elation filled him. She had not yet given herself to her intended. He was all but sure of it.

His shaking hand moved to her shoulder, then skimmed down her arm and settled on her waist. All the while, he feasted on her lips and rained kisses on her cheeks and eyelids. He nuzzled her jaw, suckled the spot just below her ear.

She slid her arms around his neck. *Gods, yes.*

"Marcus . . ."

The breathy, sensual quality she brought to his name fired a streak of desire directly to his loins. Lust dazed his mind. He calculated the distance and direction to his bed. No more than a half-dozen steps to the left. He would lay her on the mattress. Cover her body with his. Plunge into her sweet, wild heat.

She seemed to sense—and approve—his fevered decision. Her kisses grew frantic, ardent. She pressed her body against his. His tongue swept along her jaw, lapped and nibbled at the corner of her mouth. A low, growling vibration sounded in her throat.

Without warning, pain exploded in his lip.

He jerked back. "Ow!"

Gwen inhaled sharply, her eyes flicked to his mouth, then widened in horror. She looked as though she would be ill. "*Great Mother* . . . Oh, Marcus, I am sorry! I did not mean . . ."

He touched his mouth. His fingers came away smeared with blood. His blood.

She'd bitten him.

By Pollux. She'd bitten him, as a she-wolf might nip its mate. His rod hardened unmercifully. He should have been appalled. He was not. He was unbearably, insanely aroused.

Hades. What would she be like in his bed? Would loving her kill him? For an instant, he was willing to risk it.

Then sanity slammed into his brain like a load of bricks falling from the top of a scaffold. Watching a wolf turn into a woman—that experience had driven him out of his mind with lust. But taking a woman to bed, only to have her morph into a snarling, vicious beast . . .

That prospect would give any man pause.

He'd survived an encounter with Gwen as a wolf once—when she'd been weak and wounded. At full strength, he had no doubt the wolf could rip out his throat.

Abruptly, he turned and paced a few steps away. Ran his hand over his head, then glanced back at her. The self-hatred in her eyes had returned—it made him feel like the worst of louts. She thought she'd repulsed him. Not true. His phallus was throbbing and his stones were so tight they were probably blue. He was struck with an absurd urge to laugh.

He cursed under his breath instead. "Forgive me. I should not have . . . accosted you. You're Rhys's sister. He'd kill me if he were here."

It was the wrong thing to say. She stiffened, her fingers curling into small fists. "Rhys does not command me."

"No. I doubt any man could."

Then why was he struck with an irrational urge to order her behind the screen and into his bed? He shook his head slightly and cast about for something safe— or at least something *safer*—to say. He could think of nothing, except, maybe, yesterday's rain.

"Tell me more about this sword you require," he said at last, plunging headlong into the next dangerous topic. "You don't want a *gladius*, I'm sure. Do you mean for me to forge a Celt sword?"

"I . . . hardly know. I know nothing of swords. There are no weapons on Avalon—Cyric does not allow it. The sword I need . . . I held it in a dream. I fought Strabo's magic. The blade shone like polished silver."

"*Chalybs* shines, just as you've described." He paused, thinking on her words. "Why do you believe you were fighting Strabo's magic in your dream? It might have been a meaningless nightmare."

"Nay, the magic was real. I saw the Lady. It was she who handed me the sword. I used it to counter a dread beast. The creature was shrouded with the same Dark aura I'd seen about Strabo's head."

"Aura?"

"A glow that clings to someone touched by magic. Not many Druids can sense auras, but Rhys and I have a strong talent for it. The color we see tells us the type of magic a person is bound to. Seers are surrounded in white light. Yellow means a healer, green denotes a nurturing magic. Those with a light blue aura—like Rhys and me—are protectors."

"Ah. I know what you mean. Old Aiden claims to see such things."

Gwen smiled. "Aye, Owein told me. He says it's the only magic the old man has."

"So you can see magic whenever you look at a person?"

" 'Tis a magical sort of looking. The colors come into my mind."

He didn't understand, but then, he hadn't expected to. Magic was beyond his comprehension. "And when you cast your senses toward someone with no magic—like me—you see nothing?"

Sudden mischief danced in her eyes. "I see many things when I look at ye, Marcus Aquila."

The lightening of her expression made her look like a girl—carefree and happy. She should smile more often, he decided.

He grinned in return. "Many things? Like what?"

But she only shook her head slightly and turned away, as if she'd suddenly realized she'd been too light-hearted. "What ye say is true. Those who have no magic, have no aura."

He wished he could bring the teasing light back into her eyes, but he wasn't sure how to do it. "So," he said slowly. "If I forge this sword for you, what would you do with it? Attempt an attack on Strabo? Because if that's your intent—"

"'Tis not. The Druids of Avalon use magic only for good, or in defense." She hesitated, biting her lip. "I intend to bind powerful spells of Light to the sword. The presence of the blade on Avalon will strengthen the mist."

Marcus considered her words. The Light, he knew, was not as dangerous as Deep Magic. But it was magic nonetheless, and powerful. He wanted nothing to do with it. And yet—could he afford to refuse her? There was Breena to consider.

Gwen sensed his hesitation. "I know ye have no love of magic. No doubt ye do not wish to help me."

"I'm not completely unwilling. But if I agree to do this for you, I will require a service in return."

She looked wary. "What service?"

He expelled a breath. "It has to do with Breena. I don't want her to go to Avalon, but she's troubled by visions . . ." He paced in front of the furnace, stirring up puffs of ash. "The dreams stopped last summer, but now they're back with a vengeance. She won't complain, because she doesn't want to upset Rhiannon, but I'm afraid she's close to breaking. I fear for her health." He stopped and looked at her. "Rhys told Breena you helped Owein overcome the pain of his visions, and that you could do the same for her."

"I have a talent for spellcraft. I weave the ancient Words of the Old Ones into new patterns. I crafted a spell that helped Owein greatly. If Breena came to the sacred isle, 'tis likely I could do the same for her."

"I want you to help her here, in Isca. Then there will be no need for her to leave."

Gwen's brows rose. "Rhys has been given the task of bringing Breena to Avalon. He would be furious if I were to do such a thing."

"As you said, Rhys's anger is not an unusual occurrence."

She gave a reluctant laugh. "Nay, it is not." Her expression turned serious. "Are ye saying that if I teach Breena to control her visions, ye will forge my sword?"

"There is one other condition as well." One that would allow him to endure her presence without going mad.

"Tell me, then, and let us come to an agreement."

Instead of replying, he asked another question. "You traveled here as a wolf, didn't you?"

"You cannot know that."

"You carried no pack and wore only the thinnest cloak, despite the chill. No woman would travel so far with so little."

For a moment, he thought she would deny it. But then she shrugged. "I needed to travel swiftly, and a wolf is a poor packhorse."

"Shape-shifting is Deep Magic. Forbidden magic."

"I know what it is," Gwen said sharply.

"You have little respect for Cyric's teachings, then."

"Nay! I, more than anyone, know the dangers of Deep Magic. I do not call it lightly."

Marcus crossed his arms and hardened his voice to match hers. "If my father knew you'd run here as a wolf, he would throw you out. He has no more love for Deep Magic than I do."

"Do ye mean to tell him?"

"No. No one in my family knows of your power. I

never told them. And only Breena knows about Rhys's shape-shifting. Your secret is safe."

Her shoulders eased. "I thank ye for that." She looked up. "What is this last condition you mean to insist upon?"

He captured her gaze. "You must promise not to call the wolf while you are here."

She crossed her arms and rubbed her hands over her upper arms, as if suddenly realizing she was cold. She bit her lip. Silence stretched between them.

"I must have your word," Marcus said.

"And if I give it, ye will forge the sword? Help me bind my magic to it?"

He nodded once, slowly.

"Then aye, Marcus. Ye have my promise. I will not call the wolf."

Chapter Five

It was not really a lie.

Gwen told herself that as she exited the smithy with Marcus. She kept a careful distance between them as she walked at his side along the path to the main house. She'd told him she would not call the wolf. She could keep that promise. What she couldn't promise was that the wolf would not call her.

Somehow, she did not think Marcus would appreciate the distinction.

And yet, what could she do? If she refused his terms, he would not forge her sword. And Avalon had need of the weapon in her dream. She was sure of it. Her vision had been a true one.

Why hadn't she told Rhys?

Pride. She had not wanted to present her vision to her brother and listen to a disapproving litany. She was sure of her path, and she would take it, despite the fact that she'd had to break her promises to Cyric in order to do so. Once she returned to Avalon with the sword, the Elders would understand. And it was not as if she'd left Avalon unprotected, even if Cyric grew too weak to hold the mist. Rhys was there. Rhys was Cyric's blood as much as she. His power could hold the mist.

Rhys, who had shifted and never told her. Rhys, who had berated her for giving in to the Deep Magic of the wolf.

Resentment hit like a storm, turning her vision red. She would never have guessed that Rhys—honest, honorable Rhys—was such a hypocrite. His power was not less than hers, as he'd always claimed. Nay, as she'd suspected, his magic mirrored hers.

"Gwen?"

She was so absorbed in her anger that at first she thought she'd imagined her brother's voice in her mind. Then it came again.

"Gwen. Do ye hear me?"

She closed her eyes briefly. She and Rhys had been constantly in each other's minds as children, but when they reached adolescence, and grew apart, they'd let the link lapse. Until last year, when Gwen, trapped in wolf form and desperate for help, had reached out to her twin with her mind. After her rescue, the renewed intimacy had been awkward. They had not spoken silently since then. Until now.

"I am here, Rhys."

His relief—and his anger—flowed into her mind. She fought to control her own anger. He had lied to her! Well, she allowed, perhaps he hadn't lied, but he had omitted telling her that he was bound to Deep Magic as surely as she was.

"Why are ye calling to me? Has something happened?" Anxiety snaked through her gut. *"Has Strabo pierced the mist?"*

"Not yet. Where are ye?"

"I . . . I cannot say."

"What are ye doing, then? Tell me that, at least."

Gwen hesitated. *"I do what I must. Trust me, Rhys."*

"What ye must do is come home, Gwen."

She did not answer.

"Gwen, so far I've kept your absence from Cyric, but I cannot keep up the pretense much longer."

"Then I pray ye do not. I will be gone for some time. But be assured what I do, I do for the good of Avalon."

"Or for what ye think is the good of Avalon. But it does not bode well that ye think ye need to do it in secret. I can think of only one reason for that. Deep Magic."

Again, she was silent.

"Whatever your plan, abandon it, Gwen."

"How can ye ask that of me? Ye do not even know what I intend!"

"I do not have to. If it involves Deep Magic, it is better left undone. Ye know Cyric's teaching: whatever good can be accomplished with Deep Magic is far outweighed by the danger it represents. Ye vowed to walk only in the Light, Gwen. Do not forget it. Come home, where ye belong."

She remained silent.

"Gwen? Do ye hear me? Gwen? Gwen!"

Hot with anger, she threw up a spell to block Rhys from her mind. How dare he judge her! She would do what she knew was right, what was necessary. She would be careful. Rhys should know that. He was her *twin*. He should trust her. But he did not.

She dared a sideways glance at Marcus, who had not spoken since they'd left the smithy. His expression was grim; he did not want to forge her sword, but he was willing to do it if it meant Breena could avoid traveling to Avalon. Rhys and Cyric would not be pleased, but Gwen could not refuse Marcus's bargain if it meant she would gain the Lady's sword. And a chance to be close to *him*.

She could not deceive herself—her journey to Isca had as much to do with this darkly handsome, bluntly charming Roman as it did with any message from the Lady. She'd wanted to see him. Talk to him. Know him as something more than a vague memory. She suffered a pinch of guilt when she thought of what she had not told him about the sword. Resolutely, she ignored it. It was not necessary that he know.

She could hardly believe she was walking beside him now. Nor that he had kissed her—kissed her! For the past year, her single memory of him—the expression in his beautiful eyes as he'd watched her shift—had burned in her mind. After just a few hours in his presence, that one image of him had been joined by a hundred more.

For a year, he'd been a dream. Now he was a man.

And what had she done? Bitten him.

Her cheeks burned with humiliation. And fear. The wolf had howled for freedom—what would have happened if she hadn't been able to hold it back? She could not bear to think of it, so she hastily shoved the thought from her mind. The solution was simple. Marcus could not be allowed to kiss her again.

They traveled the crushed-gravel path leading from the smithy to the main house, a rambling, one-story villa with stucco walls and a red-tiled roof. The home occupied the center of a much larger compound, which included several outbuildings, gardens, and small fields. The entire complex was enclosed by a high stone wall punctuated by iron gates. The sheer size of Marcus's home amazed her. The Aquila farm was several times larger than the entire Druid settlement on Avalon.

"What you see within the perimeter wall is only a small part of my father's land," Marcus said, breaking the silence. "The wheat and barley fields lie beyond."

"And inside? What are all these buildings used for?"

"The stable and smithy are near the main gates. My stepmother's rose garden is here in front of the house; the vegetable and herb gardens are behind the kitchen, near the bathhouse. Beyond the rear terrace are the orchard, various barns, a dovecote, a hare run, and cottages for the servants and field laborers."

"Rhys has told me ye keep no slaves, as most Romans do."

"Another reason why we're looked down upon. Father is not willing to keep his wife's kinspeople as slaves." Marcus snorted. "Even if Rhiannon would tolerate such a thing."

Gwen thought of Lucius Aquila, graciously doing his best to speak his wife's native tongue. Marcus, with his broad shoulders and shining dark hair, resembled his father greatly. Lucius, no doubt, was an image of what his son would look like in years to come, when his soulful eyes were tempered by crinkles at the corners, and his thick hair softened with hints of gray. Both men had a comforting presence about them, one that spoke of strength and constancy. But they were not precisely alike. Where Lucius's mien was almost regal, enhanced by his military bearing, Marcus's posture was more relaxed, his artist's eye more watchful. His emotions were much closer to the surface.

Marcus did not lead her back to the front door of the farmhouse, but down a path that rounded one of the house's long wings and gave out into the herb garden. As they walked between the rows, Gwen cast her senses toward the plants. No glow of magic returned. Her Light had not yet recovered from its encounter with the wolf's Deep Magic.

She paused, stifling a yawn. The brief energy the morning meal had given her was gone.

Marcus shot her a glance. "Tired from your journey?"

"Aye." She did not tell him the journey was the least of it.

"No doubt Rhiannon is already preparing your bedchamber, though I wish she wouldn't tax herself."

"Ye are very protective of her."

"We all are. Rhiannon doesn't carry babes well. She's lost several, both with her first husband and since Breena was born."

"Oh! I did not know."

"That's why Breena hasn't told Rhiannon or our father that her visions have returned. I must ask you to be discreet as well. It's best if they know nothing of Breena's lessons."

"Of course, if that's what ye want."

"It's not. What I want is for Breena's visions to disappear and never come back." He'd halted. His expression was sober—his love for his sister was plain.

Her chest squeezed a little. "I wish I could grant ye that wish, Marcus. But I cannot. Visions are sent by the Great Mother, and stop only when the Seer fulfills the Mother's purpose. But I'll do my best to ease Breena's pain."

He sighed. "I hope with all my heart that you succeed."

Trevor looked as bad as Rhys felt. Which was very bad indeed.

Rhys met the Caledonian at the rendezvous point they'd agreed upon earlier, a sheltered bit of cove in the river gorge below the Roman camp. Hefin perched on a large outcropping of rock, preening his feathers; Rhys hunkered just below, a large boulder at his back. One glance at the grim set of Trevor's jaw told Rhys all he needed to know: Trevor had not found any sign of Gwen's trail, either.

The northerner ran a hand over his blond beard as he dropped to a crouch next to Rhys. "Nothing." He jabbed a thumb in the direction of the Roman camp. "Did ye—"

"She has not been taken."

"And ye know this for a fact?"

"Aye. Do not ask me how." He let out a long breath. "But I am afraid of what she is about. Gwen is not the most cautious of women, and this sorcerer's magic is great."

Trevor's eyes were troubled. "I feel his Deep Magic, and his Darkness, probing the mist."

"Aye." Rhys felt it, too, in his bones, and it troubled him greatly. Gwen's words played in his mind. *What if the Light is not enough?* Whatever she was about, he was sure it involved Deep Magic. Worry put a bitter taste in the back of his mouth.

There was a brief silence.

"I canna believe she left without a word," Trevor said. "Strabo's magic much affects Cyric. If his hold on the mist slips, Avalon will need Gwen to act as Guardian."

Rhys stood abruptly. "If Cyric cannot hold the mist, I will." He was, after all, the only other Druid who could do so. As Gwen knew. If he hadn't been home, she would never have left.

Trevor gave a nod. Rhys felt like a fraud. No one on Avalon knew it—Rhys did not wish to risk panic in the village—but a good portion of Rhys's power was already given to bolstering Cyric's spell. Soon after Gwen's disappearance, Cyric's hold on the mist had failed.

"Gwen?" He reached for her again with his mind. He came up against the spellforms she'd erected to keep him out.

When he spoke, he did not know if the anger in his voice was directed at Gwen, or at himself. "When I find my sister, she will have much to answer for."

" 'Tis partly my fault, perhaps. I pressed her too hard. She doesna want the handfasting Cyric has requested for us."

"That's not true. She's just . . ." *Afraid,* Rhys wanted to say, but that would not be right. When had Gwen ever been afraid of anything? "She needs more time to accustom herself to the idea of marriage." When Trevor did not reply, he added, "She respects ye greatly."

"Respect isna love. Or even desire."

A movement from Hefin caught Rhys's eye. With a squawk, the merlin rose into the air. At the same time, Rhys caught sight of a raft gliding over the still waters of the swamp.

"Someone is coming. And rapidly, too."

Trevor stood. "Who?"

Rhys cast his senses toward Hefin and received a mental image in return. "Why, 'tis Penn."

The gangly, dark-haired adolescent was much changed from the dirty urchin Rhys had discovered scrounging for edible garbage in the roughest quarter of Londinium seven winters before. His gaze narrowed as Penn poled his raft frantically, jumping off before the craft had even reached the shore.

"What is it? What's wrong?"

"Cyric," Penn gasped.

Trevor caught the raft's pole before it sank into the swamp. "What of him, lad?"

"He's raving. In the midst of a vision. No one can calm him, not even Mared. Even Owein can barely restrain him."

"Impossible," Rhys exclaimed. "Why, Owein outweighs Cyric four times over!"

" 'Tis true. Mared says . . . she says 'tis not Cyric's spirit inside his body." The lad gulped a lungful of air. "She says Cyric is possessed."

If Gwen had been sleeping, she would not have heard the muffled thud.

She sat bolt upright in her unfamiliar Roman bed, all her senses abruptly focused on the noise. It had come from the bedchamber next to hers. Breena's. But now all was silent.

Another moment passed. Nothing. She started to ease back down onto the cushions when frantic scuffling launched her into action. Leaping from her bed, she ran into the passageway and yanked open Breena's closed door.

"Breena? What . . . Oh, Great Mother!"

She flew into the small room. Breena lay on the tiled floor, gasping, alarmingly close to the glowing coals in the brazier. A length of linen was wound about her neck. Gwen's hands shook as she fought to loosen the sheet. The lass's face was deathly pale, her lips tinged blue. If Gwen had been sleeping . . .

Finally—*finally*—she managed to yank the linen free. Breena gasped, her spine arching as her lungs filled. Gwen breathed an answering sigh of relief.

It was only then that Gwen became aware of something exceedingly odd. The wolf's drain on her powers had ended some hours earlier. Her senses were tingling now. She focused on Breena's aura. It was not, as she might have expected, the pure white of a Seer, but an odd shade of silver. Gwen had never seen magic that color before. A shiver chased down her spine.

Deep Magic or Light?

Sprawled on the floor beside Breena, Gwen gathered the lass in her arms. Her young body was rigid, her face etched with pain. Incredibly, Breena was still asleep.

"Wake, love. Ye are safe now."

Breena's eyes fluttered open. She stared straight ahead, but Gwen could tell she saw nothing of her bedchamber.

"No . . . *no!*" Breena's arm flailed, landing a solid blow to Gwen's left ear. "I don't want to be here. I don't want to See . . ."

I don't want to See . . . Gwen understood all too well—given a choice, no Seer would choose his talent. Looking into the future was often more curse than gift.

"Come back to me, Breena." Gwen smoothed a damp lock of red hair from the lass's forehead.

A measure of lucidity returned to Breena's eyes, though her pupils remained dilated and locked in pain. She clutched at her head, gripping her hair so tightly Gwen feared she would uproot a clump of it.

"Oh gods, it hurts." Tears squeezed from beneath Breena's eyelids; she rocked back and forth like a child. "This is the worst it's ever been. It feels like someone has used one of Marcus's hammers to crack open my skull."

Gwen could believe it. She'd witnessed the pain of

Cyric's visions all her life. In the past year, the pain Owein endured with his Seer's power had spurred Gwen to craft a unique combination of Words and Light to ease his pain.

She laid her hand on Breena's head. The lass's pain and terror spiked through her, along with a sense of deep and despairing helplessness. The odd silver aura shimmered. There was no Darkness in it, Gwen was relieved to note. But its essence remained a mystery to her.

She spoke the Words and sent Light streaming into Breena's body. "Breathe," she commanded gently. "Slowly."

Breena gave a small nod. Her chest expanded and contracted with a shudder.

"That's it, love. Now—"

There was movement in the doorway. Gwen gave an inward groan as terror snapped back into Breena's eyes and a spasm wracked her body. Rhiannon cried out, rushing into the room. Gwen held up a hand. "Stay back. Just for a moment. Please."

Rhiannon hovered uncertainly, her mother's instinct at odds with Gwen's sharp command. The reprieve would not last long. Working swiftly, Gwen poured Light into Breena's mind.

The lass's magic responded. Her power was vast and untapped, as Rhys had said. Its intensity was almost frightening, even for Gwen, whose own power was considerable. 'Twas a heavy burden. Breena would have no choice but to come to terms with it, despite Marcus's wish it would just go away.

Little by little, Breena relaxed in Gwen's arms. Gwen gazed down at her pale, freckled face, aware of a startling rush of protectiveness. She was so young. Too young for this.

By the time Breena had gone completely slack in her arms, two more figures crowded the doorway—Marcus and Lucius. Both men held their bodies taut, ready to defend. Their combined energy—so potent and so male—sliced at Gwen's frayed senses.

The wolf, scenting the challenge, raised its head.

Great Mother, nay! Not here, not now. Desperately, Gwen fought to drive the beast back, enduring a brief, tense moment when she did not know if her spell would succeed. Then, to her immense relief, the wolf settled its snout on its paws and closed its eyes.

The breath left her lungs in a trembling rush.

She took a moment to collect herself, then raised her head and looked up at Breena's anxious family. Marcus caught her gaze at once, his dark eyes intense with an expression that caused her a rush of sharp, irrational fear. Had he sensed the wolf? Nay, she was thinking nonsense. He had no magic. It was not possible he could know her inner struggle.

"She's all right now," she said in a shaky whisper. "The vision has passed."

Rhiannon started to sink to her knees, but Lucius stepped forward and caught her arm. "Let me," he murmured. Bending, he lifted Breena to the bed.

Rhiannon sank down on the mattress. Lucius moved to stand behind her while Marcus lit a lamp. "It is a long while since she's been visited by a vision," Rhiannon whispered, pressing the back of her hand to her daughter's forehead. "I hoped . . . I prayed her Sight would not return."

Gwen, rising, exchanged a glance with Marcus. He

went to Rhiannon's side and placed his hand on her shoulder. His expression was pained. "Breena's visions returned a month ago. She didn't want to tell you and Father."

Rhiannon's head came up. "Ye knew all that time, Marcus? And ye kept it from us?"

Marcus remained silent. Rhiannon clasped Breena's limp hand and then turned fearful eyes to Gwen. "Are ye sure the magic did not harm her?"

"Aye," Gwen hastened to assure her. "She's but resting from the ordeal."

"I'll sit with her." Rhiannon's eyes said clearly she wanted to be alone with her daughter.

Gwen let out an unsteady breath as she preceded the men from the room. Once in the passageway, she examined Marcus more closely. He was still dressed in the shirt and *braccas* he'd worn at dinner, but now they were tinged with soot. Grime streaked his tanned face. His black hair was disheveled, his jaw shadowed by a day's worth of stubble. He'd not been sleeping, any more than she.

She could not stop herself from staring. His shirt, dark with sweat beneath his powerful arms, clung to his torso, outlining every cord of muscle. The laces at the garment's neckline were untied, revealing a triangle of black, curling hair. Gwen's belly clenched. No man on Avalon was so dark, so exotically foreign. So beautiful in his masculinity. A curious emptiness gnawed at her stomach.

Lucius closed the door to Breena's chamber. "What happened?" he asked tightly.

Gwen made a helpless gesture. "I hardly know. I heard a noise. I found her in the grip of a vision. She was on the floor, thrashing."

"It might have been just a nightmare." Marcus's tone carried no conviction.

"I think we all know it was not," Lucius said. Worry shadowed his face, making him look older than his years. He turned to Gwen. "How were you able to calm her? Rhiannon has never been able to, not in the midst of a vision."

"I . . .'tis hard to describe." Gwen was aware Marcus was watching her closely. "Most simply put—I spoke Words of magic and sent Light into her mind. When she calmed, the vision dissolved."

"Was this the spell you described to me yesterday?" Marcus asked.

"Similar, aye."

"The two of you have spoken of Breena's visions?" Lucius interjected.

"Yes. I asked Gwen to teach Breena to control her visions with magic. If the lessons are successful, she will not have to travel to Avalon."

"You can stop these visions?" Lucius demanded of Gwen.

"Nay, that I cannot do. 'Tis not a vision sprung from Darkness, I am sure. Visions of Light and Deep Magic come from the Great Mother. No mortal can stop them. Breena's vision will only cease when she understands the Great Mother's message and acts to fulfill it."

"When will that be?" Lucius asked.

Gwen rubbed her arms, suddenly aware of the chill in the unheated passageway. "I cannot say. Breena's youth, her inexperience with magic, the intense pain she endures . . . all these things interfere with her ability to interpret her vision. I . . . can help her with the pain. I can teach her certain spellforms that will lessen the intensity of what she feels when the vision overtakes her. After that, she will need to find her own way to the Goddess's will."

She could tell Marcus did not like her answer. It was not the neat solution he'd hoped for. It was, however, the only help she could offer. Better he understand that now.

Lucius rubbed his jaw. "Rhys has long insisted that Breena can only be trained on Avalon."

Gwen spread her hands. "My brother and grandfather believe such strong magic should not be practiced away from Avalon."

"But you are willing to teach Breena here, in Isca?"

"More than willing. No one so young should suffer so."

At that moment, Breena's door opened. Rhiannon appeared in a sliver of lamplight. "She is awake. She wants ye, Lucius."

He nodded. "I will come in a moment."

Turning to Gwen, he pitched his voice low. Gwen sensed his reluctance to voice his need—he was not a man used to asking for help. "If you could ease my daughter's suffering, I would be forever in your debt."

"I will do whatever I can."

Lucius searched her gaze, then nodded. "Thank you."

He disappeared into Breena's room, leaving Gwen alone with Marcus.

"It was worse than what you led my parents to believe, wasn't it?"

Marcus watched Gwen's face closely as she weighed her response to his question. He recognized the exact moment when she decided to tell him the truth. Her shoulders slumped a little. Her eyes, troubled as they were, did not avoid his gaze.

He was struck again by the sheer improbability of

her presence in his house. She was standing so near, dressed in one of Breena's sleeping tunics. The garment was too wide and too short for her. The hem fell well above her ankles, drawing his gaze to her bare feet. Her white-blond hair was unbound. It fell to her waist like untethered moonlight.

"Aye, 'twas much worse. When I found her, the bedsheet was twisted about her neck and her lips were blue."

"*Pollux.*" Marcus experienced a wave of pure terror. "If you hadn't been sleeping nearby . . ." He couldn't finish the thought. His fingers clenched; he felt like striking something. "This is my fault. I should have listened to Rhys. I should have sent her to Avalon."

"Ye could not have known." She reached out, as if to touch his arm, then at the last moment seemed to think better of it. "Ye did what ye thought best, out of love. And Avalon is hardly the safest haven right now."

"I appreciate your saying that, even if it's only to ease my conscience. Thank the gods you heard her in time. Did she cry out?"

"Nay. It was most strange. She did not utter a sound until I called her from her trance. If she hadn't fallen from her bed, and if I hadn't been lying awake, I would have heard nothing. Perhaps the Great Mother was watching over her after all."

"I can only hope that's true." Marcus unclenched his fist and rubbed the back of his neck.

"She is fine, Marcus. Tomorrow I will begin her lessons. And I'll stay in her room at night, until I am sure she has mastered them."

"You would do that?"

"Of course."

He exhaled. "Thank you." He looked at her more closely, taking note of the dark circles under her eyes.

"You were awake? I'm surprised. During supper, you all but fell asleep atop a plate of cod."

"If I had done so, the sauce would have awakened me," Gwen said wryly. "My tongue burned unmercifully after eating that. What was in it? I dared not ask, for fear of offending Rhiannon."

Marcus chuckled. "It's *liquamen*. Fermented from anchovies, brine, and salt. We Romans pour it on everything. Rhiannon did not like it much at first either."

"And now she does?" Gwen asked dubiously.

"She tolerates it." He sobered. "Why couldn't you sleep? Was the room too cool? The mattress uncomfortable?"

"Nay, not at all! The fault was mine. I often have trouble sleeping. 'Tis a problem that's plagued me ever since . . ." Her voice trailed off.

"Since?"

She drew breath. "Since the night ye and Rhys rescued me."

"Then it seems we share an affliction. I haven't slept much since that night, either."

Her startled gaze met his. He watched her wonder whether or not to pursue the opening he'd given her. Apparently the answer was no, because she half turned to her chamber door. "I should try again to sleep."

The wise course would have been to let her go. But somehow, he couldn't. "No. Please. Stay with me."

She turned back, brows raised. He summoned an easy smile. "Why should you go back to bed? After all that's happened, you won't sleep tonight, any more than I will. Surely the ceiling beams aren't that fascinating."

She hesitated. "Just what do ye propose I do instead?"

"Talk to me," he said promptly. "But not here."

He extended a hand, but she did not take it. "Where?"

"The kitchen. I've been working all night and I'm starved. That's why I was in the house in the first place." He chuckled. "I'll feed you as well, I promise. You're in sore need of it. Will you come? Please?"

She tilted her head and touched a finger to her lips. "Since ye ask so politely, aye."

He laughed then, and she did, too. She put her hand in his, and he fought to conceal his reaction to the contact. She'd be out of his life—and married to another man—as soon as he forged her sword. But for as long as she was living under his roof, he wouldn't pass up the opportunity to be alone with her.

To his surprise, she didn't take her hand from his as he led her out of the sleeping wing of the house and into the entrance gallery. They passed the formal receiving and dining rooms and Rhiannon's hearth room; the kitchen lay beyond. When they reached it, he reluctantly dropped her hand.

He busied himself rummaging around in a cupboard for a tallow taper. Touching it to the banked coals in the oven, he used the flame to light one of the hanging oil lamps.

A cozy glow settled over the room. Gwen's gaze skimmed over the long table and the bank of brick ovens. Three tall ovens were for baking; the other two were waist high, topped with iron frying grates he'd made himself, years ago. Shelves held clay pots and copper bowls, and jars of herbs and spices. Bronze and iron skillets of all sizes hung from hooks overhead. A bronze-bladed knife with a bone handle—another example of Marcus's work—gleamed on a chopping board, beside a wooden mortar and pestle and a pebble-studded bowl used for making soft cheese. A washing basin and bins for firewood and charcoal occupied either side of the door leading to the vegetable and herb gardens. He watched Gwen's eyes go round as she took it all in. No doubt cooking facilities on Avalon were far more primitive.

He pulled out one of the high stools flanking the table with a flourish. "Your throne, my hungry queen."

Gwen laughed, and sat. He felt her eyes on him as he inspected the contents of several cloth-covered bowls and platters, the apple barrel, the cheese chest, and the bread and pastry cupboards. He piled his selections on a platter, then lifted a pitcher and filled two large mugs with *cervesia*.

Gwen shook her head, a smile playing about her lips. "Do ye always eat so much in the middle of the night? Even after all ye ate at supper? There will be nothing left for breakfast."

He pretended offense. "Would you have me starve?" A mischievous voice in his head prompted him to lean across the table and pitch his voice low. "After all, I have to keep up my strength if I'm to be of any use to you."

A becoming blush stained her cheeks, but to his surprise, she didn't back away from his teasing. "I have no doubt your . . . strength . . . is equal to any task."

Gods. Was she flirting with him? He set down his mug with a thump. "Don't you?"

"Nay." Her teasing demeanor ebbed far too quickly. "I sensed your strength that night," she said quietly. "When ye carried me from the cave."

He didn't know if her oblique reminder of the wolf he'd encountered in that cave was meant to entice him or warn him away. Studying her, he thought perhaps she didn't know, either.

The silence between them stretched into awkwardness. He reached for a plate piled high with fried dough dipped in honey.

"Try one," he said, sliding the platter toward her. "These are my favorite."

"Oh, nay. I couldn't. I'm not hungry."

Marcus frowned at her. "I can't imagine why not. You're as slender as a sapling and you ate hardly anything yesterday. You probably had even less during your journey here. It won't do you any good to get sick." He snagged one of the pastries between his thumb and forefinger and held it out to her.

She took it with a sigh. "I suppose you are right."

"I often am. It's a talent of mine."

That earned him a laugh. "Arrogant man."

Leaning forward, she bit into the pastry while he still held it, her lips closing hardly a hairsbreadth from his fingers. Drawing back, she chewed slowly and swallowed. " 'Tis delicious."

Marcus's gaze clung to a drop of honey shining at the corner of her mouth. When the tip of her tongue darted out to catch it, he nearly groaned out loud. *Hades.* Perhaps he should have let her go back to her bed—alone.

He ate the other half of her pastry—a simple act that seemed suddenly steeped in intimacy. A question hammered in his mind. He formed a casual version of it on his lips.

"Did you really tell no one in Avalon that you meant to come to Isca?"

She blinked. "I told ye I did not."

"No one at all? Not even . . . your betrothed?"

Her jaw dropped. "But—I am not betrothed!"

He met her gaze frankly. "Rhys told me you were."

"My brother should not have said such a thing. 'Tis not true. No matter how much he and Cyric may want it."

Marcus's chest expanded as his lungs filled. "You don't like the man your grandfather has picked for you?"

"Oh, I like Trevor well enough. He is a fine man. Everyone on Avalon holds him in high esteem. He's broad and strong, but also kind and respectful." She grimaced. "And quiet. 'Tis as if the man must pay in silver for each word he utters."

Marcus reached for an apple. "He sounds boring."

Gwen sighed. "The other women adore him."

"But you do not?"

She shrugged. Marcus's mood lightened rapidly as he bit into his apple. He made short work of the fruit, tossed the core in the rubbish bin, and applied himself to the bread and cheese, handing thick slices of both to Gwen. "Eat this. All of it."

She did, and washed down her meal with a long draught of *cervesia*. Meanwhile, Marcus swallowed seven honey confections.

"Ye must have truly been working hard," Gwen said, a smile in her voice.

"I was. I've done two days' worth of work in half a night. There's a commission—a set of daggers—I needed to complete before I start on your sword."

"And did ye finish?"

"Yes. Tomorrow I'll deliver them and use the money I get to purchase more ore. When I return, we'll discuss the design."

He drained his mug. He was surprised to find he was actually looking forward to the challenge of forging a magic sword. Especially if Gwen's Light could help him smelt *chalybs* . . .

"Do you know much about ironworking?" he asked.

She shook her head. "Very little. We do not have an iron forge on Avalon. It would be difficult to get enough fuel, even if we had a smith, which we do not. I work only in silver, and small quantities at that." She slipped a finger past the neckline of her tunic and drew out a chain that held a silver pendant. "Just enough for this."

He studied the Druid pendant. "It's like the one you made for Breena."

"I craft a pendant for every woman Rhys brings to Avalon."

"And the men receive tattoos of the same symbol?"

"Aye."

He examined her pendant more closely. "You couldn't have made this one. It's far too old."

She dropped the charm back inside her tunic. "Ye have a good eye, Marcus. This pendant is the pattern for the others. My great-grandmother crafted it. She was one of the twin Daughters of the Lady. Has Rhys told ye the story?"

"A little. The Lady came from the East a century ago, carrying the grail Owein and Clara searched for last year. It belonged to a powerful carpenter prophet."

"That's right. Her ship ran aground on Avalon in the days before the Romans drove the Druids from the sacred isle. She was heavy with child, and soon after gave birth to twin Daughters. One became my great-grandmother, the other, Clara's."

"And now you both are expected to bear more Daughters, to continue the Lady's line."

"That's right. The Lady's magic passes to her female descendants. That's why Cyric is so anxious that I wed. Truly, I was very happy when Clara's ancestry was discovered and she came to Avalon. It enabled me to avoid my own handfasting." She grimaced. "For a while longer, at least."

"You don't wish to marry at all?"

" 'Tis not that." She worried her lower lip with her teeth. Marcus's eye was drawn to the movement. "I know 'tis my duty to join my magic with that of another Druid and bear a Daughter. Trevor is as fine a man as any. He is quite eager to wed me."

Marcus could well imagine he was. But he obviously didn't deserve Gwen. If he did, Gwen would not be here in Isca, conversing with another man in the dead of the night.

"Why haven't you accepted him? Why did Rhys tell me you had?"

"I cannot say what is in my brother's mind, but as for me . . . Trevor does not know of the wolf. I cannot marry him with such a secret between us. But I am not ready to tell him." She crushed her last bit of bread into crumbs. "I'm not sure I ever will be ready, but the time will come when I must."

"Well," Marcus said carefully, pushing the plate containing the last honey pastry in her direction. "At least you don't have to think about him while you're here."

Gwen's startled eyes met his. A moment later, a reluctant smile curved her lips. She reached for the last sweet. "I suppose I do not."

Chapter Six

Gwen fell asleep just before dawn, with Marcus's words wrapped around her like a blanket. *You don't have to think of him while you're here.* Not of Trevor, nor of her future as his wife. Nor of the Elders' anger, nor Cyric's decline. Nor Rhys's inexplicable deception. For a short time, while she lived with Marcus and his family, she could forget all that turmoil. She would think only of the Lady's sword, and the man who would forge it.

It was almost noon when she awakened from the deepest sleep she'd enjoyed since her captivity. She hastened to the hearth room, where she found Breena and Rhiannon sitting at the table. Breena worked the pestle of a small stone mortar, grinding a pungent root, while Rhiannon mixed dried herbs from several piles, tying them into small squares of linen.

They greeted Gwen as she entered. The great mastiff lying by the hearth was less amenable to her presence. Its lips drew back in a snarl. When Gwen met its gaze calmly, it heaved to its feet and slunk out the door, head low and tail tucked between its hind legs. Breena's puzzled frown followed the animal. "That's odd. Titan is generally quite friendly."

Gwen shrugged, not surprised at all. As a rule, few animals other than Ardra and Hefin tolerated her presence. She studied Breena's face. The lass seemed much recovered from her ordeal of the night before, in the way that only the very young could manage. Her eyes were calm, and her cheeks had regained their color. Rhiannon, by contrast, looked weary.

" 'Tis good to see ye looking so well," Gwen told Breena.

"I have no headache, or fatigue, as I usually do after a vision. I have your magic to thank for that, I think." She paused. "Father told me you agreed to teach me spells to take away the pain."

"Aye. Marcus asked me yesterday to give ye lessons."

"It was Marcus's idea? I can hardly believe it. He hates magic."

"He loves ye," Rhiannon chided. "It distresses him to see ye suffer. And Gwen will be teaching ye the Light, after all. Not Deep Magic."

Gwen inspected the contents of Breena's mortar, avoiding Rhiannon's gaze. The lass was rhythmically reducing a lumpy root to a dull gray powder. The strong, pungent odor was unfamiliar. "What herb is this?"

"Valerian," Breena replied. "It aids in sleep. Though in my case, it's not effective."

"If the Great Mother wishes to send ye a message, no herb will prevent it," Gwen agreed. "How often are ye visited by visions?"

"There's no pattern to it. I can go months without one, then suddenly I'll be visited every night." A shadow passed over her expression. "That's how it's been for the past fortnight. Each night has been worse than the one before."

"Tell me a little of what ye See."

Breena met Gwen's gaze briefly, a shadow crossing her blue eyes. "I don't like to talk about it."

"Please. If I am to help . . ."

Breena's knuckles went white as her grip on the pestle tightened. "In the past—even as a small child—I'd see flashes of the future, or sometimes people and things that were lost. The visions would be repeated over and over, until the event I saw came pass, or whatever was lost came to be found. These new visions are different. I can hear nothing. I See very little. Only the figure of a woman, veiled with silver shadows."

Silver. The same color Gwen had seen in Breena's aura.

Breena set the pestle on the table. "There's nothing distinct at all, and yet I know . . ."

"What?" Gwen asked gently, exchanging a glance with Rhiannon. The older woman's eyes were very grave.

"It's not what I See that's upsetting. It's what I *feel*. The woman . . . I'm linked to her emotions. Someone is enraged with her. Beating her, choking her . . . I feel her terror, her helplessness. Somehow I know I'm the only person who can help this woman, but . . . how can I? I cannot move. I can't get to her."

Gwen absorbed Breena's words, reflecting on them for several long moments. "I cannot tell ye what the vision means. Ye must discover that on your own. But I can tell ye this: the Great Mother would not send ye a vision without guiding ye to its meaning. Once ye learn to banish the pain, perhaps ye may be able to find the vision's meaning."

"I hope so." Breena picked up a small silver spoon.

With a trembling hand, she scooped the powdered valerian root from the mortar into an earthenware jar. Gray dust spilled down the sides of the container.

Rhiannon spoke. "I thank the Great Mother for sending ye to us, Gwen. Surely your arrival here when Breena is in need of your skills was not by chance."

Gwen was grateful for the quiet conviction in Rhiannon's voice. It did much to ease her conscience. If the Great Mother had guided her steps to Isca, surely leaving Avalon had been the right decision.

Rhiannon layered her bundles of herbs in a long, low basket. "Lucius will soon return from observing the planting of the north field. And Aiden will be finishing his morning walk. They'll both be wanting the noon meal."

"Will Marcus be eating with us as well?" Breena asked. "I haven't seen him yet today."

"Marcus went into town," Rhiannon told her. "He doesna expect to return before supper." Depositing the last bundle in her basket, she rose. "I will see how Alma's meal is progressing."

Breena sprang to her feet and urged her mother back to her seat. "You'll do nothing of the sort. You were up half the night with me, and you've already done far too much this morning. Sit and rest while I make you another draught of raspberry leaves and honey."

Gwen rose. "I'll see to the meal."

Breena shot her a grateful glance. "Thank you. The kitchen is at the end of the wing."

Gwen didn't tell Breena she already knew well enough where the kitchen was. Once there, she found Alma and two helpers, a stout old Celt woman called Mab and a slight, pretty Roman girl named Celia, laying out the noon meal on two large trays. Gwen had never seen such a variety of food in her life. Meals on Avalon consisted most often of barley stew flavored with venison or fish and whatever wild greens or fruits Avalon's women gathered. Hard barley bannocks served as both bread and spoon. Only rarely did she have wheat bread, and then only dense brown loaves—never light, herbed bread that gave off such a heady aroma that it caused her mouth to water.

Alma's meal was a dizzying medley of texture and color. Gwen did not even know what most of the food was. The stout, smiling cook was more than happy to enlighten her.

"Coddled eggs to start," Alma declared. "Followed by a plate of oysters and mussels cooked in spiced wine— Master Lucius is especially fond of that dish. For the main course, a hare stuffed with chestnuts and thyme; sliced veal in a sauce made with raisins, honey, and vinegar. Leeks and asparagus. For dessert, soft cheese and fresh forest berries, and a peppered sweetcake."

Gwen could only shake her head in wonder. "It all looks delicious. May I carry one of the trays for ye?"

"Ah, no need, child. Has the master arrived yet?"

"Rhiannon expects Lucius any moment."

"Good. He hates when his dinner grows cold. Celia, tend to the drink."

The slight lass, who could not have seen more than eight summers, hefted a pitcher of *cervesia* and another filled with wine onto a tray. When Gwen offered to carry one of the pitchers for her, she shook her head with a smile. "I'm strong enough," she said proudly.

"Go back to the table," Alma admonished Gwen. "There's no work for a guest here."

Sensing it would be an insult to the cook to insist,

Gwen retreated. Being a guest in a Roman household, even one as informal as the Aquilas's, took some getting used to. On Avalon, there was always more work to be done than there were hands to do it.

Returning to the hearth room, she found Lucius and Aiden already seated with Rhiannon and Breena. Gwen slipped into an empty chair as the kitchen women entered with the meal. The food had barely been served when Gwen heard the faint tang of the gate bell.

Breena grinned. "That will be Lavina. She has uncanny knowledge of our meal hours."

Lucius rose. "I'll go see."

When her father had gone, Breena turned to Aiden, her eyes dancing. "A denarius says Lavina has brought Marcus a dessert."

"Ah, lass," Aiden responded with a croaking laugh. "Surely ye doan' think I'm fool enough to take such a losing wager. The woman never arrives without a sweet for your brother."

Rhiannon smothered a smile. "Lay an extra plate on the table, Breena. Did ye invite Lavina?"

Breena rose and took a plate from the cupboard. "I did, when she brought a pudding a few days ago. And I am vexed that Marcus isn't here to greet her. Lavina would make a lovely sister."

Gwen nearly spit out a mouthful of *cervesia.* "Marcus means to marry?"

"Oh, he doesn't *mean* to," Breena told her. Aiden chortled and sipped his beer. "But he can hardly avoid it. My brother is handsome, strong, uncommonly good-natured, and well past the age when most men marry."

"He is only five-and-twenty," Gwen protested.

"He'll fall soon—it's inevitable. Lavina isn't his only admirer, but I much prefer her to Claudia or Portia."

"What of Marcus? Whom does he prefer?" Gwen found herself asking, though she really did not wish to know.

Rhiannon sighed. "None of them, though they are all fine lasses. Marcus was smitten with Clara for such a long time—since she married Owein, no other woman has held his interest."

"Except the kind of woman a man doesn't bring home to his family," Breena interjected darkly. "At least whenever Rhys is here. The two of them spent more time at that brothel—"

Aiden coughed loudly.

"Breena." Rhiannon's tone was sharp. "Mind your tongue."

"Yes, Mother," she muttered. Then, under her breath, "It's only the truth."

Gwen took a deliberate sip of *cervesia*. It did nothing to calm her churning stomach. She knew what a brothel was—Dera, who had come to Avalon from the northern city of Eburacum, had told her of houses where men paid to couple with women. But it had never occurred to Gwen that her staid and cautious brother frequented such places.

It should not bother her. She'd never assumed Rhys was chaste, and she hardly expected Marcus to be celibate. They were men, after all. That rationalization, unfortunately, did little to ease the sudden tightness in her chest when she thought of Marcus with another woman.

She was even more discomfited when Lucius returned with Lavina. She was lovely—young, and dark and lush in the way of Roman women. Small and curvaceous, she had black hair, generous breasts, and lips the color of wine. Gwen felt suddenly scrawny and pale. Last night, Marcus had mentioned more than once how thin Gwen was—had he been comparing her to Lavina? She eyed the covered basket that swung on Lavina's shapely arm. The anticipated sweet, no doubt.

It soon became clear that Lavina's family had been friendly with the Aquilas since Lavina's childhood. Rhiannon asked after Lavina's young son. Gwen gathered the woman was a widow from a neighboring farm. She could not be more than twenty—her marriage must have been over soon after it had begun. For Lavina's benefit, and Lucius's, the conversation switched from Celtic to Latin. Gwen's head soon ached with the effort of translating.

Lavina was disappointed to find Marcus away from home, but she accepted a place at the table between Rhiannon and Gwen. Her basket contained the same honey-dipped pastries Marcus had declared his favorite the night before. Apparently, Lavina was well versed in Marcus's likes and dislikes.

She did not seem to know what to make of Gwen, whom Rhiannon introduced as a visiting cousin. Gwen did not elaborate. Lavina's eyes were inquisitive; she darted glances in Gwen's direction all through the meal. At last, her curiosity could not be contained. She addressed Gwen directly. "From what town do you come?"

The question caught Gwen off guard. "Dumnovaria," she blurted. It was the first Roman town that came to mind.

"Indeed! Why, I have an uncle who lives in Dumnovaria. Felix Cassius. Do you know him?"

"I'm sorry, I do not."

"But you must! It's such a small settlement, and my uncle is the town's only textile merchant. You must know his name, at least. It's not possible that you—"

"Lavina," a male voice said. "How good to see you."

Lavina looked up, her expression brightening with pleasure, the mystery of Gwen's home forgotten as swiftly as yesterday's weather. "Marcus! Rhiannon did not expect you."

"Nonetheless, I am here." Marcus sent Gwen a swift glance as he strode to the table.

Gwen could not take her eyes from him even after he looked away. The room seemed smaller for his presence, somehow. And warmer. He did not look like a man who had worked through the night without sleeping. His short, curly hair was tousled, and his dark eyes sparkled with health and recent exertion. He must have ridden into town, for he smelled pleasantly of horse and leather.

Rhiannon smiled as her stepson strode to the table and greeted her with a touch on the shoulder and a kiss on the cheek. "We would have waited before eating had we known ye would be home for dinner," she said.

"Don't trouble yourself about it." Marcus turned to clasp Lavina's outstretched hand. He slid into the empty seat beside her without looking again at Gwen. "My business in town concluded earlier than I expected. I trust there's still some food left?"

"Of course," Rhiannon said.

Lavina smiled sweetly and laid a proprietary hand on his arm. "And I brought dessert—honeyed pastries. Your favorite."

Marcus looked discomfited, but he managed a charming smile. "Er . . . how nice."

Breena smothered a laugh with her hand. Rhiannon shot her daughter a reproachful look. Gwen looked down at her food as Lavina fussed over filling Marcus's plate.

She was no longer hungry.

"Dumnovaria?" Marcus asked Gwen later, after Lavina's horse-drawn cart had rattled out the front gates. Gwen had never been so happy to see a woman go. Marcus had eaten fully half of her honeyed pastries. And he had clearly enjoyed every one.

It was irrational, Gwen knew, but his pleasure made her feel inadequate. She hated cooking. If she were to attempt to make a honeyed pastry, no doubt it would taste like a honeyed lump of charcoal.

"Her question surprised me. Dumnovaria was the first town that came to mind." They stood in the center of the herb garden, where Marcus had sought her out after seeing Lavina to her cart. "Rhys was in Dumnovaria last autumn," she added defensively.

"Dumnovaria is little more than a cattle track. You might have said Londinium. That city is huge, and far away. Lavina's never been there."

"Ye would know, wouldn't ye?" She did not care for the notion that Marcus had intimate knowledge of Lavina's comings and goings.

He looked at her, clearly baffled. "Why wouldn't I? I've known Lavina since she was eight years old and I was Breena's age. Her husband was one of my best friends. He died of a fever two years ago."

"Oh!" Gwen felt suddenly very mean-spirited. "Ye must have been saddened by his death."

Marcus crossed his arms, still eyeing her. "I was."

She made a show of examining some yellow mustard flowers. " 'Twould be fitting, then, if ye married Lavina."

"*Jupiter.* That's Breena's wish, not mine. I'm no more eager to marry than you are. Lavina's beginning to lose patience with me already. Soon she'll turn her efforts to a more likely prospect."

"I don't know why ye would not want to wed her," Gwen said perversely. "She's a lovely woman. Very . . . shapely."

"Yes, she's shapely enough, but she chatters incessantly."

Gwen made a dismissive gesture. "All women chatter."

"You don't."

"Aye, well, I am different from most women."

Marcus laughed. "That's true enough. Most women are not prickly, wild-born Druidesses."

Something in his tone raised her ire. "I am not *prickly.* Nor am I wild-born, much to my regret. I was born right here, in Isca Silurum."

Marcus's brows shot upward. "You were? You and Rhys both?"

She sent him a look of amused disdain. "Of course, both of us. We are twins, after all."

Marcus gave her a sheepish grin. "Right. I'm just . . . surprised." He shook his head. "No, more like astounded. Rhys never told me he was born in Isca."

She moved down the row of herbs. "My brother can be very secretive, I am learning."

"How old were you when you left Isca?"

"We had seven years, I think, no more, when Cyric took us to reclaim our heritage."

"The three of you returned to Avalon alone?"

"Nay, we traveled with Mared—she is Cyric's cousin-by-marriage. Padrig, my mother's brother, and his wife, also came with us." She paused. "Their daughter, Blodwen, had nine years."

Marcus's tone sharpened. "Blodwen is the cousin who imprisoned you with Deep Magic."

Gwen swallowed hard. It was difficult to think of those hopeless days, not least because her memories of that time were not human ones. They belonged to the wolf. She felt Marcus's hand on her arm, and realized she had turned away from him.

"It still distresses you."

She looked up into dark eyes tinged with pity. Unreasonably, his sympathy prompted a hot rush of dark emotion. The wolf, sensing her agitation, stirred. Its hackles rose. Her mind's human focus slipped.

Marcus's gaze narrowed. "Gwen? What is it? Are you all right?" His fingers tightened on her arm.

The wolf viewed his touch as a threat. The beast tensed. Gwen squeezed her eyes shut and sucked in a steadying breath. One heartbeat passed, then two, three, as she summoned Words of Light. The beast relaxed, put its head on its paws, and returned to its sleep. *Thank the Great Mother.*

When she opened her eyes, she found Marcus staring at her with a strange expression. Did he suspect how weak she was? How much the wolf controlled her? The thought made her ill.

"I . . . I do not like to think about that time."

"Of course." His voice was soothing.

His touch on her arm turned into a caress. She felt ashamed, deceiving him this way. But she didn't know what else to do. She could hardly tell him how close the wolf was to the surface of her emotions.

After a moment, he asked, "Was Cyric also born in Isca?"

Gwen shook her head. "My grandparents were born on Avalon. My grandmother's mother, as ye know, was one of the twin Daughters of the Lady. My grandparents were babes when their parents fled the sacred isle."

Marcus nodded. "It would have been soon after Queen Boudicca's revolt. Governor Paulinus was convinced Druids had stirred rebellion all over Britannia. Druidry was outlawed; Druid learning centers were ordered destroyed."

"Many Druids were killed when the Roman army marched on Avalon. But not all. Some, like my grandparents, escaped."

Marcus was silent for a moment. "So it was Cyric's idea, years later, to return to the sacred isle?"

"Aye. By then my grandmother had been dead many years. When my mother—" She stopped suddenly, swallowing her words. She hadn't meant to take the story so far.

But Marcus, of course, would not let it be. "What of your mother? And your father? Rhys rarely speaks of them."

"They died before we left Isca. First my father, then my mother. Mama was a Daughter of the Lady and Cyric's only child. He took her loss hard."

"How did they die? Illness?"

"Nay. They were murdered." Once again, she sensed he was waiting for her to say more. Strangely, she found herself wanting to confide in him. "A soldier killed them."

"What happened?"

"I hardly know. Rhys and I—we were so young. Our memories of that time are clouded. Cyric never speaks of it, nor do Mared and Padrig. They say only that the Lady's carpenter prophet teaches us to forgive our enemies."

"I would not forgive such an offense," Marcus said grimly.

"Sometimes I think Cyric has not truly forgiven, either. Certainly he still grieves. I think . . . I think that is the reason he has kept me close to him on Avalon. Mared tells me I'm the very image of my mother." She spread her hands in a helpless gesture. "Sometimes . . ."

"Sometimes, what?" Marcus prompted gently.

She did not answer until she was sure she could do so without tears. "Sometimes, I wonder if my grandfather has ever truly seen me. Or if I have always been the ghost of the daughter he lost."

Chapter Seven

*I*t was dusk before Cyric's rantings quieted completely, after Mared managed to force a calming draught down his throat. Rhys left the healer sitting by his grandfather's pallet. He was exhausted by his search for Gwen's trail, and the spell she'd erected to block his mental calls was still in place. He wanted only a quiet place where he could give himself over to oblivion for a few hours.

Unfortunately, it was not to be. When he emerged from Cyric's hut, the whole of Avalon's population was gathered in the village common. As they caught sight of him, their hushed conversation died. The youngest children hid behind the skirts of the women.

"Cyric rests peacefully," he told them. "Mared says he will sleep till dawn."

Padrig stood alone in the doorway of his roundhouse, leaning on his staff. "And the enchantment?"

Rhys looked at his uncle's sour, lined face. Never cheerful or hearty, even in youth, Padrig had grown illtempered and haggard since the disgrace of his daughter. Blodwen's power had permanently shattered when the Deep Magic spell she'd called against Avalon had turned against her. Afterward, she'd been banished from Avalon. In his shame, Padrig had also spoken of leaving. Cyric had begged him to stay.

Rhys wondered whether it might have been better if Padrig had been allowed to go. The old Druid had turned bitter. Rhys could discern little of the Light in his uncle's countenance.

"The enchantment, if indeed Cyric's affliction was an enchantment, is gone," Rhys told him.

"An enchantment it was. A Dark one." Padrig shook his staff. "If your sister were here, as she should be, the sorcerer's spell would not have taken root."

"If Gwen is gone, 'tis for a good reason."

"What reason could there be to leave Avalon, especially when Cyric forbade it?"

Rhys strangled his anger and summoned a tone of respect. "When Gwen returns, she will explain."

"*If* she returns. And if she does not, will ye do your duty and take the role of Guardian? It should be yours by right."

Rhys squared his shoulders. "There will be no need for me to hold the mist," he lied. "Gwen will return soon."

The old man made a derisive sound. Jabbing his staff into the dirt, he turned and stalked into his hut.

Rhys crossed the yard to Owein and Trevor, who had been watching the exchange. Clara sat nearby, warming herself before a small fire. Her belly was enormous—Rhys could hardly believe the babe hadn't yet emerged. He had limited experience with such things, but even his untrained eye could tell Clara's time would not be long in coming.

"Dinna mind Padrig," Owein said, clapping a hand

on Rhys's shoulder. "The old man looks for Light, but sees only Darkness."

"I fear this time he is right. The visions Cyric endured were not of the Light."

Clara cradled her belly. "Strabo has pierced the mist with his Dark spells? How can that be? Cyric's Light is strong."

"My grandfather's health fails."

"Many Druids are most powerful when they are closest to death," Owein said.

There was truth to Owein's words, and it disturbed Rhys greatly. Cyric's mists should not be thinning—if anything, his dying in the Light would strengthen Avalon's protection. But it did not seem to be so. If not for Rhys's magic, Avalon would have already been exposed.

"The Roman is strong with Outland magic," Trevor said.

"Our Druid Light is also strong," Owein argued. "It should not—" He halted as Clara went stiff, stifling a gasp.

Owein's face paled, making his red hair and beard seem even more vivid. He crouched at his wife's side and laid a steadying hand on her shoulder. "What is it, love? Is the babe coming?"

Clara's shoulders relaxed a fraction. Her hand remained on her stomach. "No, I don't think so. Not yet. There is no pain, only a tightening. Mared says my womb is preparing, but it will be some days yet before the birthing begins."

"Ye must rest. Do ye wish for me to lie with ye and rub your back? Ye look worn."

Clara looked at Rhys. "If you can spare my husband for a short while . . ."

"Go," Rhys told her. "Take care of the babe."

Owein helped his wife to her feet. Together, they disappeared into their small round hut, a dwelling that was a far cry from the Roman luxury Clara had known in Isca. But she had never, to Rhys's knowledge, voiced a complaint. A Daughter of the Lady, Clara was strong in fortitude as well as magic.

Trevor's rough northern burr claimed Rhys's attention. "Ye must take on the role of Guardian before Cyric weakens further."

"That time has already passed." Rhys met Trevor's gaze. "I've been holding the mist alone since the day after Gwen disappeared."

Trevor's expression did not change, except for a slight widening of his eyes. "Cyric's magic is spent?"

"Not spent. More like . . . frozen." Rhys was silent a moment. "Overwhelmed by Darkness and Deep Magic."

Gwen could tell Marcus wanted to know more about her childhood. She didn't want to speak of it—the memories were too painful. It was with some relief that she turned to greet Breena, who was walking toward them.

"Mother has ordered a bath for us," she told Gwen. "The water is already heating. She said it would do us both good."

Beside her, Gwen felt Marcus tense. "A bath? Now?" His voice was suddenly hoarse.

Breena frowned at him. "Yes. The water has been warming for hours. Gwen's had a long journey from Avalon, and after last night, I . . ." she trailed off. "Is that a problem, Marcus?"

Gwen was amazed to note Marcus's cheeks had gone pink. He darted her a glance, then, almost as if he couldn't help himself, his gaze swept her from head to toe. Abruptly, she understood. He was imagining her unclothed.

Her own cheeks heated.

"No problem," he muttered. "I'll be in the smithy. Meet me there, Gwen, when you're . . . when you're ready to discuss your sword's design." Turning, he stomped off through the garden, his boots barely missing a clump of pennyroyal.

Breena stared at his retreating back. "What rudeness! That's not like Marcus at all. I wonder what got into him?"

Gwen didn't enlighten her.

The bathhouse was a separate structure just beyond the kitchen—to lessen the risk of fire to the main house, Breena explained. She showed Gwen the furnace, already hot, into which two youths were shoveling additional charcoal.

"This bathhouse is new. The old one had a much smaller furnace, and the hypocaust—that's the hollow space beneath the floor where the hot air circulates— was too shallow. The water never stayed hot enough. The new bathing pools are deeper now, too. You can sink in up to your neck."

Hot water up to her neck? Gwen could not fathom it. "Where does the water come from?"

"Rainwater's collected and funneled into a cistern, then piped underground to the kitchen, baths, and latrine." Breena launched into an explanation of the mechanics of water movement, but Gwen only shook her head.

"It seems like magic."

Breena laughed. "No, I can assure you it's not. Marcus supervised the construction. There's no magic here at all."

She led Gwen into the antechamber, where there were four changing alcoves, shelves piled with linen towels, and hooks on which to store clothing. Breena handed her a pair of thick-soled sandals as she directed Gwen to one of the changing alcoves. "Wear these," she instructed. "The floor of the *calidarium* can get very hot."

She entered a second alcove, still chattering pleasantly. "There are three rooms, each with a pool. We'll clean off in the *calidarium,* which has a very hot bath, then soak for as long as we want in the *tepidarium,* where the water's more comfortable. The last step is a quick plunge in the cold bath." She made a face. "I hate that part, but it's supposed to be good for your health."

Gwen felt a little dazed. "It's hard to imagine so much hot water. And that no one had to carry it."

"How do you bathe on Avalon?"

"With a bucket of water heated on the hearth," Gwen said. "Or I swim in a stream."

Breena shuddered. "I hate swimming in streams. Too cold."

Gwen disrobed and unbraided her hair. Shaking out one of the linen towels, she wrapped it around her body and followed her young guide into the *calidarium.*

A small, deep pool nearly filled the tiled chamber. Steam curled on the water's surface. Breena tossed her towel on a stone bench, supremely unselfconscious in her nakedness. Gwen released her towel more reluctantly—she was unused to being bare in company. Though it took surprisingly little imagination to picture herself reclining naked with Marcus. His torso would be bare and glistening, his hair wet, his dark, beautiful eyes inviting her to . . .

"Here." Breena's voice brought Gwen back to herself with a start. The girl picked up a small glass pitcher and poured some of its contents into Gwen's cupped palm. "Olive oil," Breena explained. "Rub it all over before you get in the water."

Gwen did as she was told, sitting on one of the stone benches and oiling her body everywhere she could reach. Breena offered to do her back, and she did Breena's in return, trying all the while not to think of Marcus performing the same act.

Breena handed her a curved bronze blade. "Scrape off the dirt with this strigil, then we'll plunge into the hot bath."

The hot water dissolved the tension from Gwen's muscles and the dirt from her skin. She dunked her head under the surface and scrubbed her scalp. A short time later, when Breena indicated it was time to move to the next room, Gwen felt better than she had in a very long time.

The *tepidarium* was a larger room, with more ornate decoration. The pool was also larger, easily big enough for six people. The floors and walls surrounding the bath were covered with small, colorful tiles that formed intricate pictures. The figures were so lifelike, Gwen could scarcely believe it.

One scene showed fantastic fish diving among the waves. Another depicted an underwater god with a flowing beard and a three-pronged staff. Overhead, a coffered ceiling was painted in shades of blue. The entire room was illuminated by a series of high windows. Blue-green tiles lined the bathing pool. A shelf around the edge held glass bottles, sponges, bronze strigils, combs, and a polished tin mirror. A flat-bladed bronze implement left Gwen perplexed. She picked it up. "What is this?"

"Oh, that's one of Marcus's razors. He's always leaving them about."

Gwen closed her eyes and stifled a groan. Now Marcus had invaded the *tepidarium*, too.

Breena abandoned her towel once again and sank into the pool with a satisfied sigh, submersing her body to the shoulders.

"This is my favorite part. I'd stay in here all day if I could."

Gwen joined her in the water, which was warm, but not so hot as the *calidarium*. Stepping down the submersed stair, she savored the sensation of warmed water lapping at her ankles, her thighs, her waist. She settled beside Breena with a sigh, tension draining from her body. Never in her life had she dreamed of such luxury.

It was yet another facet of a life that was completely foreign to her. Could she ever learn to accept such abundance without a thought, as Breena did? She thought not. The Aquila farm was not, according to Rhys, the richest of Roman estates, but to Gwen it was a place of wonder. Heated floors, bulging storerooms, more quantity and variety of food than she had ever seen in her life. Glass and bronze cups, tiled floors, walls painted with murals. Cloud-soft mattresses perched on high wooden frames.

It was too much. It made her feel like some brutish beast from the wild. She was far too simple for the graceful life Marcus and his sister took for granted.

Even so, it was easier than she would have imagined to sink up to her shoulders in the warm bath, to enjoy the heat of the water as it slid over her oiled skin. The sensation was as intoxicating as the Roman wine she'd sipped the night before.

Breena poured some scented oil into the water, then turned to Gwen and smiled. "It's wonderful, isn't it?"

Gwen smiled back. "It's . . . very—" Unbelievable. Luxurious. *Unnatural.* "—Roman," she said at last.

Breena's light laugh bounced off the tiles. "So it is. Of course, this is nothing compared to the bathing houses in Londinium. And the ones in Rome are even more lavish. Father says that in Rome, city magistrates spend the better part of their days in their baths and massage rooms."

Gwen could not imagine it. "If that is so, when do they ever go about the business of governing?"

"Why, while bathing. And every morning, at their barbers. Father says more alliances are made in the baths and barber shops of Rome than were ever contracted in the Senate."

Gwen tried to imagine Cyric, Mared, and Padrig, wet and naked, holding council in a bathing pool on Avalon. An irreverent giggle bubbled up her throat. "Your people are very different from mine."

Breena shot her an odd look. "Your people are my people. Or have you forgotten my mother is a Celt, and a queen's granddaughter, at that?"

Gwen flushed. "I'm sorry. I meant no insult. 'Tis only that your life . . . this farm . . . it's like nothing I've ever imagined."

Breena was silent for a moment, her brow pinched. "Marcus says I could never manage in Avalon because it's so primitive there. You probably agree with him. But Rhys says . . ."

"My brother thinks mainly of Cyric's commands. My

grandfather wants ye in Avalon, so Rhys works to deliver ye to him."

Breena wiggled her fingers on the surface of the water, creating tiny, anxious ripples. "Am I . . . just a duty to Rhys then?"

Gwen thought of the abruptness with which Rhys countered any questions concerning Breena. "I do not know the answer to that, but I suspect not."

Was the hope her words lit in Breena's blue eyes a good thing or not? Gwen wasn't sure.

"Does he speak of me very often?"

"Nay," Gwen replied. Breena looked so downcast that she added, "But that means little. Rhys keeps most of his thoughts to himself."

Breena sighed. "Rhys is so unlike Marcus—my brother is an open scroll! He never fails to say exactly what he thinks." She frowned. "But he's been different since Clara's rejection. He keeps to himself more than he used to. He goes into town on business, but beyond that, he hardly leaves his smithy. I think he still pines for her." She scowled. "Although when Rhys was here last month, the two wasted no time in running off to their favorite tavern. Marcus said the tavern keeper had asked Rhys to play his harp, but that hardly takes all night! They visited the brothel next door, I'm sure of it."

"Rhys . . . and Marcus . . . do they visit this brothel often?"

"Far too often, in my opinion." Breena scowled and sat up. Water sluiced off her shoulders. "And it's Rhys who drags Marcus to them. Whenever he comes to visit, they head right into town and don't return until the next morning. That's when I sneak over to the smithy window, or into the woods where Marcus practices throwing his daggers." Her smile was grim.

"Mother would die if she knew, but I've learned quite a few interesting things from eavesdropping on those morning-after conversations."

What kinds of things? Gwen wanted to ask, but didn't dare. It was humbling to think Marcus's young sister knew more about carnal matters than Gwen did! Gwen knew the basics about coupling, but she'd grown up without a mother and she'd never felt enough at ease with Mared to ask questions.

"When Rhys is not here, I don't think Marcus ever goes alone," Breena said. "Especially not since he returned from Avalon last spring. I've often wondered what happened there. All I know is that Marcus and Rhys freed you from your cousin's Dark spell. Beyond that, Marcus won't speak of it."

Gwen forced a casual tone. "I hardly know myself. I . . . barely remember being rescued. I was unconscious for days afterward."

"I'm sorry. I've brought up memories you'd rather forget. I am so unthinking. Please forgive me."

"Of course. Everyone has pain in their lives—ye do as well. We must talk about your visions. Do ye truly remember so little? Or were ye trying to spare your mother more distress?"

"I told you all I remember. The silver light, the woman in terror, the pain." Breena's forehead pinched. "I couldn't breathe. It hurts even to think about it."

Gwen studied her young companion. It was clear Breena didn't realize how close she'd come to suffocating, and Gwen didn't think it wise to enlighten her. She would only become more frightened, and less able to call the magic she needed.

"Would ye rest easier if my bed is placed in your room? That way I will be close if ye need me."

Breena's grateful expression tightened Gwen's chest. "Would you? I would appreciate it very much. I wanted to ask Mother to stay, but didn't dare, because of the babe."

"Then think nothing of it. I am happy to stay with ye. But if ye learn the magic I teach ye, my presence will soon be unnecessary." She settled back into the warm water. "Are ye ready for your first lesson? 'Tis best that the student be relaxed, and I can think of no better place to begin than in this bath."

Breena giggled. "You want to teach me magic here? In the bath?"

"If the Senators in Rome can rule from their baths, I see no reason I cannot give lessons in magic from mine."

They shared a laugh; then, as the merriment faded, Gwen turned serious. "Close your eyes. Try to quiet your thoughts."

Breena obeyed. After a moment, her expression softened.

"Good. Let your breathing go deep and slow . . . That's it."

Gwen cast her senses toward the girl. Breena's aura leapt into her mind. The silver was still apparent, but not as strong as it had been the night before. The aura was now predominantly white, as Gwen expected a Seer's to be.

Breena's face was serene, freckles scattered across her nose and cheeks. Her thick red hair floated around her. Her long fringe of lashes, darker than her hair, cast scalloped shadows on her fair skin. Her chin was subtly pointed.

Her fine, straight nose was perhaps the only feature that had come directly from her Roman ancestors. It was a feminine version of her father's and brother's. No one would call her nose small, but Gwen decided its boldness suited Breena. A smaller feature would have been lost in her expressive face.

Breena's breathing relaxed further, her countenance peaceful. Her lips parted, revealing her straight white front teeth and the gap between them. She looked like a small lass. Gwen wondered if she herself had looked so young at Breena's age. She thought not. At fourteen, Gwen had already lived in the wilderness for seven years, with only her immediate kin to shield her from the harshness of life. She and Rhys had been expected to contribute to the clan's survival from the first, gathering what food and herbs they could find on the sacred isle and the hills across the swamp.

"Your body feels very light," she told Breena. "As if it is floating. Can ye feel that?"

"Yes." The word was distant, as if Breena were talking in her sleep. But Gwen knew the lass was awake.

"Good. Very good."

The odd silver aura flitted at the edges of Gwen's senses. She had never felt anything like it—no Druid on Avalon possessed an aura of that color. She didn't understand it, and that troubled her.

"Breena."

"Yes?"

"When a vision comes upon ye, ye must not fight it. Difficult as it may be, ye must let the pain wash through ye."

"And then it will go away?"

"Nay. The pain will still be there, though not as strong. Your fear and resistance is what causes it to grow. Do ye understand?"

"Yes. I think so."

"As the pain washes through ye, say the spell I teach

ye now. 'Tis crafted from sacred Words of the Old Ones, and it is very powerful." She paused. "Are ye ready to hear it? The Words are difficult to pronounce. Ye must learn to say them—whether with your lips or in your mind—exactly as I teach ye."

"I'm ready."

Gwen spoke the spell. "Repeat the Words back to me."

Breena did, awkwardly. Gwen corrected her gently, repeating the Words one by one, until Breena's tongue formed the ancient syllables perfectly. Finally satisfied, Gwen called Breena from her trance.

Her eyelids fluttered open.

"How do ye feel?" Gwen asked. "Do ye remember the spell?"

Breena considered the question. "Yes, I do. I—"

Gwen held up a hand. "Do not speak it. The Words are powerful, only to be uttered when absolutely needed. When the vision comes. Ye must say the spell in your dream. Can ye do it?"

Breena drew a breath. "Yes. Yes, I'm sure I can."

Gwen and Breena were in the bath.

Marcus tightened his grip on the tongs and turned the hammered iron on the anvil. He would *not* think of Gwen in the *calidarium*, her body glistening with oil, veiled only by a curling curtain of steam.

He could think of nothing else.

He touched his tongue to the wound Gwen's teeth had left on his lip. He channeled a sudden surge of lust into a savage blow to the anvil. He was working one of the iron blooms he'd smelted before Gwen's arrival. The iron was of superior quality, the result of the hottest fire he'd produced so far. It was not *chalybs*, but it was a fine target for his pent-up frustration.

He pictured Gwen rising from the bath, water cascading over her shoulders and breasts, her blond tresses clinging to her sleek, subtle curves. Was the triangle of curls between her thighs as fair as the hair on her head, or a shade darker?

Desire sliced his gut as keenly as any blade he'd ever honed. His hammer glanced off the flattened bloom at the wrong angle, leaving a deep gouge. Cursing, Marcus thrust the metal into the furnace and worked the bellows. The metal absorbed the red heat of the coals.

Sweat trickled into his eyes. He blinked rapidly against the sting, dragging the back of his sleeve across face. His shirt was grimy. He, too, needed a bath. He allowed himself a moment of fantasy in which he and Gwen spread oil on each others' naked bodies. He started with her shoulders and arms, working downward. By the time his hands mentally covered her breasts, he was so hard he was in danger of spilling his seed into the furnace.

With a curse he pulled the glowing iron from the furnace and plunged it into the water trough. Steam rose in a hiss. He could no longer remain here in the smithy—he needed to escape, to expend some energy in a different way. Banking the furnace, he strode to the shelf that held his favorite throwing daggers. He chose a set of six blades, sheathed and wrapped in oiled cloth, and headed out the door.

The field laborers were planting the north fields; the north gate stood ajar. Marcus strode the path between the wheat and barley, waving when one or two of the men called to him. His destination was the thick woods bordering the well-tended fields.

The grassy clearing where he practiced throwing his daggers was just far enough into the woods that it was

out of sight of both the workers in the fields and anyone coming from the gate. He sought this oasis of silence often, especially when he needed to think. He'd
set up two targets, thick planks fastened to the trunks
of two ancient oaks, forty paces distant from each
other. His typical routine was to stand in front of one
mark and throw to the other, then cross the clearing
and throw back to the first, over and over, until his arm
ached. Usually, this calmed his mind.

Unfortunately, today it did not.

Eventually he ceased the fruitless exercise, leaving
his daggers sunk in one of the targets. The spring day
was warm, and the forge had been hot. Stripping his
sweat-soaked shirt over his head, he flung it to the
ground and leaned against a tree trunk. He tipped his
head back until it connected with rough bark.

A long sigh escaped his lungs. His eyes closed.
Hades. He could think of nothing but Gwen. In the
bath. Without Breena.

With *him*.

She reclined in the water, the pink tips of her breasts
cresting the misty surface. He was hard and hungry before her, sitting on the edge of the pool with his legs in
the water. Languidly, she rose and moved to stand between his parted legs. Her lashes fluttered downward,
her gaze fell upon his erection.

She bit her lip. He fisted his hands in her hair.

Tilting her head up, he claimed her mouth in a long,
drugging kiss. Then he maneuvered her closer, urging
her to kneel in the water. He guided her head to his . . .

Marcus bit off a groan, pressing his spine into the
oak's rough bark, reminding himself that he was alone
in the woods, not secluded in the bathhouse with
Gwen. His shaft was rigid; he was beyond fighting his

need. His shaking fingers worked the ties of his *braccas*, loosening the fabric until his erection sprang free. He wrapped his hand around his shaft, working smooth skin over iron-hard muscle. Gods, how he wished his rough hand was Gwen's delicate, wet mouth.

He stroked once, twice, a third time, and gave himself up to the rhythm.

Chapter Eight

Gwen paced the forest trail to which Breena had directed her after they'd emerged from the deserted smithy. "Marcus is probably out throwing knives," Breena had declared when she noticed her brother's favorite set of daggers was missing. "He does that whenever he needs to think."

Curious, Gwen had gone to seek him out while Breena returned to the main house to check on her mother. Gwen's footsteps slowed as she caught a glimpse of him through the trees. She was suddenly very glad Breena had not accompanied her, because Marcus was not throwing knives. Nor was he *thinking*.

He was . . . pleasuring himself.

Gwen stopped short, staring, her heart slamming her ribs. Her head felt as though it were about to float off her shoulders. She put out a hand to steady herself, blindly reaching for the nearest tree. *Great Mother.* She hadn't realized a man might seek fulfillment without a woman. But there was no mistaking what Marcus was doing.

He stood with legs spread wide, his broad shoulders supported by the trunk of an ancient oak. He'd discarded his shirt, leaving his powerful torso, sprinkled with curly dark hair, bared to her view. His lean hips were thrust forward, his fingers wrapped firmly about his shaft. His arm moved in a jerking, almost brutal rhythm, his wrist flexing with every stroke. Each tug vibrated deep in her own belly.

His eyes were closed. He could not have heard her approach. She'd intruded on a moment of intense privacy—if she had any honor at all, she'd turn and flee. Apparently her honor was in short supply, because she stayed.

And watched.

Silently, like a moth to a flame, she crept closer, emerging from the shelter of the woods. The expressions playing on Marcus's face fascinated her. The angles of his countenance were set in harsh contours, his generous, mobile lips pressed into a grim line. His breathing was shallow, his cheeks flushed. Gwen's mouth went dry. In all her dreams of Marcus, she'd never pictured him like this—she hadn't known enough to imagine it. A peculiar hunger gnawed her belly. He was so beautiful, so purely masculine, so strong and so vulnerable, all at once. She could not look away.

She must have made a sound, for Marcus's eyes snapped open. Their gazes locked; the distance between them—barely ten paces—seemed to melt away. His hand stilled, but didn't unclench from his erection.

She bit her lip. His gaze shot to the small movement, his eyes darkening to midnight.

"Come here."

His voice was hoarse, his tone harsh. The command

vibrated with such power and need that Gwen did not even consider disobeying. Slowly, she picked her way through the sea of grass that separated them, feeling as though she had stepped onto a shifting raft adrift in tumultuous waters.

She went to him as if in a dream, where time slows and fades, and all paths merge into one. This was her path—the only one she wanted. She stopped before him. His eyes were deep, dark pools of unsated desire. Beads of sweat stood out on his temple, his jaw, his neck. She was struck with an urge to collect the drops with her tongue.

His hand dropped to his side. Her gaze flicked downward. His sex was big and thick and erect, jutting from a nest of dark hair just visible between the flaps of his *braccas*. Her womb clenched and wept; dew seeped between her thighs.

"Touch me, Gwen."

Her eyes flew to his; her lips parted.

"Touch me." His voice was strained, barely in control. "Please."

Hesitantly, she obeyed. Her fingertips brushed his broad, blunt tip. The round knob was softer than she'd expected. And hotter. A drop of moisture beaded on the crest. She touched it with her fingertip. He sucked in a sharp breath, his jaw clenching.

Gwen snatched her hand away. "Oh! I'm sorry. I did not mean to hurt—"

He made a harsh sound midway between a laugh and a groan. "You . . . didn't."

Each word he uttered seemed to cost him dearly. He stared at her, his throat working, then caught her wrist in a punishing grip. He guided her hand, pressing her palm to his hard flesh. He molded her fingers around his shaft, shaping them to his length. And holding her there.

His skin was like the softest doeskin. Beneath the unexpectedly supple veneer, he was hard as iron. She flexed her fingers and a shudder passed through him. He closed his eyes; his head tipped back against the tree. He was hot in her hand, hotter than she could have imagined. And alive. His life's blood pulsed against her palm.

"Stroke me."

"Marcus, I—"

"Stroke me, Gwen." His hand began moving as it had been just moments before—except this time, he was teaching her. Her pulse quickened as she accepted his guidance. She learned his length, from thick hilt to broad, rounded tip. The soft outer skin moved over the hardness beneath; he shuddered when she circled his shaft's wide head.

Slowly, tensely, as if he feared she would bolt, he released his hold on her hand. His arm came around her waist, pulling her tightly against his side. She laid her head on his shoulder and continued stroking. The quick, almost desperate rise and fall of his breath matched her own.

"Gwen . . . *gods* . . . that feels so good."

Urgency pooled in her stomach. Instinctively, her grip tightened and her rhythm quickened. Marcus groaned; his hand went to her nape. He grasped her damp braid and wrapped it once around his wrist, pulling the strands taut. His legs were shaking now; the muscles in his thighs rock hard. Her own limbs were no better; her knees were in danger of buckling.

He tugged her braid back, tilting her head, forcing her to look up at him. His pupils were dilated, his gaze unfocused.

"Faster," he rasped. He swallowed hard, his throat working convulsively. "Harder. *Please*."

She did as he asked, until the muscles in her upper arm burned. His mouth descended on hers, his lips hard and bruising, his tongue probing with blatant possession. One hand held her head immobile, the other came up to cover her breast. Her nipple tightened into a hard, aching pebble. He caught it between his thumb and forefinger and squeezed gently.

Fire streaked to the dark place between her thighs. The hot, coiling ache inside was becoming unbearable. She pressed into the jut of Marcus's hip, seeking relief. Somehow, the contact made the ache better and worse at the same time. Her grip on Marcus's rod tightened. Incredibly, it grew even harder inside her palm. His body went taut. His breath was harsh; his male scent surrounded her. She sensed his savage satisfaction, his masculine triumph, his urge to dominate her completely.

The wolf inside her sensed it, too. It raised its head.

Nay! She jerked back, snatching her hand away, summoning the spell that banished the beast. At the same time, Marcus released her, gasping, wrenching himself roughly to one side and milking his shaft with such violent motion that Gwen feared he would injure himself. He braced his free hand on the oak, his big body shuddering. A groan tore from his lips as his seed spurted on the grass.

He stood motionless for a long time afterward, his eyes closed. Gwen did not move; she couldn't. Her heart pounded as if she'd been running full pace in the forest. The wolf had retreated, but the effort of banishing it so abruptly had left her dizzy. Witnessing Marcus's release had not helped her composure. The place between her thighs throbbed with dark, relentless yearning. She felt so . . . empty. Her body was weeping. She wanted him inside her.

But even if she'd known how to ask a man for such a thing, she didn't dare. Not with the wolf lying in wait.

Marcus's eyes opened. His beautiful, dark, expressive eyes. The emotion they conveyed took her breath away. He devoured her with his gaze—and she was shocked to realize his hunger had been barely sated by what they'd shared. His shaft had not softened in the least.

She wanted to touch him again; feel him touch her as intimately as she'd handled him. Her lust was like a towline drawing her across endless black water to a dark and dangerous place. And, Goddess help her, she wanted to go.

Then Marcus drew a breath and seemed to come back to himself. The hunger in his eyes changed into wry embarrassment. The bridge of his nose reddened; he shot her a sheepish smile as he did up his *braccas.*

"Next time," he said mildly, "perhaps you could make a bit more noise when you approach me." Retrieving his shirt from the grass, he shook off a few insects and pulled it over his head.

Gwen blinked, unsure of how to answer. Her face flamed; Marcus, for all his forced naturalness, was studiously avoiding her gaze. Striding across the clearing, he began retrieving daggers, one by one, from a scarred wooden target.

Gwen started to follow him, then drew up short and blurted, "Was this . . . was this like an encounter with one of your brothel women?"

His hand stilled on the grip of a dagger. "What do you know of brothel women?"

"Breena told me—"

"*Pollux.* Breena should keep her mouth shut. No doubt she's filled your head with nonsense."

"Nonsense." Her tone sharpened. She was angry, she realized. Though she was not precisely sure why. "Is that what ye call what we just did? Nonsense?"

He spun about. "No." The word echoed across the clearing. "*No.* This was . . . nothing like . . . *gods.*" His hand shook as he wiped the blade of a dagger with a small rag, slid it into its sheath, and laid it atop an oiled cloth he'd spread on the ground. "Is that what you believe? That I consider you no better than a *meretrix?* A whore?"

The ugly words shook her. "I . . . I don't know what to think."

The look he gave her was unreadable. He cleaned and sheathed three more daggers, then bound them together in a heavy roll of oilskin. Only when he was done did he straighten and face her again.

"Gwendolyn."

The sound of her name on his tongue felt like a caress on her skin. His voice was low and vibrant, touching her in places already sensitive from the intimacy they'd shared. "I have burned for you with an unquenched fire for more than a year. I have done things to you in my dreams that would shock you so badly that you would turn and run were I to tell them to you. Then, one morning, you appear out of nowhere, on my doorstep. And I realize the . . . *reality* of you is so much more than any pale, thin dream could ever be."

Approaching her, he took her hand and pressed it once more against his groin. Her fingers closed on him convulsively, remembering and wanting him again. He was still hard, the bulge of his rod straining the seams of his *braccas*. When she would have taken her hand away, he did not let her go.

"Do you feel that? *You* do that to me. And you're not even aware of it, are you? All you have to do is look in my direction, and I can hardly breathe from the force of wanting you."

"I . . . do not know what to say."

"Say you want me, too. Say you'll come to my bed."

"Marcus . . . I . . ."

"You want me, too." He kissed her lips and drew her flush against him. "Tell me I'm wrong."

That was one lie she couldn't bring herself to speak. He took advantage of her silence, kissing her again, then drawing her body tight against his. He fingered the sleeve of her borrowed tunic.

"This is Rhiannon's."

"Aye. Breena gave it to me. She sent my old tunic to be washed." It felt odd, speaking of something so ordinary with her breasts pressed to his chest. "I'm taller than she is. 'Tis too short."

"The color suits you, though. Green, like springtime." A small smile played on his lips as he traced the neckline, his finger leaving a hot trail on her skin. He toyed with the lacing at the shoulder. His hand drifted lower, cupping her breast. With a sudden motion, his head dipped. Before Gwen quite knew what had happened, he'd covered her breast with his mouth, his teeth dragging the moistened linen across her sensitized nipple.

She gasped at the sensations that shot through her body. Desperately, she grasped a handful of his hair and tried to push him away. "Marcus, this—"

He bit her softly.

She couldn't repress her moan. "This . . . is not right. I am to marry another m—"

His head came up, his eyes sober and intense. "You haven't yet accepted the Caledonian."

"That makes no difference." She tried to pull back. His arm tightened around her. "I will accept Trevor eventually. Or another Druid."

"But for now, you are free."

She shook her head. "Ye don't understand. There are other reasons we cannot do this. I—"

He silenced her with a kiss, his tongue slipping into her gasp of protest to stroke the slick inner lining of her mouth. He plundered her mouth like a conqueror, giving her no quarter. His palms molded her buttocks, pulling her close. His arousal pressed against the part of her that ached for him.

By the time he released her mouth, she was panting. He kissed a trail along her jaw to her ear. "You'll return to Avalon and your lifetime of duty soon enough. It's likely we'll never see each other again. But while you're here with me—your life is your own. Not your grandfather's, not your Elders', not Rhys's. Yours. You can choose to whom to give yourself." He nuzzled her neck. "Choose me, Gwen. Please. I will treasure the gift all my days."

Gwen shut her eyes against a sudden wash of tears. Marcus was right—she wanted him. Wanted a memory to take into her loveless future on Avalon. How could she make him understand why she dared not accept what he offered?

She eased out of his arms, her eyes fixed on the ground. He let her go, reluctantly. She couldn't bear to utter the words that would turn him away. *I cannot lie with ye because I do not control the wolf. I do not control my own magic. I am afraid it will destroy you.*

She should say those words. Set him free. But oh,

how it would hurt when he turned away! She summoned her courage and opened her mouth, but Breena's sudden call through the woods silenced her.

"Marcus? Gwen? Are you here?"

Marcus quickly stepped away, bending to roll his daggers inside the oilcloth as his sister tromped into view.

"Oh, there you are! I told Father I'd likely find you here. He's looking for you, Marcus."

"What does he want?"

Gwen was astonished at how calm Marcus sounded. If she were to attempt speech, she knew her voice would fail.

"Some problem with one of the plows," Breena told her brother. "He's in the west field."

"I'll go to him," Marcus said, tucking his oilcloth bundle under his arm. He sent a meaningful glance toward Gwen. "We'll continue our discussion later."

She watched him stride away. Breena turned to her, her eyes bright with curiosity. "What were you speaking of? The sword Marcus is to make for you? No doubt he already has a good idea of how to proceed."

"Aye. He does." She had no idea if it were true.

"Ah, well," Breena replied. "If that's the case, you're assured of success. Marcus never fails once he's set a goal."

That, Gwen thought grimly, was precisely what she was afraid of.

The smithy door was open. Intent on his drawing, Marcus was not aware of Gwen's presence until she stood almost at his elbow. He jerked, his head whipping around. The back of his hand smacked the ink jar, knocking it over.

"Hades!" He righted the jar, but not before the ink spattered across the table.

"Oh! I'm sorry."

"No matter," Marcus mumbled, grabbing a rag he kept nearby for just this purpose. He sopped up the mess, scrubbing across his worktable as Gwen snatched several drawings out of the path of the spreading ink. "You can tell from the stains on the table I've spilled ink before," he muttered under his breath.

He was a bumbling fool. And he'd proven it by nearly assaulting Gwen in the forest, spilling his seed at her feet, then insulting her by insinuating she was needy enough to fall into his bed. Even if she were inclined to take a lover before sacrificing her life to her grandfather's whims, what possessed him to think she would choose *him?* She hadn't even appeared at dinner afterward, pleading a headache. It had been plain enough to discern what *that* meant. He'd disgusted her with his crudity. He'd retreated to his smithy and spent half the night trying not to think about it.

But he'd known sooner or later he would have to face her. She needed him to forge her sword.

"Did ye not hear me enter?" she asked, laying his drawings on a clean spot on the table.

He straightened and looked at her. Her front teeth worried her lower lip, and her eyes avoided his gaze. Her cheeks were pink. She was nervous, he realized. Perhaps even as nervous as he. His mood abruptly improved. "I get very absorbed in my work," he told her. "Breena knows to bang loudly on the door."

"I'll remember that trick in the future."

Marcus felt her eyes on him as he crossed the room to dispose of the soiled rag in the barrel by the door. He was a disheveled mess, he knew. He'd slept in his clothes, and he had ink stains on his sleeves. He'd meant to bathe at dawn . . .

He glanced out the door. "Why, it must be near

noon," he said with some surprise. Last night, contemplating the problem of Gwen's sword, inspiration had struck. Once he'd put pen to paper, he'd completely lost track of the time.

"Past midday." Reluctant amusement threaded her voice. "Do not tell me ye were up all night again."

"No, I dropped like a stone right after dinner. I woke just after midnight, with a dream of a sword vivid in my mind. I started drawing . . ." he spread his hands. "It's often like this for me. I don't keep regular hours. Sometimes I get days and night completely switched around, arriving at dinner as if it were the morning meal. Other times I forget to eat at all." For the first time, he noticed the basket on her arm. His stomach rumbled in sudden hope. "Is that food?"

She laughed. The sound went right to his groin. He half-turned back to the table, not wanting her to notice his burgeoning erection.

"When ye did not appear to break your fast, nor to eat the midday meal, Rhiannon asked me to bring ye a bite. Meat and bread, and some cheese and apples."

Marcus had already uncovered the basket and downed his first mouthful. "Thank you. I'm half-starved." He finished off a hunk of cheese and rooted around for an apple. He eyed her. "You look a little tired. Did you spend the night with Breena? Did she have another one of her dreams?"

"I stayed with Breena, but she had no dreams."

"Because of a spell you taught her?"

"Nay. She had no cause to try it. No vision came. She slept peacefully till morn."

"But you didn't?"

She blushed and looked away. " 'Tis nothing new. I told ye, I have difficulty sleeping."

He set his half-eaten apple aside. "I could help with that," he said softly.

The flush on her cheeks intensified. "I do not know what you mean."

"Let me do for you what you did for me in the woods yesterday. Believe me, I'd make sure you could do nothing but sleep afterward. I'd leave you as boneless as a cream pudding."

Her embarrassment warred with her laughter, as he knew it would. He smiled. She wasn't used to being teased.

"A cream pudding? Do ye think of nothing but food, then?"

"I'm a growing lad. I need nourishment. I need . . ." He caught her gaze. "I need *you*, Gwen. Let me love you. You won't regret it."

The laughter evaporated from her eyes. "*Ye* would regret it, Marcus."

"Never."

She shook her head. "Let us speak of it no more. I came to discuss the sword, that is all." Reaching around him, she picked up one of his rejected drawings.

He sighed. "Not that one." He eased it from her hand and located the correct one. Ink had splattered in one corner, but luckily, it hadn't obliterated any crucial lines.

He waved the papyrus in the air to dry it, then placed it in her hands. "What do you think?"

He waited while she examined the intricate drawing. The blade of the sword he'd drawn was long and sleek, with Celtic tracework on the flat. An intricate design decorated the wide crosspiece. At the opposite end of the hilt, to balance the weight of the long blade,

Marcus had set a round pommel embossed with the mark of the Druids of Avalon.

She examined the drawing for a long time, without comment. The odd expression on her face worried him, until she looked up and he saw that her eyes were filled with wonder.

" 'Tis beautiful, Marcus. 'Tis the sword of my dream. How could ye know?"

He shrugged, taken aback. "It just came to me. In my own dream." The thought was unsettling.

Gwen seemed pleased with the explanation, though. "The Great Mother sent you this inspiration, I am sure." For the first time since she'd entered the smithy, she bestowed him upon a wide, generous smile. "When shall we begin?"

"Today, if you'd like." He propped his hip against the table and nodded toward the furnace, trying to project a sense of nonchalance. In truth, he'd avoided thinking of how close he'd have to work with Gwen's magic. But now, to his surprise, he realized the prospect of experiencing her Light didn't unsettle him nearly as much as it should have. All he could think of was that it would take a fortnight or more to forge her sword, and for much of that time, she would be here beside him. Alone. Hour after hour, bathed by the heat and solitude of the smithy.

She was Rhys's sister, and all but promised to another man, but when he looked at her, he could not seem to remember his honor. All logic and reason were blotted out by the fierce urge to possess her. A blunt voice in his brain ordered him to claim her. Conquer her. Mark her as his own.

The sheer violence of his feelings shocked him to

the bone. This was not at all what he had felt for Clara. *That* emotion had been tender. Protective. He would not have dared to touch Clara before wedding her. Perhaps that was why he had managed to step aside and let Owein have her. In contrast, whenever Marcus thought of Gwen's betrothed, a murderous rage overtook him.

The faceless Druid would not be the first man to love Gwen—Marcus meant to claim that prize himself. His and Gwen's physical joining was inevitable. He knew it, as she did, even if she hadn't yet acknowledged it. There was nothing, save abandoning the sword, that would stop it.

Gwen looked at the furnace, then back at him. He was still leaning against the table; their eyes were on a level.

"The ore I purchased yesterday will be delivered this afternoon," he said steadily. "We can smelt it tonight. Then we will see what my skill, and your magic, can create."

"The mist is thinning."

"I know that," Rhys snapped.

He did not turn toward Owein, nor rise from his seated position on Avalon's shore. Owein, approaching from behind, came to stand beside him. Rhys continued his brooding, gazing out over the swamp in silence. He was weary with a fatigue that went far beyond the effort of holding the mist, beyond the sleepless nights he spent at Cyric's bedside, though those trials were bad enough.

Cyric's nightmares were turbulent. When he woke, he could not say what they had been, but Rhys had a good idea. *Tamar,* Cyric sobbed over and over in his sleep. *Tamar.*

Rhys's mother.

Rhys had been visited with his own nightmares of his mother's death. During the day, when Mared or one of the other Druids sat with Cyric, Rhys had tried to sleep. Though spells of Light surrounded his pallet, he could not close his eyes without seeing the waxen face of Mama's corpse. Now he did all he could to stay awake, so the nightmares could not reach him. But it was impossible for a man to eschew sleep entirely.

He shredded a willow frond in his fingers. His gaze was fixed on the faint glow of torchlight that had sprung up on the hills beyond the swamp as dusk fell. The Romans had returned to their camp for the night. The thought did not calm Rhys. He should not be able to see the camp at all through the mist.

Despite his best effort to hold the mist, it was thinning. Strabo's Deep Magic was taunting him, as it taunted Cyric. Gods. If only Gwen were here, they could combine their power and face the threat together. But she would not answer him.

Putting aside his pride, he tried once more. *"Gwen. Please. I need ye here. Strabo's Deep Magic has strengthened. I do not know if I can guard Avalon without your help."*

He held his breath, listening for Gwen's response. He sensed nothing but the faint hum of the spell she'd erected to block him. Where was she? Why did she persist in maintaining this silence between them? Did she not realize how much she was needed?

Owein, fortunately, did not speak for a long time. He lowered his large frame to the ground at Rhys's side and joined him in gazing out over the swamp.

"How is Clara?" Rhys asked at last.

"Her belly tightens and relaxes, but Mared says it

will be a sennight or more before the babe comes." He paused. "I wish very much that Rhiannon were here."

Rhys heard the worry in the older man's voice. Owein's mother had died birthing him; Rhiannon was more mother than sister to him.

"It does no good to worry," Rhys told him. When had he become so hypocritical? "Mared will see Clara through her time safely."

"Mared's healing skills are stretched thin. Cyric commands much of her attention. The Darkness covering him grows stronger."

"Aye. He sobs my mother's name. He speaks of leaving Isca and traveling to Avalon—a journey he took long ago."

"He is lost in the past."

Rhys grimaced. "My own dreams are mired in the past as well."

"As are mine," Owein admitted.

Rhys looked up in surprise. With Owein's gift of Sight, he was sometimes visited by dreams that were something more. "Have ye received a vision, then? Guidance from the Great Mother?"

"Nay. I see only memories I thought long dead. Memories I do not wish to revive. It has been the same for Clara, and I suspect for Trevor and many of the other villagers as well."

Rhys shredded the last of the willow frond. "Strabo's Deep Magic affects us all."

"He is a dreamcaster."

"Aye. 'Tis very likely." Cyric had once told Rhys of dreamcasting—the talent of forming images from a person's most intense memories. It was a rare gift. Rhys had never encountered it on his travels, and no one on

Avalon claimed that talent. Rhys did not know how to fight it.

"Gwen should be here to face this with us." Rhys couldn't keep the bitter edge from his tone. "She insults us all by staying away."

"If I have learned anything about your sister in the past year, 'tis that Gwen doesna easily dismiss her duties. If anything, she feels them too keenly."

"She's never accepted Cyric's authority. She's always done as she wished, even as a child."

"While ye have never done as ye wished."

"You make me sound churlish in my obedience." Though his obedience, Rhys reflected, was far from untarnished. The memory of his leap into the forbidden—flying as a merlin—was a weight on his conscience. He'd berated Gwen for succumbing to the lure of Deep Magic when in truth he was no better than she. Pride had kept him from confiding in his twin. He *wanted* her to believe he was perfect. That he was better than she.

No wonder she would not answer him.

Owein's voice cut through Rhys's dark thoughts. "Ye dinna take my meaning. Of course I dinna think ill of ye for obeying Cyric. He is a powerful Seer, and has his reasons for what he commands. Ye live a hard life without complaint, and Avalon is strong because of it. I only mean to suggest that though ye and Gwen shared your mother's womb, ye are different people."

"I know that only too well."

"I've come to admire Gwen very much in the past year. Her skill in crafting new spells from the sacred Words of the Old Ones is unique. She's helped me banish much of the pain my visions bring, relieving Clara of that burden. She ever has the good of Avalon at heart."

"Mared says . . ."

"Mared is too close to Gwen. She sees only her faults. Not the war Gwen wages within her own soul. If Gwen is gone, if she doesna answer your calls, there is a good reason. Trust her, Rhys."

Trust? Gwen had asked him to do the same, but Rhys wasn't sure he could. Or should. He had, after all, known Gwen far longer than Owein had. True, Owein had reminded Rhys of Gwen's loyalty, but Rhys knew his twin's recklessness was just as strong.

And he did not know how much longer he could hold the mist without her.

The spring days were growing long; though the evening meal was done, the sky was still very bright. Gwen walked slowly toward the smithy, where Marcus awaited her. Marcus, with his teasing laughter. Marcus, with his beautiful dark eyes and his shameless coaxing.

The forge was already hot; smoke rose from the vent in the furnace. She'd almost reached the door when she felt a whisper in her mind, and realized she had let her defenses down.

"Gwen."

She stopped dead and stiffened, trying to push Rhys away. But it was too late.

"Gwen. I know ye can hear me."

There was a weary edge to her brother's silent communication. Guilt warred with anger; her first instinct was to comfort her twin, but close upon the heels of that impulse came a deep sense of betrayal. Rhys had kept his own secret from her. She was entitled to hers.

"Gwen, please. Ye must stop this folly and come home."

Folly? She bristled. What she was doing was not *folly*.

"Gwen, please. I need ye here. Strabo's Deep Magic has strengthened. I do not know if I can guard Avalon without your help. Strabo . . . he's a dreamcaster, Gwen. He's assaulting Avalon with nightmares. Cyric is much affected. He no longer holds the mist.

Her chest contracted so tightly she had to remind herself to breathe. She answered before she could silence her thought. *"The mist is gone?"*

"Nay. Not gone. I am holding it. But Gwen, Strabo's magic affects me, too. I need ye here beside me."

"I am coming, Rhys."

"When?"

She bit her lip. *"Soon. When I can. Trust me, Rhys."*

"Gwen—"

She threw up the blocking spell. She could not bear to listen. He needed her, and her instinct was to go to him. But not yet. Not without the Lady's sword.

"Gwen?" She started at Marcus's greeting. He stood in the doorway of the smithy, wearing a soot-stained apron. "Are you coming in, or do you intend to stand on the path all night?"

She pushed Rhys and Avalon from her mind. "I'm coming in, of course. But I'd best not stay past midnight. I need to be with Breena in case—"

"Of course."

The coals in the main furnace glowed red. The newer chamber, in which the bright iron was to be smelted, was no longer empty.

Marcus's tone turned businesslike. "I've laid the layers of ore and charcoal. Heat causes the ore to melt and change. Afterward, the molten iron—the bloom—is found under the ashes. If we can produce enough heat, and sustain it long enough, the bloom will yield *chalybs.*" He took a second apron, similar to his own, from a hook on the wall. "Put this on. Sparks are a danger."

Gwen accepted the apron, fastening the ties around her neck and waist.

"I've designed the bellows to keep a steady flow of air over the coals." He demonstrated the two-handed apparatus. When one bellows rose, the other lowered, so that the flow of air was never interrupted. They were positioned so one person could sit between them and operate both at once. "Once the fire is lit, the temperature will rise quickly." He glanced at her. "But I don't know if it will rise high enough."

"It will," Gwen said quietly. "I will see to it."

"With magic."

"Aye."

"What will you do?"

"I . . . I will need to touch ye."

He sent her a slow smile. "I've no objection to that." The heat in his eyes matched that in the furnace. His voice was pitched low. "Where?"

She ignored the fluttering in her stomach. Harder to ignore was the memory of Marcus standing half naked in the woods, of touching him intimately. She placed her hand on his shoulder and felt the muscle leap.

He was remembering, too.

She drew a breath and considered her next step. She had thought long and hard about the spells and methods she would employ to enchant the sword Marcus created. "I . . . I will send my magic through ye, as ye work the bellows."

"That will make the heat rise?"

"Aye, I think so."

For a moment he looked as though he would ask another question, but then he seemed to think better of it. He offered her a crooked smile. "Are you ready, then?"

His voice was low and intimate and sent swirls of sensation through her body. Ready? Most likely not.

She took a steadying breath. "Aye. Let us begin."

Using a coal from the main furnace, Marcus lit the charcoal in the new chamber in several places. Folding his large body onto a low stool in front of the forge, he placed one hand on each bellows and began a steady up-and-down motion, sending air into the fire.

The coals flared. A red glow spread slowly through the layers of ore. Heat rose in waves, bathing her face. Soon sweat was trickling down her temples.

"The heat takes some getting used to," Marcus said.

"I do not mind it."

She fell silent as he worked the bellows. The rush of air over the coals was like the breath of the earth. Like the breath in her own body. Like the call of Deep Magic.

Suddenly, doubt assailed her. Doubt and guilt. Marcus thought she called only the Light, when in truth, she was prepared to call both Light and Deep Magic. She was well aware that there was not a single Druid on Avalon who would approve of her plan. Cyric, especially, would be devastated by her disobedience.

And if she held back? If she sent only Light to meet the Deep Magic threatening Avalon? Rhys's communication had disturbed her. Strabo's Deep Magic had cowed Cyric, and Rhys was wavering as well. Her own Light had been no match for the powers the Roman had commanded.

She'd always run with her instincts—the wolf had taught her that. Her heart told her that despite the danger, Deep Magic was Avalon's best hope. But she dared not call only Deep Magic—she was not so reckless as that. She meant to bind Deep Magic with Light.

Would such a binding work?

She did not know. She could only try, and pray—and hope that her pride did not destroy her.

Deliberately, she moved behind Marcus and laid both hands on his shoulders. He flinched at her touch, but his rhythm on the bellows didn't falter. She sucked in a breath. She could feel his desire for her beneath her fingertips, flaring as hot as the coals in the furnace. Her eyes were drawn to the gap between his short hair and the neckline of his dampened shirt. His skin glistened with sweat; the musky scent caused her nostrils to flare. Her tongue swiped her lower lip; it was only with great effort that she resisted the urge to dip her head and taste him.

She closed her eyes. Better that she did not see—feeling him was bad enough. Each flex of his muscles sent a ripple of lust to her loins. His desire seared her, opened her, softened her. Tightened the tips of her breasts until she longed to lean forward and rub them against the hard planes of his back.

Her fingers tightened on his shoulders, her nails digging into his flesh though the fabric of his shirt. If she caused him pain, he gave no indication of it.

A long hiss and a shifting of the fuel in the furnace brought her attention back to the fire. There was a popping noise and a shower of sparks. The fire snapped.

It was time.

She let her focus on the fire soften, seeking the lightening of her mind in which magic grew. Gathering her power, her Light, she sent it flowing down her arms and into Marcus's body. He stiffened as it touched him, surprising her. She hadn't expected him to feel it.

"Do not fight it," she whispered.

She felt his spirit hesitate, then relax. She rode his

acceptance, chanting Words of Light. Magic flowed into the furnace, into the coals, into the iron. The rise and fall of the bellows echoed inside her mind. She let her mind grow soft, wrapping it loosely around Marcus's. It felt so natural, to hold him this way. She swayed forward, giving in to her yearning to press herself against him. The contact felt so good. She couldn't pull back.

How long she stood, with her body and mind touching him, she did not know. Light flowed between them, around them, binding them. His rhythm on the bellows quickened. Heat hissed from the furnace. Sweat ran from her pores. The fire rose, consuming the ore, melting it, changing it. The magic swirled and danced around it.

Light infused her spirit. Her knees felt weak; her hands slid from Marcus's shoulders to wrap around his torso. The rocking motion of his body as he worked the bellows intensified the tingling in her nipples. She rubbed them against Marcus's shirt, seeking relief. Her leather apron muted the sensation. Goddess! She needed him closer. Clumsily, she tore at the apron's ties, groaning in thanks when the heavy garment slumped to the ground.

"Gwen . . ." He made a noise in his throat, half pleasure, half pain. His lungs worked in tandem with the bellows, the rhythm quickening yet again. Her arms tightened convulsively about him. He was slick with sweat, his shirt plastered to his skin, his hair dripping. She pressed her cheek on the top of his head and clung to him.

She'd released the Light. Now it remained to call Deep Magic. Anxiety seeped through her veins. Once Deep Magic was called, there would be no turning it back. No way to undo what she started.

There was still time for retreat. If she drew back now, the sword would still be powerful, infused with Light. The Elders would accept that, perhaps even applaud it.

And yet . . . what if it were not enough? What if Avalon were destroyed, because she had given in to her fear? Light danced behind her closed eyelids. It had to be now. The power—the Words—were there, within her, waiting to be set free.

She summoned the Words to her lips. Cast them into the world.

Deep Magic, set free.

Power exploded inside her, poured through her contact with Marcus and into the furnace. A rushing noise sounded in her ears. Her head spun. Her body felt as though it would whirl into a thousand pieces, as if her human flesh could no longer contain her.

It could not.

The wolf leaped to its feet and howled.

Chapter Nine

$\mathcal{M}$arcus wasn't quite sure what was happening.

The heat in the furnace was tremendous. Sweat poured off his skin, running in rivulets down the side of his face and neck, and into his shirt. He was acutely aware of Gwen's soft breasts squashed against his back. The peaks were hard little nubs pressed into his skin, tantalizing and unreachable. The combination of her body pressed against him, and yet out of view, inflamed him to a peak of lust beyond anything he'd ever experienced.

He had a death grip on the handles of the bellows. He couldn't stop pumping, couldn't risk the furnace cooling. He'd felt a tingle when Gwen had first laid her hands on him, a slight spark as her magic passed through him. His first instinct had been to resist, but once he'd relaxed, the sensation had disappeared. If Gwen's Light were still flowing—and he expected it was—his dull, mundane senses couldn't feel it.

But he could feel her arousal. The scent of it surrounded him, musky and dark and enticing. Her body moved on his, rubbing up and down along his spine. Her open mouth pressed on the back of his neck, her tongue rasped his skin. Her questing hands ran under his apron, down his chest, over his stomach, tore at the laces on his *braccas* . . .

Jupiter and Pollux. Her fingers closed on his erection. He jerked his hands from the bellows just as her teeth sank—*hard*—into his neck.

Pain—and something far more primitive—exploded inside him. A deep, primal part of him forced its way to the surface of his psyche. Instinctive, feral power gripped him. The next heartbeat found him on his feet, yanking at the ties of his own apron. He spun about, grabbing Gwen as she stumbled against him, his fingers biting into the soft flesh of her upper arms. She fought his control, thrashing and biting. He felt her knee connect with the inside of his thigh. There was a wildness about her that stirred his lust. His mind spun; his vision turned bright red. He wanted her; he needed her. He pinioned her wrists between their bodies. She kicked at him; he covered her mouth with his. She bit his lip, then sucked the wound into her mouth. The next thing he knew, she was on her back on the ground, surrounded by heat and ash and the odor of burning charcoal. He straddled her, stretching her arms over her head, and holding them there with one hand. His lower body imprisoned her legs.

"Gods, Gwen. What—"

"Marcus. Please . . ." Her voice sounded strange. He did not know what she was asking. Her back arched, thrusting her breasts toward him. Reflexively, he covered one with his free hand.

Her breath was pulsing in sharp, shallow puffs. Her

eyes were not focused. She jerked her arms, but he didn't let go. He was rock hard and throbbing painfully, his stones heavy and tight.

"Marcus . . . please. I need . . . something, or I won't be able to stop it—"

His hand covered her breast.

She gasped, writhing under him. And then he saw it. A shimmer passing over her body. He felt it like a tingling on his skin. Her eyes changed, the pupils narrowing. They were human eyes no longer.

Gwen was shifting.

"Marcus." Her voice was a thready gasp. "Help me. I don't want—"

Horror warred with a bolt of pure, raw lust. He felt something inside him shift, some part of his own humanity falling away. The wolf had been the guardian of his own ancestors; perhaps the spirit of that ancient beast had risen in him now, to accept the challenge of Gwen's Deep Magic.

With a shudder, he gave himself over to the primitive madness. He heard fabric rending, and barely understood that he'd torn Gwen's tunic from neckline to hem. He shoved his *braccas* down over his hips. He sprung free, hard and pounding and relentless.

With one hand, he rolled Gwen over, holding her by the neck as he ripped the shredded tunic from her body. She was trembling now. Struggling but not. Her legs parted. Rising on all fours, her hands braced on the ground, she thrust her buttocks backward in unmistakable invitation. The soft round globes ground into his groin. He slipped between them and encountered slick heat.

His brain spun beyond thought, beyond caution, beyond any notion of restraint. He hardly knew who he was—hardly knew *what* he was. He only knew he needed this woman's complete submission. Now.

"Mine," he growled. "You are mine, Gwen. Say it."

"Yours," she gasped.

He covered her, caging her body with his legs and arms. A whirling vortex sucked at his sanity. Every touch, every sound, every smell left him reeling. Her scent inflamed him; he dragged his tongue across her neck, pressed his open mouth to the fleshy mound of her shoulder. She tasted of salt, of honey, of feminine mystery.

His body was on fire for her. His shaft jabbed between her legs, the broad head finding the entrance to her body. He surged forward and penetrated her, touching the barrier that was proof no man had preceded him. His teeth scraped her skin. Her head dropped, and tilted slightly, like a wolf bitch offering her jugular to her mate.

His teeth sank into her flesh. The same instant, his hips jerked forward. He surged into her heat, driving through her maidenhead, impaling her with one deep, primitive thrust. A cry tore from her throat. The sound filled him with savage satisfaction. Gods, she was tight. Her slick, hot passageway closed on him like a fist. Held him. He licked her shoulder and tasted her blood.

Reality slammed into him.

"*Hades.*" What was he doing? He was rutting on Gwen like an animal. Gods, had he lost his mind? Had her magic crippled his brain? He started to withdraw, then stopped, frozen by her strangled cry.

"Nay," she gasped, reaching around with one hand,

her fingernails biting his hip. "Do not stop, Marcus. Finish it."

Finish it.

The words set him ablaze again. The top of his skull felt as though it had separated from the rest of his head. Blood rushed hot and urgent to his groin. He grasped her hips, hard, and slid into her a second time, the head of his phallus dragging on the hot walls of her slick inner passage. The pleasure was so sharp, so intoxicating, that the smithy walls might have collapsed around him and he would not have noticed. He closed his eyes, his world narrowing to his cock, to the flex of his fingers on Gwen's hipbones, to the shuddering surrender of Gwen's sweet body.

His hips jerked again and again, pulling and plunging. The rhythm took over his will; only death could have stopped him. A bright light burned in his mind, then spread to fill his body. His stones grew heavy; Gwen's inner passage contracted.

He thrust with all his strength, one last, glorious time. She let out a strangled cry, her body convulsing in his hands. His world exploded in a rush of pleasure so intense he was sure he'd been lifted off the ground. For a moment he hung suspended in a place of perfect bliss; the next instant he collapsed, barely managing to avoid crushing the woman under him. He rolled onto his back on the warm stone floor, snagging her about the waist and pulling her on top of him to sprawl across his chest.

His heart pounded convulsively. Gwen trembled. They were both struggling to gasp air. Sanity, as unwelcome as it was, crept back into his skull. *Jupiter and Apollo.* What had he done?

Coward that he was, he waited until she lifted her head and spoke his name before he dared to open his eyes. The sight of her made his heart contract painfully. Gods, she was lovely. Her braid had come completely undone. Her hair cascaded over her shoulders like pure moonlight. Her face was flushed, her cheeks red, her mouth swollen. Her eyes were clear and gray. He searched them intently. Incredibly, he saw no anger.

His shaking hand stroked up her arm. She flinched when she reached her shoulder. With a muttered curse, he lifted her hair and stared at the wound he'd inflicted. He'd *bitten* her. Gods. Bitten her, and used her more violently than he'd ever used any practiced whore. To add to the insult, his body was not even ashamed. He was still hard. He wanted her again.

"Gods, Gwen. I'm sorry. I have never in my life treated a woman so shamefully. I . . . I don't know what to say."

Her hands smoothed over his shirt, her fingers playing with the curling hair below his throat. "Do not apologize to me, Marcus. There is no need." She kissed his lips. "Do ye not realize what ye did? Ye stopped it."

Stopped it? He'd stopped *nothing*. He hadn't been able to. He'd let the basest part of his nature consume them both. He'd torn her clothes from her body, not even stopping to remove his own. He'd bitten her, put bruises on her body. And Gwen looked happy about it. Or, more precisely, *relieved*, as if his unforgivable assault had lifted some incredible burden from her shoulders. He pushed himself up on one elbow, suddenly aware they were lying atop a layer of ash.

"You should be furious with me. Or crying."

She shook her head, a smile touching her lips. "Ye

do not understand. The wolf wanted freedom. Ye stopped it, after I had already begun to shift. That has never happened before."

Suddenly, he remembered. "But why would you call the wolf here? Now? You promised—"

"I did not call it." She looked away, biting her lip.

Her reached up and touched her mouth, smoothing the ragged skin. "Then what happened? Tell me."

"I misled ye, Marcus. I promised not to call the wolf, but that was a promise I could not make. I do not control the wolf. Not entirely. Aye, I can call it, and sometimes do, but most often . . . the magic comes unbidden, especially when my emotions rise strongly. I cannot control it."

Marcus sat up the rest of the way, shifting her into his lap. His erection prodded her bottom. "You can't control when the wolf will emerge?"

"Not entirely. Not since my time in the cave. I spent so many nights in the wolf's body, my human soul had begun to fade. Now when the wolf wants freedom, my Light cannot always subdue it. But ye . . ." She blushed and started to scramble off his lap.

Reluctantly, he let her go and rose.

She stood twisting her fingers together. "My Deep Magic has never struck so quickly and violently. Never have I been able to stop it once it's gotten so far. But when ye turned on me . . ." She clamped her lips together, her cheeks flushing bright red. Ducking her head, she searched the floor for her tunic. When she found it, under the anvil, she stared at the shredded garment as if she'd never seen it before. Hugging it to her chest, she looked back at him.

"The wolf yielded to ye, Marcus. Surely ye felt it."

"I did. But what does it mean?"

"I hardly know. I did not even think such a thing was possible."

His gaze traveled over her. Her cheeks were still flushed, her pale skin smudged with soot. The imprint of his fingers was on her hip; she'd have a nasty bruise there tomorrow.

He touched it gently, his remorse sharp. "You're going to be sore."

"It does not matter." Her fingers clutched the ruined tunic. "But how will I explain to Rhiannon that I ruined her tunic?"

"No difficulty there. We'll blame it on the soot and sparks from the furnace. My clothes are destroyed with alarming regularity." He approached her, relieved when she didn't flinch. Not willing to give her more chance to protest, he lifted her off her feet and into his arms.

"What—? Put me down, Marcus."

"Aye, my lady," he said, imitating her Celt accent. She snorted, and he grinned. Striding across the smithy, he rounded the wooden screen and laid her gently on his bed. Easing the ruined tunic from her fingers, he scooped a blanket off the floor and offered it to her instead. "Wait here."

He returned a moment later with a filled washbowl, a linen towel slung over his shoulder. He set the bowl on the trunk next to the bed and dipped the rag in the water. "You're a mess."

"This water is hot," she said with some surprise as he dabbed at the soot on her face.

"I keep a full cauldron in an alcove on the far side of the furnace. The water heats while I work. It's useful for washing up."

He finished cleaning her face. She sat up, and he

drew back her hair from her neck, exposing his bite. He washed the wound, frowning.

"I can't explain what came over me," he muttered. He kept his head down, running the cloth over her shoulders and arms, washing away soot and sweat.

"Magic," Gwen said. "Did ye feel it?"

His hand stilled. "I felt something. Light. Some tingling." He met her gaze. "Lust. Was that magic, too?"

"I do not know." Her gaze drifted to the furnace, where a faint aura shone. Her pulse quickened. "The iron. May I see it?"

"The bloom is too hot to pull out. Give it some time to cool."

The towel dipped between her breasts. He bent his head, circling the rag around her areole. Her nipples puckered to tight buds. She let the blanket slip to her stomach. His mouth went dry; he tried to swallow, but couldn't. Dimly he was aware of her easing the rag from his fingers.

She rinsed it in the warm water, then, with light strokes that he felt deep in his belly, washed his face. "Ye are a fright as well."

"I never said you were a fright."

She guided the towel down his neck. "Take off your shirt."

He obeyed, shucking the garment and tossing it on the floor. His *braccas* followed. Naked, he held himself very still as she stroked the rag over his chest. She instructed him to turn so she could reach his back. He did.

When the rag dipped to his waist, he stood and captured her gaze. "If I make love to you again, will the wolf remain in its lair?"

A shadow passed through her eyes. "I do not know."

"There's only one way to find out, then." When she didn't answer, he added. "I want you, Gwen. I want to make love to you. Not mount you like a rutting boar." He placed a kiss on her forehead. "Tell me you want that, too."

"But the wolf—"

"I'm not afraid of the wolf."

"Ye should be."

Perhaps she was right. Perhaps lust had eaten all the sense in his brain. It made no difference; he wanted her again. Desperately. Wetting the clean towel, he bent over her, stroking a circle around her navel. Her belly quivered; she made no move to stop him. He tugged the blanket completely away, revealing a triangle of white-blond curls.

"Lean back, Gwen, and part your legs for me."

Slowly, she did as he requested, lying back on the mattress. She wasn't certain, he could tell, but all doubt had fled Marcus's mind. He'd forced the wolf's retreat once. Surely he could do it again. If not . . . well, it was a risk he was willing to take.

He dipped the wet towel between her legs. She flinched a little; she must be sore, after the way he'd he used her. He clamped down on his self-loathing. She'd said his roughness was due to magic—it was an excuse that meant little to him. A man's actions were his own, and Marcus could not deny he'd reveled in his harsh treatment of her body. His orgasm has been the most intense he'd ever known. Had Gwen even found release? He didn't know—he'd been so lost in his own pleasure that he hadn't been aware of hers.

He could correct that, at least. Kneeling before her, he ran his hands up her legs, parting them more fully, opening her completely. He placed a kiss high on the inside of her thigh.

"What . . . are ye doing?" she asked unsteadily.

"This," he said, and covered her with his mouth.

The shudder that shook her body was so strong Gwen found herself grabbing fistfuls of blanket. Marcus's mouth was hot, his lips and tongue relentless. He nipped and licked and suckled, consuming her intimate flesh in a way she had never dreamed was possible. It was too much; she couldn't think. She tried to bring her knees together.

She couldn't. His broad shoulders were between her legs. His hands had slipped under her bottom, lifting her, giving him better access to take whatever he wanted. *Give* whatever he wanted. Swells of pleasure cascaded over her, each one higher than the one before. She clutched at his hair, not knowing whether to shove him away or pull him closer.

He lifted his head and slipped a finger inside her, pressing deep. She gasped at the invasion, gasped again when a wave of indescribable pleasure broke over her. A second finger joined the first, stretching her. His mouth covered her again, seeking in her folds for the hard nub from which all sensation radiated.

He went on and on, driving her to ever-increasing peaks of pleasure, then drawing back until the sensations faded. As soon as she caught her breath, he began again, pushing her toward some unknown goal. The rough coupling on the floor of the smithy had been nothing like this. That had shocked her—first with pain as her maidenhead broke, then with brief, violent pleasure when Marcus exploded inside her. But

this . . . this rise and fall of bliss, this sweet aching pleasure, was completely unexpected. Was this what lovemaking was? She had never imagined something
so . . . personal.

The low points of her pleasure were shallower now,
the peaks more pronounced. Each one hung higher,
endured longer, was more intense. There was something just beyond, something that frightened her. It was
akin to the joy she felt when the pain of her shifting fell
away, leaving her wholly in the body of the wolf. It was
a wild joy, an abandon she associated with Deep
Magic. She was afraid if she reached for it, claimed it
as her own, it would rouse the wolf.

A sharp wave of bliss crashed over her; she all but
drowned in it. She twisted to one side. "Marcus . . .
nay . . ."

"Come for me, Gwen." His voice was ragged, his
breath hot on her belly. His thumb found the place
where his mouth had been. All coherent thought spun
away. "Let go. Let me give this to you."

It was beyond her power to deny him. She gave herself over to his care, to his lips and tongue, to the heat
of his body and the urgency of his desire. A bright light
shattered behind her eyes as she came apart in his
hands, carried on the brilliance of a pleasure so deep,
so intense, that she was sure what she was, *who* she
was, had ceased to be

And through it all, even when Marcus moved over
her and slid inside, the wolf did not stir.

She woke some time later wrapped securely in Marcus's arms. His bed was not meant for two—she was
sprawled half atop him, one leg flung over his thigh.
The fire in the furnace had dimmed to a low glow.

Through the smithy's single window, she saw the sky had faded to pale gray.

For a time she listened to the sounds of the farm drifting through the open window. Birdsong, the bark of a dog, the call of a voice from the stables. The scent of rain and the promises of spring teased her nostrils. For the first time in years she did not want to be anywhere other than where she was.

If only it could last.

"Night is falling," she said with a sigh.

Marcus kissed the top of her head. "So it is."

She pushed herself up, looking down at him. His brown eyes were soft and warm, and . . . satisfied.

"How do you feel?" he asked, rubbing her back.

"I . . ." She shook her head. "Truly, I do not know. Not like myself, in any case."

His expression turned wary. "Regrets?"

"Nay." It was the truth. She scooted higher on his body and kissed his mouth. He made a low sound in his throat and pulled her closer. His shaft lengthened against her belly, causing her insides to dissolve in liquid heat. Shifting ever so slightly, she opened to him and welcomed him inside.

He slipped in easily. "I don't want to hurt you. You're sure to be tender . . ."

"I do not care."

He needed no more encouragement. Guiding her hips with his hands, he began a slow, languid lovemaking that soon had her gasping. Her release was a quick-spreading heat that reached every part of her body—even to her toes and fingers. Marcus closed his eyes and groaned, his hips flexing in one, long upward thrust as he spilled his seed. He gathered her to his chest and kissed her again.

She would have liked to stay in his arms forever, but night was falling. "I . . . I should go. I don't want to leave Breena alone. Last night was peaceful, but—"

"Of course," he said, instantly lifting them both to a sitting position. "But you'll need clothes first. Wait here—I'll find something."

He disappeared out the smithy door. Gwen set her feet on the floor, wrapping the blanket under her arms. She walked barefoot to the furnace, gazing at the red coals. She cast her senses, searching for magic she'd sensed there before. It was there. A steady glow of Light, wrapped around something even more vibrant.

Deep Magic. It pulsed like a thing alive. She felt a thrill of triumph, tempered by a healthy dose of apprehension. Would the Deep Magic submit to the Light? The spells she would set in the days to come, as Marcus fashioned the sword, would be crucial.

Marcus soon returned, carrying her old tunic, freshly laundered. "I found it drying behind the bathhouse."

Gwen dressed and braided her hair the best she could. She bent to fasten her shoes, nodding toward the forge. "When will ye look at what we've wrought?"

"The furnace is too hot to pull out the bloom now. I'll tend to it after I walk you back to the house. In the morning, I'll show you what we've created." He touched her chin, lifting her gaze to his. "Together."

Marcus returned to the smithy alone after seeing Gwen to the main house. Restless, he hefted an iron rake and worked over the smoldering coals, seeking the new bloom that lay in the bottom of the furnace chamber. Misshapen, pitted lumps of various sizes, they looked like nothing so much as worthless lumps of rock. Taking up a pair of long prongs, he lifted one from the ashes and laid it on the anvil.

He traded the long prongs for a shorter pair. Hammer in hand, he struck the newly smelted metal, mindful of a hot spurt of slag. Turning it over, he struck again.

He settled into a familiar rhythm, hammering away ash and soot, smoothing imperfections, turning the bloom from one side to another as it flattened. Finally, he stopped, wiped his sleeve across his brow and stared.

The metal gleamed like moonlight.

Bright iron.

Chapter Ten

Gwen slept fitfully; dawn was far too long in coming. She lay on her back, staring at the shadows cast by the ceiling beams, reliving each touch of Marcus's hands and mouth on her body. He'd tamed the wolf. She had not thought it possible, even for a Druid. But Marcus, a man with no magic, had done it.

How? And would the beast stay away? Or was it merely biding its time?

She had no answer—only hopes, mingled with fears. The night seemed to pass at a snail's pace; the wind had risen, sending the shutter tapping erratically against the window frame. She dozed fitfully. Toward daybreak, Breena moaned in her sleep, then started muttering. Gwen was at the lass's side in a heartbeat. She hovered uncertainly. Would Breena, while walking in her vision, remember the spell Gwen had taught her? If she did, would it be enough?

Breena's young face contorted in pain. Gwen resisted the urge to wake her; Marcus's sister had to learn to navigate her visions on her own, especially if she meant to stay in Isca. Her breathing became labored and her slim body started to writhe. When Gwen drew the bed linens away from Breena's neck, a choked cry erupted from the girl's lips. She bolted upright, her hands clutching at her throat, her eyes wild. The strange silver aura flared and sputtered around her. She tried to draw breath, but couldn't; a gulp of air became a sickening wheeze. Before Gwen could react, the girl's body twisted, flopping like a fish in the mud. She lurched sideways. Gwen caught her as she rolled off the bed. They landed in a heap on the floor.

Breena rolled, her sleeping tunic tangling in her legs, her lungs straining for air. Gwen lurched after her, grasped her upper arms and gave her a violent shake.

"Breena! Wake up!" The back of Breena's head thunked against the tiles. The jolt shocked her out of her trance. She gasped, her chest heaving as air whooshed into her lungs. Her eyes snapped open. With a moan she broke Gwen's grip and rolled away. She curled in upon herself, her knees drawn up to her chest, and let out a keening sob. "Oh, Goddess, it hurts . . ."

Once the vision was upon her, she must not have been able to recall the spell Gwen had taught her. Gwen molded her palms to Breena's skull. Light flowed into the silver shimmer surrounding Breena's body. Pain rebounded into Gwen's palms, scoring them like a jagged blade. Gwen gasped another spell, summoned more Light. Breena's pain receded only slightly. Tears cascaded over the lass's face as she rocked and sobbed and gasped. Gwen redoubled her efforts, summoning all the Light she possessed. Finally, Breena's sobs quieted; her body slowly uncoiled. She lay on her side, panting.

When she thought the girl could stand, Gwen

helped her to her bed. Breena sat down heavily, gripping the wooden frame tightly. "I did as you said," she rasped. "I cast the spell exactly as you taught me. But nothing happened."

" 'Twas your first time," Gwen said, sitting beside her, more disturbed than she wanted Marcus's sister to know. She massaged Breena's scalp.

Tears oozed from beneath the girl's eyelids. "I'm sorry. I'm a poor student."

Gwen's heart twisted. She concentrated on sending healing Light through her fingertips. Breena's shoulders relaxed, and her breathing became more even. She drifted off to sleep. Gwen eased her down on the bed and covered her with a blanket.

She sat for a long time, watching Marcus's sister sleep, dreading what she would have to do if her Light were not strong enough to keep Breena safe.

The knock on the smithy door was firm and loud. It was hardly past dawn. Not Gwen, Marcus decided, as he finished tying the laces on a clean pair of *braccas*. Not Breena or his stepmother, either. He shrugged an unsoiled shirt over his head and went to answer the door. His brows went up when he found Lucius standing on the threshold.

Marcus waved his father inside. "To what do I owe this rare honor?"

Lucius shook his head. "Surely it has not been so long since I've visited the smithy."

"Surely it has been," Marcus replied good-naturedly. His father had long ago resigned himself to his son's unorthodox choice of vocation, but he'd never become truly comfortable with it. Nor was he especially enamored of the space's usual disarray.

Lucius advanced into the heart of the chaos, first inspecting the rack of unfinished swords and daggers, then coming to stand before Marcus's worktable. Marcus squelched the urge to scuttle about, to replace pens and stack parchment in neat piles. He'd spent his life listening to his father extol the virtues of discipline and organization. Lately, Breena had taken up the cause as well. But Marcus had long ago accepted the fact that he had no talent for order.

Today, however, his father did not comment on the mess. Turning from the worktable, he strode to the forge. His brows lifted when he spied the newly worked metal lying on the anvil.

"You were successful, then."

"With Gwen's help," Marcus said. He came to stand beside his father, gazing meditatively at the *chalybs*. "There is magic in that metal, I am sure. But I can't see it, or feel it."

"Nor can I. How long will it take you to forge Gwen's sword?"

"The bright iron is more difficult to work than the black. A fortnight, at least."

"Good. Breena needs Gwen here. I am not sure her first lessons in magic have done her any good. She was haggard this morning. But she would not speak of it."

The news was troubling. "She will improve."

"I hope that is true. But I cannot help considering that Rhys is right—Breena needs to learn magic on Avalon."

Marcus studied his father. Lucius was five-and-forty. Old, by anyone's standard. But though more strands of white wove though Lucius's dark hair with each passing year, his bearing was that of a much younger man. He'd never developed the paunch most retired soldiers sported; he didn't lounge in the tavern, drinking unwatered wine and telling tales of past glory. Still, Marcus's father wasn't getting any younger. Today, the lines of worry in his face almost made him look his age.

"Rhiannon is sorely troubled," Lucius continued. "It cannot be good for the babe." He paused. "You remember how it was when Breena was born."

Marcus nodded. He remembered vividly, though he'd been only eleven years old at the time. Breena had come early, and had nearly died. "Gwen will make progress with Breena." She had to.

"And if she does not, we will send Breena to Avalon once the babe is born."

It wasn't a pleasant thought, but it was far preferable to the possibility that Breena's visions would do her real harm if she remained here in Isca. "Perhaps that would be wise."

Lucius looked at his son with some surprise. "You offer no argument against Breena traveling to Avalon? Has Gwen changed your opinion of magic, then, where Rhys could not?"

Marcus only shrugged.

There was a moment of silence, and then Lucius said, "She is a striking woman."

"It hardly matters how striking she is. She'll be gone once I forge her sword."

"But you don't want her to leave."

"What I want makes no difference."

"And all this time I thought you brooded for Clara. Now I begin to wonder if it hasn't been Gwen in your thoughts since you returned from Avalon."

"What if it has been? It changes nothing. She cannot stay here, and the Druids wouldn't even let me set foot into their pitiful village."

"Her eyes follow you. And yours follow her. It's clear enough there is something between you."

Marcus looked up at the ceiling and grimaced. "So much for discretion. But it doesn't change who she is."

"I was once at war with Rhiannon's clan. Owein tried his best to kill me."

"That has nothing to do with Gwen and me."

"No?" Lucius shrugged. A smile played about his lips. "My mistake, then."

Barefoot, his face and arms darkened with a thin layer of swamp muck, Rhys crouched in a shadowed crevice directly below the entrance to the Druid silver mine. Despite his best efforts to bolster the spell of protection shielding the cave's bounty from Roman eyes, soldiers had discovered a trace of silver ore two days earlier. The deep, twisting passage had suddenly become the main focus of the Roman mining exploration.

Riders had been dispatched eastward. Within a day, an officer had arrived on horseback, accompanied by an armed escort. Rhys recognized the man; Tribune Valgus, the arrogant senator's son who had once been betrothed to Clara—a man with an endless need for coin to fund his enormous gambling losses. Valgus and Strabo had disappeared into the mine some time ago.

Rhys glanced toward the swamps. If not for the mists, Avalon would be plainly visible. He could feel Strabo's Deep Magic, searching. So far Rhys's Light had confounded it, but the effort had cost him dearly. Occupied with Strabo's magic, Rhys hadn't been able to completely hold the spell on the Druid mine.

Once the Romans realized what riches lay under the hill, they would build a permanent fort. Trevor would have to abandon his barley fields. Avalon would suffer—it would be difficult to grow all their grain on the sacred isle. Assuming that Rhys could even keep Avalon hidden.

Where, *where* was Gwen? Together, they might be able to ensure Avalon's safety. *Trust me,* she had begged. But Rhys found his trust had grown dangerously thin. A deep, twisting resentment—an emotion reserved solely for his twin—snaked through his gut.

Tribune Valgus and Legate Strabo emerged from the mine, coming to a halt just above Rhys's hiding place. Rhys tensed, his ears straining for their murmured conversation.

Valgus's voice was laced with satisfaction. "I knew that misshapen dwarf's wild tale of a hidden mine in these hills was true. I found a sizeable chunk of ore in his pack, after all."

Rhys swallowed his anger. Valgus could only be referring to Cormac, a Celt spy and sometime visitor to Avalon whom Rhys had never trusted, even before the man had aided Blodwen's campaign against Avalon. Cormac had claimed Blodwen after her banishment; no doubt she'd told him of the mine's exact location. Rhys might have expected the dwarf to pilfer some of the ore—but relay the mine's location to the Romans? That betrayal was inexcusable.

Valgus chuckled. "Prying information out of that dirty *Brittunculus* was quite an enjoyable task. By the time my men finished with him, he'd have sold his mother for a denarius."

Strabo made a derisive sound in his throat. "If your men had done their job correctly, the slippery bastard would not have been able to escape. His guidance would have saved you a month of searching."

"It will all be the same in the end. We've found the vein. We cannot be far from the lode."

"I hope you are correct."

Rhys had heard enough. He waited until the Romans moved away, then eased off the ledge and down the mountain. He found Trevor where he'd left him, guarding the raft that would take them back across the swamp.

With so many soldiers on the hill, they no longer dared risk the crossing in daylight, even with the mist's protection. Hunkering down, they waited for dusk. When dusk fell at last, Trevor poled the raft while Rhys laid a trail of illusion in their wake. He hoped Strabo was occupied—he was not at all sure the spell would hold up to the sorcerer's close scrutiny.

The raft bumped Avalon's shore. Rhys's muscles unwound. They tightened again almost immediately when he spotted Owein on the dock. His expression was grim.

" 'Tis Cyric," the red-haired northerner said. "His dreams have darkened. He wanders, sobbing a woman's name. Tamar."

Rhys's chest tightened painfully. "My mother."

"She didna die a kind death, did she?"

"Nay." Rhys's heart shrank from the memory. "She did not."

Gwen's days settled into a steady rhythm, much like the melody of Marcus's hammer on the newly smelted *chalybs*. She never tired of gazing upon the bright iron, nor of watching Marcus's arms flex as he heated and worked the misshapen blooms into one mass of shining metal. When she cast her senses, a nimbus of white

179

light appeared around it. Within the Light, there was a flicker of blue.

Deep Magic, pure and steady, encased in Light. The blade was truly awesome in its power. Marcus had taken to calling it Exchalybur—"cutting bright iron." Gwen only hoped her magic was equal to the task of wielding such a weapon, and that Rhys could hold off Strabo until it was ready.

While Marcus worked steadily, hammering and folding the metal, Gwen crafted intricate spells she hoped would ensure that the Deep Magic stayed subject to the Light. She sent the magic through Marcus into the bright iron. Each day, she grew more hopeful that she would reach her goal.

But there was an unexpected quality to Gwen's collaboration with Marcus—each spell she set fanned the heat smoldering between them. Her instinct was to shy away from the intimacy, because she was not so sure the wolf had been cowed completely. Marcus, however, would not allow it.

Each day he made love to her—most days, more than once. He pleasured her in his narrow bed, or while she sat with legs spread on his worktable, or with her spine pressed against the warm walls of the smithy. He took her hand and led her through the north gates and into the woods, to lie with her in the place where she had first touched him intimately. As he moved deep inside her, Gwen gazed up at the sky and wished her life, her duty, belonged to another woman. But it did not. It was hers alone, and she could not abandon it. She could only savor each moment with Marcus, hoarding them like gems in her heart.

If Gwen's days were wreathed with bittersweet love, her nights contained only worry. Rhys still called, each time more desperately. Strabo's spells affected Cyric deeply, and Rhys was not sure he could hold the illusion on the Druid mines and grain field as well as the mist around the sacred isle. "*Come home,*" he called. "*Soon,*" she wanted to tell him. But she kept her silence.

Rhys's calls were not the only trouble of the night. Despite Gwen's most fervent efforts, the ill effects of Breena's visions did not lessen. Though Breena had learned the Words of the protective spell perfectly, the Light the lass called did not lessen her pain, nor her terror. Over and over, Gwen's Light was needed to draw Breena out of her vision before she suffocated. What would happen when the sword was completed? If Breena did not travel to Avalon with Gwen, she would be completely at the mercy of her visions. But the thought of putting Marcus's sister in the way of Strabo's Deep Magic was equally chilling.

And so Gwen made the decision she'd been dreading.

She sought out Breena—she found her in the hearth room, sitting before Rhiannon's loom, passing the shuttle listlessly through the warp of a half-finished blanket. The stones that weighted the threads swayed and clacked. The last few lines of the weave were lumpy and uneven, and no wonder. Gwen doubted the lass managed even two hours of sleep each night.

Breena grimaced as Gwen approached. She sent the shuttle back along the path it had just taken, undoing the weft thread. She wound the unraveled wool back in place on the shuttle with a sigh. "I'm horrible at weaving, even on a good day."

"The design is pleasant," Gwen said.

"That's because it's Mother's. I'm no artist, not like Marcus."

"The Great Mother does not give everyone the same talents."

"That is true, of course, but it would have been nice to have been born with only two thumbs, rather than ten."

Gwen smiled. "Surely it's not that bad."

"Oh, it is. I have no talent for any craft. I dislike working with my hands." She fingered the upper half of the blanket, where Rhiannon's weave was tight and even. "I shouldn't touch Mother's work, but . . . I need something to occupy my days, or I'll go mad with worry about the nights."

"The spell I taught ye does not help at all."

"Perhaps I didn't learn it correctly."

"Nay, ye say the Words perfectly. The magic of the vision interferes with your Light." Gwen paused. "The aura of silver that surrounds ye—"

"I cannot break through it, no matter what I try. I know I must—the woman in my vision needs me, but . . ." She rose abruptly, a sound of frustration in her throat. "I am blind and deaf, and cannot help her! Is there nothing else I can do?"

"There is another spell I might teach ye. More powerful than the first." She drew a breath. "Deep Magic."

Breena's eyes widened. "Is that permitted?"

"Nay," Gwen said truthfully. "But I do not know what else to do. Ye cannot go on as ye have been, especially after I leave Isca. And what good is the Great Mother's message if ye cannot understand it?"

"True enough," Breena replied shakily. Her chin came up, and her slender shoulders squared. "If you think this spell will help, I am willing to learn it."

"Then we will begin immediately. But . . ." Gwen glanced at the loom. "Not here, I think. Your mind needs to be as untroubled as possible. Is there a place where ye feel more at ease? A personal sanctuary?"

"You mean like Marcus's clearing in the woods?"

Gwen blushed, thinking of what she and Marcus had done in that sanctuary just that morning. "Aye. Like that. Do ye have your own place in the woods, perhaps?"

Breena took Gwen's arm. "No, not in the woods. My sanctuary is here, in the house. It is Father's library. I'll take you there now—Father has gone to town, so no one is likely to bother us."

The library was indeed empty. "Marcus never comes here," Breena explained. "And no one else on the farm is able to read."

Gwen regarded the room with amazement. She'd never seen anything like it—this dark, slightly musty space was so far removed from her life on Avalon as to belong to a different world entirely. If this were Breena's sanctuary, it was no wonder Marcus believed his sister would not be happy on Avalon.

How odd Rhys had never mentioned Breena's intense love for books and learning. But then, she reflected, Rhys was reticent on most things having to do with Breena.

The room was almost oppressively neat. No wonder Marcus did not come here! The space was high, long, and narrow. Six square windows punctuated the wall just below the coffered ceiling, providing diffuse illumination. Each wall was covered with shelves taller than Gwen could reach. The wooden planks all but groaned under the weight of their treasures. A polished oak table flanked with cross-legged chairs occupied the center of the room. Wax tablets, styluses, parchment, pens, inkwells, and other paraphernalia marched neatly down its center. Three hanging sconces, each holding four oil lamps, hovered over the table ready to provide increased illumination.

"We have over two hundred scrolls," Breena announced proudly. "Each is labeled with a brass tag. We also have a good number of codices, which are not so old as the scrolls." Breena lifted a sheath of square-cut leafs, bound along one edge, and demonstrated turning the pages. "Parchment is sturdier than papyrus," she explained, "and reading pages bound this way is much less trouble than unrolling a scroll." She beamed at Gwen. "Is it not a wonderful invention?"

"Aye, certainly," Gwen murmured politely.

Breena replaced the codex and went to close the door that led to the entrance gallery. Gwen would have preferred to leave it open; the library shelving seemed to loom inward, giving her a feeling of being pressed in upon. The slight odor of mold turned her stomach. She'd always preferred open spaces to closed ones, even more so after her imprisonment. She chafed her cold hands, reminding herself that it was not her feelings about the library that mattered, but Breena's.

"Father had most of these scrolls sent from Rome when he sold his properties there." Breena lifted a scroll and reverently unrolled it. "There are texts in both Latin and Greek, of course."

Gwen squinted at the incomprehensible Roman runes. Her own language did not have a written form. Her people passed on knowledge in stories and songs. "Ye can read them all?"

"Yes. Father taught me. We've spent hours upon hours here together. I love it. Mathematics is my favorite subject, but I also like philosophy and medicine,

GET UP TO
4 FREE BOOKS!

You can have the best romance delivered to your door for less than what you'd pay in a bookstore or online. Sign up for one of our book clubs today, and we'll send you **FREE* BOOKS** just for trying it out...**with no obligation to buy, ever!**

HISTORICAL ROMANCE BOOK CLUB

Travel from the Scottish Highlands to the American West, the decadent ballrooms of Regency England to Viking ships. Your shipments will include authors such as CONNIE MASON, CASSIE EDWARDS, LYNSAY SANDS, LEIGH GREENWOOD, and many, many more.

LOVE SPELL BOOK CLUB

Bring a little magic into your life with the romances of Love Spell—fun contemporaries, paranormals, time-travels, futuristics, and more. Your shipments will include authors such as KATIE MACALISTER, SUSAN GRANT, NINA BANGS, SANDRA HILL, and more.

As a book club member you also receive the following special benefits:

- **30% OFF all orders through our website & telecenter!**
  (Plus, you still get 1 book FREE for every 5 books you buy!)

- **Exclusive access to special discounts!**

- **Convenient home delivery and 10 days to return any books you don't want to keep.**

There is no minimum number of books to buy, and you may cancel membership at any time. See back to sign up!

*Please include $2.00 for shipping and handling.

YES! ☐

Sign me up for the **Historical Romance Book Club** and send my TWO FREE BOOKS! If I choose to stay in the club, I will pay only $8.50* each month, a savings of $5.48!

YES! ☐

Sign me up for the **Love Spell Book Club** and send my TWO FREE BOOKS! If I choose to stay in the club, I will pay only $8.50* each month, a savings of $5.48!

NAME: _____

ADDRESS: _____

_____

TELEPHONE: _____

E-MAIL: _____

☐ **I WANT TO PAY BY CREDIT CARD.**

☐ VISA   ☐ MasterCard   ☐ DISCOVER

ACCOUNT #: _____

EXPIRATION DATE: _____

SIGNATURE: _____

Send this card along with $2.00 shipping & handling for each club you wish to join, to:

Romance Book Clubs
1 Mechanic Street
Norwalk, CT 06850-3431

Or fax (must include credit card information!) to: 610.995.9274.
You can also sign up online at www.dorchesterpub.com.

*Plus $2.00 for shipping. Offer open to residents of the U.S. and Canada only.
Canadian residents please call 1.800.481.9191 for pricing information.

If under 18, a parent or guardian must sign. Terms, prices and conditions subject to change. Subscription subject
to acceptance. Dorchester Publishing reserves the right to reject any order or cancel any subscription.

JOIN NOW!

and the great epics of Homer." She nodded to the scroll she'd opened. "This is a text by Titus Livius. It's a history of Rome."

"I'm afraid the runes mean nothing to me. I cannot read Latin."

"How did you come to speak it at all?" Breena asked as she carefully rerolled the scroll.

"Cyric taught Rhys. Rhys and I did not understand why our grandfather did not teach me as well—we didn't know at the time that Cyric meant for Rhys to leave Avalon. But in those days, Rhys and I shared everything. He would receive his lesson, then come and teach me everything he learned."

At the mention of Rhys, Breena's eyes lit up. "But Rhys can read and write Latin. Why did he not teach you?"

"He learned those skills after he left Avalon. We were not . . . often together after that."

"I can teach you, if you'd like."

Gwen smiled faintly. "I thank ye, but I will not be here long enough to learn."

"I will miss you when you're gone."

Gwen watched as Breena replaced the scroll on the shelf with the sort of care most women reserved for a newborn babe. Her love for the scrolls was clear. Marcus was right. It was difficult to imagine Breena in a primitive Celt settlement.

Breena motioned to the sconces above the table. "Shall I light the lamps for our lesson?"

"Nay. There will be no need."

She motioned for Breena to take one of the chairs flanking the table. "The Deep Magic spell I will teach ye now is very powerful."

"And dangerous."

Gwen exhaled. "Aye. Dangerous. Deep Magic is the

power of the gods. It can turn against any human who dares to call it. And it always demands a price—often in the form of weakness after the spell has abated. Though not always. Sometimes the gods do not demand their payment right away."

"Is there no other way to control my vision?"

"Not without journeying to Avalon. Even then, I'm not sure the pain could be assuaged with Light only."

Breena raised her small, pointed chin. "Then show me."

"All right. Clear your mind, as I taught ye before."

Breena nodded and closed her eyes. Soon her breathing slowed. Gwen positioned herself behind the girl and placed her hands on Breena's shoulders.

"Feel how heavy my hands are," she murmured. "Let them press your body into the chair, into the floor. When I speak, repeat the Words exactly."

Closing her eyes, Gwen summoned Words from the deepest depth of her being. They were Words no one had taught her. Certainly Cyric had not allowed them to be uttered on Avalon. But Gwen, soon after her first woman's blood—when she'd discovered the wolf that lived inside her—had found the Words waiting inside her.

It was her emerging talent as a spellcrafter that had led her to use the Words of the Old Ones—syllables of Light as well as sounds of Deep Magic—in new ways and unique patterns. She said such a spell for Breena now. The lass repeated the Words carefully, with precision.

Her silver aura flared, then settled into a gentle glow.

Gwen swallowed hard. Leaving Breena's side, she retrieved a small knife used to trim the wicks on the oil lamps, which had been lying in the center of the table among the pens and wax tablets. Taking Breena's hand in hers, she cradled it, palm up, her conscience prickling. Breena was so trusting.

She contemplated the small sharp blade. Had Marcus made it? Most likely. The thought made Gwen even more uneasy about what she had to do. Shoving her doubt roughly aside, she said a single Word. At the same time, she slashed the blade across the fleshy part of Breena's hand, just below her left thumb. Blood welled from the wound, pooling inside her pale palm. Breena did not so much as flinch. Her eyes remained closed, her breathing sure and deep.

Gwen let out a shaking breath. "Open your eyes."

Breena's eyelids fluttered open. For a moment, she stared at her bloody palm, her brow pursed in confusion. Her gaze shifted to the knife's red-stained edge.

"Did . . . did you cut me? How could that be? I felt nothing."

"The Deep Magic spell ye spoke shielded ye from the pain."

Breena sucked on the cut, her eyes meeting Gwen's. "And this spell will wipe out the pain of my visions? The same way it blocked the pain of this cut?"

"Aye."

"Why, that is wonderful!"

"And perilous. Most pain serves a purpose, and the spell cannot distinguish one type of pain from another. A person who feels no pain when it's vital that he should . . ."

Breena's eyes widened. "Might be destroyed, without ever feeling a thing."

"Ye understand, then. Ye must not use this spell outside your vision."

"I . . . understand. I'll be careful, I promise." Breena's expression was troubled. "Marcus . . . he would be furious if he knew what you've taught me. Promise me you won't tell him."

Gwen ignored a pinch of guilt. "I assure ye, I would not dream of it."

Rhys struggled to match his short strides to his father's long ones. Da did not like it when Rhys lagged behind. But when they reached the forum market, Da surprised Rhys by catching him around the waist and lifting him into the air. Rhys laughed aloud at the brief, heady feeling of weightlessness. It was almost as if he were rising into the air on bird's wings! An instant later, Rhys found himself on Da's broad shoulders, gazing out over the crowd.

His eyes widened as he clutched at Da's hair. He had to see everything, no matter how large or small, so he could describe it to Gwen. She'd been very angry to be stuck at home, helping Mared with the weaving.

It was her own fault, Rhys reflected. She shouldn't have run off into the fields last night after supper. For once, he hadn't let her talk him into joining her in disobeying Mama. But he had worried about her the entire time she'd been gone. Especially after Da had gone looking for her.

Da had whipped Gwen's arse soundly, but she hadn't cried even one tear. Rhys didn't know whether to be proud or envious. He would have bawled.

It was market day in Isca, and the merchant stalls were piled high with wares. Fruits and vegetables, cookware and pottery, livestock and clothing, fabric and jewelry. The market, a jumble of stalls squeezed between the fortress gates and the amphitheater, was packed to overflowing.

"Two Roman soldiers are shopping for boots," *Rhys told Gwen in his mind.*

"I hate soldiers," *his sister replied.*

"A Roman matron is frowning over some blue glassware," *he reported. Glass was very costly. He'd never touched it. Was it cold, like the ice it resembled?*

"How many slaves does the matron have with her?" *Gwen wanted to know.*

"Two. A maid and a lad to carry packages."

He told Gwen about two patricians coming out of the barber's shop, their chins scraped clean. They were wearing short white togas and their limbs looked like chicken legs. Gwen giggled.

Rhys thought the Celt women, in their colorful plaid and checkered tunics, were much prettier than the Roman women in their pale stolae. *Gwen agreed.*

Da turned down the aisle leading to the stall where Mama sold the blankets she and Mared and Aunt Carys wove. Rhys loved climbing the piles of soft, colorful wool. But it was more fun climbing with Gwen. Everything was more fun with Gwen.

"I wish ye were here," *he told her.*

"Me, too," *she sighed.*

They were nearly at Mama's stall when Da stopped so abruptly Rhys nearly pitched over his head. He clutched Da's ears, suddenly pierced with fear. Da had gone still, the muscles in his shoulders tensing until they were hard as rocks.

Angry. Da was angry.

Had Rhys done something wrong? Or maybe forgotten to do something he was supposed to do? He racked his brain, but could not think of a single thing. And Da seemed to have forgotten all about him, so it was probably not Rhys who had angered him.

Nay, not Rhys—but just as bad. Da was staring at Mama. A Roman soldier had stopped at her stall. Mama stood with her hands on her hips and her head tilted to one side, smiling up at her visitor. The Roman reached out and brushed a lock of blond hair from Mama's forehead. Mama laughed, her eyes sparkling.

Da made a low, growling sound, deep in his throat. Gripping Rhys about the waist, he jerked him off his shoulders and set him roughly on the ground. Without a word, without even glancing down, Da strode away.

Rhys darted after him, only to run into the legs of a portly middle-aged merchant. The man grunted and cursed, landing a sound kick to Rhys's ribs. "Little rat."

Rhys sprawled on the ground, tasting dust. He coughed and spit, then rolled once and jumped to his feet to dash after Da. By the time he reached Mama's stall, the soldier had gone. The leather flap that separated the rear of the stall from the front was down. The barrier did little to mute the voices behind it. Da's was deep and angry, Mama's soft and pleading.

There was a loud thump and a sharp, feminine cry. Rhys yanked on the flap. It did not open. Da had tied it down.

"Mama!"

The voices stopped, but no answer came. Rhys's chest squeezed so tight he could not breathe.

"Rhys? What's wrong?"

"Gwen . . . Da is beating Mama. Again."

His twin's frightened silence joined his own. Tears squeezed past Rhys's closed eyelids. He wished with all his might that his twin were there beside him.

Cyric's low moan dragged Rhys from his nightmare. He rolled from his pallet into a crouch in one smooth motion. The peat fire in the hearth smoldered, sending herb-laden smoke into his lungs. Cyric thrashed on his pallet, his thin limbs flailing.

"Tamar . . . nay . . ."

Should he wake his grandfather from his private torment? He wasn't sure. He hunkered by the old man's bed, tensed and ready to intervene should the nightmare turn violent. But Cyric's sobs remained muted until he shuddered and slipped back into sleep.

Rhys exhaled a long sigh. The dread of his own nightmare still clung to him like sodden swamp grass. The horror of that long-ago day remained vivid in his mind, no less so because it had marked the beginning of a long, dark slide into misery.

It hadn't been long after that fateful argument and beating that his father had been found lying facedown in a ditch.

Dead.

Chapter Eleven

The face was familiar to Gwen, yet not.

" 'Tis not Mama," she told Rhys. " 'Tis not!"

Mama's skin was soft and warm, not white and waxy and cold. She always had a hug ready for Gwen. Often, she would whisper stories about the Lost Grail of Avalon, and what it meant to be a Daughter of the Lady. Or at least she had until the start of the summer. Since then, it had seemed, Mama had always been crying. After Da's death, she had cried even more.

Gwen did not understand that. Gwen had not cried at all when Da died.

But Gwen had tried to be good, so that Mama would be happy again. It was hard. It was so tempting to slip outside the hut and run toward town, or in the opposite direction into the fields. So she had not made Mama happy, and Mama was still and white, and Grandfather was sobbing.

Gwen thought she should remember how it had happened, but whenever she tried to find the memory in her head, she came up against a wall of darkness. It was the same for Rhys. There was a blank hole where the memory should have been.

Mared knelt beside Grandfather, her arm around his shoulders, murmuring soft words in his ear. Aunt Carys was pacing, trying to quiet little Blodwen, who seemed to enjoy wailing more than any other activity. Uncle Padrig stood by the doorway, stiff with anger.

"Ye should not have faced the bastard alone," he said to Grandfather.

Mared hushed him. "Your advice does no good now."

"He should have told me," Padrig muttered. He opened the door a crack and peered out into the night.

Grandfather did not reply, except with another sob. Gwen did not like it. Grandfather had never cried before! The sound made her chest hurt so badly she could hardly breathe.

She held onto Rhys and looked at Mama's face. Rhys squeezed her hand; she thought her fingers might break.

"She's dead, Gwen."

"Dead." Dead.

Gwen's brain poked at the hideous word as her dirty fingernails might have picked at a scab on her knee. Her stomach lurched. She thought she might throw up.

"Rhys, do people ever stop being dead?"

"Nay. When someone is dead, they stay that way. Always."

Her brother's eyes were rimmed in red. A large tear escaped and rolled down his cheek. Rhys cried more easily than Gwen, and sometimes she envied him for it. Her own hurts lodged painfully in her chest and throat.

She tried to swallow around the swelling. It burned.

"Always?"

Rhys nodded. His sob emerged as a gasp, and he started shaking. Gwen put her arms around his waist, and his own thin arms wrapped her in return. She clung to her twin, the other half of herself. She had Rhys. As long as he was here with her, she could bear anything.

Dead, dead, dead.

Gwen clung to her brother for a long time, the words beating a gruesome rhythm in her skull.

Dead, dead, dead.

Gwen woke with a shudder, her heart pounding so hard she thought it might leap from her chest.

Dead, dead, dead.

Her throat was raw; unshed tears burned her eyes. The pain her seven-year-old self had endured—pain she had thought long buried—was suddenly fresh and raw. Her heart was bleeding.

The wolf raised its head.

Quickly, Gwen pushed the emotions of her childhood back into the black depths from which they had risen. Closing her eyes, she whispered a spell to calm the wolf.

The beast growled.

She threw off her blanket, suddenly hot. The room was too small; the walls too rigid. Her sleeping tunic was unbearably heavy on her skin. Rising shakily, she was careful to make no noise that might disturb Breena. The lass was sleeping peacefully. If a vision had come, she had banished it without waking Gwen.

A vibration strummed deep inside her. The wolf. The nightmare had roused it; she did not know if she could hold it back. She had to get out, away from the farm and into the woods.

Her bare feet hurried down the passageway. She let herself out one of the doors leading from the entrance gallery to the rear terrace. Once free of the house, she ran, past the kitchen gardens and into the orchard. The north gate was not far. Surely she could reach it before the change came upon her! But when she drew up short before the iron bars, she realized the gate had been locked for the night, and she did not have the key.

She sank to the ground. The wolf inside clamored for release, but she could not shift here, inside the farm compound, so near to the sheep and pig barns. Within sight of the servants' huts.

Great Mother, help me.

Fighting the urge to rip off her clothes, she pulled her knees up to her chest and wrapped her arms tightly around them. She pressed her forehead to her knees, chanting her most powerful spell of Light, interspersing the Words with desperate prayers to the Goddess.

A shudder wracked her body. She braced herself for the pain. It never came.

The wolf receded.

Gwen stayed motionless for a long time afterward, sobbing.

Later, after she'd crept back to her bed, her head aching and her throat raw, she felt the familiar stirring in her mind.

"Gwen. Sister, are ye there?"

She squeezed her eyes closed and focused all her power into blocking Rhys's call. It was no use. His thoughts vibrated in her mind. But she did not answer. She couldn't, not with her emotions in such turmoil.

"I am trying to hold the mist, but I haven't your power. Avalon needs ye, Gwen. Cyric . . . he cannot resist Strabo's Deep Magic. Owein believes the Roman is a dreamcaster, Gwen. His spells reach into each soul, into its darkest corners, and rip open wounds of the past. Cyric is the most affected, but all of Avalon feels Strabo's spell.

"The worst dream was tonight, Gwen. I saw the day Da beat Mama in the market."

Oh, Rhys.

She wanted so much to comfort him, but she didn't dare. The wolf was so close to the surface. She would not be able to banish it a second time.

Rhys's call faded. She rolled over in her bed, replaying his words in her mind. Rhys had dreamed of Mama's death, and so had Gwen. It could not be a coincidence.

Had Strabo's dreamcaster magic found Gwen here, in Isca? It did not seem possible. More likely, Rhys had unwittingly channeled Strabo's magic to Gwen through their mental link. And the Deep Magic had stirred the wolf.

Unsettled, she rose from the bed. Breena still slept peacefully, a slight smile on her young face. Cautiously, Gwen opened the shutters, letting in the pre-dawn breeze.

Rhys needed her. Strabo's Deep Magic was thinning the mist, putting Avalon in grave danger. It was Gwen's duty to defend her people, but now, more than ever, she believed her Light would not be enough. She needed the Lady's sword.

Exchalybur was Gwen's best hope. It was almost complete; she would press Marcus to work more quickly. She pushed away the pain the thought of leaving him brought. She'd given him her body, and her heart. She would stay with him forever if the choice were her own. It was not.

She prayed Rhys could hold the mists without her just a little while longer.

Breena woke to a clear dawn. Her head did not hurt and her lungs were clear. There was a dim memory of a vision, silver silence into which she had spoken Words of Deep Magic. Once the spell had been cast, the vision had faded away.

She stretched her arms overhead and grinned. It had been almost two months since she'd felt so well in the morning. There was none of the fatigue Gwen had warned her of—on the contrary, exuberant energy infused her limbs. She swung her legs over the side of the bed, eager to begin the day.

Gwen had already risen. She didn't seem to have rested as well as Breena had. She stood by the window, staring out at the garden, her shoulders hunched, her hair hanging in tangles. When Breena greeted her, she did not immediately respond.

Breena rose and went to her. "You did not sleep well?"

"Well enough, for a few hours." She turned and straightened, and Breena could see the effort she made to hide whatever troubled her. Her expression smoothed into a smile that did not reach her eyes. "You look fine this morn."

"I feel wonderful."

"Did the vision not come last night?"

Breena couldn't suppress a grin. "Yes, it came—that's what's so wonderful! I used the Deep Magic spell. Once I said the words, the vision disappeared."

Gwen frowned. "The vision and pain disappeared, yet ye feel no effect of the Deep Magic now?"

"None at all." Breena's smile faded. "Is that not good?"

" 'Tis . . . unexpected. I'd hoped the Great Mother's message to ye would become clearer, not vanish completely. But perhaps it is not a bad turn of events. Your body and spirit have been strained. Some nights of rest can only do ye good. When the Great Mother's favor returns, ye will be more receptive to it."

Breena was not so sure. She was glad the vision had faded, and did not wish it back. The joy she'd felt upon awakening dried like morning dew. She truly did not want to reject the Great Mother's message, but if the Goddess's favor came with pain and terror, she was not sure she wanted to be blessed.

Rhys lay on his back, listening to the steady rasp of night breathing in the small hut. Gwen's was closest, right beside him. She was not sleeping any more than Rhys was, but that was not unusual. His twin much preferred night to day. Sometimes Rhys wondered if she slept at all.

He resumed his inventory. Cyric . . . Mared . . . Carys . . . Padrig . . . Blodwen—the babe snuffled, as she always did . . . Da's heavy snore . . . and . . .

He frowned. Mama. Where was Mama?

He sent a out a thought. "Gwen. Ye are awake, aye?"

"Aye."

"Where is Mama?"

Gwen wriggled across the pallet until she lay with her lips close to his ear.

"Gone. She crept out the door a little while ago, right after Da started snoring."

Rhys digested this information. He didn't like it. The

night was dark. Dark was dangerous. Mama told them that again and again.

Gwen folded her lithe body into a crouch. "Let's go find her."

Rhys was appalled. "Ye mean leave the hut? At night?"

"Mama could be in trouble."

"Then . . . we should wake Da. Or Grandfather."

There was a short silence, then Gwen shook her head violently. She was right. That would only make more trouble.

"We have to make sure she gets back before Da wakes," *Gwen said silently.*

Rhys gathered his courage. "Aye."

He crawled out from beneath the blanket. Gwen found his hand and clasped it tightly, as though she were the timid one, rather than he. The sleeping pallets filled the entire floor of the hut with very little room to spare. Together, they crept through the maze toward the door.

Mama had left it a bit ajar. It was simple to slip out into the starless night without waking anyone.

"She could not have gone far, if she left just a little while ago," he told Gwen once they were a safe distance from the hut.

"True."

Rhys looked uphill, toward the town, then downhill, toward the forest. "Which way?"

Gwen peered through the night as though she were an owl.

"To the river, I think."

Now that the end of her time with Marcus was so quickly approaching, Gwen could not seem to take her eyes from him. She was with Breena in the hearth room the next morning when he entered, his hair wet from his bath. His shirt clung damply to his torso, outlining every muscle. His jaw was freshly shaven; if she looked closely, she could see the scrape of the razor on his skin.

She felt his presence in every part of her body—her stomach tightened, her breath went shallow, and her palms began to sweat. A warm, tingling feeling settled low in her belly. She shut her eyes and relived the sensation of his mouth on hers, of his knee parting her legs, of his body moving inside her. When she met his gaze, she knew he was remembering, too.

Soon memories would be all she had.

She turned quickly and busied herself with raking coals into a pile beneath the cauldron, though the fire was already hot enough. She felt Marcus's gaze on her back as he greeted his sister. When he spoke Gwen's name, she turned and nodded.

Then he looked at Breena's bandaged hand and frowned. "What happened?"

Breena froze in the act of pouring her brother's *cervesia*. Her gaze darted to Gwen as she answered. "I cut it in the kitchen."

"It's not like you to be so careless. Has Mother looked at it?"

"There's no need. Gwen cleansed it with honey." The girl's laugh was strained. "Really Marcus, since when do you concern yourself with my every little scrape?"

Marcus shrugged. Gwen thought he might have said more, but Lucius and Aiden entered and the opportunity faded. Rhiannon and Alma emerged from the kitchen. The cook set a tray of cold mutton and bread on the table and departed.

Gwen took a place at the table next to Breena. A thrill shot through her as Marcus slid into the empty seat beside her. He reached past her for a piece of bread, intentionally brushing her breast with his arm.

"Pardon," he said, his breath on her cheek.

She said nothing.

"Is something wrong?" he asked in an undertone. "You don't look well." His gaze darted at Breena. "Did she—"

"Nay, Breena slept peacefully last night." She bit her lip. "But I need to talk to ye. Later, when we are alone."

"Of course," he said, frowning.

Rhiannon, Gwen noted, watched their private exchange with interest. Gwen, uncomfortable since Marcus had told her that his father suspected the long hours they spent together were not entirely occupied with bladesmithing, kept her head down for the rest of the meal. She had little appetite. After a fortnight of being almost a member of the Aquila family, suddenly she felt very much like an outsider. She listened with only half an ear while Lucius and Marcus discussed the advantages of free-threshing triticum wheat over the more common hulled varieties.

Once the meal was done, Marcus clasped Gwen by the elbow, nodded to his family, and steered her out of the house and into the rose garden.

"Now," he demanded. "Tell me what is wrong."

"When will the sword be finished?"

"Ten days or so."

"That's far too long! I . . . Rhys has been calling me, Marcus."

"You mean . . . in your mind?" He knew Rhys had communicated with his sister silently when she'd been trapped in wolf form.

"Aye. Strabo's magic has caused Cyric's hold on the mist to falter. Rhys is holding the spell, but with Deep Magic assaulting Avalon, it is difficult. I must return with the Lady's sword as soon as I can. How quickly can ye finish it?"

"It will take three days at least to temper the bright iron. Another day to attach the hilt and complete the scabbard."

"I pray that will be soon enough."

They walked to the smithy. Marcus said nothing as he pushed open the door. As soon as she entered, she became aware of the magic of Exchalybur.

She approached the forge and gazed down at the blade on the stone cooling ledge. The weapon was long and straight, but the edges were still rough, and the grip was missing. A nimbus of white light radiated from the bright iron. Laced through it were streaks of shining sky blue.

The sword's aura pulsed gently, as a human aura did. When Gwen reached out her hand, the metal was warm to the touch. As if it were alive.

This was Deep Magic indeed, deeper than anything she had guessed she could create. In the past two days, she had crafted spells designed to hide the sword from its enemies. She hoped to retain an element of surprise when she returned to face Strabo.

"There's great magic in this sword, isn't there?"

She looked at Marcus with surprise. And guilt. "Can ye feel it?" she asked carefully.

"No." He was silent for a moment. "I can see it in your face, when you look at it. The Light must be very strong."

She could not meet his gaze. "It is." She bit her lip to stop herself from confessing the whole—that Light was not the only magic bound to the Lady's sword. The heart of the metal was Deep Magic. If Marcus knew, would he refuse to finish the weapon? She could not take that chance.

And so she let her lie stand.

Marcus lifted the unfinished sword. Its aura flared at his touch, but he did not seem at all affected by it. He sighted down the length of the piece, then turned it in his hand, inspecting the flat and the blunt edges.

"What would Rhys say about it, do you think?" he asked.

Gwen gave a guilty start. "I . . . I am not sure. Cyric . . . he does not allow weapons on Avalon."

"Even weapons of Light?"

"Nay. And Rhys . . . he is obedient to Cyric. He is ever chiding me that I am not." She bit her lip. "I am a disappointment to my brother."

"That's not true."

"I am sure that it is."

Marcus replaced the sword on the stone ledge and gave a decisive shake of his head. "No. If anything, I think it's more likely that Rhys is jealous of you."

"Ye are daft, Marcus! Rhys is not jealous of me. Why, the man does not hesitate to point out my every flaw!"

"Perhaps he is envious of your flaws."

She shot him a disbelieving look. "Oh, aye, to be sure."

"I mean it. Rhys has never been happy with his life, it seems to me. He roams Britain because Cyric has ordered it, when all he wants to do is live on Avalon. I think he wishes he had the courage to disobey your grandfather, as you do."

"If that is a compliment, Marcus, it is not a very flattering one."

Marcus shrugged. "It's what I think, that is all." He slid her another look, his eyes suddenly glinting with mischief. "So, while we are speaking of your faults, may I ask which in particular Rhys most disapproves of? Your sharp tongue? Your rash nature?"

She laughed. "Ye would have me lay out my short-comings before you?"

"I'll confess my own flaws first, if that would make you more comfortable." He extended a thumb. "First, I dislike Father's library. I especially hate philosophy, history, and rhetoric. And my Greek is abysmal."

A genuine smile tugged at Gwen's lips. It was hard to be anxious when Marcus joked. "None of those things are shortcomings to my mind."

His forefinger extended. "Two, I am a hopeless swordsman. Surely that counts against me."

She laughed outright. "That cannot be true."

"I assure you it is. Oh, I know the moves and can wave a blade about—that's essential if I am to learn the proper balance of a weapon—but in a true fight I'm as good as dead. Father tried his best to teach me, but I endured the lessons with poor grace, and did not practice. As a child, I spent all my free time drawing."

"Drawing is a worthy skill." She glanced at the papyrus, parchment, and wax tablets cluttering Marcus's worktable, all filled with intricate images.

Her gaze strayed to Marcus's hands. His fingers were strong and blunt, rough with callouses, marred by puckered burns. And yet, those hands held pen or stylus with utmost delicacy. Those hands worshiped her breasts and stroked between her thighs like pure magic.

Without thinking, she touched his bare chin. Another part of him that fascinated her. Another thing she would miss when she left him. The only other man she ever saw without a beard was Rhys.

He caught her wrist and held it. The inner ring of his

iris expanded, leaving her to plunge into the dark of his pupils. It was a seductive darkness, like the depths of the forest on a starless night. It was no place she should go.

She had vowed to walk in the Light.

And yet, she did not want to.

His gaze locked with hers, Marcus turned her palm to his lips and kissed it.

She closed her eyes as delicious, familiar fire streaked through her body, pooling in her breasts, her belly, her loins. He had the power to melt her, with only the touch of his lips. His tongue stroked a small, vivid circle in the center of her palm, then licked a line to the fleshy mound at the base of her thumb. He set his lips to the inside of her wrist and scraped her pulse point with his teeth.

"Marcus . . ."

He searched her gaze. "Were you happy, living on Avalon?"

"I . . . what do ye mean? Avalon is my home."

"I know that. I asked if you were happy there. Do you miss it?"

Gwen shook her head. Did she miss Avalon? Certainly, her thoughts were consumed by the threat to her home, except during those hours when Marcus's lovemaking chased all else from her mind. She missed Ardra, and wondered how the cubs were growing. She missed laughing with Clara. But Mared's disapproving scowl? Nay, she did not miss that. Padrig's pursed lips? If she never saw them again, she would not be sorry. And she was ashamed to admit she felt only relief at the loss of Trevor's hopeful gaze and Cyric's patient disappointment.

Here in Isca, her days were filled with Rhiannon's

welcoming smile, Lucius's grave concern, Breena's cheerful friendship. And Marcus. Especially Marcus.

Nay, she did not miss Avalon. Not at all.

The thought disturbed her greatly.

She met Marcus's soft, dark eyes. "Avalon is all I know."

"It *was* all you knew. Not anymore. Now you know me, and my home. I want you to stay."

Her heart squeezed painfully. "Ye know that cannot be! Did ye hear nothing I told ye? I must return to Avalon as soon as possible."

"You must return, yes, but do you have to remain?"

She stared at him. "Of course I do."

"Why? Can't another Druid wield Exchalybur? What about Owein? He's very powerful, and a Seer, like your grandfather. Apart from that, he's a trained warrior."

"He could never be Guardian of Avalon. The mist is Cyric's. Only those of his blood can hold it. 'Tis yet another reason I must return, and marry."

"Let Rhys become Guardian. He'd welcome the role."

"Cyric would never allow it."

Marcus swore. "It all comes back to that old man's whims."

"They are not whims, Marcus. Cyric is a Seer. He follows the will of the Great Mother."

"I don't see how it can be the will of the Great Mother for you to live in a place where you do not wish to be, with people who do not value you, married to a man you do not love. If I were to consult with the Great Mother, I am sure she would tell me you should stay here and marry me."

Gwen's lips parted. "Ye wish to *marry* me?"

Marcus crossed his arms. "Yes. I do. And you, unless I am very much mistaken, want to marry me."

"Nay, I do not—"

He uncrossed his arms and took two angry steps toward her. "Do not lie to me, Gwen."

She sucked in a breath. "Even if I do want to marry ye, Marcus. I . . . cannot. The wolf—"

"I am not afraid of the wolf."

"Ye should be! So far, the beast has yielded to ye, but it is a creature of Deep Magic. I've told ye before—I cannot control or predict what will happen when it comes to the wolf. I could shift in your bed . . . I could hurt ye—"

"You would never do that."

"Nay, ye do not understand. 'Tis not just that I cannot control when the wolf comes. There is something else—" She closed her eyes, fighting back hot, searing tears.

"What?" Marcus said. His hands were on her shoulders, his breath hot on her forehead. "Gwen, trust me. Tell me everything. Whatever it is, I'll prove to you that it doesn't matter."

"That is not possible, Marcus. As ye know, before I was trapped by my cousin's Dark spell, I shifted only when I wished to. I called the wolf; it did not call me. Now my control is gone. When the wolf calls, I cannot always deny it. But there is more. Each time I run as a beast, 'tis harder and harder to return to myself. I'm afraid that someday . . ."

Marcus's grip on her shoulders tightened. "Afraid of what, Gwen?" True horror crept into his voice. "Gods, Gwen. Are you telling me that one day you won't be able to come back? That you'll become a wolf . . . forever?"

She swallowed hard and nodded. "That is why I can never be your wife, Marcus. Do not speak of it again, because I will not listen. As soon as the sword is forged, I'll be gone. Ye will do well to forget me."

Chapter Twelve

*G*ripping Rhys's hand tightly, Gwen kept to the side of the road leading out of the village. Just a short way downhill, near the river, stood a dense thicket of elms. The arms of the largest tree—the one Gwen had named grandmother—sagged all the way to the ground, creating a space with moss for a floor and sunlight-dappled leaves for walls. She and Rhys snuck off to play there whenever they could.

But once, they'd arrived at the secret place and found Mama there, crying. That time, they hadn't stayed. Later, when Mama came home, she was smiling. Gwen figured the grandmother tree had cheered her. So if Mama was troubled now, perhaps she'd gone to the grandmother tree again.

They'd almost reached the thicket when low voices drifted through the curtain of leaves. The woman sounded like Mama, but the man was definitely not Da.

"Mama's in trouble!" Gwen cried. She started to run, but Rhys drew her up short, nearly pulling her arm from its socket.

"Nay. She's not."

The man let out a guttural cry. Mama responded with a moan.

"He's hurting her, Rhys, like Da does! We have to stop him!" She tried to wrench her arm from her brother's hand.

Rhys clung to her, his fingers digging into her skin. "Nay, Gwen. I'm . . . I do not think he's hurting her."

Mama moaned again. "He is!" Gwen declared.

"Perhaps that is not even Mama." Rhys sounded desperate. His face was pale under the moon, his eyes wide and frightened.

"Ye are a coward, Rhys," Gwen whispered violently. "Even if 'tis not Mama, 'tis someone who needs our help." She tried again to break his grasp on her arm. "Let me go!"

"Nay."

She scowled. "Fine. Come with me, then." She set out for the tree, dragging him along with her.

Together they crept to the edge of the veil of branches and peeked inside. And Gwen discovered Rhys was right. The man was not hurting the woman. He was on top of her, rocking back and forth the way Da and Mama, or Aunt Carys and Uncle Padrig, sometimes did under their blankets at night. And though it did not look like much fun, neither Mama or Aunt Carys had ever complained in the morning.

Gwen gave a silent shudder of disgust. "Ye were right," she told Rhys in her mind. "'Tis not Mama."

Rhys made a strangled sound. "Look again, Gwen."

Something in Rhys's tone made Gwen's stomach twist into a knot. Slowly, she turned and peered through the branches again. And became aware of the woman's long white-blond hair—hair the same color as hers and Rhys's—spread out over the moss like spilled silver.

'Twas Mama.

"The man—he's the soldier I saw talking to Mama in the market," *Rhys said.* "The day that Da beat her."

"Nay!" *Gwen spun and ran, bolting up the hill.*

"Gwen!" *Rhys's call chased her.* "Gwen, wait!"

She did not stop.

A blow to the head shocked Marcus from a deep sleep. He grabbed Gwen's wrist before she could hit him again. She snarled, twisting desperately to free herself. He rolled, trapping her with his weight.

"Shh, Gwen. It's just a dream."

At least he hoped it was.

He continued gentling her with his hands and voice. Her eyes remained closed, but at some level she must have understood him. Gradually she quieted, her body going soft beneath him. But he didn't immediately lift himself off her.

He smoothed a damp lock of hair from her face. Gwen had been so peaceful after they'd made love, nestling into his arms and saying she wanted to rest just for a moment before returning to the room she shared with Breena. Breena had been sleeping peacefully of late, untroubled by visions, so when a moment's rest had turned into a deep slumber, Marcus had succumbed to the comfort of holding Gwen and slipped into sleep himself—only to be awakened by her flailing arm.

"Gwen." She seemed to be awakening. "Open your eyes, love. You're safe. It was just a dream."

Her eyelids fluttered open. She stared at him a moment before recognition sparked. "Marcus?"

Her voice was small and frightened, like a child's. Marcus's heart clenched. He placed a kiss on her forehead.

"Yes, it's me. Nothing to fear."

It must have been the wrong thing to say, because tears flooded her eyes. She moved slightly beneath him and he was abruptly aware he was half hard and prodding her thigh. Thank the gods, she didn't seem aware of his inappropriate lust.

He started to ease his body from hers.

"Nay." She clutched at his upper arms. He looked down at her, uncertain. She was heartbreakingly beautiful with moonlight on her tousled hair. She was like some magical creature—a naiad or a forest sprite. Or a goddess. Like Vulcan, Marcus had somehow lured Venus to his bed. He was not worthy of her, and yet she clung to him as if he were her only anchor.

"A dream?" she whispered.

"Yes."

She closed her eyes. "Oh, Marcus." He felt the tension go out of her body, though she still clutched his arms tightly. Tears leaked from the corners of her eyelids.

"Shh . . ." He shifted, only to have her clutch at him again. He froze as his arousal responded. Surely she felt it. But if she did, she said nothing.

"Do you . . . will you tell me about it?"

"Nay. I want to forget it."

"Was it like Breena's dreams? A vision?"

Her gray eyes met his, completely lucid now. And fearful. "Nay. Not a vision." She sounded as though she were trying to convince herself. "It was . . . a dream. Of when I was a child."

"It stirred the wolf."

She swallowed, hard. "Aye. But then ye . . . ye calmed it, I think. Ye chased the beast away. Again. Thank ye." Her eyes were wet. "I am the weakest of fools," she muttered, dashing at her tears.

He caught her hand. "Don't be afraid to cry. Not with me."

She stared at him. He smoothed her tears with his thumbs and kissed her. With a small sigh, she let him draw her close.

"Make love to me again, Marcus."

Her plea fogged his brain. It would be a wiser choice to put some distance between them; if he were not careful, she'd take his heart with her when she left. But he was too weak to turn away from what she offered. She slid a leg over his hips. He lifted her atop him and slid into her with one smooth motion.

She tilted her hips, urging him deeper.

"Nay! Ye will not keep me from her!"

Cyric lurched from his pallet, grappling with his blanket as if the threadbare wool meant to do him mortal harm. His thin frame lunged across the hut. The hem of his tunic dragged at the hearth, scattering sparks and ashes.

Rhys grabbed for a fistful of his grandfather's robe. The old man eluded Rhys's grasp with a spry leap. Rhys lunged after him and tripped. Cyric dashed through the door before Rhys could heave himself to his feet.

Swearing, Rhys bolted out of the hut, catching up to Cyric in the village common area. Cyric spun around. Rhys's blood ran cold. Not a single spark of recognition lit Cyric's eyes.

"Grandfather." Rhys caught his grandfather's elbow. "Come back to bed."

"Unhand me!" Cyric's palm connected with Rhys's cheek.

Rhys staggered backward, stunned. Cyric had never

raised a hand to him in all his life. The eyes he thought
he knew so well—eyes that held unfathomable depths
of calm and wisdom—now burned hot with mad rage.
"Ye should have stopped her!"

"Gwen?" Rhys asked, bewildered.

"My daughter. Can ye nay utter her name?"

"Tamar," Rhys breathed.

"How long have ye known she had a Roman lover?
Ye and Carys and Mared? And yet, ye did not tell me!"

Cyric was caught in a dream. A scene from the past
in which Rhys was cast in the role played by his uncle,
Padrig. Rhys opened his mouth, then shut it. He had
no idea what to say.

A door opened, then another. Dera emerged, with
Howell at her side. Rhys caught a glimpse of young
Penn and Siane, sheltering the children. Mared clutched the edge of her hut's door, white-faced and grim.
Padrig stood rigid inside his own doorway. Owein
and Trevor were present as well, their expressions
grave.

Cyric's eyes glowed with madness. "Stand aside! I
will take Tamar back, if I have to break down the
fortress to do it!"

Owein advanced toward Cyric. Trevor closed in from
the other side. Rhys raised a hand. A physical interven-
tion might cause Cyric to hurt himself.

"Grandfather—"

"Nay! Ye canna stop me." Cyric flung up a hand and
shouted a Word Rhys had never heard fall from his
grandfather's lips.

Deep Magic. The spell's power gathered like a coiling
snake. Rhys threw up his arms, a counterspell on his
lips. Owein flung himself at Cyric. Light flashed. Trev-

or's broad body hit Rhys with the force of a rolling boulder, sending Rhys airborne. He fell hard, his head impacting on solid ground.

Everything went black.

Chapter Thirteen

Someone was using the back of Rhys's skull as a gong. He shoved himself upright, then fell back on his elbows when the ringing got louder and the world listed sharply to one side.

"Easy, man."

Gingerly, he swung his head toward the sound of Trevor's voice. The walls of his friend's hut swayed only a little, and he took that to be a good thing. He was lying on Trevor's pallet, he realized. Trevor sat on a stool nearby, his forearms on his thighs, his hands dangling between his legs. His expression was grave.

"What happened?"

"Ye dinna remember?"

"Not . . . entirely. Cyric was lost in a dream of the past. He thought I was . . . Padrig, I think. He was very angry. He blamed me—I mean, Padrig—for . . . something." He shook his head, then winced at the movement. ". . . Something to do with my mother."

"Aye, he was angry. So angry he almost killed ye." A muscle in Trevor's jaw ticked. "With Deep Magic."

Rhys stared. "Nay. That cannot be. Cyric would never use Deep Magic. Why, he is the one who has forbidden it!"

"He did, nonetheless. A death strike. I've known only one other Druid strong enough to call such power. If it had hit ye, ye would not be talking to me now."

The memory surfaced. "Ye shoved me out of the way."

"Not entirely. The blow glanced off your head."

"This ache is not completely because my skull struck the ground?"

"I think not. Is your magic affected? What of the mist?"

Rhys cast his senses. Vibrations of the earth's magic echoed back at him. He sought his connection to the mists. It was still strong. "Other than the headache, I feel nothing wrong." He paused. "Trevor, ye should not have risked yourself. Ye might have been killed."

Trevor looked down at his clasped hands. "Better I should die than ye."

"I would not have your life in barter for mine."

"Nay? Well, I willna argue with ye, then. 'Twould be a useless discussion in any case, since both of us are still breathing."

"Where is Cryic now?"

"Resting. He doesna know what he did."

"Thank the Great Mother for that. It would destroy him. He has devoted his life to peace, and forgiveness."

"Mared is preparing the strongest sleeping draught she dares administer. Let us hope it silences Cyric's nightmares." Trevor regarded Rhys gravely. "Can ye stand, do ye think?"

Rhys shoved himself to his feet. The hut swayed a bit, then steadied. The throbbing in his head lessened somewhat, and the ringing faded. He touched the back of his skull and found a lump there. Pressing it, he winced.

"I'm well enough," he told Trevor.

"Well, ye look like a corpse," the Caledonian replied bluntly. "Are ye sure your magic is unaffected? With Deep Magic, there is always some effect."

"Nothing seems wrong," Rhys said.

He hoped it was true.

Something was happening in the Roman camp.

The evening before, Trevor, who had been keeping an eye on the comings and goings of the soldiers, reported two riders approaching from the east. The soldiers had halted at the gate, then, at the sentry's nod, disappeared into the camp.

Now, just past dawn, the camp was abuzz with activity. Had the soldiers carried a message from the fortress? If so, what did that mean for Avalon?

From his position across the gorge, Rhys squinted against the sun, watching the camp. Soldiers bustled to and fro, both inside and outside the palisade. What they were doing, Rhys couldn't tell. He was too far away.

Hefin swooped down and perched beside him.

"Ah, good. I could use your help," Rhys told the bird.

The merlin's head swiveled. Unblinking, Hefin fixed his eyes on Rhys.

"Fly, then, and see what ye may."

He sent the suggestion to Hefin not in words, since the falcon did not comprehend human language, but as a subtle pulse of intent. The small falcon spread its wings and rose.

Rhys watched the bird soar into the gorge, dive, then ride high on an updraft. Once above the Roman camp, it tilted its wings and turned lazy circles above the tents. The arcs tightened as Hefin dropped altitude and came to rest on the palisade.

Rhys hunkered down on the shadow side of a large boulder. As far as he could tell, none of the soldiers milling about the camp took note of the merlin. Rhys hoped Strabo would not suspect the bird was more than it seemed. Hefin had no magic of his own; it was Rhys's power that allowed them to communicate. Still, Rhys had no idea what the limits of Strabo's talent might be. Because of Cyric's restrictions, his practical knowledge of Deep Magic was sorely lacking.

Gwen, he thought testily, knew far more.

Eventually, Hefin returned, his wings flapping with slow precision as he flew across the gorge. Rhys stretched out his arm for the merlin's landing. Hefin gave a small screech as he folded his wings over his back.

Rhys cast his senses toward his companion. Images came, sharp but oddly distorted; a bird's sight was not like a human's. Rhys saw the tops of the Roman tents, and the helmets of soldiers. Strabo and Tribune Valgus emerged from the commander's tent, dressed for travel.

"Why, they are leaving," he murmured.

He could not quite believe this good fortune. Reflecting further, however, he supposed he might have anticipated it. Strabo commanded the Roman army's Second Legion. Such a man could hardly huddle in the wilderness indefinitely. No doubt his presence was needed at the fortress.

Avalon had gained a much-needed reprieve. Rhys closed his eyes and whispered a fervent prayer of thanks.

* * *

Strabo left at dawn, accompanied by an escort of four soldiers, all mounted. As they rode away from the camp, Hefin spread his wings, following the entourage. Rhys frowned. He hadn't instructed the bird to trail the sorcerer. But then, Hefin often obeyed his own instincts.

The Dark spell probing the mist receded with Strabo's departure. Rhys returned to the village and took up his usual post by Cyric's bed. Toward midday, Cyric sat up and rubbed his eyes as if banishing the remnants of a bad dream.

"Grandfather?"

"Rhys." Cyric's brow furrowed. "When did ye return home?"

Rhys let out a breath. "A fortnight past, Grandfather."

"That is not possible. I have no memory of your arrival."

"Ye've been ill," Rhys said carefully. He dipped a cup into a bucket of clear water and offered it to Cyric.

"I prefer *cervesia,* Rhys. Ye know that."

Rhys put the cup aside as he rose. "I'll fetch ye some."

"Send Gwen with it. I would speak with her."

Rhys halted and turned. "Gwen is not here."

"Gone again?" Cyric's sigh was weary. "Ah, well, she cannot be far. When she returns, tell her to come to me." He shifted on his pallet. "She has taken the burden of Guardian. I may have been ill, but I am well now. She may release the mist to me."

"Gwen is not holding the mist," Rhys said slowly. "I am."

Cyric's gaze narrowed. Rhys felt a subtle probe at the edges of his mind.

"Why, 'tis true."

Rhys felt a surge of annoyance. "Of course 'tis true. Have I ever spoken false to ye?"

"Ah, Rhys. I did not mean to question ye." Cyric shook his head. "But I must admonish ye. 'Tis not your duty to act as Guardian. In fact, it *must* not be. I have Seen . . ."

"What? What have ye Seen?"

Cyric fell silent for a moment. "That is not for ye to know," he said eventually. Rhys ground his teeth, but did not question further. He knew it would do no good.

" 'Tis Gwen who must hold the mist, Rhys. She and no other."

Rhys's laugh was bitter. "She cannot hold the mist if she is not here. She is gone, Grandfather."

"For how long?"

"She disappeared a fortnight past—the day before ye fell ill. Several days after a Roman sorcerer began casting Deep Magic spells into Avalon's mist. Do ye not remember at all?"

Cyric frowned. "I sense no Deep Magic near Avalon."

"The sorcerer has withdrawn. For now. But while he was here, ye were . . . not yourself." Rhys was not eager to describe to Cyric the extent of his infirmity.

"And so with Gwen gone, ye took the protection of Avalon upon yourself."

"Aye," Rhys said. "It was necessary."

Cyric rubbed a hand over his beard and sighed. "And ye always do what is necessary."

For some reason, the praise sounded more like an accusation. Rhys swallowed a surge of anger. Cyric was not at fault here. Gwen was.

"Help me rise, Rhys."

Rhys lent him an arm. The old man gained his feet, leaning heavily on his staff. In the farthest recesses of his mind, Rhys felt the burden of the mist lift.

"Nay, Grandfather—ye are not well. Let me hold the

mist until—" But the vibration of the spell was already gone.

"The protection of Avalon is not your task, Rhys. 'Tis mine, and Gwen's."

"Gwen is not here!"

"Then 'tis your task to find her, and bring her back."

"Bring her back," Rhys muttered. "And how, I ask ye, am I to do that? I have no idea where she is!"

Owein shook his head. " 'Tis a difficult task, to be sure. I am sorry, Rhys, that the vision I sought of your sister showed me nothing." And the attempt had wearied the burly warrior, Rhys thought, at a time when Avalon's defenders could not afford to be weak.

Rhys's gaze swung to Clara, who was resting by the hearth, her hands folded over her enormous belly. "Ye are a friend to her. Do ye have any idea where she might have gone?"

Clara frowned into the flames. "It's true I am Gwen's friend, but that means little, I'm afraid. She is a difficult person to understand."

" 'Tis true," Rhys said, reflecting privately that there had once been a time when he understood his twin as well as he knew himself. But no more.

"Perhaps the Great Mother will send ye a sign," Owein suggested, "once ye start the search."

"I'm not eager to embark on an aimless journey. I'm needed here. Cyric's strength and faculties may have returned, but I cannot forget how vulnerable he was to Strabo's spells. I cannot take the chance the sorcerer will return while I am away."

A voice sounded behind Rhys. "Ye might follow the Roman, then. And perhaps ensure he does not return."

Rhys turned to find Trevor's broad torso filling the doorway. "Aye," he said slowly. "I might."

The Caledonian advanced into the hut. "The more we learn of Strabo, the more effective our defense will be. If he discovers us following . . ." He shrugged. "Better we should fight him far from Avalon."

"We?"

"Aye," Trevor said. "When ye go, I mean to accompany ye."

Chapter Fourteen

*B*ut Gwen, you must come with us to the market! You've been here more than a fortnight and you haven't even left the farm."

Gwen looked into Breena's eager blue eyes. "I cannot spare the time. Marcus and I—"

"Marcus must come to town as well. There's a slave auction today. He cannot miss it."

Gwen hesitated. For the past three days, Marcus had worked almost without stop on the Lady's sword. He'd tempered the blade, heating the bright iron until it was red-hot, then plunging it into a water trough, over and over. He'd finished fitting the grip and fashioning the scabbard yesterday. All that was left was the final honing of the blade. If he completed that step today, she would be able to leave in the morning.

Would a delay of a few hours mean so much? Marcus had spoken to her of his ongoing mission of buying and freeing Celt slaves from the markets, especially those in the worst situations. Every servant on the farm was free. She couldn't insist he miss this opportunity to liberate more of her own people.

"And besides," Breena continued. "You lived in Isca when you were small. Don't you want to see if you remember anything of the city?"

Gwen had no desire to revisit the town. Nevertheless, a short time later she found herself and Breena seated amid a pile of empty baskets, in a cart driven by the stable hand called Linus. A wiry, barefooted boy, Matius, sat at his side. The white mare hitched in front was not happy to have Gwen as a passenger; it sensed the wolf, no doubt. It was a testament to Linus's skill that the animal kept to the road at all. Marcus and Lucius, on their own mounts, rode ahead.

Rhiannon, at Lucius's insistence, had remained behind, but not before giving Breena extensive instructions, which Breena had taken down on a wax tablet. Stylus still in hand, she studied the list.

"Mother wants dates and olives," she told Gwen. "And oysters and mussels, but only if they look fresh. And some dyed linen . . ."

They left the horses and cart at a field just outside town, crowded alongside other carts and wagons belonging to market-goers traveling into town from the countryside surrounding Isca. Linus remained behind to watch over the horses while Matius jumped off the cart, eager to carry Breena's purchases. As Gwen rose from her seat on the cart, Marcus appeared at her elbow. She shook off his offer of assistance.

"I'm perfectly capable of climbing down on my own." In truth, her refusal had more to do with the sudden change in his appearance than any sense of virtuous independence.

Marcus and his father had donned Roman-style

clothing for the trip into town. It gave them the advantage at the slave auctions, Marcus had explained before they left, to appear as the patricians they were. Gwen supposed she could understood his reasoning, but she didn't have to like it. Seeing Marcus dressed in a tunic and toga unsettled her. The pristine white linen contrasted deeply with his dark hair and olive complexion. The draping of the fabric hid the muscular form she knew so well. Dressed this way he looked so . . . *Roman*. Not at all like the man she loved.

And she *did* love him, with all her heart.

He noticed her reticence, and guessed at its source. "The toga puts you off," he said, falling into step beside her as they followed the stream of people into town.

"Ye don't look like yourself."

"And that bothers you."

She sighed. "Aye, it does."

He rolled his shoulders. "I dislike dressing this way, myself. I'm accustomed to wearing *braccas*. Bare legs make me feel like a woman."

Gwen couldn't repress a snort of laughter. "I doubt Isca has ever seen such a large and hairy female."

Marcus grinned back at her. Her breath caught in her throat. Goddess, he was beautiful. Turned to stone, he might have easily graced the pedestal outside the Roman temple they'd just passed. But as he was . . . living, breathing, vital . . . he was more appealing than any marble god. It was hard to believe that after tomorrow, his face and his touch would be just a memory.

She averted her eyes, not wanting him to see how rapidly she was blinking. They'd passed into the main part of town. Buildings crowded the road on either side. The fortress loomed over the village, its stone walls gray and forbidding.

"The entire Second Legion is stationed here in Isca," Marcus said. "Almost five thousand Legionary soldiers, plus auxiliary troops and cavalry."

"I . . . I can hardly imagine." Just thinking about so many soldiers made her queasy. What if hundreds were sent to the hills near Avalon? The Druids would never evade them.

They joined the press of the crowd in the market square, which was dominated by the high curved walls of the amphitheater. "Games are held there," Marcus told her, "and other entertainments." His jaw hardened. "And slave auctions."

"Is that where ye and Lucius will go?"

"Yes. But there is some time yet. I thought I'd take a look through the market for a bit." He paused. "Does it seem familiar at all? It's been a long time since you've been here."

Gwen moved farther into the medley of colors, scents, and sounds of the merchant stalls as if in a daze. She was hardly aware of Marcus on her right, Breena and Lucius on her left. The market did indeed tug at her memory. But she could not quite reconcile it with her childish recollections.

"The stalls seem much smaller than they were."

"They would have looked bigger to a seven-year-old," Marcus pointed out.

"Aye," Gwen said, automatically counting off the aisles before she realized what she was doing. She stopped, a strange familiarity coming over her. She used to count like this when she came looking for Mama's and Da's stall. Five was the number. But was it five rows from the fortress wall? Or five from the opposite side, starting at the amphitheater? She wasn't sure.

A chattering trio of women passed by, jostling her. A

scant second later, a slave boy, running with his master's purchases, clipped her legs. Close behind him was a uniformed centurion.

Her heart pounded. She shrank back with a cry, earning a frown and a narrowed glance from the man. Marcus's arm came around her as he sent a pleasant nod toward the soldier. The centurion took in Marcus's attire and moved aside with a deferential bow.

Gwen nearly sagged in relief. "Steady," Marcus murmured in her ear. "Is something wrong? You don't know that man, do you?"

"Nay, of course not." How could she? "It's just . . . there are so many people here."

"I suppose it's overwhelming if you're not used to it."

"Exactly." She eased his arm from her waist. "I'm fine now."

Breena, walking on Gwen's other side, sent her a sympathetic look. "Mother says she felt much the same when she first came to Isca. And that was fifteen years ago! I'm sure the market is even bigger now."

"Gwen lived here eighteen years ago," Marcus said.

"I've hardly thought of it since then," Gwen admitted. "I remember my father had a stall where he and Mama sold the blankets my mother and aunt wove. I remember coming here, to the market, with Rhys. I felt sorry for the goats in their pens and the hares in their baskets. Once, I convinced Rhys to create a diversion while I let a family of hares hop out." She smiled. "The merchant never even saw me. But oh, was he furious!"

She focused on a blanket mounded high with piles of peas, wild nettles, and a red root vegetable Marcus identified as radishes. A memory flashed—Gwen had stood before a similar display holding Mama's skirt as Mama haggled with a toothless old woman. Gwen closed her eyes. The image expanded to include a young, dark-skinned centurion. He stood at the next booth, watching with hooded eyes as Mama enacted a barter—a small blanket for a basket of vegetables and one of plover's eggs.

The transaction completed, Mama had glanced in the soldier's direction. He'd straightened. Mama had ducked her head, blushed, and looked away. A rare smile lingered on her lips for some time afterward.

Gwen opened her eyes, startled at the emotion the memory stirred. Sour fear, and something akin to jealousy. She'd forgotten how her mother's pinched face had softened whenever she'd seen her Roman lover. The man who had killed her. Of course, at the time, Gwen hadn't understood what the man was. Only that he could make Mama smile, when Gwen herself most often made Mama frown.

Now, eighteen years later, pity seeped into the mix of emotions Gwen felt. How terrible, to be killed by someone you loved.

She drew a breath and allowed Marcus to guide her through the crowd, his hand placed protectively on her lower back. The market was teeming—had the entire population of Isca and the surrounding countryside come to town? She saw Romans of all social strata—patricians in their togas, merchants in their white wool tunics, workers and slaves in rougher garments. Women with braids coiled high on their heads, their faces framed with short curls, walked with their maids. A dog chained to a potter's stall gave a low growl as Gwen passed, its fur rising on its neck. Marcus frowned at the animal.

The buzz of conversation around her was largely in rapid Latin. Most of it flowed past in a meaningless stream. There was a fair bit of conversation in her own tongue, though, as Celts mingled freely with the Romans. Some were as finely garbed as the conquerors, others less so. Farmers and merchants, buying and selling foodstuffs and other wares, switched between Latin and Celtic with fluent ease. Many, Gwen thought, were of mixed blood, like Breena. Nearly two centuries after Julius Caesar's invasion, Romans and Celts were blending into one people. Britons, they called themselves.

There were many soldiers, of course. Some wore bloodred tunics and segmented Legionary armor, others dressed in *braccas,* their wool shirts covered with more flexible chain mail. No matter what their garb, she couldn't stop her pulse from pounding whenever one of them passed too close. She reminded herself she was nothing to them. Just a faceless woman in the crowd. They couldn't feel her magic. Had no reason to single her out. Still, she was glad for Marcus's presence beside her.

Breena and Lucius stopped before a spice merchant's stall. She and Marcus strolled on to the next shop, which featured an elaborate display of iron and bronze cookware. There were also long-handled Roman cooking pans of various sizes as well as Celt-style cauldrons.

"Great Mother, how many cauldrons there are!" She began to count, and was past twenty before she stopped. "The entire village of Avalon has only three."

The vendor, an older woman with a sharp face, spoke in Celtic. "A new pot, miss?"

"Nay, I think not. But thank ye."

The next booth was a potter's. The man's wares—redware plates, bowls, and pitchers—were exquisitely etched with black figures of people and animals. Past the potter was a mercer's. Fabrics unlike anything

Gwen had ever seen cascaded over the edge of a long table like a rainbow-hued waterfall.

"The finest wools and linens," the middle-aged Roman woman sitting behind the display declared with a smile. "Just arrived from Rome and Egypt."

Her husband took a slightly different tack. "Your wife is very beautiful," he told Marcus, inclining his head in a slight bow. "You are a fortunate man."

"I'm not—" Gwen began, but Marcus cut her off. "Yes. She is lovely, isn't she?"

The merchant grinned widely and spread his hands. A jeweled ring glittered on each of his thick fingers. "Such a beautiful woman must be adorned with beautiful cloth. As my own beautiful wife is."

His wife blushed. Gwen could not tell if her reaction to her husband's compliment was genuine or part of a practiced sales effort. The merchant turned back to his wares, making a show of lifting and examining each fabric with a critical eye.

"None of these common cloths will do your wife justice," he told Marcus seriously. "With hair like moonlight, she should be clothed in radiance. If you will wait just a moment . . ."

Rising, he inclined his head and disappeared through the leather flap that served as the door to the rear of the stall. A moment later, he called his wife to help him locate something. The woman rose. "Please stay just a moment longer. It will be worth the wait, I promise you."

"Let us go," Gwen whispered as the tent flap closed behind her. "Before they come back."

Marcus covered her hand with his and leaned close. "That would be quite rude. And anyway, don't you want to see what they bring out?"

"Nay. I do not. He thinks—"

"You don't like being mistaken for my wife?" Marcus's tone was light, but his eyes were grave.

Her heart lurched; her next words were sharper than she'd intended. "That man cannot truly think we are married!"

"Why not?"

"Because ye are a Roman and I am—"

"Perhaps he simply believes we are lovers," Marcus said bluntly. "But does not wish to embarrass you."

"Marcus . . ."

The merchant, followed by his wife, emerged from the back of the stall, carrying a large package wrapped in oilcloth. Sweeping a fine blue wool aside, the man laid it on the table and unrolled the covering.

"When my eyes beheld your lady, even before you approached my humble shop, I knew she must have this. Only one as fair as she could do it justice."

The oilcloth fell away, revealing a silver fabric so fine and delicate it looked like liquid moonlight. The merchant reverently lifted the material, shaking out the folds. It rippled over his outstretched forearm.

Gwen stared. She had never envisioned such finery. Hesitantly, and only after much urging by the merchant, she reached out and touched it. The fabric was cool and smooth, almost like water—it felt as if she were dabbling her fingers in a stream. What would it feel like on her bare shoulders and breasts?

"Silk," the merchant said proudly. "From the East. It looks delicate, but I assure you it will not tear. When I purchased this particular length, I vowed I would not sell it until I found a woman worthy of its brilliance."

Leaning forward, he draped a length of the fabric across her torso. "You, my lady, are that woman." His gaze shifted to Marcus. "Your wife is a rare treasure."

"Yes, she is," Marcus agreed. He paused. "How much do you want for it?"

The merchant named a sum that had Gwen gasping. Even with her limited knowledge of Roman coins and prices, she knew it was exorbitant. It was very near to the amount Marcus carried in the purse hidden in the folds of his toga, with which he meant to purchase two Celt slaves.

He caught her gaze. "If you'd like the cloth . . ."

"Nay," she said swiftly, taking a step back, away from the sensation of the silk on her skin. It was beautiful beyond anything she'd ever imagined, but it was not for her.

Nothing of Marcus's Roman life was for her.

"I do not want it."

It was a lie, and from the look Marcus sent her, he knew it. But he did not insist. "I'm sorry," he told the man.

The merchant gave a theatrical sigh as he folded and rewrapped the silk. "Your wife is a modest woman. Such a prize is indeed worth far more than silk." Leaning toward Marcus, he added in a low voice, "All the more reason to reward your lady's virtue. I am not at all sure the fabric will be here tomorrow. I am afraid if you pass it by now, and later change your mind . . ." He trailed off suggestively.

Marcus smiled and shook his head. "I'm sure such a rare and beautiful cloth will be gone before the day is out. Regrettably, I will not be its new owner."

He guided Gwen toward Lucius and Breena, who'd already moved several stalls past them and stood inspecting a brace of haddock at a fishmonger's. "The mercer spoke truly. That silk was made for you."

"I cannot agree. It was beautiful, aye, but not for someone like me."

"You sell yourself short. You deserve to be draped in silks."

"Silk has no place on Avalon."

He sighed, and she felt him withdraw a bit into himself. "I suppose it doesn't."

She stopped and turned to him. "And I would not have ye waste your money on something so trivial. Far better you grant freedom to some of my people instead. That's worth far more than all the silk in the East."

"Still, I would not have minded seeing you lying in my bed with nothing but that silk draped across your body."

She felt her cheeks heat.

"Tonight I'll spread furs for you to lie on. I'll—"

Fortunately, Breena's call interrupted Marcus's erotic musings. "Marcus! Gwen!" She waved from across the aisle. "Father and I were wondering where you had gotten to."

"We were giving you an opportunity to shop," Marcus said with a laugh. Matius's arms were already overflowing with parcels. "And it looks like you took advantage of it."

"I'm hungry," Breena declared. "We should find some food and drink."

"I'll leave you to it, then," Marcus said. His gaze strayed to the far end of the market, where the temporary slave pens had been erected. "Father and I need to leave now," he said to Gwen. "Will you be all right in the crowd without me?"

Stay, she wanted to tell him, but his purpose at the slave auction was far more important than her petty fears and memories. "Go. I'll be fine with your sister."

"I'll take good care of her, Marcus," Breena said, linking arms with Gwen. "Matius won't let us be crushed."

"Oh, well, that's all right, then," Marcus said with a wink at the lad.

They made an agreement to meet at the cart for the ride home, then Marcus and Lucius strode toward the slave pens. A toga-clad patrician coming out of the viewing area gave them the barest of nods as he passed.

"The other patricians think they are crazy, to buy slaves and then free them," Breena said with some amusement.

"And they truly don't care that they are ridiculed behind their backs?"

"They are mocked to their faces as well. Father barely notices—he was a soldier, after all. He says after what he's seen in battle, no idle talk can ever have power over him. And Marcus? He has the thickest skin imaginable. He does what he wants, always."

They stopped at a food vendor's stall, where Breena ordered Gwen and herself sausage and warmed spiced wine. By the time the sun was overhead, and they had visited a dozen more stalls, Gwen was more than ready to abandon the shopping expedition. The crowds frayed her nerves. The odors of people, spices, perfumes, and garbage, combined with the greasy meal she'd eaten, made her head ache and her stomach churn. Each time a passerby jostled her, she fought a fresh surge of panic. She desperately needed some open space and fresh air.

She breathed a sigh of relief when Breena declared her purchases complete. They left the crush of the market and headed down the road leading out of town. They'd almost reached the field where they'd left their cart when several mounted Legionary soldiers came pounding up the road. Sunlight glinted off their crested helmets; their horses' hooves sprayed mud. Immediately, Breena and Matius moved to the side of the road.

Gwen didn't follow. Sudden fear had paralyzed her limbs. One of the two lead soldiers shouted at her; the pair of riders split, flowing around her, leaving her staring at the officer riding in their wake. The man reined in his mount, drawing up sharply an instant before he would have trampled her.

His head and shoulders were cloaked with blue-black light.

Strabo.

"Gwen! What are you *doing?*" Breena shouted as Strabo's escort reined in around their commander. She hurried to Gwen's side and tugged her arm. "Get out of the way!"

Gwen barely heard her. Strabo, here in Isca! What did it mean? Had he given up the search for Avalon? Abruptly, Gwen realized several days had passed since she'd felt Rhys in her mind. Was she too late? Had Avalon already fallen? Merciless fingers of fear closed about her throat.

Strabo's angry voice accosted her. "What is the meaning of this? Get out of—" He stopped, his dark eyes widening above the cheek guards of his helmet.

Gwen's breath left her. Breena's grip was firm on her arm, and Matius had moved to stand beside her. Strabo's aura flared dangerously, then settled into a dark, angry glow. His eyes challenged her. The wolf inside her responded, rising on all fours, its hackles lifting. Its silent growl vibrated deep in her bones.

Great Mother! She could not shift here, in front of half the population of Isca! A Roman sword would slice her in two before the transformation was complete. Closing her eyes, she fought the Deep Magic with every shred of her will.

The wolf snarled, but backed off. Gwen exhaled a long breath.

"Good day, Legate," she heard Breena say. "Please excuse my cousin. She should be more careful."

"Indeed."

Gwen's eyes flew open. Breena had stepped in front of her, attempting to shield her from Strabo's scrutiny. As Gwen stood half a head taller than her would-be defender, it was a fruitless effort.

Strabo examined Breena intently for a moment, then, to Gwen's great surprise, he inclined his head. "I am sorry to have startled your . . . *cousin*, is it?" He eyed the mud splattered on Gwen's tunic. "I fear I may have ruined your clothing," he said to Gwen. "Where may I send reparations?"

" 'Tis not necessary," Gwen choked out.

"Is it not?" His dark aura flared.

The wolf, barely settled, raised its head. Hastily, Gwen averted her eyes. The beast laid its head on its paws, but remained watchful.

"May I respectfully suggest, ladies, that you keep to the side of the road in the future?"

"Of course, Legate," Breena replied. "Good day to you."

"Good day."

Gwen's knees went weak as Strabo kicked his mount's flanks and continued toward the fortress. She had to grip Breena's arm to keep herself upright.

"Don't worry," Breena said, her arm encircling Gwen's waist. "I don't think he recognized you."

On the contrary. Gwen was sure that he had.

Marcus did not know if the woman he'd bought, or her newborn son, would live.

Heart heavy, he carried the young mother's slight

body through the maze of carts. She weighed next to nothing. Malnourished and still ill from the delivery of her child, she'd lapsed into unconsciousness soon after Marcus had bought her, as if she'd been waiting for a safe haven in which to close her eyes.

Her chestnut hair was tinged with auburn, but her tiny son's hair was as dark as Marcus's own. "It's a miracle she lived through the birthing," he muttered to Lucius.

"Yes." Lucius peered down at the bundle in his arms. "Though this babe is so thin and quiet, I wonder if he will survive."

Marcus had wondered the same thing. Perhaps he should have passed over these two wretched souls in favor of two who might have lived. But when he'd seen the woman's eyes—a vivid green, filled with lost hope—he'd not been able to pass her by.

He turned up the aisle leading to their cart. Breena was already seated in the vehicle while Gwen paced between the rows. When she saw him, she halted. Her eyes were haunted. He thought he knew why. Governor Julius Severus had arrived unexpectedly from Londinium two days before. The market was abuzz with gossip; Severus had not been pleased to find Legate Strabo away from the fortress. Swift riders were sent to summon him, and the legate had just ridden into town. Had Gwen seen him? Marcus thought she must have.

But if Gwen meant to speak of Strabo, her intention abruptly changed when she saw the woman in his arms. "Oh, Marcus! She is so ill!"

"I'm not sure she will live."

Gwen touched the woman's flushed cheek. "She's hot."

"Childbed fever, no doubt." He nodded toward his father.

Gwen's gaze shot to Lucius, her eyes widening as she realized what he held. "Her babe lives?"

"Yes. The slaver knew how much I wanted them, and raised his price accordingly." He grimaced. "No one but me would have made such a poor bargain."

"I'm very glad that ye did," Gwen said softly. Her eyes did not waver from the babe. She lifted the infant from Lucius's arms, drawing back the swaddling rags from his face.

The child was strangely silent. His eyes were the same vivid green as his mother's. Gwen gazed down at the babe, and at the mother, and for a long time said nothing. Then she lifted her head.

"The Great Mother must have led ye to this child," she said in a low voice. "His aura is very strong. He is touched by magic. As is his mother."

Marcus exhaled. More magic. He could not seem to get away from it.

That evening, Gwen helped Breena settle the ailing mother in a small servants' hut that often served as an infirmary. The woman regained consciousness briefly, moaning for her son. Gwen eased the baby into his mother's arms, but the woman held the infant only long enough to press a kiss to his brow.

The babe did not utter a sound. His mother's hand fell from his bottom, and Gwen caught the child before he wriggled to the ground. She handed the tiny lad to one of the female field workers, who had offered to put the child to breast with her own infant.

Breena bathed the woman's face with a damp cloth. Rhiannon had brewed a potion of willow bark, but Lucius had forbidden her to visit the sickroom. Rhiannon acceded to her husband's order grudgingly.

Gwen watched Breena and Mab tend the unconscious woman. Rhiannon's draught had done the patient some good; her fever no longer raged so hot, and her slumber was peaceful.

"I think she will live," Breena told Gwen.

"I hope ye are right," Gwen replied. The woman showed signs of having been beaten, but her aura was strong and steady. Green, the color of the earth. The babe's aura held all the colors of the rainbow, as was often the case with children. It was impossible to know what his talent would be. But it would be strong, of that much Gwen was certain.

"You look ready to drop," Breena told Gwen. "You had a fright, encountering Legate Strabo in the road as you did. Go to bed. Alma will look after the woman during the night. I doubt she'll awaken, in any case."

Gwen *was* sorely fatigued, but she knew she would not rest tonight. She and Marcus had to complete Exchalybur. By this time tomorrow, she meant to be well on her way to Avalon.

She nodded and slipped out the door. As she walked up the orchard path to the main house, voices drifted toward her, and Gwen's steps slowed. Rhiannon and Marcus stood on the rear terrace of the farmhouse, talking and looking out over the herb garden. As Gwen neared, Rhiannon reached up and touched her stepson's jaw.

"Ye have sore need of a razor, Marcus."

"And *you* have need of rest. I don't want my new brother or sister coming early, as Breena did."

Rhiannon's hand went to her stomach. "Dinna worry. I am tired, aye, but the babe is fine."

"You shouldn't take chances."

"Nor will I. But I am not as frail as your father seems

to think, despite my age. Lucius will gain another son, and you will get a brother."

Marcus grinned. "It's a boy, then? Are you sure?"

"Aye, I believe so."

A note of humor crept into Marcus's voice. "Father will be happy for a second chance at a son who loves philosophy and rhetoric."

Rhiannon chuckled. "Lucius already has a daughter so enamored. And a son who is a fine artist and a sensitive soul. Whatever this new babe's inclinations, your father will accept them without murmur."

"I don't doubt it." Marcus's arm went around Rhiannon's shoulders. He placed a kiss on top of her head. Marcus's love for his stepmother was palpable, as was Rhiannon's love for the son she had not birthed. Gwen found herself blinking back tears.

"Thank ye for being who ye are, Marcus," Rhiannon said. "And for saving that woman and her babe."

"I could hardly leave them to die." He paused. "Gwen says they are touched by magic."

"Truly?" Rhiannon sighed. "Then they will go to Avalon, no doubt."

"If Avalon is safe, yes. If not . . ." He sighed and turned to the darkness of the gardens, leaning his forearm on the stone railing.

Rhiannon touched his arm. "Do not worry so. The Druids' Light is strong. They will prevail."

"I wish I had your faith. But I—"

Marcus's words went unsaid as Lucius emerged from the house with swift steps.

"Rhiannon. What are you doing out here? You should be off your feet."

Rhiannon smiled and stepped toward her husband. "I am coming, Lucius. There is no need to scold."

Lucius fitted Rhiannon to his side, his arm curved about her shoulders. "I will not have you taxing yourself," he admonished as he escorted her down the path to the house. "You will come to bed now, and stay there until morning."

"Aye?" Rhiannon laughed and drew her husband's head down to whisper in his ear.

"Yes, certainly, if that's what it takes to keep you there," Lucius said with a grin much like the one Marcus gave Gwen just before he kissed her. Gwen dashed a tear from her eye as the couple disappeared into the house.

Marcus shifted his stance and looked directly at Gwen. "Hiding in the shadows?"

With a wry smile, Gwen moved into the moonlight. "I did not wish to intrude on your talk with Rhiannon."

"Eavesdropping is not intruding, I suppose," Marcus said mildly. He held out his hand. Gwen went to him readily. He enfolded her in his arms. His kiss was tender and unhurried, as if he'd been kissing her that way for years and would continue for years to come. The casual familiarity of it stole her breath, and once again, Gwen found herself fighting back tears.

She felt Marcus's gaze on her as she blinked them away. "We are so close to the house. Someone might see—"

"I do not care. I'm not ashamed of wanting you."

But she was ashamed of wanting *him*. Because of Avalon. Because of Trevor. She didn't say it, but the unspoken words hung in the air between them. Marcus's hand had been on her waist; now it fell away.

She cleared her throat. "Rhiannon is not too weary?"

"Father will see that she rests." He descended the terrace steps, taking the path that led to the smithy. Gwen fell into step beside him.

" 'Tis fortunate you found the slave woman before it was too late. So many women die bearing children."

"Rhiannon's mother did, when Owein was born," Marcus said. "My own mother as well. The child died with her."

"I did not know that. How old were you?"

"Nine years. I came to Britain with my father soon after."

"Was your mother very different from Rhiannon?" Gwen asked.

"As day is from night. Mother loved new clothes and parties. She and I lived in Rome, and we hardly ever left the city. She never accompanied Father to any of his posts." He paused. "The child she died giving birth to was not his."

"Truly?" Gwen was stunned. "I cannot believe it! No sane woman would reject Lucius for another man."

"Apparently, Mother did not find it difficult, as Father was rarely home. Even when he was, they didn't deal well together. But that is hardly surprising, I suppose, given the fact that they did not choose each other. Their marriage was contracted by their parents."

He sent her a meaningful glance—one she chose to ignore. They walked on for a moment in silence, and then Gwen asked, "Did you know your mother had taken a lover?"

"That's an odd question."

"I'm sorry. Perhaps I should not have asked—"

"I don't mind telling you," Marcus interrupted. "The truth is, I didn't know." He gave a rueful laugh. "I was a rather thickheaded child, and whoever the man was, he did not visit our house. I thought the babe was Father's, even though he'd been away for more than a year when the infant came."

"Ye jest."

Marcus snorted. "I'm sorry to tell you that I do not. Even at the advanced age of nine, I knew little about carnal relations." He touched her, his hand coming to rest on her lower back as he guided her over a protruding root on the path.

"My mother—her name was Tamar—she also had a lover." The words tumbled from Gwen's lips before she'd even realized she'd said them. She stopped on the path, aghast. She'd never spoken of it since Mama's death. Not even with Rhys.

Marcus's astonishment was evident. "And you knew this? But you were only seven years old."

"Rhys and I . . . we saw Mama . . . coupling with the man. At night. She left our hut when she thought everyone was asleep. Rhys and I followed her to a hidden spot near the river."

Marcus let out an oath. "Who was he?"

"A Roman soldier. A centurion. We'd seen him before, at Mama's market stall."

"Did they know you'd seen them?"

"No. We snuck away immediately. By the time Mama returned to our hut, we were under our blankets, feigning sleep. But I think . . . I think my father knew. They argued often, and sometimes . . . sometimes he beat her. She had bruises the day after Rhys and I saw her lying with the soldier. The very next day, Uncle Padrig found Father dead."

"The centurion killed him?"

"We suspected he did, but we never knew for certain. Not long after, the centurion's anger turned toward Mama. He killed her."

"Why?"

"I think he must have asked her to run away with

him, and she would not. At least, that is what Rhys and I heard Mared tell Padrig. Grandfather gave no explanation at all, and Rhys and I knew better than to ask. We buried Mama and left Isca the same day."

"You went to Avalon."

"Aye. And none of them—Cyric, Padrig, or Mared—ever spoke of Mama's death again, except to say that the Lady teaches us to forgive those who wrong us."

They'd arrived at the smithy door. "These memories aren't the only thing bothering you tonight," Marcus said. "Rhiannon told me of your encounter with Strabo—"

An icy finger moved down Gwen's spine. "He recognized me."

"Are you sure?"

She nodded. "The sooner I leave here, the better. If we work through the night, the sword will be completed by morning. I'll leave then. Strabo's return to Isca may prove to be a boon. I will be able to set new protections around Avalon while the governor distracts him here."

"And once the sacred isle is safely hidden, will you marry the man your grandfather has chosen for you?"

She drew a breath. "Aye. I will marry Trevor. He is a good man. He says he loves me."

"He could not love you half as much as I," Marcus said, causing Gwen's heart to lurch. He had never before offered such blunt words of love. "And you do not love him. Will you go from my bed to his? Will you tell him to whom you gave your maidenhood?" His tone turned bitter. "Or will you lie and say that you are untouched?"

She winced. "Do not make this harder for me than it already is, Marcus. If I were free, I would stay here with you gladly. But I am not. 'Tis my duty to become

Guardian of Avalon. To marry as Cyric asks. Even if it were not, there is the wolf—"

"I am not afraid of the wolf. And I do not care for your grandfather's machinations." He all but kicked open the smithy door. "I'll take you to Avalon, Gwen. When we get there, I want you to give Exchalybur to Rhys and return home with me."

"Marcus, ye cannot accompany me to Avalon! A Roman with no magic is not welcome—"

"I am well aware of that," he said grimly, "but I'll see you safely there, regardless. I mean to make you understand you need not sacrifice your life to an old man's whims. Clara and Owein will ensure the Lady's line remains unbroken. Rhys will become Avalon's Guardian, and wield Exchalybur in its defense."

Gwen swallowed. She could hardly tell Marcus Rhys would not touch Exchalybur once he realized Deep Magic lived at its core. "I cannot do that, Marcus. There is . . . more to this than ye know."

He dragged a hand over his hair, making the ends stick up. "What is it, then? Tell me and I'll find a way around it. I don't want to be without you, Gwen. I love you."

Her chest squeezed so tightly, her next breath caused a streak of pain. "Do not ask me to explain, Marcus. Just trust me when I say I cannot leave the protection of Avalon to Rhys."

He studied her for a long time, his eyes shadowed by night and emotion. "I will not accept that, Gwen."

She did not answer.

At last he sighed and entered the smithy. "I'll complete my work on the sword before morning," he said as he lit the lamps. "But this discussion isn't over, Gwen. Not at all."

* * *

Exchalybur shone like a sliver of moonlight. Marcus even imagined he could feel the magic Gwen had woven into the bright iron. But surely, that was a figment of his overactive imagination. He had no magic; he could feel nothing.

And yet, even to his mundane eye it was plain that he'd never crafted a sword so beautiful, nor so deadly. Its weight was slight for such a large weapon, but the blade would not bend or break. It would be lethal in battle, even without its magic.

He honed the edges to perfection while Gwen dozed on his bed. This was not how he'd envisioned her last night in Isca. In that dream, he had made love to her until dawn, and she had whispered words of devotion—to *him,* not to Avalon. She'd agreed to give up the sword to Rhys and become Marcus's wife.

He could not dismiss that dream as easily as she had.

When he at last put the sharpening stone aside, he didn't have the heart to wake her from her much-needed slumber. There was yet an hour or two before dawn. The night was quiet. The gates were locked. Gwen had set magical protections all around the perimeter wall; if Strabo was searching for her, as she'd feared he might, he had not found her.

He left the finished sword on his worktable, eased open the smithy door, and went to see about provisions for their journey.

Chapter Fifteen

Sweet warmth enveloped Gwen. She was lying on the softest of cushions, her spine pressed against Marcus's chest, his strong arms entwined about her body. She arched back, into his heat. His breath caressed her temple. His hips flexed.

His arousal prodded between the soft globes of her naked buttocks. Moisture gathered between her thighs.

His big hand moved over her belly, dipping low, his clever fingers finding her body's dew. His fingertips skated over her mound and through the slick folds between her legs. His thumb circled the tight bud where her pleasure centered.

Urgent heat spread through her body. She pressed her hips backward with a moan.

"Marcus . . ."

He chuckled, his amusement vibrating through her body. His touch grew bolder. His hand swept up to her breast. He kneaded one breast, then the other. Rolled one nipple between his thumb and forefinger.

Then he pinched. Hard.

She cried out, twisting and flailing, turning to catch a glimpse of a hard, unforgiving face.

Not Marcus.

Strabo.

A strangled cry froze in her throat. She scrambled to summon a Word of protection, but it would not come. Shock blanked her brain, and her power.

Nay. More than shock. Blue-black sparks flashed around her. The scent of burning flesh choked her senses. Strabo's arms banded about her body, his arousal pressed insistently between her legs.

"Did you think I would let you leave me, too?"

Panicked, she curled her fingers into a fist and struck behind her. The angle was awkward; with her arms pinned above the elbows, all she managed was a glancing blow to his thigh. He caught her wrists with ease, first one, then the other. Rolling atop her, he lifted her arms above her head, pinning them with one hand. His lower body trapped her legs. She was caught like a fly in honey.

His Dark aura pulsed ominously.

She bared her teeth. "This is not real. 'Tis but a dream."

"A dream now, perhaps, but soon . . ." His free hand roamed her body. "Ah, soon enough, it will be truth, my little she-wolf."

She started. "Ye know about the wolf."

His white teeth flashed in cruel smile. "Of course. You should not have run, that first night I spied you. It was not worthy of what you are." His dark eyes regarded her with an intensity that made her skin crawl. "I thought I came for the old man, but now—I am not so sure. I begin to think you are the better prize. You are so like her."

"Like who?"

He did not answer. She tried again to call a spell—a spell of Deep Magic this time—but she could not make the Words form in her head, nor on her lips. Strabo's blue-black essence flowed to her from the places their bodies touched, tingling painfully on her skin. Darkness compressed her chest, forcing her to struggle for every breath.

"Do not tire yourself," Strabo said. "Your magic is no match for what mine has become. And his . . . his cannot stand much longer. He cannot save himself, and he cannot save you."

"Who?" She did not understand. Strabo was insane, she was sure of it. His eyes blazed darkly. She tried to look away, but his hand came up to catch her chin, preventing it.

"It will be . . . almost as it was. How I have longed for that."

His head dipped. His mouth covered hers, roughly. What little breath she had was drawn into his lungs. Magic ran in dark waves to her core. Fire kindled in the pit of her stomach, turning her soul to ash.

He kissed her ruthlessly, as if he could command the response he desired. Dimly, she was aware of his knee sliding between her legs, opening her.

Finally, the Words she so desperately sought came to her, ringing like the clearest bells in her mind. The wolf sprang from its stupor. The change began, twisting deep inside her.

The dream broke; Strabo vanished.

But she heard him laughing as the wolf took control.

The instant Marcus opened the door to the smithy, he knew something was terribly wrong. Ill-feeling swept over him like a noxious sewer odor, wrenching his stomach and making his limbs tense with dread. Fighting panic, he took two steps toward his bed, then stopped.

Gwen was gone.

A faint impression on the blanket was all that was left of her presence. Had she fled alone to Avalon, rather than suffer his escort? But no, that could not be it. Exchalybur lay untouched on his worktable. Gwen might leave Marcus behind, but she would not have left the sword.

Where was she? He considered the possibility that she might be visiting the latrine near the bathhouse, with its running water, rather than use the covered pot he kept handy for such purposes. A moment later, when he noticed the empty hook where the gate key normally hung, he ground out a foul oath. She'd gone out to the forest. In the middle of the night.

He ran to the gate leading to the fields. She had not bothered to lock it behind her; the iron bars swung free on their hinges. His foreboding accelerated when the moon came from behind a cloud, illuminating a clear path through the barley where the new plants had been broken. She'd been in such a hurry she hadn't even taken the time to find the path between the fields. What had disturbed her so? Strabo? Or the wolf?

As he plunged into the woods, he wished he'd taken a few moments to bring a lamp from the smithy. No time to go back for one now. He'd have to rely on the uncertain moonlight. He ran to the clearing where they'd made love—if she were looking for a refuge, perhaps that would be it.

He drew up short when he burst into the open, quickly scanning the area. "Gwen!"

He cocked his head, listening. Nothing.

But she had been here. A swath of trampled grass led to the tree where she had come upon him that first time. At the base of the trunk, a glint of silver caught his eye. Gwen's pendant, lying in the grass. He picked it up, and closed his fist around it. He'd never seen her take the chain from around her neck. Not even while they'd made love. The gate key lay nearby, half-hidden by a lichen-covered branch. A few steps beyond, Gwen's tunic lay in a crumpled heap.

His blood ran cold. Strabo? Or the wolf? He circled the area, searching the shadowed ground for tracks.

To his relief, he found none that belonged to a man, save his own. Instead he discovered the imprint of a soft pad and four spread toes. A second print, and more, led out of the clearing and deeper into the forest.

Marcus stood staring in the direction Gwen had gone. As if to taunt him, the moon chose that moment to disappear behind a silver-rimmed cloud. He swallowed hard. He'd never be able to track her in the dark, and even if he could, he would not be able to catch a wolf. But she would return to the clearing for her tunic and pendant.

Would she come as a wolf, and shift before him? Or would she shift in darkness, and come to him as a woman, naked in moonlight? Or—and this dread thought arrested his growing desire quite effectively— would Gwen's worst fear come to pass?

Would the wolf claim her completely?

Jaw clenched and stomach churning, Marcus returned to the tree with Gwen's pendant and tunic, and sat down to wait.

She did not know this forest.

She ran blindly, sharp brambles tearing at her fur.

She did not care how far or in which direction she traveled. It was often so when the wolf had not been free for some time. It was as if the beast longed to outrun everything human.

This time, Gwen wanted to outrun her nightmare as well. The memory of Strabo's intimate assault pursued her through the shadows more ruthlessly than any hunter. Had the horror come from her own mind? Or had the sorcerer cast a Dark dream? As disturbing as the first notion was, she infinitely preferred it to the second.

But the second was much more likely. Strabo had recognized her on the road into town. Now he was telling her he knew about the wolf. And boasting to her of what she feared was all too true: that his magic was greater than hers.

She raced deeper into the forest. Was he here, in these woods, waiting for her? He would not catch her. The wolf would not allow it. The beast was the strongest part of her.

She called a spell of protection to mind. A spell of Deep Magic. As they had not in her dream, the Words came easily. Because of the wolf. The beast was closer to the magic of the gods than her human form could ever hope to be.

A small falcon flew overhead, swooping low. The sudden motion disturbed her. She stumbled to a halt, disoriented. It was then that she became aware of a familiar scent in the air. She lifted her nose and sniffed.

Marcus.

He was part of her now; she would know his scent anywhere. The wolf had accepted him as her mate and master, sensing, perhaps, that his domination would never hurt her. She could feel his desire, pulsing with the night wind. He wanted her to come to him. Unerringly, she turned and padded toward him.

She had no clear idea of how much time had passed since she'd left the smithy. Not long, perhaps, because the eastern sky was only just beginning to lighten. Her body hummed like a plucked string on Rhys's harp. It was only when she was almost upon the clearing—just as her eyes found Marcus, standing with his back to her, peering intently through the trees—that she fully understood what he wanted.

For her to shift in front of him.

Her paws froze in midstep. Her human mind recoiled. She could not do it. She could *not*. He'd said watching her shift had not been a horror, but she did not believe him. She could not bear to see the revulsion in his eyes when he looked upon her.

She backed away, slowly, praying he would not sense her presence. He did not turn, did not so much as move. Creeping slowly through the underbrush, she did not stop until she'd put a good distance and a solid outcrop of rock between them. She fell into a deep crouch on the damp, shadowed loam. She would shift here, then go to him. That, she could bear.

She let the Words seep into her mind. After only a brief hesitation, the wolf lowered its head in acquiescence. Brilliant pain suffused her limbs, sinking deep into her bones. She did not dull it with a numbing spell. The pain reminded her that the wolf would always be a part of her. If she did not keep that thought foremost in her mind, she would never be able to turn her back on the life Marcus offered her.

She endured the suffering as she always did—silently and without tears. Once she felt secure enough in her woman's form, she opened her eyes. All around her, the world was flat, devoid of magic. Like the life ahead of her, lived without Marcus. She felt as though a hole had been ripped in her heart.

Perhaps she'd not been made for happiness. Perhaps this penance was the price of her mother's dishonor.

Her woman's body fully re-formed, she heaved her aching limbs into a crouch, steadying herself with one hand as a rush of light-headedness pulsed and receded.

Behind her, a twig snapped.

She turned her head quickly, sucked in a breath. Marcus stood just three strides before her, her pendant dangling from his fingers. His eyes glittered with dangerous emotion. Not horror. Not disgust. Not even pity.

Lust.

"Get up."

The note of absolute command in his voice caused her stomach to clench. Heat pooled in her belly, slipped slickly between her thighs. Her nipples tightened.

Slowly, not taking her eyes from him, she obeyed.

"Lift your arms above your head. Clasp your elbows."

The motion lifted and parted her breasts, increasing her vulnerability. His eyes consumed her. She thought her skin would burst into flames from the heat of his gaze. Erotic fire flashed through her, every bit as potent as the magic that, in the wake of her shifting, she could not feel.

He took a step toward her, her pendant slowly swinging on its chain. She could smell his heat, his lust. Her body responded, softening in preparation for her inevitable surrender. The wolf could not deny its mate. Nor did the woman want to.

But her shame would not abate. "Ye . . . saw?"

"Yes."

"I wish ye had not. I wish ye had stayed away."

He gave a harsh laugh. "I'd have sooner cut off my right arm."

He advanced another step. She arched her back, silently offering him her breasts. He did not touch them. Instead, he placed her chain over her head. With studious deliberation, he lifted her hair, guiding the long, tangled locks through the silver circlet. The metal, warm with the heat of his touch, nestled against her bare skin.

His gaze drifted to the spot where she'd shifted, then slid back to her. His hands dropped to his waist, unlacing his braccas. His erection sprang free from a thatch of dark, curling hair. He wrapped his fingers around it.

"Nay." Before she quite knew what she intended, she'd abandoned the pose he'd ordered her to take and gone down on her knees before him. Her parted lips bathed the tip of his erection. His fingers threaded through her hair, gripping tightly at the base of her skull. She was not sure if he meant to pull her close or push her away.

She made the decision for him. Her hands slipped beneath the waist of his braccas and shoved them down over his hips. Filling her palms with the tight globes of his buttocks, she pulled him to her.

He tasted salty. She liked it, and liked how the glide of her lips over the broad round head of his shaft dragged a groan from his lips. She teased with her tongue, scraped with her teeth. His big body shuddered.

She parted her lips wider and slid the full length of him into her mouth. His grip on her hair tightened painfully. His arms moved, guiding her. She gave herself over to his command, letting him set the pace as he wished, reveling in her ability to offer him this pleasure. She would even take his seed this way, if he wanted it. But the instant she felt his shaft hardening in anticipation of release, he hooked his hands under her arms and dragged her to her feet. She felt her spine press against the rough trunk of a tree.

His hips pinned her in place. He pressed his forehead to hers, his eyes closed. "Gods, you make me crazed. Have you cast a spell on me?"

"Nay! Never. Do not think it."

"I hunger for you, Gwen, but having you does nothing to ease my appetite. It only inflames me more." His hand found her nipple and plucked it into an exquisitely sensitive peak.

She gasped as fire streaked to her loins. She wriggled against him, hooking one leg around his calf. Her body wept for him. She needed him where her yearning was fiercest.

"Come inside me, Marcus."

"Gladly."

He joined them with one powerful thrust of his hips, seating himself so deeply that she saw stars. His breath warmed her face. He rained kisses on her cheeks, her forehead, her eyelids. Took her mouth in a hot, wet kiss as he moved inside her body. Inside her soul.

She gave herself over to the beauty of it, granting him mastery of her body. He drove her to the edge of her pleasure, then slowed, allowing the bliss to retreat. When next it rose, the pleasure was sharper, her need greater. But he let that ebb, too.

"Marcus . . ."

He gave no indication he'd heard her plea. Again the peak rushed at her, only to slip away when she reached for it. Her heart felt as though it were being shredded with pleasure. Tears of frustration flooded her eyes.

"Please, Marcus . . ."

He anchored her hips with his hands and withdrew almost completely. She struggled, trying to follow him.

"Marcus, please. I . . . I love ye so. I—"

His head came up. "What did you say?"

"I love ye, Marcus. I do. I—"

"*Gods, Gwen.*" Something inside him seemed to snap; he surged forward so violently that Gwen's head smacked against the tree trunk. With an oath he slipped one arm behind her head, another behind her hips, cushioning her body as he rammed himself inside her.

Her world exploded, her body convulsing as pure pleasure took possession of every fiber of her being. She clutched Marcus's head as he rode her into the storm and beyond. Incredibly, once the first wave receded, a second, higher wave rose.

She clung to him. She felt his teeth on her shoulder, the small burst of pain pushing her higher. Then her climax took her, hard and fast and stunning.

This time he came with her, her name a prayer on his lips.

Hefin landed in a flurry of beating feathers.

Rhys looked up from the meager campfire he'd built to chase off the dawn chill while Trevor occupied himself with a search for clean water.

He frowned at the merlin. "About time ye showed yourself."

The bird lifted its wings and squawked, its head cocking first to one side, than the other. Rhys's gaze narrowed. Hefin was rarely so agitated.

"What have ye seen, little one?" He closed his eyes and extended his senses, aligning himself with the bird's primitive brain. An image coalesced in his mind. A silver wolf, running in moonlight.

Rhys jumped to his feet. *Gwen.*

"Where?" He sent the thought into Hefin's mind.

The dream image continued. The silver wolf came to a sudden halt. Its nose came up, sniffing the air. There was a shifting of light. The shadow of a man lingered in the wood, watching.

Marcus Aquila.

A twig snapped. The image shattered. Rhys started, swinging toward the disturbance. Trevor stood a short distance away, waterskin in hand, his countenance filled with dismay.

"I've interfered with your magic."

"Aye," Rhys said shortly. He was already throwing handfuls of dirt on the fire. "But I've seen enough." He described his vision to Trevor, revealing Gwen's link to the wolf's Deep Magic in terse sentences. A shocking confession, clumsily made, but Trevor absorbed the information silently, in his usual stoic manner.

"Gwen is a shifter?" was all he asked.

"Aye. And I . . . I am as well. My form is that of a merlin."

If Trevor was surprised by this further admission, he gave no indication of it. "And ye know, now, where she is? Hefin has seen her?"

"Aye," Rhys said. "My sister is in Isca. With . . . with Marcus Aquila."

Chapter Sixteen

$\mathcal{M}$arcus woke with Gwen's naked body wrapped around him. The furnace had burned itself out. A glance at the smithy window told him dawn was long past. Last night, their explosive lovemaking had given way to a bitter poignancy that left Marcus feeling as though his heart had been scooped out of his chest. In its place was a hollow ache that worsened with each passing moment.

Gwen had wanted to set out for Avalon before dawn—alone. Marcus had refused; she had argued. In the end, it had been sheer exhaustion more than persuasive rhetoric that had conquered her. Her shifting had left her pale and drained. She'd barely been able to stand, let alone travel.

She lay, for now, pliant and peaceful in his arms. He let the soft, even rhythm of her breathing work its way into his soul. Her expression was untroubled; in sleep she seemed much younger than her twenty-five years. He wanted to keep her here always, sheltered by his body, safe from the worry and responsibilities that weighed upon her soul.

She should not be so burdened. Resentment simmered in his chest. Cyric, Rhys, and the rest of the Druids valued Gwen only for her magic and her role in continuing the line of their Lady. They knew nothing of her heart, her courage, her abiding love for them. He was sure she would not hesitate to sacrifice her life for Avalon. The Druids dismissed that gift as their due.

She deserved so much more.

His arms tightened. She stirred, but did not awaken. She snuggled more securely into the crook of his arm, her palm spread possessively on his chest. He could feel the imprint of each finger.

She had said that she loved him. *Loved* him. And yet, she was still determined to leave.

The day was advancing; he could not hide here with Gwen much longer. But he could snatch a few more peaceful moments before they began arguing about the journey to Avalon. She did not want him to accompany her, but it didn't matter; he would not let her go alone. Unwilling to hasten the departure, he closed his eyes. They flew open a moment later when a sharp knock sounded on the smithy door.

"Marcus?"

Breena. Inwardly, he groaned. Gwen, still sleeping, turned her face into his chest.

"Marcus, are you in there? Is Gwen? Please answer."

The latch on the door rattled. Thank the gods he'd had the presence of mind to lock it. If he didn't answer, maybe she'd take the hint and go away.

She didn't. She pounded on the door. "Marcus! Answer me!"

Her tone had taken on a hint of desperation. Something was wrong. Gently, he disentangled himself from Gwen's arms. She must have been even more exhausted than he realized, because she rolled onto her stomach without opening her eyes. He shoved his legs into his *braccas*. He reached the door just as Breena's pounding started again.

"I'm here, Bree," he called. "Settle down." He pulled the door open.

"Marcus! What took you so long?"

"I—"

He stopped abruptly. Breena was not alone. Rhys, accompanied by a tall, blond-bearded Celt, stood behind her.

"Rhys," he said, letting his voice rise. He only hoped Gwen was awake enough to heed his warning. "Well met. Have you only just arrived?"

"Aye." Rhys's gray eyes, unnervingly like Gwen's, took in Marcus's half-dressed state. His expression hardened.

"Marcus," Breena said, "is Gwen with you? Rhys needs to—"

"Who is your companion, Rhys?" Marcus's interruption earned him a glare from Breena. He ignored it; his gaze was fixed on the bearded giant hovering at Rhys's elbow. His clothing was simple—fur vest, *braccas,* and boots of rough-cured animal skin. His dark blond hair, drawn back in a tight queue, nearly reached his waist. A tarnished silver torc encircled his neck. He said nothing.

Marcus had a sudden, unwelcome premonition as to his identity.

"This is . . ." Rhys paused, his gaze flicking past Marcus, then returning to his face. "A friend."

"Trevor," Marcus said.

Surprise flashed across Rhys's face. "Aye."

Trevor's expression did not change.

How Marcus managed to keep his own expression impassive, he did not know. His fingers curled into fists; a slow burn began in his gut. Rhys and Cyric expected Gwen to *marry* this barbarian behemoth? And Gwen herself was—what had she said? *Not unwilling.* The thought made him ill.

He resisted the urge to glance in the direction of the wooden screen. She was his. His *mate.* He had marked her with his teeth, taken her maidenhood, earned her love. He would not surrender her to any man, Druid or no. His instinct to shield Gwen from embarrassment warred with the wholly masculine impulse to strike down the screen and assert his claim.

Somehow, civility reigned over passion. "Trevor," he said. "Well met." He took a step toward the door, intending to remove his unwanted guests from the smithy while Gwen's good sense kept her safely hidden behind the screen.

Unfortunately, Gwen's good sense had fled.

She emerged from behind the screen, her hastily donned tunic dirty and rumpled. Her feet were bare, her hair hung in wild, erotic disarray. Her lips were swollen from his kisses. A bite mark from their forest encounter stood out against the pale skin of her neck.

Breena's gasp merged with Rhys's muttered curse.

A rush of pure masculine triumph swept over Marcus. There could be only one reason Gwen would appear like this before Rhys and Trevor. She was declaring herself bound to Marcus.

"Gwen." Rhys's tone held a wealth of anger and disappointment.

Marcus's resentment intensified. He was barely aware

of his body moving, until he found himself at Gwen's side. His arm encircled her waist.

Gwen did not look at him. Nor did she look at Trevor. Her gaze was wholly for Rhys. "Why are ye here? What of the mists?"

"I could ask ye the same, sister." He swallowed hard, his throat working.

"I haven't heard ye in my mind for days. Now ye and Strabo are both here in Isca. What does that mean for Avalon?"

"Soon after Strabo rode out, Cyric's affliction vanished, and he is once again holding the mists in place. Until ye return. Then he will hand the duty to ye, Gwen. He says it is time."

"That's not going to—" Marcus began.

Rhys cut him off. "Cyric commanded me to find ye. And so I have. Here, warming Marcus Aquila's bed like a whore."

Breena made a choking sound. Marcus's vision went red. Angrily, he angled his body between Gwen and her brother. "Take care what you say, Rhys. I will not tolerate any disrespect to Gwen."

It was as if he'd never spoken. "Rhys," Gwen said softly, stepping around Marcus. "Ye do not understand—"

"I understand more than I want to. Ye've disobeyed Cyric, and ye've called the wolf."

"Ah, and ye are the perfect grandson, are ye not? Ye are a hypocrite, Rhys! Ye've called Deep Magic yourself, without Cyric's knowledge."

Guilt flashed across Rhys's face. "Marcus told ye."

"Aye. Did ye think he would not?"

"I called the merlin only once. To save ye."

Tears glistened in Gwen's eyes. "Ye might have helped me even more if ye'd been truthful about it afterward."

"I . . . ye are right, of course." Rhys's gaze flicked to Marcus, then back to Gwen. "We . . . will speak of it later, when we're alone. Right now . . . just gather your belongings. We must return to Avalon at once."

Gwen locked gazes with her brother. For several heart-beats, they just stared at each other. Then Gwen's shoulders slumped slightly, and she nodded once. Marcus watched, stunned, as she disappeared behind the screen.

She could not truly be meaning to leave. Not after what they'd shared. Not after she'd returned his words of love. No. It was not possible.

He swung back to Rhys. "Gwen is not going anywhere. She's staying here, with me."

"What? Ye think since ye've broken her maidenhead, ye have the right to command her?"

"I have that right far more than you do. Gwen is—"

Pain exploded as Rhys's fist cracked against Marcus's jaw. *Hades*, he hadn't even seen the blow coming. His head whipped around. He staggered and nearly fell.

Breena screamed. Trevor broke his silence to utter a curse, and Gwen rushed from behind the screen. Marcus barely registered any of it. His every sense, his every thought, exploded in a blinding rush of rage.

"You self-righteous pig!"

He launched himself at Rhys. Wrapping his arms around Rhys's torso, he heaved him into the air before throwing him to the ground. Rhys grabbed Marcus's shirt with both hands, pulling him down, too. Marcus fell hard and rolled, slamming Rhys into the wooden bench near the door. The heavy piece teetered, then toppled with a crash.

Marcus tried to use his greater weight to shove Rhys

onto his back. Rhys's quick reaction prevented it. He slammed a fist into Marcus's gut.

"Ye *swine*. Could ye not keep your cock in your pants? She was a maid! Unused to men like ye."

Marcus landed a blow to Rhys's left jaw. "Yes, unused to men who treat her with respect!" Dodging Rhys's return jab, he managed a glancing blow to Rhys's ear. "Unused to men who care about her happiness!" His hands reached for Rhys's neck. "Unused to—"

Marcus gagged as a large arm was wrapped around him from behind, closing his windpipe. He ducked his chin and clawed at the beefy arm. He succeeded in moving it only enough to rasp a thin breath of air.

"Enough." Trevor's quiet voice held not a trace of anger.

The man's unnerving calm was more effective than any impassioned command might have been. Marcus wrenched himself out of the giant's grip and jumped to his feet.

Breena had gone deathly pale, her attention suspended between Marcus and Rhys, as if uncertain which man deserved her loyalty. Marcus felt his sister's indecision like a blow.

Gwen, however, did not look at Rhys at all. Nor at Trevor. She came to Marcus. Her fingers slid over his bruised jaw. He winced. She swung about and glowered at Rhys. The Druid's eye was nearly swollen shut, Marcus noted smugly.

"Ye are a beast," Gwen told her twin.

"Me?" Rhys's jaw dropped. "He threw me down!"

"I would not have," Marcus growled, "if you hadn't hurled the basest of insults at the woman who is to be my wife."

"Wife?" Rhys spit out a curse. "Are ye insane? Gwen is promised to Trevor. Though why he should want her now, after watching her come from another man's bed—"

Marcus made a sound deep in his throat and made to launch himself at Rhys again. Trevor's hand clamped down on his shoulder, holding him back.

Gwen spoke, her voice calm. "I have not promised myself to Trevor."

"But ye did promise to guard Avalon," her brother replied. "And to shun Deep Magic."

"Ye of all people have no right to lecture me about Deep Magic!"

"Gwen." Rhys's voice vibrated. "Does Marcus speak truly? Do ye intend to stay here and become his wife?"

The air in Marcus's lungs stalled as he waited for Gwen's reply. She was standing so close, he could have reached out and touched her. He did not.

A tear slipped down Gwen's cheek. Something inside Marcus broke. He sought her gaze, but she would not look at him.

"You could be carrying my child," he said baldly.

Rhys started. "*Gods.* I pray she is not."

Marcus ignored him. "Gwen. Look at me. Please."

When she did, her tears fell faster.

"Gwen, I love you. I'll give you my life, my home, my children. Everything I have and everything I am." When she didn't answer, he added simply, "You'd be happy here. I would make sure of it."

"It would be false happiness, Marcus."

"No, it—"

"Gwen speaks truly," Rhys cut in. "Her duty lies on Avalon." He turned to his sister. "Let this be the last of your resistance to Cyric's will. This disappearance . . .

running here to some fantasy ye know ye cannot keep . . . it was not worthy of ye, Gwen."

"You are an ass," Marcus interjected. "What right do you have to judge her? You don't even know why she came here."

"To indulge her whim of seeing ye again. To—"

"She came here out of love and loyalty to Avalon. To create a weapon that can stand against Strabo's Deep Magic. Though I begin to wonder if Avalon deserves such a gift."

Rhys looked as though he would reply, until Trevor silenced him with a frown. The big man looked at Gwen. "There is an unusual power here, lass. In this room. What is it?"

Rhys's eyes turned to Gwen. "Aye, I feel it now as well. Gwen, what have ye done?"

"I—" Gwen opened her mouth, then closed it. Her shoulders tensed; Marcus could feel the agitation thrumming through her body. She eased from his side, her chin rising as she strode to his worktable like a soldier marching to battle.

She lifted the sword, one hand on the hilt, the other supporting the scabbard.

"I came to Isca for one purpose: to beg Marcus to forge a sword for Avalon. A weapon of magic that will stand against our darkest enemies." With a slow, deliberate stroke, she slid the shining blade from its sheath.

"This is the blade he created. Crafted from bright iron. Marcus calls it Exchalybur."

Rhys stared at the weapon. Briefly, he closed his eyes. When they snapped open an instant later, Marcus was taken aback by the expression of stunned rage in them.

"Gwen." Rhys's voice vibrated with fury. "This time ye have truly gone too far."

"Is Avalon's very survival too far, Rhys? For that is what's at stake."

Rhys uttered the foulest oath Marcus had ever heard fall from his friend's lips.

"You're angry about this?" Marcus demanded. He could not believe it. "That Gwen bound Light to a sword for the defense of Avalon?"

"Is that what she told ye this is? A weapon of defense? Of Light magic?" Rhys sent Gwen a withering look. "'Tis not true. This sword is bound to Deep Magic."

Marcus's gaze shot to Gwen. "Is that true?"

She bit her lip. "Aye."

He stared at the weapon. "Why didn't you tell me that's what you intended?"

"If I had, would ye have forged it?"

"I—" He felt as if he'd been punched in the gut. "No. Of course not."

"Then ye have your answer."

Her expression became carefully blank. At the same time, her shoulders squared as she drew herself up to her full height. Despite the lines of fatigue about her eyes and mouth, despite her tangled hair and frayed tunic, she had the air of a queen.

She slid the sword back into its sheath, but did not release her grip on it as she turned to Rhys and Trevor. "I felt the danger to Avalon even before Strabo's Dark spells seeped into the mist. I knew from the start that Light alone would not turn him away."

"And so ye thought to forge a sword of Deep Magic?" The question, surprisingly, came from Trevor.

"I saw the sword in a dream."

"A dream that might have been sent by Strabo," Rhys said.

"Nay. The dream came from the Lady."

"How can ye be sure?"

"Because I saw her. I felt her power. Can ye nay trust me, Rhys? Strabo is sure to return to Avalon. When he does, we must be ready to counter his Deep Magic with our own. Exchalybur is our only hope."

"Hope? What hope is that?" Rhys's fingers flexed. "Deep Magic will destroy us. Ye know that as well as I."

"I do not know it. I only know Cyric says it will."

"Do ye think he lies? Have ye forgotten the terror of Blodwen's Deep Magic so quickly? Or do ye, perhaps, nurture a remnant of our cousin's folly in your own soul?"

A tightening of her mouth was Gwen's only reaction to Rhys's barb. "The Deep Magic I've bound to this sword is entwined with Light. It will not turn against us."

"Ye cannot be sure of that. This sword—it could be a far greater danger to Avalon than any magic Strabo sends against us. It must be destroyed. Now."

"Nay. I *will* take it to Avalon, Rhys."

"And what do ye think Cyric and the Elders will say? Or any of the Druids? Gwen, the Druids of Avalon are keepers of the Light! Not men and women who grasp at the forbidden power of the gods. That sword must be melted down and buried in as deep a hole as can be dug."

"I'll not allow that. Cyric chose me as Avalon's next Guardian, Rhys. Not ye. I've often wondered at the reason. Perhaps it was because he knew I was the one with the courage to disobey him when the need turned dire."

Marcus stood to one side, watching the exchange between the siblings as if through a haze. Had he really thought Gwen would abandon Avalon out of love for him? She seemed to have forgotten he was even in the room.

"Ye have felt Strabo's power," Gwen went on. "Ye know Light alone cannot stand against him. What would ye have the Druids do? Flee?"

Rhys hesitated. Gwen did not relent. Angling the hilt of the sword toward her brother, she offered him the weapon. From the look on his face, she might have been presenting him a poisonous snake.

"Take it, Rhys. Once ye hold it, ye will understand."

Rhys's hand closed reluctantly around the sword's hilt. Marcus imagined the blade glowed brighter at his touch, then dismissed the notion as a trick of the light. Rhys closed his eyes and remained silent for a long moment.

When he opened his eyes, his expression was no longer so confident. "The Light is strong within the blade. But Deep Magic lies within it. We cannot be certain it will not turn on us."

Gwen's voice was soft. "Have ye ever considered, Rhys, that uncertainty is part of the test the Great Mother has set for her children?"

Rhys only shook his head.

"When ye took the form of a merlin," Gwen asked her twin softly. "How did ye feel?"

Color rose to Rhys's cheeks. "Happy," he admitted bitterly. "Free. When I took wing, I felt I had found the best part of me. It should not have felt so . . . right."

" 'Tis the same when I am the wolf. I felt that joy when Marcus and I forged the Lady's sword. It holds the same force that's inside us, Rhys. No matter what Cyric would have us do, we cannot deny what we are."

"No mortal can command Deep Magic. Only a god can."

"Then we must serve the Great Mother, and the Lady, and hope that is enough. Support me in this, Rhys. I beg of ye. Stand by me when I present the sword to Cyric and the Elders. Without this sword, without Deep Magic, we may as well scatter like dust before Strabo's ill wind."

Indecision played across Rhys's face. At last, he sighed and handed the sword, still sheathed, back to Gwen. "All right. Bring the sword to Avalon. And I will stand at your side when ye present it to Cyric and the Elders, if ye abide by Cyric's decision whether to use the sword or destroy it."

"What? Rhys, ye cannot—"

A muscle worked in Rhys's throat. "Ye must agree to this condition, Gwen. Or I will see that weapon destroyed before it gets anywhere near Avalon."

She hesitated, then nodded once.

"That is not all. Ye must also give Trevor the promise of your hand. Now. Before we leave."

Gwen's gaze darted to Trevor. "But . . . he cannot still be willing to have me, not after . . ." Her words trailed off.

Trevor, brawny arms crossed over his massive chest, regarded Gwen seriously. "I am willing."

Marcus itched to smash his fist into the giant's stolid face. "Gwen, you cannot marry this man!"

She made no answer.

"Gwen," he said more loudly, grabbing her and spinning her around to face him. She gripped the sword tightly, holding it upright between them.

He placed his hands on her shoulders and spoke in a low, urgent voice. "Gwen. This isn't right. You cannot marry Trevor! Not when you love me. And if you're willing to abide by Cyric's judgment, you don't need to return to Avalon at all. Rhys and Trevor can take the sword to Cyric, and if he agrees, one of them can wield it in your place. Rhys can take your place as Guardian. It's what he wants, as fiercely as you want to be free. Why shouldn't you both live as you wish?"

A small, sad smile touched Gwen's lips. "That cannot be, Marcus. I am bound to Deep Magic. How can I live my life here in your Roman world? I cannot, as much as I may want to. I belong to Avalon."

"In another man's bed."

She flinched. "Trevor is a fine man."

He went cold inside. "So you've said."

He felt Trevor's eyes upon him. The giant's expression was impassive, but he made no move to remove Marcus's hands from his would-be betrothed. The Druid's lack of emotion made Marcus's stomach turn. The thought of Gwen giving herself to this emotionless giant sickened him. Again he was struck with the urge to smash his fist into the man's rigid jaw.

He settled for a more subtle taunt. Jerking Gwen's body toward him, he covered her mouth with his, thrusting his tongue deep. His hands moved on Gwen's body, molding her breasts, her hips, her buttocks. The sword's hilt pressed between.

He all but assaulted her with his frustration and hurt. She seemed to understand, because she made a small sound in the back of her throat and kissed him back. All the while, Marcus waited for the giant's big hand to pull him up by the scruff of his neck and throw him against the wall.

Trevor was silent. The man had no more emotion than a rock.

Finally, Marcus tore himself away, panting. Gwen's eyes were huge in her face. Tears streamed down her face, unheeded.

"Stay with me," he begged.

She closed her eyes and shook her head. "'Tis a dream that can never be."

He stepped back. Without a glance at Rhys or Trevor, he turned on his heel and left the smithy.

Chapter Seventeen

"You have to eat *something*, Rhys."

Breena set her tray down on the table. Rhys looked horrible. His complexion was waxen, his eyes ringed with fatigue. He spoke in monosyllables, a sharp contrast to his usual affability. She had never seen him like this—so tired and so unsure of himself.

She'd coaxed him back to the main house. His large, silent companion, Trevor, had gone to the kitchen to see about provisions for the journey back to Avalon. Gwen was still in the smithy, and Marcus—Breena did not know where Marcus was. He'd taken a horse from the stables and had not told Linus where he was going nor when he would return.

"Where is Rhiannon?" Rhys asked as she set a mug of *cervesia* before him.

"Gone to visit a friend who is also with child. Father took her early this morning."

"Ah." He lifted the mug and drank.

She could not tear her eyes from him. Even when tired and troubled, he was the most beautiful man she had ever seen. His long legs stretched under the table. His arms and shoulders were not as bulky as Marcus's, but lean, wiry strength suited him. His white-blond hair was mussed, and his beard was longer than she had ever seen it. He looked more like a wild Celt now than he ever had. Breena was startled to find that she found his roughness appealing.

She'd watched the scene in the smithy with wide, disbelieving eyes. Rhys had been embarrassed for her, she thought, when Gwen had emerged from Marcus's bed, but later, he seemed to forget she was even there, until the shouting was over and Marcus had stormed out.

She set a plate of savory roasted lamb and fresh bread, baked with herbs, in front of him. His stomach growled audibly. She smiled, and he sent her a rueful look.

She took the seat beside him. "You look like you've just come out of Hades. How long has it been since you've slept?"

He rubbed his eyes. "Two days," he admitted. "And even longer since any sleep I've had has been untroubled. Strabo's dreams . . ."

"You must rest here before you go back to Avalon."

"There is no time."

"There will be even less if Trevor has to carry you."

Rhys frowned into his cup. "I have to get Gwen away from this place."

"Away from Marcus, you mean."

He leaned back in his chair and sighed. "Aye. Away from Marcus."

"Is it . . . is it so bad that they have found each other? Marcus loves Gwen. He would be a good husband to her."

"Perhaps. But Gwen is not free to choose."

"She's been happy here. She's not happy, I think, on Avalon."

His expression became shuttered. "Gwen and I . . . our lives are not our own. Our paths were chosen long before we were born. We have duties that have nothing to do with happiness."

"Are you saying you aren't happy, either?" She had never considered the possibility. For the whole of Breena's life, whenever Rhys was visiting, he'd always been ready with a jest and a smile for her.

"My happiness is hardly relevant, Bree. The Great Mother, through my grandfather's visions, has given me a task. I complete it as best I can."

"But what if . . . what would you do if you couldn't tell what the Great Mother wanted you to do? What if her message were clouded?"

"What do ye mean?" Understanding slowly dawned in his eyes. "Ye speak of yourself. Your visions. Have they worsened?"

Breena twisted her fingers in her lap. "They did, for a time, until Gwen taught me how to stop them."

"*Stop* them?" Rhys's head jerked up. "Gwen taught ye to stop your visions?"

She nodded.

"Only a spell of Deep Magic could halt a true vision." He cursed. "My sister has no respect at all for Cyric's teachings."

"She only did it because I was in such pain—and choking! One night . . . one night, I almost died!"

"*What?*" He was on his feet, gripping her upper arms. "What happened? Tell me."

Briefly, Breena recounted her ordeal. "If Gwen had not come in time, I would have died! She only taught me to stop the visions so it wouldn't happen again.

And . . . nothing bad has come from the spells she taught me."

"Except that your visions have stopped."

"I don't consider that a bad thing."

"And the Great Mother's message? What of that, Bree?"

"I couldn't see what it was, in any case! Everything was silent, and draped in silver."

"When you were ready to understand, the vision would have cleared. Gwen should not have interfered."

His fingers bit into her flesh. "You're hurting me, Rhys."

He looked down at his hands as if he'd forgotten he'd taken hold of her arms. Abruptly, he let go, his scowl deepening. "My apologies."

Breena rubbed her arm. "It's all right."

He turned and paced toward the hearth, his meal forgotten. "Gwen should not have done this. If your need was so urgent, she should have brought ye to Avalon, to gain the wisdom of the Elders and the protection of the sacred isle."

"With Legate Strabo assaulting the mist? My parents and Marcus would never have agreed to let me travel into such danger." She paused. "Would you?"

He pressed two fingers to his temples and winced. "I do not know."

"Does your head hurt?"

"Aye," he said after a moment.

His pallor alarmed her. "You look ready to drop from exhaustion. I know you and Trevor want to leave soon, but how can you travel without rest? You have to sleep, if only for a few hours."

She thought he would protest, but after a moment he looked up and nodded.

"Aye. But two hours only, and no more."

* * *

The bed was soft. The closed shutters cast the room in gloom. Sleep descended upon Rhys almost immediately. And with it, came another dream . . .

Rhys crouched at the edge of the grandmother elm's drooping branches, peering into the space formed by the curtain of leaves. He and Gwen had stopped coming here to play ever since they'd seen Mama with . . . him.

Mama and her centurion were here again, now. He caught a glimpse of Mama's white-blond hair and the soldier's red cape. The Roman's voice was low and urgent.

"Tonight, Tamar. It must be tonight. I've received my orders. I'm to leave at dawn."

"But the children . . . they've only just lost their father . . ."

The soldier gave a harsh laugh. "No doubt they will be grateful to me for that someday."

"But . . . what of my father?"

"Tell him you mean to marry again. He will understand."

"Nay. He will not. You are Roman, and we are Celts. Druids."

"I am not so different, Tamar. You have shown me that. My magic may be as powerful as Cyric's."

"It will not matter to him. I am a Daughter of the Lady, and Gwen is as well. My father will not allow us to leave Britain."

"I do not care. I only care that you believe in me. In us."

"But, Titus—Egypt? 'Tis so far away. How can I carry my children to a place so unlike their home? There will be sand and heat and wind . . ."

Rhys felt for Gwen's hand. She squeezed his fingers tightly.

"Rhys and Gwen will be happy there," the soldier

said. "It will not be forever, I promise you. When I am able, I will bring you back to Britain." A pause, then, "Tamar. Tell me you will come with me."

"Oh, Titus—"

"Tamar!" Grandfather's voice called from the road behind Rhys and Gwen, sharp and angry. "Tamar! Where are ye? Answer me, lass!"

The scene dissolved into darkness, but the dream did not end. Rhys was running now, but slowly, as if his feet were stuck in mud. He heard a man's shout, a woman's terrified scream.

A nauseating roll of power shook the ground. Rhys stood paralyzed, his chest heaving with the effort of drawing breath. Up ahead, in the darkness, shone blue-black light.

Deep Magic, pulsing like life. Like death. Rhys wanted to run away. He couldn't move. He felt for Gwen with his mind.

"Gwen?"

"Rhys! Where are ye?" She sounded as terrified as he felt.

"I . . . don't know. Where are you?"

If there was an answer, he didn't hear it. A deep rumble shook the ground. The next instant, the blue-black orb exploded in a shower of sparks.

"Rhys!" Gwen was beside him, her grip on his arm painful. She hauled him to his feet. "Come quick!"

She was sobbing. It scared him; Gwen never cried. He clung to her as she pulled him after her. He could see more clearly now. They were on the path leading to the river.

"What happened?"

"The soldier. The one who Mama . . ." She bit her lip. "Something happened. Something bad."

279

"Where?"

"Under the grandmother elm."

They lunged down the hill toward the tree, skidding to a stop when a figure emerged from behind the charred branches that had once been a green, leafy curtain.

Grandfather, carrying Mama. Her body was limp, her dangling arm rocking with every heavy step Grandfather took. Tears ran down Grandfather's face. Rhys's whole body went cold.

Nausea churned his stomach.

"She's dead, Gwen. Mama is dead."

Rhys sat bolt upright in bed, gasping. Strabo. *Strabo* had been his mother's lover.

He'd seen the legate's face clearly in his dream. The man had been eighteen years younger, but his identity was unmistakable.

Rhys thought he might be ill. His shirt was little more than a sweaty rag plastered to his body. The contact was unbearable. He tore at it, ripping the wool as he stripped the garment over his head.

He rose and paced the tiled floor, covering the distance from one smooth wall to the other, then moving to the window to throw open the shutters. His stomach was in knots, the nightmare images shifting sickeningly. The fresh air did little good. He did not want to remember.

But now that he did, there was no undoing it. Mama had loved the Roman; she'd helped him discover the magic within him. Strabo had wanted Mama to accompany him to a posting in Egypt. Mama had refused, and he'd become enraged. Magic had exploded. Deep Magic. When it cleared, Mama was dead.

Now, eighteen years later, Strabo was the commander of the Second Legion, in the town where he'd killed Rhys's mother. He must have seen Rhys on one of Rhys's many trips to Isca. Rhys's age, his unusual white-blond hair, his gray eyes, his features and height—all were clues to his parentage. Strabo must have suspected the itinerant minstrel was Tamar's son. And when he had encountered Gwen near Avalon— well, it was apparent to anyone with eyes that she was Rhys's twin. But why would Strabo pursue the children of his Celt lover so many years after her murder?

Rhys's nausea intensified. Bile seared a path up his throat. Quickly, he crossed to the washbasin, bracing himself over it on rigid arms. He wanted to call Gwen in his mind, to tell her what he'd dreamed and ask if she remembered, too. His pride would not let him. He was a man. He did not cling to his sister's skirts.

He started trembling, cold sweat beading on his brow. His stomach heaved, emptying its contents into the washbasin. At the exact same moment, the door behind him creaked open. He gripped the edge of the washstand, too dizzy to lift his head, or even speak to his unwelcome visitor.

"Rhys! You're ill!" Breena's soft footsteps flew across the room. She touched his shoulder, his brow.

Great Mother. Now his agony was complete.

He focused all his will on drawing his next breath. Then, hoping his head would allow it, he slowly straightened and turned.

Breena, practical soul that she was, was already busy. She located a clean linen towel and dampened it with water from the washstand's pitcher. She offered it to him; he took it and mopped his face. Still breathing hard, he watched her pour a cup of watered wine from a second pitcher on a sideboard.

She offered it to him. He took it and drained it, then surrendered the empty cup. "My thanks."

Her blue eyes were soft with concern. "You're very pale, Rhys."

"I'm fine." He took a step, then, afraid his stomach would heave again, sat down on the edge of the bed.

A mistake, because Breena sat down next to him, far too close. She smelled faintly of perfume from her bath. Not rose or lavender, though. Breena shunned the lighter floral scents, preferring earthier musks and spices. *Great Mother.* This was more than any man could be expected to bear.

He was aware of a choking wave of self-loathing. This was Breena, who not long ago had been a sticky-faced little lass he'd tickle and swing over his head. He used to love her squeal of glee when he teased her. She was as much a sister to him as Gwen—and a much younger one, at that. She was an innocent, barely more than a lass, though many girls married at her age. But Breena was destined for a life on Avalon, while he . . . was not. He could not be attracted to her.

And yet, he was.

He covered his face with his hands and groaned.

Which only made Breena more anxious. She leaned into him, her breast pressing against his arm as she laid a cool hand on his forehead. "Are you going to be sick again? Do you want me to bring the basin?"

"Nay," he said quickly, shifting away from her on the bed. He bent one knee to hide his reaction to her nearness. "I am well. Truly. It was just . . . a bad reaction to a dream."

She frowned. "I have never known a mere dream to cause anyone to vomit. And I'm sure I've never read about it in Hippocrates's *Book of Prognostics*."

He almost laughed. Breena could not know how re-freshing her bluntness was. In Rhys's experience, few people were brave enough to be so genuine. But Breena . . . since the day he'd met her, when she'd been barely three summers old, she had disarmed him with her honesty.

"Was it truly a dream, Rhys? Or something more? You look as though you've seen the dead." His expression must have changed, because her eyes widened. "*Have* you seen the dead? In a vision?"

"Not precisely. I saw the past." His temple throbbed again; he rubbed it and Breena frowned. "Another of Strabo's spells."

"Then he knows you are here."

"Most likely. I need to leave, soon. Where is Gwen? I need to—" He tried to stand. The sudden movement made the room sway. He sat back down.

"You're unsettled still." Breena fussed over him like a little mama. Or a wife. He blocked off *that* thought the instant it rose.

"I'll be fine in a moment. Go. Find Gwen and Trevor and tell them—"

"You can tell them yourself. I've already awakened Trevor, and he went to find Gwen. You're to meet them in the hearth room. Until then . . . will you tell me what you dreamt that upset you so?" When he did not an-swer, she added, "Please?"

Her clear, blue gaze disarmed him. She was young, yes, but her eyes held the promise of uncommon ma-turity and strength. He found himself wanting to tell her everything, though she was hardly the person he should confide in. Gwen would be a far more logical choice. Or Trevor. And yet, the words tumbled from his lips.

"I dreamt . . . of my mother's death. It was not something I remembered until now. I had thought—"

He broke off as Breena slipped behind him on the mattress and started massaging his shoulders. Belatedly, he realized his shirt was still on the floor. The sensation of her strong fingers on his bare skin was intoxicating.

He went very still.

"You had thought what?" Breena prompted gently.

He struggled to remember their conversation, but for a moment all he could think of were her fingers, kneading and soothing. Then he gathered his wits and shook his head.

"Gwen and I . . . neither of us remember seeing our mother die. Cyric never spoke of it; Mared and Padrig would not answer any of our questions. We knew she was killed by a Roman soldier, a man she'd taken as a lover. In my dream . . . Gwen and I were there, just before Mama's death. I saw her lover's face. It was Strabo."

Her hands stilled. "But how could that be?"

"He was a centurion eighteen years ago. Unknown to him, he had magic. Mama helped him discover his power. He wanted her to accompany him to Egypt, but she refused. He became enraged and killed her with the same magic she had helped him discover."

"Oh, Rhys. I'm so sorry." Her fingers started working on his rigid muscles again. She put all her weight into loosening a particularly tight knot. He let out a gasp, then a groan of deep pleasure. He felt her body go quiet.

"Lean forward," she whispered.

Some subtle shift had occurred in their rapport. It had become much more intimate than anything he'd shared with Breena before. It was wrong—he should not be sitting half naked, taking a fierce and guilty pleasure in her touch. She was too young, too innocent. Even if she were older, and his life were not that of a homeless wanderer, he did not have the luxury of time. He should be gone, already on the road to Avalon with Trevor and his sister.

But he made no move to rise.

Instead, he did as she asked. He leaned forward, propping his elbows on his knees and letting his hands dangle between them. She went up on her knees behind him, pressing into him more deeply, using the weight of her body as leverage. He closed his eyes as her warm palms covered his shoulders. Her thumbs kneaded the tight muscles on either side of his neck.

She did not speak—sensing, perhaps, that he wanted silence. That was another quality that drew him to Breena. She had the uncanny knack of knowing just what he needed, and providing it.

Her soft hands urged his upper body toward the mattress. "Lie down."

Gods.

"That's not a good idea," he replied shakily.

"You're wrong, Rhys." Her voice dipped so low he had to strain to hear it. "And . . . I think it's time I showed you just how wrong you are."

Her lips touched his neck, just below his earlobe.

Pure lust spiraled through his body. Her kiss felt like a brand on his skin. Her teeth, when they caught his earlobe and nibbled, sent a rush of fire to his groin. And when her tongue swirled into the shell of his ear . . .

Great Mother. How did she know to do such things?

His mind reeled with shock as she licked a wet path along his jaw. She shifted onto his lap and entwined her arms around his neck. He was stunned. Paralyzed.

If the entire Second Legion had chosen that instant to pound down the door, demanding his head on a spear, he could not have moved.

"Rhys."

She brought a heady breathlessness to his name. Unbidden, he began to harden. She melted against him with a sigh. Sanity slammed back into his brain; wrenching his mouth from hers, he gripped her shoulders and pushed her back. Blue eyes, filled with an adulation he absolutely did not deserve, blinked up at him.

He tried to keep his voice as gentle as possible, but his words came out rough. "Breena. What is this?"

"I love you, Rhys." She shut her eyes briefly. "There. I've said it."

"You don't mean that," he said hoarsely.

"Oh, but I do! I've always loved you!"

He swallowed around the lump in his throat. "Aye, Bree, but not like this. Ye love me as a sister loves a brother. Like ye love Marcus."

"No." She shook her head for emphasis. "*Never* like that. Not even when I was small. I always knew you were different. That you would marry me someday."

"You cannot be serious." A note of desperation crept into his voice. "It cannot be like that between us. I am fond of ye, 'tis true—"

"Fond? Is *that* what you call it? Odd, it felt more like—"

He launched himself off the bed, all but throwing her across the room. She stumbled and fell, landing with a sharp thump on the floor. Rhys caught a glimpse of the stunned hurt in her eyes before he turned his back to her.

He fled to the opposite corner of the room, shame obliterating every trace of desire. He schooled his features into a blank mask and pivoted.

Breena stared up at him from the floor, having made no effort to pick herself up. Crossing his arms, he stood looking down at her with what he hoped was an expression of amused condescension.

Her eyes filled with tears, making them bluer. "Rhys."

"Get up, Breena. What could ye have been thinking, to shame yourself so?"

She scrambled to her feet, choking on a sob. "I . . . I thought you'd be pleased—"

"*Pleased?* That ye would throw yourself at me?"

"Yes. And you *were* pleased, at first. You wanted me." *Gods, how would he survive this?*

"Breena, any man would respond so, to any woman. It means nothing. When you are grown, ye will understand."

Her chin came up, her lips thinning with anger as her tears abated. Good. He preferred her angry to sobbing. At least, he thought he did.

"I *am* grown. I am nearly fifteen. Many girls my age are already married!"

"Ye know as well as I do that your father will not allow ye to marry for several years yet."

"He would not object to *you*, Rhys. I've loved you forever, and I would make you a good wife."

He felt a tugging sensation in the vicinity of his heart, but refused to be swayed by it. He let his tone grow harsh. "Put this fantasy out of your head. I am not the man for ye. I am too old, for one thing."

"You are only five-and-twenty!"

"And ye are fourteen, and like a little sister to me."

"You wouldn't kiss a sister the way you just kissed me."

His throat nearly closed. "Breena. I have no home, and seldom stay in one town or village for more than a fortnight. I travel long and hard, sleep in the forest, or someone's barn, or, if I am very lucky, on the floor before a stranger's hearth. It is not a life into which I would bring a wife, even one who is accustomed to hardship, as you are not."

"I . . . don't care." But her voice wavered.

Thank the Goddess, her pouting expression reminded him of the child she'd been, rather than the woman she was rapidly becoming. He seized on her uncertainty. He summoned just the right tone—patronizing, with a large dose of amusement.

"Ah, but ye do care, Bree. Ye are so young, and have lived all your life in luxury. Ye have no conception of a grown woman's life, especially a woman with no home of her own." He forced a chuckle, because he knew she hated to be laughed at. "Ye are a child yet."

"I am not a child!" She stamped her foot, looking so much like she had when she was a small lass that he would have laughed in truth, if the situation hadn't been so delicate. Aye, he wanted her to abandon her romantic notions, but he didn't want her to hate him.

"Ye dream of marrying me only because I'm familiar, Breena. Ye do not love me. Not really."

"I do."

"Well, I do not love ye. Not that way."

"But—"

"Stop, lass. Before ye shame yourself even more."

"You . . . truly do not want me?"

"As a wife? Nay, I do not. And I never will."

She stared at him, light fading from her beautiful blue eyes even as her spine stiffened and her chin came up. Rhys's chest tightened painfully. He ignored the discomfort. The sooner Bree accepted that her future did not lie with him, the better off she would be.

"Your life is just beginning, Bree. Ye are strong in the

Light, and visited by powerful visions. One day ye will journey to Avalon to find your power. And join with a Druid worthy of being your husband. But that man will not be me. Put the notion from your mind."

She stared at him for a long time, her tears drying on her cheeks, her hands clasped in front of her. The neckline of her tunic had slipped off one shoulder. Rhys kept his expression stern, his gaze fixed on her eyes.

"I understand," she said finally. Her shoulders straightened. "I am sorry to have disturbed you with my childish fantasies."

He gave a brief nod. "I accept your apology. Do not trouble yourself about it. A child is not fully responsible for her actions."

Her eyes widened at this final insult. With a strangled sound, she turned and fled through the door. Rhys strode to the threshold just in time to see Trevor, who was coming up the passageway, stand aside to let her run past.

"What was that about?"

"Ye do not want to know."

Trevor took him at his word. "Have ye seen Gwen, then?"

Rhys frowned. "Breena said she was with ye."

"I went to look for her, aye, but she was not in the smithy. Nor anywhere else, and no one I questioned has seen her." He paused, his expression grave.

"The sword is gone as well."

The elm where Gwen and Rhys had played, where they'd seen Mama with Strabo—where Mama had met her death—was gone.

In its place was a warehouse, used to store goods arriving by boat; extensive docks marked the place where the River Usk ran into an inlet of the sea. Gwen hesitated, considering her path. Rhys and Trevor would surely assume she'd taken the shortest route to Avalon: south to Venta Silurum, across the Sabrina channel by boat, then along the edge of the Mendips until she reached the swamps surrounding Avalon.

But Gwen had no coin to pay a fisherman to take her across the channel. Also, she did not wish to argue again with Rhys. Aye, he'd agreed to see the sword presented to Cyric and the Elders, but it was very likely the Elders would order the sword destroyed. Gwen could not allow that. She would call the sword's Deep Magic herself, once she neared Avalon—alone.

Rhys and Trevor would reach Avalon before her, but that did not matter. When she reached the coast road, she turned east. She'd take the same route home she'd traveled when she'd run to Isca as a wolf: east along the channel, until the inlet narrowed into a river and she was able to cross. Then she would travel south and west into the swamps.

She was not sure if Strabo would know immediately that she had left Isca, but she suspected he might—he'd known enough to appear in her dream. He might, even now, be following her.

Quickly, she put the thought out of her mind and adjusted the sword's belt across her shoulder. The weapon was long; it hung almost to her knees, striking her hip with every step that took her farther from Isca. From Marcus.

Thinking of Marcus made her stomach turn to lead. She hadn't wanted to hurt him, but she knew she had—deeply. But she'd had no choice! She was the only Druid willing to do whatever was necessary to protect Avalon. She couldn't abandon that responsibility.

She'd known from the first that her time with Marcus would be brief. Her fantasy of living in Isca as his wife, was just that—a fantasy. She could not live in the Roman world; magic was the root from which her life had grown. And despite Marcus's confidence that the wolf would never turn on him, she could not be completely sure that was true. The wolf was a creature of Deep Magic. And Deep Magic, ultimately, was out of her control.

Deep Magic. It sang within the bright iron, calling her, urging her to set it free. It reminded her of the wolf. Forging this sword had been a grave risk. Despite the confidence she'd feigned before Rhys and Trevor, Gwen had no way of knowing whether the spells of Light she'd woven into Exchalybur would fully contain the Deep Magic at its heart.

She set a swift pace. The dull no-magic aftermath of the wolf had passed, allowing her to lay spells of confusion in her wake. She did not want Strabo to overtake her until after she had set strong, Deep Magic spells of protection around the sacred isle. When Avalon was cloaked, then she would be free to turn and fight to keep it that way.

Day gave way to night. She did not stop, even when darkness descended. Rhys did not call to her in her mind. That was odd—she had expected to feel his anger as soon as he discovered she was gone. Which he surely had by now. But his voice in her mind was silent, as it had been for days before his arrival.

It was nearly dawn when she sensed she was being followed. She could feel a subtle vibration beneath her feet. The wolf inside her sprang up and held its body completely motionless, absorbing the threat. It raised its snout and sniffed the air.

She rebuffed the beast. If the wolf emerged now, she'd be unable to carry the sword to Avalon. That would be a disaster.

The vibrations resolved into the pounding of horses' hooves. She moved off the road, angling her path towards the darkest part of the woods. She should have kept to the woods from the start, despite the slower pace that would have meant. Too late now. Casting her most potent *not-there* spell around herself, she prayed the rider would pass her by.

He did not. He left the road, closing the distance between them. Gwen slipped deeper into the woods, cast another spell, but her pursuer did not hesitate. Strabo. Could she face him here, so far from Avalon? She would have to. She moved into the shelter of a rocky cove. Reaching up over her shoulder, she grasped the sword's hilt and eased the weapon from its scabbard. Holding it before her, point raised, both hands wrapped around the hilt, she opened herself to its magic. And waited.

He dismounted. His footsteps drew closer. Her fingers tightened on the sword's grip. Light flashed along the blade, from crosspiece to tip, ending in a white streak of lightning. Wind filled her ears. It felt as if her body were expanding, rising. She was ready. She would battle him here.

And then, without warning, the unthinkable happened.

She began to change.

Chapter Eighteen

Gwen?"

Marcus glimpsed a flash of light through the trees. It had to be Gwen—his horse had become increasingly nervous with every step it took. Dismounting, he tethered the fretful animal to a tree and moved toward her.

"Gwen?"

He called louder this time, but no answer came. Forging ahead, he kept his gaze fixed on the flickering glow between the trees. He was almost upon it when a blurred form leaped from the shadows, striking him squarely in the chest. Its weight threw him backward. He landed hard on his back in the dirt.

The silver-gray wolf loomed over him, paws pinning him to the ground, jaws open, teeth bared, ears flattened. Its eyes gleamed with a feral light. Hot breath bathed his exposed neck.

A low, menacing growl sounded in the back of its throat. The beast did not recognize him.

"Gwen . . ." he choked out. "It's me. Marcus."

The wolf stiffened. Marcus locked eyes with the beast and kept his breathing even. A difficult task, when his heart was pounding so madly in his chest, he was sure the wolf could hear.

Did she know who he was? Or had the wolf taken over completely? No. He would not believe that.

He lifted one hand, very slowly. "Gwen. It's all right. I won't hurt you. I would never hurt you. Let me up. Please."

The wolf blinked once, then cocked its head as if considering his words. Its ears rose.

It backed away, until it stood at his feet. Pulse still pounding, Marcus rose first onto his elbows, then to a sitting position, careful to keep his movements unthreatening. The wolf went down on its haunches, watching him with wary eyes.

The creature's silver fur shone in the subtle moonlight. The animal was so beautiful. Gwen, he reminded himself. This was Gwen. The part of her that was bound to Deep Magic.

He loved her. All of her. Even this. Even if, as she feared, her magic could destroy him.

He gladly accepted that risk.

He waited, thinking she would shift back to her human form. After a time, when she did not, he stood up. The wolf did the same.

He studied the animal. Gwen. What did she want from him? Was this a test, to see if he would run in the face of the magic he'd once despised so completely? If it was a test, he had no intention of failing. His feelings about Deep Magic had become much more complicated since he'd come to love her.

No, he would not fail.

Slowly, he approached the wolf. Laid a hand on its head.

"Where is Exchalybur?"

Gwen paused on the trail and looked back at Marcus, towering above her on the back of a very nervous horse. The animal clearly did not like the wolf; it was a testament to Marcus's skill as a horseman that he was able to follow her at all.

But follow he did, and closely, too.

Gwen's clothes were stuffed in a pack tied to his saddle hook. Her pendant was around his neck. The Lady's sword was strapped to his back, the hilt protruding above his left shoulder. She was struck by the dark beauty of him, even viewed through wolf's eyes. She felt his unwavering gaze even when her back was turned.

She'd thought he would leave her when she deliberately did not shift back into human form. He hadn't. He'd found the sword and her clothing and calmly told her to continue her journey. Confused, she obeyed. She understood that he'd been looking for her, but wasn't completely sure how he'd managed to break through her spells. He should not have been able to.

Her mind flickered, and for a moment she forgot what she'd been thinking of. The wolf's instinct came to the fore, concerned only with the scents and sensations of the path ahead. Time passed; how much, she couldn't be sure—the wolf did not concern itself with such things.

When her human mind finally surfaced, it was with an undercurrent of panic. On the trip from Avalon to Isca, she'd traveled three days as a wolf, but had no problem retaining her human mind or regaining her woman's form. Now it seemed the wolf had been made stronger by her increasing willingness to call and use Deep Magic.

They'd traveled past dawn and well into the next day. Soon a second night would fall—it would be pure folly to stay in wolf form for another full day of travel. Avalon could not be much farther. Losing her wolf form meant temporarily losing her magic. She would need a full day to recover before she could use the sword to raise a veil of Deep Magic around Avalon.

She halted in a sheltered clearing. Marcus reined in his mount and waited, watching her with silent eyes. When she didn't resume the journey, he stopped and dismounted, tethering the horse a fair distance away, out of sight of Gwen. She listened to him speak to the animal, his voice low and gentle. Finally, he left the horse and rejoined her.

He crouched before her and offered her his hand. She approached shyly, licking it, then retreating. She knew what she had to do next. She also knew that Marcus would not let her hide it. She told herself that he'd already seen her shift, not once, but twice. The thought did little to reassure her. The first time she'd been wounded and half-mad. The second time she hadn't known he was watching.

This time, she knew what she was doing. She knew he would be watching. She knew, too, how it would affect him.

Heat flowed through her body. She felt so vulnerable, so uncertain. So . . . aroused.

She let the Words seep into her mind. She felt the change begin, deep inside her. Marcus's attention did not waver; the light in his dark eyes flared. Gwen wanted to look away; she could not.

Bone and muscle twisted; fur melted into skin. Light shimmered, reclaiming her soul, stretching and molding her wolf's body into that of a woman. When it was over, she lay naked and panting, slick with sweat. She opened her eyes to find Marcus crouching before her. Wordlessly, he reached out and cupped her cheek. Dipping his head, he caught her lips with his.

She ran her hands over his body as he kissed her. Her fingers brushed his sex. He was aroused, enormously so, as she had known he would be.

"Why does my shifting affect ye like this?"

He gave her a wry, embarrassed smile. "I don't know. But it has, ever since the first time. Just thinking about it makes me hard."

His desire fanned hers. She stroked him through his *braccas*. "Then take me, Marcus."

"Here?"

"Aye." She started unlacing his *braccas*.

He needed no further encouragement. He shrugged the sword and its belt from his shoulder and laid it aside. His shirt, pants, and boots soon followed. She drew him down on top of her, stroking his back, his shoulders, his face. She'd thought she would never lie with him again—now she had one more chance.

She lay back on the soft moss, cradling his face between her hands and kissing him. She loved him so—her heart nearly burst with it. He shifted to lie beside her, his arousal hot and insistent against her thigh. She rolled to face him, hooking one leg over his hip. He pulled it higher over his hip bone, his other hand cupping her bottom. She encircled his neck with her arms; he joined their bodies with a powerful thrust that touched the very center of her soul.

"Gods, Gwen."

Their coupling was slow and fierce. Marcus's thrusts took her with deep, deliberate possession. He anchored her gaze with his, and would not let her look away.

"You are mine."

The vow was low and vibrant in his throat, as it had been during that first violent joining, when he'd tamed the wolf. He thrust into her, at the same time pulling her toward him, leaving her no space or opportunity for retreat.

"There will be no other man. Not Trevor, not anyone. Not ever. You'll give your body only to me."

She shut her eyes. "Marcus, ye know I cannot promise . . ."

"You *will* promise." His hips stilled, leaving him buried deep inside her. She could feel him pulsing, hotly. Slipping a hand between their bodies, he pressed the tight bud just above their joining.

Stars exploded behind her eyelids. She flexed her hips, wanting more, wanting him to *move*, but he tightened his grip on her hip, stopping her. Then he jerked his hand away.

"Nay, Marcus! Do not—"

"Promise me, Gwen. You will not take Trevor—or any man—into your body." He flicked his thumb again, drawing a gasp from her lips. "Say it, Gwen."

"I'll not marry Trevor," she whispered. How could she? She would feel like a whore, lying with one man while dreaming of another.

He touched her again, too lightly. And still did not move.

She writhed, trying to make him relent. "Marcus . . ."

"Again, Gwen. Tell me again. No one else. No one but me."

"Aye. I promise. No one but you."

He started moving again—long, sweet strokes of mindless pleasure. She buried her face in his chest, inhaling his scent, his arousal, his passion. A coil wound tight in her belly.

"Gwen. You feel so good. So right."

He stiffened inside her, causing her inner muscles to tighten. Her climax rushed at her. Marcus growled and thrust deep, and the pleasure sliced like a white-hot knife. She gave herself to it. To him. This was magic, deeper than anything she'd ever imagined. More than anything she deserved.

He was right. There could be no other. Not when he possessed her heart, her mind, and her soul.

Too soon, the mindless bliss receded, leaving her trembling. She clung to his neck, drinking air in gulps while his hand stroked rhythmically up and down her spine.

"Mine," he said.

She let out a long, shuddering breath. "Aye, Marcus. Yours."

"Ye should not have come after me," she told him later, after she had dressed and regained her wits. "I might have killed ye."

"No. You would not have. Don't you realize that by now? The wolf will never hurt me."

She did not agree. He shrugged into his shirt, then picked up the sword and offered it to her.

She shook her head. "I don't have the strength to carry it." She'd spent far too much time as a wolf in the last few days.

He gave her a long look, then buckled the sword belt over his own shoulder.

"When I heard ye pursuing me, I thought ye were

Strabo, coming after me. He spoke to me in my dream . . . I was afraid he could sense that I had left Isca."

"Even if he has, he won't be able to come after you before tomorrow at the earliest."

"How can ye know that?"

"I heard talk in the tavern while I was trying to cool my temper in a mug of *cervesia*. There's a formal dinner at the fortress tonight in honor of the Governor. Strabo and all his high-ranking officers will be in attendance, along with every civilian of note in Isca."

"A short reprieve, then. That is good. But what I don't understand is, how did *ye* find me? Ye should not have been able to. I laid spells of confusion . . ."

"I don't know myself how I did it. All I know is that when I returned to the farm, Breena met me at the gate. She said you'd taken the sword and left while Rhys and Trevor were sleeping. As soon as they realized you'd gone, they left as well. But then . . ." He frowned and gave a shrug. "It's difficult to explain how I felt. Somehow I knew they'd gone in the wrong direction. That they wouldn't find you. And I was right, because I found you, and they didn't."

"That sounds like magic, Marcus."

Discomfort flashed across his face. "I thought of that, too. But it can't be possible."

"It might, because of Exchalybur. Ye forged the sword . . . perhaps ye retain a connection to it. Perhaps ye were drawn to me because I carry it."

"Maybe. Or perhaps I was drawn to *you*. Perhaps the Deep Magic you sent through me and into the sword bound us together in ways we don't yet understand."

It was a troubling—and thrilling—thought. "Ye could well be right."

He held out his hand to her. "Come, then. The sky is already lightening. If I can convince my mount to accept you as a rider, we can reach Avalon before nightfall."

The boatman put Rhys and Trevor ashore in a clear dawn, not far from Avalon.

By midday they were hopelessly lost.

Thick mist obscured their vision. Not Cyric's mist of Light. This was a darker fog. Unfathomable and impenetrable.

Deep Magic.

Rhys cast out his senses, searching for a path that would lead him home. Not the slightest nuance of the correct bearing entered his consciousness. The grim set of Trevor's jaw told him the Caledonian was just as blind.

They forged on, the charcoal mist taunting them with every step. Each tree, each rock, each ditch and mound appeared and disappeared like a dream. Though they were moving, Rhys had the distinct feeling that he and Trevor were standing still. Treading water.

And then he felt it.

A shiver of magic, vibrating in his mind. A touch as familiar to him as his own breath.

"Rhys."

"Gwen. Where are ye?"

"Near, brother. Come, I'll guide you to me."

He closed his eyes and let her power draw him.

Gwen had sat down only for a moment, while Marcus led his horse to the muddy stream bank for a much-needed drink. The poor beast was distraught from the trauma of carrying what it thought was a wolf. Gwen hadn't meant to close her eyes, but leaning her head back against the trunk of an ash tree, she did just that. The sounds of the forest faded as sleep dropped over her like a shroud.

She woke some time later with a start. A familiar figure stood before her.

"Rhys," she said in astonishment. "Ye found me. Where . . ." She looked about. "Where is Trevor?"

He frowned. "Why did ye run?"

"I thought . . . I thought 'twould be better if I faced Strabo alone."

"Ye were not meant to stand alone, Gwen. And now that I am here, ye will not have to, ever again."

She found herself blinking back tears.

"Come." Rhys held out his hand.

After a brief hesitation, she took it and allowed him to pull her to her feet. "Go? Go where?"

Rhys turned and frowned at her. "Do not question me, Gwendolyn."

He tugged her along a trail she had not noticed earlier. He did not stop, or even look back at her.

"Rhys. Stop. This isn't right."

He did not heed her, or release her wrist. She stumbled after him, her limbs saturated with the heaviness that always followed her shifting. She almost fell, but he did not pause. "Rhys, wait! Ye walk too fast—"

He turned. The expression in his eyes drew her up short.

"Ye are angry," she said.

"Aye. Did ye imagine I would not be? Ye ran from me. From what ye know must be."

"I had to run. I must follow my own conscience. And I cannot marry Trevor, Rhys. I won't."

"True," he said. "Ye are meant for another."

She stared at him. "Another? But who—" She broke

off as Rhys's gray eyes took on an unearthly glow.

"Rhys?" She tried again to yank her arm from his grasp. His fingers bit into her flesh. "Let go. Ye are hurting me."

"That is my right." Rhys's voice had gone strange, all trace of his Celtic lilt vanished. His next words came in Latin. "You, Gwendolyn, are mine."

Rhys's face and body wavered. The forest around him dissolved, colors smearing and blending together, darkening to a deep, pulsing blue. The ground dropped away and Gwen fell, tumbling through space, arms outstretched, reaching . . . but finding nothing. She landed with a sickening jolt, with a sense of the world falling to pieces around her. But there was no impact, no pain. As if the whole thing had been a dream.

A dream. Of course. That was what it had been. With a prayer of thanks to the Great Mother, she opened her eyes.

And beheld Strabo standing before her, dressed in full Legionary armor. His dark eyes regarded her calmly from beneath the rim of his helmet.

She made a noise in her throat and scrambled to her feet. The forest around her was unfamiliar. She was not in the place where she'd fallen asleep.

"Ah," he said. "Finally, you understand."

"How . . . how did I get here?"

"You came to me, of course. You will always come when I call. Remember that."

With swift strides, he closed the distance between them and clamped his fingers on her chin. He leaned close, his face blurring in her vision. Panic flooded her. With her Light still numb from the wolf, how could she fight him?

She struck out blindly, her balled fist connecting

painfully with the side of his helmet. Strabo laughed. In a heartbeat, she found herself immobile, her body caged by his arms.

"Come now, my little Druidess, can you do no better than that? Or has the wolf taken all your strength?"

"How do you know of the wolf?"

"How could I not know?" His fingers delved into her hair. "I *felt* you. Like I once felt my Tamar."

Gwen twisted in his arms. "Ye were her lover."

"Yes."

"And ye guessed Rhys was her son. That was why ye followed him."

"You and your brother favor Tamar greatly. A blessing, since your father was a hulking brute of a man. I much enjoyed killing him." He used his grip on her hair to tilt her head up. "You, my dear, have a fascinating power. You take the form of a beast. Do you know how rare that is? Your twin, does he have the same power?"

"What . . . what do ye want of us?"

His tone held an edge that made Gwen's blood run cold. "From him—nothing. It's you I want. You and your grandfather." He stroked the side of her face.

She fought back nausea. "Why?"

He did not immediately answer. When he did, his eyes went oddly soft. "You are so like Tamar. Tall and proud, like a warrior queen. I met her in the market. I sensed her magic, and her sadness. Both drew me to her." His arms tightened around her. "She wanted to denounce the brute her father had given her to. But Cyric would not hear of it. When he learned of our love, he turned his Dark arts on me. He sent me ailments . . . rashes, boils, a fever. None of it mattered. He could not keep me away from her."

"That's . . . not possible. Cyric practices only the Light. He would never inflict illness. That requires Deep Magic."

"I assure you, Cyric did not hesitate to conjure Deep Magic against me." His tone went flat. "Tamar died because of it."

Suddenly, he shifted her body in his arms, lifting her easily. He started walking, his strides swift.

"Put me down!"

"That, I will not do."

Goddess, help me. If she could only conjure a spell, however slight, she might be able to break his hold. She dug deep into her consciousness, calling for her magic. *Nothing.*

"Where are ye taking me?"

"I told you. You are mine. You will, I think, be a wife I will not easily tire of."

"Wife?"

He paused on the trail, looking down at her. "Why, of course you will become my wife. Your mother would have wanted it."

Gwen couldn't have gone far.

Marcus kept telling himself that, even long after he'd ceased to believe it. She'd slipped off so quietly, so completely, he might have thought she'd run away again. Despite the intimacy they'd shared, and the vow he'd forced from her, he still was not sure of her. But she had not run, he was sure of that. She might have left Marcus behind, but she would never have left the sword.

He kept the weapon strapped on his back as he scouted for tracks. The ground was soft; he soon found what he sought. A single set of footprints, leading north.

Some distance down the trail, Gwen's tracks were joined by another set. These were larger, deeper impressions on the soft loam. A man, he was sure.

He fingered the hilt of the dagger at his belt. A brigand? Not likely. The soles of the newcomer's boots were studded with iron nubs. Legionary footwear. There had been a struggle; scuffs and gouges in the dirt. Then the soldier's tracks had deepened, and Gwen's had disappeared. The man had carried her off.

Fear clutched his throat. Had Strabo come after her, as she had expected? Because of her recent transformation, Gwen would have been unable to call her magic against him. The sword that might have saved her was dangling uselessly on Marcus's back.

He followed the trail to the crest of the hill, where the sorcerer's tracks, and all trace of Gwen, abruptly vanished.

Gwen woke within a cloud of thick Deep Magic. She'd passed out in Strabo's arms—how long ago? She had no idea. Fear for Marcus consumed her. Had Strabo assaulted him? Killed him and taken Exchalybur? Or had the spells of illusion she'd woven into the metal shielded Marcus from the sorcerer's sight? She prayed the latter was true.

A deadening force sapped her strength. She remembered Strabo calling the spell, remembered feeling as though her lungs couldn't take in enough air. The spell was much like the one she'd endured a year before, when her cousin had trapped her in wolf form. Deep Magic, all but unbreakable.

Bile burned the back of her throat. When she reached inside for her magic, she could barely feel it.

It was there, but very far away. She could not rouse it. She sought her connection to Rhys and was alarmed to realize she could not feel him at all.

Even the wolf, when she called it, did not stir.

She pushed herself upright. She was in a room with soft fabric walls—a tent, more richly appointed than the Aquilas' home. Furs and skins covered the plank flooring. She lay on an elaborately carved bed strewn with more furs, and more silk. The other furnishings were just as opulent—a writing table, cross-legged chairs, a washstand, a trunk. An armor stand, draped with Strabo's armor. Unfortunately, his war belt—which held his sword and battle dagger—was nowhere in sight.

A table was set for a meal for two. Bread, cheese, oysters, dried figs . . . but no knife. A bowl filled with wildflowers. The romantic arrangement was far too intimate for comfort.

Voices drew her gaze to the narrow slice of light at the edge of the tent flap. Just outside, two men were conversing in rough Latin. Guards?

Shoving herself off the bed, she crept toward the opening on shaking legs. Peering through the gap, she found her fear confirmed. She was in a Roman camp—was it the mining camp near Avalon? Fear became a living thing inside her. Stripped of her power, surrounded by Legionaries, she was all but helpless against anything Strabo chose to do to her.

You will, I think, be a wife I will not easily tire of.

She fought off a surge of nausea. She'd survived Blodwen's spell. She would survive this as well. She would wait, and watch, and seize whatever opportunity for escape presented itself.

She concentrated on the conversation outside the tent, translating the rough, rapid Latin. The guards spoke of their recent shift in the mine, resentment plain in their voices. They were fed up with working in the dark, dank passageways. A thin vein of silver had been found several days ago, but it had petered out the day Legate Strabo had left for Isca. Tribune Valgus had been furious, and had doubled their shifts in the hope they would discover the lode he insisted was there. The men hoped that Legate Strabo's reappearance would put an end to the folly. They wanted to pack up camp and return to the fortress.

Their grumblings halted abruptly. Words of respectful salute followed. Gwen had just enough time to retreat to the opposite side of the tent before the tent flap lifted.

Strabo entered, garbed in a simple red tunic. His blue-black aura trailed gently behind him as he took in the empty bed, then scanned the recesses of the tent. When his gaze alighted on Gwen, he smiled.

"You are awake, my love. I am very glad."

His tone chilled her. It was not the tone of a captor, but the soft, gentle voice of a lover. She stood frozen as he strode toward her—there was nowhere to go. He halted before her and looked down. He was a tall man. She might have kept her eyes downcast, on his boots, or level, looking at his mouth. Instead, she tipped her chin up, meeting his gaze. She did not realize until she had done it what a submissive pose she had taken. The wolf inside did not like baring her neck to him.

He placed one finger under her chin and tipped her head back even farther. Dark magic pulsed at the point of contact, making her stomach rebel even more.

"You are pale. Did you not rest well?"

She did not answer.

He gave her an indulgent smile and placed a kiss on her forehead. "What is your desire? Food? Wine? More pillows? Tell me."

Gwen swallowed a curse. She sensed it would do no good to antagonize her captor.

"Nothing? That cannot be. All women have whims." He gazed down at her with a tenderness that, incredibly, seemed genuine.

Her terror expanded. The man was insane. He had to be.

With an effort, she kept her loathing from her face. She sensed that scorn, more than anything, would spark his rage. How could Mama have loved this man? It was incomprehensible.

He cupped her cheek. One large thumb rubbed back and forth over her lower lip. His thumb pressed, parting her lower lip from the upper.

"Do not be afraid. I will treat you like a queen. You will enjoy your life with me. The life your mother should have had."

His mouth covered her lips, as if to seal the vow.

Chapter Nineteen

Cyric thrashed wildly on his pallet. An agitated Siane was trying to calm him. When Owein ducked into the hut, she choked back a sob. The red mark of a hand showed on her cheek.

"He hit ye?" Owein moved quickly to Cyric's side and caught the old Druid's flailing arm.

"He did not mean to! A vision is upon him. I tried to comfort him—" She burst into tears.

"Go," Owein said tersely. "Fetch Mared. She is with Clara." He didn't like to take Mared away from Clara—Clara's birth travails had started at midday the day before, and he wanted the healer at his wife's side. But he had little choice.

Siane jumped up and nodded.

"Nay!" Cyric shouted as the lass reached the door. He clawed at Owein, trying to launch himself off the pallet. "Ye will not go! Ye will not abandon your people! Your clan!"

Siane hesitated at the door, her expression stricken.

"He doesna know what he is saying," Owein muttered. "Go now, quickly, as I told ye. Fetch Mared."

The girl threw a fearful glance at Cyric and fled. As the door thumped shut, Cyric went limp. Tears streamed down his weathered cheeks. "She goes to him."

Owein eased the old man back onto the bed. "She will return. All is well."

"Nay. Ye do not understand. Nothing will ever be right again. My Tamar . . . she is gone. Dead."

Blessedly, the old Druid soon lapsed into unconsciousness. Owein stood, frowning down at him. All of Avalon was suffering from a renewed assault of Deep Magic—Owein could only surmise that Strabo had returned. Even the youngest of the Druids could not sleep without fear. The mist was thinning once again, and this time, Dark dreams were affecting everyone on the sacred isle.

Owein's own nightmares were brutal, mired in the pain of his past—war and slavery and torture. He did not want to remember those days, had fought long and hard to forgive his enemies and bury his anger against them. Now, like bones dug from a grave, his past had returned. But painful as those memories were, they did not rule him as they once had. Clara had helped him face that Darkness, and conquer it.

He could not say that Cyric had conquered his past.

The old man's anguish bled from a wound that had never healed. One that ran deep into his soul. A noise sounded behind Owein—he turned and nodded to Mared. He was not surprised to see Padrig follow close behind. Their expressions were grave.

"Ye have remained silent," Owein told them. "But I

suspect ye know more about Cyric's affliction than ye say. Ye must tell me."

"We promised Cyric long ago never to speak of it," Mared said.

"If the story can help him now, I pray ye dinna keep his confidence."

"I am not sure it can help him," Padrig said wearily. "The horror of that night never faded for Cyric."

"The night Tamar died?"

"Aye." Mared moved to a stool and sat, her frail body bending with difficulty. " 'Twas eighteen summers past. Rhys and Gwen had but seven years. Their mother, Tamar, was . . . unhappy in her marriage. Morvyn, her husband, was overly fond of unwatered Roman wine. When he drank, he became crude."

"I dinna understand. Why would Cyric choose such a man for his daughter?"

"Cyric agreed to the match when Tamar and Morvyn were children," Padrig said. "Morvyn's father had been a Druid of Avalon, a friend to Cyric in his youth. Cyric could not go back on his word, especially after his friend's death."

Owein nodded. "Go on."

"Tamar wanted to break her handfasting with Morvyn," Mared said. " 'Twas her right, after all. But Cyric would not agree to it, especially after Rhys and Gwen were born. He thought, perhaps, that father-hood would improve Morvyn's demeanor. It did not." The healer's gnarled hand tightened on her staff. "The twins had four summers when Tamar found a lover. A Roman centurion."

Owein made a sound of disbelief.

"Tamar could not have chosen a worse man with which to cuckold her husband," Mared said. "When

Morvyn discovered her perfidy, he beat her. Tamar was defiant—she continued to meet her lover. Morvyn's beatings worsened. Then one night, he did not return home."

"I found him dead," Padrig put in. "His throat had been slit. Not many days later, Tamar went to Cyric and told him she wished to marry her Roman lover—not only marry, but leave Britain, because he'd received orders to a new posting. Cyric refused. Tamar declared she would go without his blessing. Cyric realized he could not stop her, but he would not allow her to take Avalon's future with her. Rhys and Gwen would stay in Britain."

"Tamar loved her children fiercely," Mared said. "She did not want to take them from their clan and their homeland. Truth be told, she did not want to leave Britain herself. We thought the centurion would leave, and she would forget him. We never realized that he had magic—Deep Magic—and that Tamar had been teaching him to call it. In the end, the magic she helped him discover was turned against her."

"He killed her with Deep Magic?" Owein said.

"Aye. One night, she went down to the river. Cyric followed. When he returned, he was carrying Tamar's body. We never saw the centurion again."

"But he is here now," Padrig said. "Unless I am very much mistaken."

Owein's gaze cut to Rhys's uncle. "What do ye mean?"

"We never knew the name of Tamar's Roman lover. Cyric would not allow her to speak it in his presence. But this Roman sorcerer . . . Strabo . . . I sense it is the same man. Tamar's lover. Indeed, I am almost certain of it."

* * *

Marcus thought, at first, that the silver-gray wolf was Gwen.

The animal appeared on the trail before him, emerging from the shadows like a dream. His horse reared with a frantic snort, hooves pawing wildly. It took all Marcus's strength to regain control of the animal.

When he glanced back at the wolf, he saw it had not moved.

It was not Gwen. This she-wolf's teats were pink and swollen; it had recently birthed a litter of cubs. Most likely Marcus had stumbled upon its lair and roused its protective instinct.

"My apologies." He must be insane, conversing with the beast. He was not Rhys; the animal could not possibly understand him. He started to back his mount away.

The wolf advanced, matching his progress step for step. Marcus halted. The creature did not seem hostile. It seemed . . . expectant.

Could this be *Gwen's* wolf? He could not be entirely certain. He'd seen the animal only once, a year before, when it had led Marcus and Rhys to Gwen. If it meant to do the same now . . .

"Where is she?" he asked. "Where is Gwen?"

The wolf's tail rose. Turning, it loped a short way down the trail, then looked back expectantly. His heart clenching in his chest, Marcus steadied his anxious mount and followed.

The wolf led him along a high ridge overlooking a deep gorge. It paused at a rocky promontory. Dismounting, Marcus tethered his horse and approached. He peered around the outcropping. Less than a quarter mile away, directly across the gorge, stood a Roman military camp. The mining camp Gwen had spoken of?

A steep trail led from the camp gate to the cave below it. Excavated dirt dribbled down the face of the cliff.

Mentally, he considered the size of the camp. It likely housed thirty soldiers or more. Two armed men loitered on either side of the gate set in a sturdy encircling palisade. A contingent of ten men trudged up the trail from the mines, apparently just finishing their shift.

"Gwen is inside the camp?"

The wolf just looked back at him.

Marcus swore. Never in his life had he felt more useless. Even if he could cross the gorge unseen, he could hardly march up to the camp gate and demand entrance. Still less likely was the prospect of scaling the sharpened spikes of the palisade unnoticed, even if he waited for nightfall. And even supposing he could accomplish one of those feats, it would remain to locate Gwen and carry her past thirty armed Legionaries to safety without getting both her and himself killed.

And he hadn't even begun to consider Strabo's magic.

Exchalybur hung heavily on his back. If he had any magic at all, he wouldn't hesitate to use the weapon, Deep Magic or no. But in his hands, the sword was just a sword. And he was not the most able of swordsmen.

He needed help. Desperately. He looked down the gorge, out over the swamps. Somewhere, hidden in the mist, was an island that was forbidden to him.

He turned to the wolf. "Avalon," he said. "Take me there."

Shouts and curses erupted from Cyric's hut. Sounds of struggle followed. Owein tried to shove the disturbance from his mind. Clara was gripping his hand so tightly, he thought his bones might crack. He would not leave her now, not even if Strabo and the entire Roman army landed on Avalon's shore.

She let out a moan. Her pain echoed through their linked minds. She'd been visited by her own nightmares, full of grief for her dead father and fear for her babe. Owein absorbed what he could into his own soul, through the mental link they shared. But it was not enough. Clara was pale with agony, gasping for each breath.

He did not know much about such things, but this could not be right. She'd labored more than a day. The babe was not coming. Gods, how he wished Rhiannon were here. His sister would know what to do.

Cyric's cries seeped around the edges of the closed door. Owein ground his teeth. Dimly, he was aware of the women around him—Eleri, and Howell's wife, Dera. Mared was with Cyric.

"Can ye nay *do* something?" he barked as Clara choked off another cry. Her eyes were glazed with pain.

"Fetch Mared," Dera told Eleri. "If ye can."

The lass nodded and rushed from the hut. Clara's spasm passed; her body went limp. Owein smoothed a wet strand of hair from his wife's forehead. He was utterly gutted by helplessness.

"Owein?"

"I'm here, love."

"I don't think . . . I don't think I can birth our son."

His insides twisted. "Ye *can,* Clara. Ye must."

"No, I—ah!"

Another pain hit, harder than all the ones before. Her small body went so taut, he thought it might snap. And all he could do was heap curses on top of his prayers.

The door opened and Mared entered. Another of Cyric's screams entered with her.

Clara's eyes fluttered open. "Cyric . . . he's gone mad."

"Put it from your mind," Owein said sharply. "Think only of our babe."

"Our babe." Clara closed her eyes. "I . . . I'm sorry, Owein. I'm not strong enough. I'm . . . so tired."

"All birthing women grow weary," Mared told Clara briskly. " 'Tis only natural."

The old healer laid her palms on Clara's stomach. Her eyes closed; her brow creased. Long moments passed, in which Owein's panic mounted.

"What is it?" he asked when he could wait no longer. "Is the babe d—" His throat closed on the word.

Clara's face contorted as another spasm hit. The pain tore a keening scream from her throat; Mared slipped an arm around her waist and murmured soothing words. The contraction went on so long that Owein almost found himself moaning along with Clara. When at last she collapsed, he felt as though he'd been pounded into the dirt.

He scrubbed a hand down his face. When his fingers came away wet, he realized he was crying.

"She is dying." He was dying, too. He could not breathe. He'd fought many battles, but none had been as bad as this.

Mared frowned at him. "Nay. 'Tis a long labor, to be sure, but it goes well."

"Well? *Well?* You lie! I've watched men perish in battle with less pain. She is dying, and ye willna tell me!"

"Hush!" Mared's tone was sharp, her grip on his arm sharper. "She isna dying. And her pain is no more or less than any birthing woman endures. By the morrow, 'twill be forgotten."

Forgotten? Owein could not conceive of such a thing. He was sure *he* would not forget.

"Tell me true, old woman. She is dying, aye?"

Mared glowered. "Get a grip on yourself, man! Truly, 'tis best ye leave. Ye are only upsetting her."

"Nay, I willna—"

"Go out. Now. Dera will fetch ye when your son arrives."

"But—"

A bloodcurdling scream drowned out his protest. Not Clara's. *Cyric's.* Clara's eyes went wide. Dera gasped a prayer to the Great Mother. Owein's gaze locked with Mared's as Cyric's enraged howl rent the air.

"Get out! Get out, ye Roman swine! *Or I will kill ye where ye stand!*"

Chapter Twenty

Strabo's kiss was that of a lover. Gentle. Coaxing. The sheer horror of it suffocated Gwen. *This man killed Mama.*

His dark aura was a noxious oil on her skin and in her nostrils. His tongue stroked her lips. In desperation, she reached for her magic. It did not answer.

He drew back, regarding her with a hooded gaze. "You are so like Tamar. It is as if she's come back to me."

He lifted her hand to his lips. Gwen endured the kiss he brushed on her knuckles. He had not mentioned Marcus or Exchalybur. Once again, she prayed the spells she'd put on the Lady's sword had deflected Strabo's attention. If so, then surely Marcus was searching for her. If she could find him, and get her hands on Exchalybur, then perhaps she could shake off the effects of Strabo's magic-deadening spell.

But even as she plotted, she feared her plan was futile. Each time she reached for her magic, she could not grasp it. And even if Marcus succeeded in tracing her to the Roman camp, what could he do to rescue her? There were so many soldiers. Strabo would not even have to use magic to kill him.

But perhaps help could come from another quarter. She sought her brother with her mind. *"Rhys?"*

He did not answer; she cast her senses, but could not feel him at all. It was as if their connection had been completely severed. Another effect of Strabo's spell?

The voices of the guards rose in laughter at some crude jest. Strabo looked toward the tent flap and frowned. Releasing Gwen, he strode to the entrance and issued a sharp reprimand. The soldiers murmured apologies.

When Strabo returned to Gwen, she offered him what she hoped looked like a shy smile. He leaned forward to kiss her; she stopped him with a demure hand on his chest.

"There are so many men about," she whispered with an embarrassed glance at the tent flap. "I . . . I confess I cannot feel easy about . . . being with ye. If they should hear us . . ."

Strabo's thick brows met in a single line. "I will send them away."

"Nay. 'Twould be so much better if . . ." She touched his lower lip with her finger.

His dark gaze flared. "Tell me."

She forced herself to go up on tiptoe, her hand sliding around his neck as she whispered near his ear. "If we could find a place in the forest. A private place, surrounded by a screen of branches. Near the river, perhaps . . ."

His arm tightened around her. "Tamar and I had such a place, once."

"Then let us find our own. Away from the camp, where none of your men will disturb us."

He caught her hand and pressed a kiss to her palm. "I can easily grant that request, my love."

"Get out, Roman swine! Get out, or I will kill ye where ye stand!"

Marcus drew up short at the edge of the village common. A tattered old Celt was brandishing an oaken staff in Marcus's direction. He was clad in a stained robe, his long white hair and beard bristling wildly, framing a mottled red face.

It could only be Cyric. Was he mad? Had Strabo's Deep Magic unhinged his mind? Perhaps that was why, once Marcus had launched the raft Gwen's wolf had shown him, the mist had parted so easily.

Once on Avalon's dock, Marcus had made the trek to the village with ease. There had been no sign of the spells he'd encountered the previous year, which had prevented him from reaching Gwen while she recovered from her ordeal. Clearly, all was not right in Avalon.

Avalon's Druids clustered behind their crazed leader. Marcus scanned the group quickly—a man, a youth, two women, several children. Rhys was not among them, nor was Trevor, nor even Owein and Clara. He did not recognize a single face.

"By the Great Mother," the man muttered, catching sight of Marcus. "A Roman! Is the mist gone?"

"He brings soldiers," a small, plump woman replied fearfully. "They'll cut us down where we stand."

Cyric's staff sliced the air. "Nay. I will kill him."

He leveled the staff's tip at Marcus. Several of the younger Druids shrank back, as if fearing the thing would explode. Marcus had no doubt that it could. Slowly, he reached up and behind, his fingers closing on the hilt of Gwen's sword. Though what protection the weapon could afford a man with no magic, Marcus did not know.

"Wait! Cyric, nay!" A second old man surged from one of the huts, barking a warning. "Dinna—"

Cyric's head whipped around. "Stay back, Padrig. He will pay the price of his insult to Tamar."

Tamar. That had been Gwen's mother's name. Marcus stood motionless, his fingers flexing on the sword's hilt. He fought the urge to wrench it from its sheath. Was Cyric caught in a dream, reliving his daughter's death? If so, and if he thought Marcus was the soldier who had killed her, there was no doubt that Marcus would be dead before his blade cleared its sheath.

"I have not come for Tamar," he said in Celtic, pronouncing each word with deliberate emphasis. "I have come begging your help."

"Treacherous Roman! Do ye think me a fool? How can ye spew such lies with Deep Magic flowing all around ye? Ye wish to make my daughter your whore. Ye will not. I will kill ye."

At the edge of his vision, Marcus saw Owein's broad form emerge from one of the huts. *Thank the gods!* Finally, someone who might be termed—however loosely—a friend.

He kept his voice low, his gaze fixed on Cyric, but Marcus's next words were for Rhiannon's brother. "I need your help. Gwen has been taken by—" He checked himself, wary of uttering Strabo's name. "She's been taken by a soldier."

"Ye are a soldier," Cyric muttered.

"No. I am not. I am a smith."

Cyric blinked, seemingly taken aback. "A smith? Nay. That is not right. Ye are a soldier."

Owein had begun a stealthy movement toward the old Druid. His gaze was fixed on Cyric's staff. Marcus blinked. Was that a spark of blue light, running the length of the wood?

"Ye lie. As all Romans do. Your Deep Magic destroyed her." The glowing tip of Cyric's staff rose, pointing directly at Marcus's chest. "For this, ye will die."

Cyric's staff exploded. A woman screamed. In the same instant, Owein launched himself at the old man. "Cyric, nay!"

The shot drove into the ground at Marcus's feet. The old Druid railed against Owein. "Stay back, man. This battle is mine!"

"By all that is holy, Cyric," Owein shouted, "stop this!"

"Nay!" With a power born of some force beyond his own frail body, the old man threw the bulky warrior off. "This time, I will not fail!"

Cyric's staff swung around, seeking Marcus. The time for talk was done, Marcus decided. He yanked Exchalybur from its sheath and brandished the weapon before him. What good would the sword be against a magical attack? He did not know. Marcus was no Druid. In his hands, the Lady's weapon was just a sword.

"Die, Roman swine!"

Dark flame exploded. Marcus gripped the sword with both hands and grimly met the attack.

It had not been Gwen's voice he'd heard in his mind. It had been another of Strabo's tricks, leading Rhys and Trevor farther astray. Once Rhys realized the sorcerer's trickery, the voice faded, and the mist began to thin.

They'd found themselves far to the west of Avalon, and it had taken some time to circle back, and more time still to find one of the Druid's hidden rafts. Now, as Trevor plied the craft's pole through the cloudy water, Rhys closed his eyes and felt for Cyric's failing spell. He caught it just before it evaporated completely.

Centering himself, he plucked each delicate thread of his grandfather's broken spellcraft and bound it to the next. It was difficult work. The spell had deteriorated almost beyond repair. Rhys knew he should never have left Avalon. When Cyric had ordered him to go after Gwen, he should have refused.

"The mist returns."

Trevor's spoken relief ran as a silent tremor through Rhys's body. He opened his eyes and watched wisps of white vapor curl at the edges of the raft. *Thank the Great Mother.* He'd done it. But had he been too late? Was Avalon discovered?

Rhys's worst fear erupted scant moments later when the raft touched shore. A blast of fire shot into the sky on the far slope of the isle, above the village. Blue and white sparks spewed high into the air. Trevor cursed and dropped the raft's rope.

Rhys was already pounding up the trail to the village, his heart in his throat. He burst into the village common, gasping. The scene before him was nothing he might have imagined. Marcus Aquila stood in the center of the village, brandishing Gwen's shining, dangerous sword. But where was Gwen?

Trevor's heavy tread thumped to a halt behind Rhys. *"Goddess."*

The sword's magic was blinding. Rhys blinked against a flash of white light, laced with a clear, true blue. It was like looking into the center of a flame. Into the center of life.

The fire burning on the tip of Cyric's staff was far

more ominous, however. Dark and fathomless, it carried the color of pure Deep Magic. Black flame shot toward Marcus. Marcus, incredibly, stood firm, catching the assault on the flat of Gwen's magic blade. Cyric's flame ricocheted, scudding into the earth.

"This willna last," Trevor muttered. "The Roman is mundane. Cyric will kill him."

"Aye," Rhys said as Exchalybur wrenched itself to one side. The weapon, glowing white and blue, seemed to have a life and a will of its own. "Marcus cannot hope to control Deep Magic."

Cyric's next blast went wide, whizzing toward Rhys and Trevor. They both ducked.

"Nor can Cyric," Trevor said grimly.

Owein was behind Cyric, stealthily approaching. Rhys caught the warrior's gaze, then sent a glance to Trevor. Immediately, Trevor circled to the right. Rhys went to the left. Soon Cyric stood in the center of a triangle, while the three Druids stood at the points. Marcus was outside the invisible boundary, midway between Rhys and Trevor.

Rhys spoke the first Word. The syllable of Light was echoed by Trevor, then by Owein. Light shot between them, enclosing Cyric within. The fire issuing from his staff faltered as it struck the magic boundary.

Outside the limits of the spell, Marcus lowered his sword, watching. At Rhys's signal, the three Druids advanced. The nimbus of Light brightened as it shrank. Cyric's Deep Magic crackled like lightning within it.

Cyric's arm came up. For one terrifying moment, Rhys feared his grandfather would break the spell. But then the old man's eyes changed. His spirit seemed to crumple, and with it, the forbidden magic he commanded. The blue-black fire died. Cyric's oaken staff fell from his fingers; his legs crumpled. He dropped to his knees, frail shoulders heaving, hands covering his face.

"What have I done?"

Rhys signaled to Owein and Trevor to dissolve the protective spell. The Light vanished. Rhys ran to Cyric, crouching before him. Trevor and Owein hovered nearby. Rhys felt a third man approach. Padrig. He did not look up.

Cyric's eyes clung to Rhys's. "He has . . . he has returned."

"Strabo, ye mean."

"Is that his name? I never wished to know it. But I recognize his power in my dreams. He has come for me, as I knew he would."

His words were a whisper. Cyric's eyelids, thin as old parchment, closed. Tears slipped from beneath. "As I deserve."

His heart heavy, Rhys lifted his grandfather in his arms and carried him to his hut. Padrig followed. Rhys left his uncle with the now unconscious Cyric and returned to the village common, where he found Marcus, his sword sheathed, in agitated conversation with Trevor and Owein.

"What is this about?" Rhys demanded. "Where is Gwen?"

"Strabo has her. We were traveling together. I left her sleeping for just a moment while I watered my horse; when I returned, she was gone. I followed her tracks. There were signs of struggle. A man carried her off."

"It might have been any man," Rhys said. "A brigand, a soldier . . ."

"No. The tracks—they just vanished."

"Magic," Trevor muttered. "One spell to draw her

away, another to cover the trail. But why would she not fight? Her magic is strong."

"It wasn't," Marcus said. "She'd just shifted. Her magic . . . it fades after she regains her human form."

Rhys had suffered the same effect the one time he'd shifted into merlin form. He'd thought it had been because of the newness of the skill. Why had he never sought Gwen's counsel?

He closed his eyes, reaching for her with his mind.

"Gwen. Can ye hear me?"

Dread burned in his gut. "I can feel nothing. Not even a spark of her life force. She . . . she could be dead."

"No," Marcus said sharply. "She isn't. She is in the Roman camp, with Strabo."

"How do ye know?" Trevor asked.

"Her companion—the she-wolf that just gave birth—"

"Ardra," Rhys said.

"Yes. The animal found me in the forest and guided me to the Roman camp. I'm sure Ardra knew Gwen was there. Surrounded by thirty soldiers, there was no way I could get to her. So I asked Ardra to guide me here. Gwen needs your help. Your magic."

"I will go at once," Rhys said.

"As will I," Trevor said. "Gwen is my responsibility."

Marcus sucked in a breath, his color heightening. His fingers flexed into a fist, but to Rhys's surprise, his friend kept his temper in check. "Good. Let's go, then. We are wasting time."

"I will come—" Owein stopped abruptly as a woman's cry sounded from his hut.

"Clara is laboring?" Rhys asked.

"Aye. And not well, though Mared insists there is no danger." There was uncharacteristic panic in the big warrior's voice. "The old hag sent me out of my own hut. Can ye believe that?"

"I can, with no trouble," Rhys told him.

Another scream rent the air. Owein started for the hut, then, with effort, he stopped and turned back to Rhys. "I will come with ye."

Rhys shook his head. "Nay. With Clara laboring, ye could not summon the calm needed to fight Deep Magic."

"I fear ye are right," Owein replied, dragging a hand down his face. "But what of ye, Rhys? Ye hold Avalon's mist. Can ye fight Strabo at the same time?"

Could he? Rhys did not know.

"The man murdered my mother. I will do what I must."

Gwen's power was out of reach, beyond a veil of blue-black darkness. Perhaps that was why Strabo's war-horse did not protest her approach.

The sorcerer's grip settled on her waist. With little effort, he lifted her into the saddle and mounted behind her. One arm kept her in place while the other commanded the reins.

They left the camp amid the speculative gazes of Strabo's men. Not a single soldier dared to question him, but Gwen did not miss the leers and knowing winks that followed her. Once they rode through the camp gates and rounded a bend in the trail, Gwen felt easier. Until Strabo placed a kiss on her bared shoulder.

Her stomach began to churn. Aye, she'd succeeded in getting out of the camp, but without her magic, how could she fight her captor? She could not even raise a spell strong enough to serve as a distraction while she made a mundane escape.

They descended the slope of the mountain, moving

into the woods bordering the swamp. As the horse picked its way down the trail, Gwen closed her eyes and dug deep into her mind. A day had passed since she'd shifted. Her Light should be strengthening.

Suffocated by Strabo's spell, it was not. Even her Deep Magic was quiescent, the wolf slumbering through her calls.

Raw fear dug claws into her heart.

Strabo led his mount to a grassy copse and dismounted, sliding from the saddle in one smooth motion. Gwen saw her chance, slight though it was. Throwing herself from the saddle on the horse's opposite side, she ran.

Stumbling blindly, driven by a desperate instinct, she darted through the forest, ducking under a low branch, leaping over a fallen log. Her lungs worked madly to fuel her flight.

Until a Word stopped her.

It was a syllable unlike any she had ever heard. Strong and ancient, born of a foreign land, it was wholly unlike the sacred language from which she crafted her own spells. This Word was a silky, sibilant resonance. It melted her strength, stole her will. Her mind blurred.

The forest grew watery, as if she were viewing its reflection in a pond. Trees and sky dripped away, leaving nothing but a void. She spun around, panic closing her throat. It was as if the world had just . . . disappeared.

"What . . . have ye done?" she cried.

Strabo's voice was soft in her ear. "Ah, my love, do you not understand? You cannot run. Not from me."

He was there, beside her, enveloped in a nimbus of Darkness. He lifted his hand, and spoke another Word.

A low bed, strewn with silk and furs, appeared. A

garden bower arched overhead; long leafy fronds hung all around. A gilded table held honeyed pastries and wine. Gwen's ragged tunic was transformed into a Roman gown that left her left arm and shoulder bare. Her hair was unbound, her feet unshod. A delicate chain encircled her right ankle.

Strabo's Legionary armor melted into a long silken robe, striped with every color of the rainbow. "This place was your mother's favorite. I conjured it often when we were together."

"An illusion."

"A dream. Where else can one have everything?" He touched her bare shoulder and traced a delicate line down her arm. "And now, at last, I will have what I've dreamed of these last eighteen years. You will take the place of the woman I lost."

Gwen jerked away. "The woman you murdered."

A beat of silence ensued. When Strabo's voice came again, his tone was deadly. "He told you that?"

"Can ye deny it? Ye killed my father as well."

"The drunken bastard deserved it. My only regret is that I did not end his life sooner."

"And afterward . . . Mama realized what ye were. A murderer. She refused to run away with ye, and ye killed her as well. With Deep Magic."

"No. I loved Tamar. I would never have harmed even one hair on her head."

"She died by your hand! Because she rejected ye."

"Tamar did not reject me. She was to accompany me to Egypt—with you and your brother. If only I'd taken her away an hour earlier . . . but Cyric found out she meant to leave, after she had told him she would stay. He came after her . . ."

"And when he did, ye cast a blue ball of flame. I remember now. I saw it. *Rhys* saw it. Your Deep Magic killed her."

Strabo's eyes lit with fury. "Your memory lies. Yes, a spell of Deep Magic was cast, but it was not mine. I did not know how to call such power, not then. If I had, I would surely have turned it on Cyric when Tamar fell."

Cold dread iced Gwen's blood. Suddenly, her memory of Mama's last moments did not seem so clear. "Ye cannot mean—"

"That Cyric's Deep Magic killed Tamar? Yes. He killed her. With a blast that was meant for me. She tried to stop him—and died in my place. Not by my hand. Never that. Her own father destroyed her. I barely escaped with my life."

"That . . . that cannot be," Gwen whispered.

Strabo's laugh was harsh. "Do you know how many times in the past eighteen years I have wished it had not happened? That I had been killed, as Cyric intended, and she had lived? More than I can count. All the time I lived in Egypt, I plotted my revenge. Every spell of Deep Magic I have learned, every dream illusion I have cast, all the pain I have endured—it was all for one purpose only. To return to Britain and kill the Druid who destroyed the woman I loved."

His fingers bit into Gwen's shoulders. "Cyric took what was mine. Now I will claim what is his. His life, and you. And he will die knowing his own magic has turned against him once again."

Chapter Twenty-one

$\mathcal{M}$arcus, accompanied by Rhys and Trevor, had just reached the shore below the Roman camp when Gwen's voice sounded in his skull as clearly as if she'd spoken in his ear.

"Rhys. Brother, where are ye? Ye must hear me!"

He nearly jumped out of his skin. Spinning about, he scanned the trees. Nothing.

"Rhys!" Gwen's voice. Again. But where?

Marcus grabbed Rhys's shoulder and spun him about. "Did you hear that?"

Trevor looked up from securing his raft and grunted. "Hear what?"

"Gwen, calling Rhys."

"Rhys, brother, I need ye. Please answer."

Rhys shook his head. "I hear nothing."

Marcus spit out a curse. "How can you not? She's in trouble. She's calling you."

He scanned the forest. Surely Gwen was nearby. Her voice . . . it couldn't be magic. It was impossible. He *had* no magic. "I hear her . . ." He swallowed. "It sounds like she's inside my head."

Rhys stared. "Ye hear Gwen in your mind?"

Marcus nodded.

"Has . . . has this happened before?"

"No. Of course not. How could I—" He broke off. "I have not heard her in my mind. Not like this. But I've *felt* her there. Ever since . . ." Ever since the night they'd made love in the woods near the barley fields, after he'd watched her shift. The night she'd told him she loved him. "I didn't realize what it meant until Gwen left Isca and I went after her. I found her because I . . . sensed her. And now I hear her. She's calling you."

"Answer her," Rhys said tersely.

"What? *How?*"

Rhys made an impatient gesture. "Just concentrate . . . and direct your thoughts to her."

"But . . . that's magic."

"Aye. It is."

Marcus hesitated, then nodded. Drawing a deep breath, he reached inside for Gwen's presence. It felt . . . ridiculous.

"Gwen?"

There was an instant of startled silence, then, tentatively, incredulously . . .

"Marcus?"

"Yes. I . . . can hear you. Gwen, are you with Strabo? Has he . . . has he harmed you?"

"Not yet. But Marcus, he intends to have me. Soon. I convinced him to leave the mining camp. I told him I wanted privacy. I thought I could get away, but he's smothered my magic. I cannot fight him. I could not call Rhys. But ye . . ."

"I'm coming for you."

"But Marcus, I do not know where I am! Strabo has conjured an illusion around us."

"It doesn't matter. I can find you. As I did before. Do whatever you can to delay him. We're not far from you, I think."

"We?"

"Rhys and Trevor are with me."

"Ye met them on the road?"

"No. In Avalon."

"Avalon? But how did ye find your way—" Gwen broke off abruptly.

Her fear burned hot in Marcus's mind. *"Gwen? What is it?"*

"Oh, Marcus—hurry."

"Come, my love. It's time." Strabo held out a hand. He gave no indication he was aware Gwen had spoken with Marcus in her mind. Marcus! Not Rhys. She could not quite believe it.

She kept her voice steady. "I am not the woman ye . . . lost. Having me will not bring Tamar back."

"You are the very image of her. Tamar would be glad to see us together."

"She would not, knowing that I do not wish it."

He gave an impatient shake of his head. "You do not understand. You are mine now. You have no choice. And truly, there is nothing to fear. I will give you pleasure." His lips twisted. "And power. Power that flows from a desert land."

"Egypt."

"Yes."

Delay, Marcus had told her. She seized on the subject. "Tell me of that land. It is vast and dry, is it not?"

"Yes. The desert goes on and on, like a sea. A sea of sand and heat. The gods there are ancient, their powers vast. And for one who has learned their secrets, as I have—"

"Secrets of Deep Magic."

"Yes." He waved an arm. "I have gained the favor of a god—some call him a demon. Men know him as Apep. Ah, I see you cannot conceive of the power he has granted me. I will show you a taste of it."

He spoke a Word. A ball of Dark flame appeared in his right hand. As Gwen watched in horror, Strabo passed the flame over the bare skin of his forearms. Flesh puckered and burned, its stench assaulting her nostrils. Strabo's face was rigid with pain; his teeth clenched and beads of sweat stood out on his brow. "Apep," he said softly. "I am ready."

Gwen was aghast. What manner of Deep Magic was this?

She bit back a cry as the flame expanded, consuming his body until it burned like a hideous human torch. Then she blinked, as his outline shifted. Reformed. *Great Mother*. Strabo was a shifter, like herself. Like Rhys.

The flame burned out, leaving Gwen to gape at what Strabo had become—a beast far beyond Gwen's darkest nightmare. Twice as large as a man, its long, sinuous body glittered darkly, supported by thick, squat legs. Sharp, jagged teeth protruded from an elongated jaw. Dark wings, webbed like a bat's, unfurled from its back.

Its roar was like thunder. When it reared, tongues of fire shot from its mouth. She fought to keep her voice steady. "The beast . . . it cannot be real. It must be an illusion."

Abruptly, the creature collapsed in upon itself, reforming into the shape of a man. Strabo stood before her once more, obscenely calm and unruffled. His forearms, which she had seen hideously burned, were smooth and unmarred.

His white teeth flashed. "No illusion. My demon form is real. More real, perhaps, than my human form."

"What . . . what did ye become?"

"A son of the god Apep, who is the sworn enemy of the Egyptian sun god, Ra. Apep is the Darkest aspect of Deep Magic. His is a power that can never be defeated."

"He grants ye that form in return for your pain?"

"A small price to pay for the powers of Darkness and Deep Magic."

"And yet, ye have yet to smother Avalon's Light."

"Light." Strabo spat the word. "Cyric may shroud his sacred isle with Light, but eighteen years ago, he did not hesitate to call Darkness down upon his enemies. Upon me. He should have killed me along with Tamar. Since then, I have dreamed of nothing but Cyric groveling at my feet, begging for mercy that I do not grant him. I *will* destroy his loathsome mist. When I do, I will show him I have taken you as my own, in Tamar's place. And then, I will kill him."

Strabo reached out and grabbed a handful of her hair. Gwen stifled a scream as he yanked her down on the fur-strewn bed.

"Enough talk. You are mine. The sooner you understand that, the easier it will be. I will give you pleasure, that I promise you. And you will love me, as your mother did."

He pressed her into the cloud-soft mattress, aligning his body with hers. Gwen felt his arousal, hard and heavy on her thigh. How had Mama loved this man? Was it true what he said? That Cyric had killed Tamar?

Or was Strabo lying to gain Gwen's favor? Her senses filled with horror. She struggled to get free of him; he caught her arms and pinned them to the furs.

Panic clogged her throat. She closed her eyes and summoned the wolf. Her Deep Magic was dim, but present. She reached for it, only to have it recede into a blue-black fog. And Marcus? Where was he? She called for him with her mind. Strabo's magic flared, smothering her call.

His hips shifted. His shaft prodded, his knee forced her legs to part. Pure terror struck; Gwen twisted, gasping and kicking with all her strength. But all her strength was like nothing compared with his. When she realized her struggles only inflamed his lust further, she stilled.

He buried his face in her neck, inhaling deeply. "Ah, Tamar, how I've longed for you. How lonely these years have been without you."

"I am not my mother," Gwen whispered. "If ye truly loved her, ye would not do this."

"Hush, my sweet." He nibbled the corner of her mouth. His hand came up to cup her breast. "We will be together at last. I swear it."

Chapter Twenty-two

"No," a hard voice said. "You will not. Release her. Now."

Marcus! Gwen tensed. Strabo's head jerked up. Without moving even a fraction from Gwen's body, he glanced behind him.

Marcus stood with sword drawn and murder in his eyes. Rough and dirty and forbidding, he was an incongruous figure within Strabo's elegant garden bower illusion. More warrior than smith. With Exchalybur's tip trained on Strabo, he advanced.

Strabo laughed. Dark smoke began to seep from the ground. The mist rose quickly, partially obscuring Marcus behind a hazy veil. He slashed at the barrier. The sword struck it and rebounded as if the smoke were solid.

"Who is this man? No sorcerer, though his sword holds some slight magic. You are Roman, so I will be kind. Go now, and perhaps I will forget you were here."

Marcus's expression did not change. Twisting Exchalybur's angle slightly, he slashed again at the Dark mist. This time, the sword cleaved it in two, creating a clear path through Strabo's enchantment. "Get away from her. Now."

Strabo released Gwen's wrists and shoved himself off the mattress. Gwen scrambled backward. Her feet hit the ground on the opposite side of the bed just as two figures materialized behind Marcus. Rhys and Trevor, with Words of Light on their lips. White Light arced between them. Strabo's garden illusion cracked, then dissolved, running into the ground like muddy water. The edge of the swamp melted into view. The silken bed changed into a patch of moss.

Strabo threw back his head and laughed. "Do you think your spells of Light will stand against me? I can kill you where you stand. But for what purpose? I do not bear hatred for any of you." He addressed Rhys. "Especially you, Tamar's son. I only claim what is mine. This woman and Cyric's life. But know this: I *will* kill you if you persist in this folly."

Rhys and Trevor continued their chant as if the sorcerer had never spoken. Gwen recognized the spell they invoked—a powerful protection of Light. It beat back Strabo's Darkness; her own magic surged in response, suddenly free.

Strabo countered with a guttural Word. Gwen felt the evil even before the fire appeared in his palm. Dark flame consumed his body; his form began to change. The wolf, recognizing its enemy, rose on all fours, fur bristling. In the marrow of her bones, she felt the shift begin. In that moment Gwen understood she had no choice. The beast inside her would not be restrained. As the wolf, she could not wield the Lady's sword. The weapon would remain with its maker. Marcus.

His gaze swung to her. He felt the wolf, she realized,

even before it had emerged. "Gwen, no. You must take the sword."

She tore off her tunic, wrenched the pendant from about her neck. "Nay. The Lady's sword is yours. Use it, Marcus. Help me defeat him."

They were her last words before the wolf took possession of her body.

Marcus gripped Exchalybur. Magic swirled, Light mingling with Deep Magic and Darkness. How he was able to stand in the middle of it unscathed, he did not know. Did the sword protect him? Or was Rhys shielding him with Light? He did not know.

He could feel Gwen changing. She'd left the Lady's sword to him. He was no Druid; he did not have the magic to wield the sword. And yet, it seemed the duty had fallen to him.

The ground heaved under his feet. He shifted his stance. The scent of burning flesh filled the air. He blinked into a Dark mist, searching for Strabo. There.

Rhys's chant faltered. Trevor bit off a curse as Strabo laughed. The sorcerer held fire in his hands; as Marcus watched in disbelief, Strabo allowed the tongues of fire to consume his flesh. An unearthly sound emerged from his throat as his body went up in flames. His outline shifted and re-formed; black smoke thickened and folded back upon itself. Marcus blinked as it congealed into a creature with a snakelike body, squat legs, and a hideous, sharp-toothed snout.

He reached for Gwen with his mind. *"What is it?"*

"Strabo. In the shape of a demon of Egypt."

Flames spewed from the thing's mouth, blistering the air. Exchalybur vibrated. Marcus held it aloft; the bright iron absorbed the fire. The demon turned on Rhys and

Trevor; a Dark blast of fire issued from its mouth. The Druids' Light sputtered and died as black smoke enveloped them. When it cleared, they lay unmoving.

"Rhys!" Gwen's horror burst into Marcus's mind. He could not see the wolf; it was somewhere behind him. But he could feel her human agitation, merged with the panic of her animal mind.

"Steady," he told her.

She didn't reply.

The demon swung toward Marcus. Its eyes glowed red; its jaws gaped. As the monster charged, Marcus leaped to one side and swung his sword. Exchalybur connected with scaled skin. Thick black blood spurted forth. The impact nearly caused Marcus to drop the sword. Then it righted itself. The bright iron seemed almost . . . alive. As if it possessed intelligence of its own.

That intelligence hated its opponent with a rare and deadly zeal. It wanted to fling itself into the demon's jaw, and did not care if it took Marcus with it. Marcus fought with all his strength to keep the weapon under some semblance of control.

He swung about, anticipating the demon's next charge. But the thing hung back, circling slowly, swiping almost leisurely at its prey. Marcus met each attack with a slash from Exchalybur. Some blows missed, others struck deep, drawing blood. Marcus continued this course until he realized each injury seemed, paradoxically, to strengthen the demon.

With a flash of insight, he understood. Strabo was absorbing the Deep Magic of the Lady's sword, and making it his own. With an oath, Marcus retreated. There was no merit in fighting if his every blow only made his enemy stronger.

* * *

Rhys and Trevor lay prostrate; Marcus was faltering. Strabo's demon form was drawing power from Exchalybur. Gwen fought the terror welling in her human mind. Consciously, she allowed the wolf to take control. The animal was a creature of Deep Magic as much as Strabo's demon was. It could fight him, where Gwen's Light could not.

The demon's long neck twisted, its horrifying mouth spewing flames in Marcus's direction. He met it with Exchalybur's blade, absorbing the Dark fire. As he did, the demon seemed to grow larger. It reared back, gathering its strength; Gwen was sure its next blast would kill.

With feral strength, she leaped, skidding to a halt between Marcus and the beast. Ignoring his shout, she darted between the demon's heavy legs, evading one of its sharp talons by less than the length of her tail. Flames shot out, singing her fur.

Circling behind the beast, she attacked its limbs and tail. Marcus shouted a curse. Metal flashed above her head; Marcus had launched a mundane dagger at the demon. The blade sliced deeply into the demon's flank. Enraged, it swung around and swiped at Marcus, striking his chest. Crimson blood spread across his white shirt.

He staggered backward. Gwen's human mind blanked with sheer terror. He could not die. The wolf would not allow it.

Kill the demon.

She crouched, teeth bared, preparing for her attack.

"No, Gwen!" Marcus's shout rang in her ears. He leaped after her and grabbed the scruff of her neck.

"Let me go, Marcus! I can kill it. Ye cannot."

"Don't be so sure of that."

"How can ye fight it? The beast draws power from Exchalybur each time ye attack."

"But it weakens when you strike."

"Aye. That is why ye must let me fight it."

The demon went up on its hind legs.

"We can defeat it together," Marcus said urgently. *"You sent magic through me before, when we created the sword. Do it again. Now, Gwen. Through this mental link we've forged."*

She understood. Marcus wanted the wolf's Deep Magic to take control of Exchalybur, thereby preventing Strabo from absorbing the blade's magic. Would it work? She did not know.

She sent a Word of Deep Magic into Marcus's mind. Exchalybur flared, its power wild and unfocused. She summoned more Words, weaving a spell designed to bend the sword's Deep Magic to the will of Light.

Marcus struck at the beast. This time, the sword's power remained its own. Gwen felt Strabo's surprise, then his anger. He struck out, blasting Marcus with a stream of fire. Marcus countered the attack, absorbing the demon's breath on his blade.

"It's working, Gwen."

It was true. The power of the sword was once again hers. Hers and Marcus's. As the demon struck again, Gwen gathered each facet of the sword's power. Light Magic and Deep Magic. Protection and attack. Both forces were needed to win.

When the demon roared, Marcus went on the offensive, darting forward and slashing at its underbelly. Strabo countered with a blast of fire. Marcus staggered. The beast rose above him, wings beating, readying itself for a killing blow.

With an animal snarl, Gwen loosed her wildest, deepest magic. The force passed through her mind and into Marcus's. Blue-white fire erupted from Exchalybur. Strabo's darker blast faltered. The demon reared in fury, wings beating searing waves of air into Marcus's face. But Marcus did not waver.

He advanced through the hot storm, Exchalybur raised before him. The bright iron sang as it sliced the beast's belly. The demon let out a roar of rage and scuttled backward. Marcus struck again, nearly severing a squat foreleg. A third slash opened a gash in the demon's neck. Black fluid spurted. The creature's hind legs sank into the muck bordering the swamp.

Marcus struck a killing blow. The creature let out an unearthly squeal. Victory. Gwen could taste it. The demon teetered and fell into the murky water.

Deep Magic sang in Gwen's veins. Her wolf's body felt as though it were expanding, filling the universe. She felt like a goddess. A god. She could command life. Create death. The power was awesome, intoxicating.

The beast's death throes churned the black water. Gwen padded to the edge of the swamp. Strabo's Deep Magic was seeping into the earth—suddenly, Gwen realized the power did not have to disappear. She could take it for her own. Combined, the demon's power and the wolf's magic would be unsurpassed. No authority would be above her. Not Cyric, not Rhys, not Avalon's Elders. Not even the gods.

Exultant, she cast the spell that would make Strabo's powers hers.

"Gwen! Gods! What are you doing?"

Her head jerked toward Marcus. Exchalybur had gone wild in his hands. He fought to control it. The weapon had taken on a life of its own. The bright iron pulsed darkly, absorbing the demon's expiring Deep Magic. Black power ran the length of the blade and passed into Marcus's body.

He cried out. Gwen felt his pain, his fear. Great Mother! This was her doing. In fulfilling her greed, she'd abandoned every lesson Cyric had ever taught her. And she had not considered that her bid to absorb Strabo's Deep Magic would turn the Lady's sword against Marcus. Shame engulfed her.

Black sparks flew wildly. Marcus fell to his knees, grappling with the sword.

"*Get rid of it,*" Gwen screamed in his mind.

"*I can't. It . . . won't let me go.*"

Because Gwen had called the power to herself— through Marcus. Abruptly, she broke their mental contact. Marcus heaved the sword out over the swamp. It hurtled through the air, trailing blue and white stars behind it. It landed with a splash in the murky water, and quickly sank out of sight.

Marcus, relieved of his burden, wavered on his feet. A moment later, his legs gave way and he collapsed facedown in the mud.

Chapter Twenty-three

Gwen placed a paw on the man's shoulder. He did not move.

She tilted her head. His scent was familiar. Not an enemy. That much she knew.

Beyond that, nothing.

The edge of the swamp was silent. The battle that had taken place there was over. Her paws sank into the mud, too deeply. She did not like that. She scuttled onto firmer ground.

Two other men lay nearby, unmoving. Something nagged at the back of her mind. She should *care* about these men. Especially the fairer one. But that made no sense. They were human.

She was not.

She turned and loped into the forest, leaving them behind.

Marcus's lungs were bursting. He couldn't breathe.

Panic infused his limbs with sudden strength. He jerked himself out of the mud, somehow simultaneously sucking in air and gasping with pain. His hands were burnt, and his body felt as though it had been thoroughly pummeled by brigands.

He remembered striking the demon down at the edge of the swamp. He'd seen it fall; now, in place of its hideous body lay the bloated body of a man. Marcus staggered to it and kicked it over. Strabo. Dead.

When the beast fell, Exchalybur had erupted with deadly power. The bright iron had tried to absorb Strabo's Deep Magic. Because Gwen had commanded it.

Gwen. He jerked his head around. She was gone. But where?

A groan sounded. "Rhys!" Marcus lurched to his friend's side. By the time he reached him, Rhys was struggling into a sitting position.

"Are you hurt?" Marcus demanded.

Rhys winced. "Not permanently, I hope."

Marcus's gaze moved to Trevor. The Caledonian lay deathly still. His right arm was burnt, the skin charred black. Marcus felt Trevor's throat for the throb of his pulse. "Alive."

Rhys shook the big man's shoulders. "Trevor. Can ye hear me, man?"

Trevor groaned. "Aye," he said, his eyes opening. But he did not rise. "Strabo? The demon—?"

"Dead." With terse words, Marcus described the battle he and Gwen had fought, the sword's savage mutiny, how he'd awakened to find Gwen gone. "She could be hurt."

Rhys gained his feet. "She can't have gone far. We'll find her." He looked at Marcus. "Can ye . . . feel her?"

Marcus closed his eyes, searching his mind for Gwen's essence. It was there, but . . . he swallowed hard. "She is not in human form." He shot a look at Trevor. "You'd better get him back to Avalon. I'll go after Gwen." When Rhys hesitated, he added, "It's best if I confront the wolf alone."

Rhys nodded. Marcus helped him carry Trevor to a raft, then he returned to search for the wolf's tracks in the muddy ground. He followed Gwen's trail into the forest. She had run in circles, then veered uphill. He found her a short time later, crouching in a shallow cave. Her ears were flat, her tail down. When he tried to approach, she rose on all fours and bared her teeth. Her hackles rose. A low snarl vibrated in her throat.

Her eyes had gone completely feral. He reached for her with his mind. There was nothing human about her essence. Nothing human at all.

Gwen had become the wolf.

The big man made himself suddenly smaller, his legs bending beneath him. Crouching, he slowly extended one hand.

The wolf paused, uncertain whether the man represented danger. His scent was not comforting. It was human. Male. Humans—especially male humans—were not to be trusted.

She bared her teeth again, snarling. Took a warning step in his direction. The man did not waver. Did not turn and flee.

She smelled no fear. She didn't understand that, because even though the man was not afraid, he didn't challenge her. He stayed small, close to the ground, reaching out to her.

She did not know what to make of it.

She wanted him gone. If he did not flee, she would have to attack. She growled again. The man's only reaction was a softening about his eyes. That was good. It showed weakness.

She readied herself to pounce.

"Gwen."

The word was a soft whisper. Like wind. A human sound—she did not know what it meant. But it was . . . familiar.

She hesitated.

The man moved. Closer, not away. That was not good. She wanted him to leave. But he was creeping nearer. And nearer.

His head was still low. Lower than hers. That was confusing—if he meant to attack, he would rise.

She snarled, warning him away.

He gave no indication he understood.

"Gwen," he said again. "Come back to me. Please."

She did not understand the words, but they made her feel uncomfortable. Vulnerable. She didn't like them. Didn't like *him*. He wasn't like her. She had to drive him off. If she let him live, he would hurt her.

But she couldn't bring herself to spring. Not while his head was low. Not when he wasn't afraid. She should run. She couldn't. He was too close, and there was a solid wall of rock at her back. She'd been foolish to take refuge here.

His long legs started to unfold. His head rose. She wanted to pounce, but somehow she couldn't. His eyes were on her.

They were dark and . . . *safe*. But that made no sense. He was a man. Her enemy. His outstretched hand was coming closer. He wanted to touch her. She couldn't allow it. If she surrendered, she would never be free. She would never truly be wild.

She would belong to him, always.

"Gwen."

His face was very close to hers now. He'd bared his throat to her. He would not attack. It would be nothing to kill him. Nothing at all.

"Gwen." His urgency arrested her. His voice was hoarse, trembling with an emotion she did not understand. "I know you are not lost to the wolf. Not completely, or I would already be dead. Look inside, Gwen. Find yourself. Come back to me."

She cocked her head.

His beautiful eyes shimmered with moisture.

"Come back, Gwen. Love me. As I love you."

I love you.

The words touched something deep inside. The vibration touched a dark, hidden place—a part of her soul she hardly knew.

Love.

What was love? Did she know? She thought perhaps she *had* known . . . once.

"Love me, Gwen." His voice broke on the words. Water ran down his face.

She did not like that. She went to him. Nuzzled his hand. Licked his cheek. His arms came around her, pulling her to him, clutching her tightly to his chest. Trapping her. She should have been afraid. Enraged. Panicked. She was not. His big body heaved, his shoulders shook. His grief flooded into her mind.

She wanted his pain to stop. *She* could stop it.

A Word formed in her mind. A Word of Light. A Word that meant . . . surrender. A Word the wolf hated.

And yet, she let it come. Because somehow, she knew it would bring her back to *him*.

Chapter Twenty-four

Gwen woke in Marcus's arms. She was naked, and he was crying.

For a long moment, she couldn't find her voice. He wasn't trying to hide his tears, or wipe them away. The emotion in his eyes was so deep, so true. She was truly humbled.

She reached up and wiped a tear from his cheek with her thumb. Catching her hand, he shut his eyes and pressed his lips to her palm.

"Gods, Gwen. I thought I'd lost you."

"I'm not so easily put aside," she said shakily.

"I thank the Great Mother for that. Are you hurt?"

"Nay. I do not think so." She moved slightly in his arms and he winced.

"Your wound!" His shirt gaped open; blood was crusted on the angry gash left by the demon's claws. "And your hands are burned. Strabo's fire—"

"It's nothing." He exhaled and shook his head, as if to clear the horror from it. "What was that thing Strabo turned into? I wouldn't have believed it was real if it hadn't been trying so hard to kill me."

"A Dark god. Strabo traded his pain for its foul magic."

"It wasn't equal to the power of Exchalybur."

She shuddered. "The Lady's sword . . . I am not sure I should have asked ye to forge it, Marcus. I almost lost myself to its power."

"If we hadn't forged it, we would most likely be dead. And Rhys and Trevor, as well."

"And Cyric. My grandfather is the one Strabo wanted."

"So Rhys said. But I don't completely understand. Why come after Cyric after all these years? Strabo killed your mother long ago."

Gwen was silent for a moment. "I do not think Strabo killed her, Marcus. He claimed he did not. He may truly have loved her, when he was young and capable of that emotion. He told me it was Cyric's Deep Magic that killed Mama. My grandfather tried to kill Strabo, but struck Mama instead."

Marcus swore. "Do you believe that?"

"Aye. I think I do. It explains much about my grandfather's refusal to talk of the past, and his abiding hatred for Deep Magic. Strabo vowed vengeance—it took him eighteen years to return to Britain to enact it. He meant to kill Cyric and take me as wife in Mama's place."

"He may have been wronged all those years ago," Marcus said. "But I cannot say I am sorry he is dead now. The man was mad."

"He was lost in Deep Magic. As I very nearly was. Until ye came for me. Until ye called me back."

"I will always come for you. The wolf will never take you away from me."

She did not answer. He stood and helped her to her

feet. "You can hardly return to Avalon unclothed," he muttered. "I'd offer you my shirt, but—" He spread his arms. His shirt was little more than bloody rags.

"We should be able to find my tunic. And my pendant."

They returned to the site of the battle. Gwen dressed, shuddering when her gaze fell on Strabo's charred and bloated body. "Rhys and Trevor," she asked shakily. "They are both unharmed?"

"Rhys is well enough. Trevor took the brunt of Strabo's assault. He was barely conscious when Rhys and I carried him to the raft. Rhys took him to Avalon."

Gwen gave a cry of dismay. "Trevor cannot die because of me! I must go to him at once."

Marcus stiffened. "Of course. I'll take you to him."

Rhys's stomach churned as Mared straightened from Trevor's pallet. "How bad is he?"

"He sleeps," the old healer replied. "His wound is clean, and the Deep Magic that touched his soul did not enter. He is strong. He will live."

"Thank the Great Mother," Rhys said. He looked up. "And Clara's babe—?"

Mared laid a hand on his shoulder. "A fine little lad, who is at his mother's breast this moment. But 'tis not Trevor and Clara ye should worry over, Rhys. 'Tis Cyric. He has not stirred from his pallet since he tried to kill Marcus Aquila."

"But surely he will recover now that Strabo is dead."

Mared shook her head. "I do not believe he will. The past weighs too heavily on him. Losing your mother was a blow from which your grandfather never recovered. Strabo's magic has brought too much of that time back."

Rhys ran a hand down his face. "What happened that night, Mared? I remember so little. Gwen and I . . . we were there, I think, when Strabo cast his spell."

"Padrig and I know little more than ye do," the healer replied. "Tamar had taken ye and Gwen. When Cyric realized she'd gone to her Roman lover, he went after her. He returned carrying her body. We buried her and fled that same night—we were afraid soldiers would kick down the door by morning. We came to Avalon and dedicated our lives to the Light and the teachings of the Lady. But Cyric . . . for all his talk of forgiveness and comfort, he never knew peace after that night. A part of his soul has remained untouched by the Lady's Light. That Darkness consumes him now."

"Where is he?"

"We have carried him to the high slope, to await the Great Mother's call near the stone that marks the entrance to Annwyn. It will not be long now."

When Rhys ascended the hill and set eyes upon his grandfather, he knew Mared had spoken the truth. Cyric's countenance was as waxen as that of a corpse. He slept fitfully, muttering in his sleep. Death would not be long in coming.

Mared and Eleri, who had been watching Cyric, slipped away. Not willing to disturb his grandfather's sleep, however troubled, Rhys lowered his aching body to the ground by Cyric's pallet, and waited.

He was still sitting motionless some time later when Gwen appeared, tired and wary, but whole and— thank the Goddess—*human*. Her gaze went immediately to Cyric. "He lives still?"

"For now." He stood. "Ye are unharmed?"

"Thanks to Marcus."

"He is here? In the village?"

"Aye. Your mist did not prevent his approach."

"Cyric's mist did not keep him from Avalon before, when he came here seeking help to rescue you from Strabo."

"How is that possible?"

"Perhaps it had to do with the sword."

"The sword is gone now," Gwen pointed out. "But the connection Marcus and I created in forging it remains. I feel and hear him in my mind."

"But now you do not hear me."

Gwen's eyes were infinitely sad. "Aye. It would seem so, brother."

He clasped her hands. "It was the blow from Cyric's staff that severed our connection, I think. Not Strabo's magic. Now the place I once occupied in your mind and in your heart has been filled by Marcus. I will miss ye, Gwen."

She did not blink back her tears. "Ah, Rhys. Ye will be in my heart always. That will never change. But I need to know . . . why did ye never tell me ye had shifted?"

He studied their joined hands. Why, indeed? "I was too proud," he said at last. "I've always envied ye, Gwen. I used my righteousness to hold myself above ye. It was wrong of me. I hurt ye deeply." He met her gaze. "Can ye forgive me?"

"Oh, Rhys." She was crying in earnest now. "How can I not? Ye are a part of me. The better part of me."

"Not better, Gwen. Our strengths are different, that is all."

She smiled through her tears. "Perhaps that is true. After all, a wolf could make a short meal of a falcon."

Rhys flashed her a grin. "If she could catch him."

He embraced her then. Gwen clutched his neck fiercely for a moment before drawing away. "There's something ye should know, Rhys."

He searched her gaze. "I think I already do know it. Ye do not intend to stay in Avalon."

"Aye. I want to be with Marcus. And ye—ye want to be here, I know ye do. Ye can hold the mist as well as I. If we exchange roles, we will both be happier."

Rhys shot a troubled look toward Cyric, who had begun to mutter in his sleep, almost as if in protest of Gwen's declaration. "Is that what ye truly want?"

"More than anything, Rhys. And I will visit often. If ye wish to leave the sacred isle, ye have only to send for me."

It was the life he'd always dreamed of, during eleven long years of roaming. "But Cyric—"

Gwen's expression grew sober. Her voice was low. "There is something ye should know, Rhys, about the night Mama died. Something I've only just—"

A deep moan cut off her words. Rhys and Gwen both started; an instant later they were kneeling on either side of Cyric's pallet. Gwen took her grandfather's hand.

"So cold," she whispered.

Cyric's thin breath rattled in his lungs. His eyes opened. They were weary and rimmed with red, but lucid.

"I am sorry. So sorry, my children."

Gwen leaned close and placed a kiss on Cyric's forehead. "Ye have grieved for so long. Have ye not always preached the wisdom of forgiveness? 'Tis time to forgive yourself."

Rhys's brow furrowed.

Cyric clutched at Gwen's hand. "Ye know."

"Aye."

The old man's shoulders shook as tears spilled from his eyes. "I did not mean for it to happen. I wanted only to keep her by my side. I wanted to kill *him*. Not her. Never *her*. My child, my light."

Horror seeped into Rhys's brain. "Ye killed Mama?" His gaze cut to Gwen. "Ye knew this."

"Strabo told me," she whispered. "I did not want to believe it either, but . . . now I know for certain."

Cyric covered his eyes, his hand shaking. "Aye, 'tis true. The Deep Magic I called to drive back Strabo . . . it went away. I tried to call it back—I could not." He shuddered. "Deep Magic. Power of the gods. No human can control it. No human should try. Remember that always, my children."

Rhys felt as though the earth beneath his feet had fallen away. He struggled to find some sense of balance. He opened his mouth to ask Cyric more, but Gwen caught his gaze and shook her head. Rhys shut his mouth. It would do no good to question Cyric. Not now.

Gwen's voice was low and soothing. "Ye carried this guilt so long, Grandfather. Ye must let it go now. Be at peace."

"Ah, peace. I think . . . aye, I think 'tis close. It will come with death. 'Tis time, Gwendolyn. Soon. I hear the Great Mother's call." His chest rose and fell with a wheezing sound. "When I am gone, carry out your duties. Guard Avalon as I have taught ye. The mist will protect the sacred isle as long as ye are here."

Gwen exchanged a glance with Rhys. "Grandfather . . . I cannot make that promise. I wish to leave. To marry elsewhere. Rhys has agreed to hold the mist in my place."

Cyric's gaze swung wildly to Rhys. His bony hand

clutched Rhys's arm as the old man struggled to rise. "Nay, Rhys! Ye cannot. That is not your role! Ye must never stop seeking those touched by magic. There is no other way!"

A fit of coughing overtook him. Alarmed, Rhys eased Cyric back onto the cushions. "Rest, Grandfather. We will speak of this later."

"Nay—" He broke off, gasping for breath. "I know . . . I know ye do not understand. I know ye both feel the weight of your burdens. Many times have I asked the Great Mother if her will could not be served another way. The answer is always the same. If Avalon is to live, if the Light of the sacred isle is to nurture the King who is to come, then the Son and Daughter of the Lady must fulfill the roles the Goddess has revealed to me. If ye do not . . ." Another fit overtook him.

Gwen hastened to fill a cup with water. Rhys supported Cyric's thin shoulders and pressed the rim to the old man's parched lips. He took but a sip, then waved the cup away.

He took Gwen's hand in his left, Rhys's in his right. "Listen well, my children, for this I have Seen many times, in visions the Great Mother has sent to me since your birth. Her will is clear. The Daughter must stay, the Son must roam. Only then will the King be born. Only then will the King call Light to battle Darkness. If he does not . . . Britain will be lost. The world will be lost.

"Ye two . . . ye have so much Light inside. Ye must fight against Dark Magic, always. Ye must fulfill your duty as I have taught ye. There is no other way."

"Grandfather—" Rhys began.

Cyric's grip closed painfully on Rhys's fingers. "Promise me, Rhys. Gwen."

Rhys was never quite sure what happened in the

next instant. Cyric's voice rose. His infirmity seemed to fall away. His voice strengthened, his bleary eyes cleared. Light lit his features, making his white hair and beard glow with ethereal radiance. Magic filled the air, causing Rhys's skin to prickle.

"You promised your obedience to me long ago," Cyric rasped. "I will have those promises again. Gwen, ye will hold the mist. Rhys, ye will seek outside it. 'Tis the only way. *The only way.*"

White Light shimmered about Cyric's head and shoulders. It flowed from Cyric to Rhys and Gwen, enveloping all three in a nimbus of deep, unearthly power. The flash of a vision appeared—a man, a king, clothed in Light. Astride a tall horse, the man surveyed a peaceful, fertile countryside. Another flash, and Rhys saw the same countryside cloaked in Darkness, fields burned, cottages laid to waste. And in that instant Rhys knew—*knew,* in the marrow of his bones—that Cyric spoke the truth.

There *was* no other way.

Something inside him broke.

He would never call Avalon home. And Gwen—He met his sister's gaze and his heart twisted. She understood as well as he did. And her anguish was even greater.

"Promise me, my children," Cyric begged.

"Aye, Grandfather," Gwen whispered. "We promise."

And so Rhys's future, and Gwen's, slipped into place.

Chapter Twenty-five

"Will you be leaving soon, then, Marcus?"

"On the morrow," Marcus told Clara. "Now that Cyric is buried and Gwen has assumed the role of Guardian, I have little choice." He still could not quite believe it. When he'd brought Gwen back to Avalon after the wolf had released her, he'd been sure she was his. Then she'd disappeared with Rhys to the high slope of Avalon, where Cyric lay dying. Two days later, when she finally returned to the village, after Cyric had breathed his last, she had told Marcus in calm tones that she would not marry him.

She had not shed so much as a tear. And since that moment, Marcus had not heard her thoughts in his mind, and she had not answered his unspoken questions. But Marcus was not fooled by Gwen's silence. He knew that behind her stoic facade, she was breaking.

It had been left to Rhys to explain Cyric's vision to Marcus. And after he had, Marcus had seen clearly enough that Gwen truly had no choice but the one she had made.

Cold comfort, that.

Clara's dark eyes told him she understood his grief. She looked so peaceful, nestled in a bed of furs, nursing her infant son. The babe's fuzzy red head—his hair was exactly the color of his father's—was just visible amid the swath of blankets. A new life, so small and innocent.

Marcus felt something clutch in his chest. Gwen would never hold his child at her breast. Not now. He shut his eyes briefly against the pain the realization brought.

"Marcus? Are you all right?"

He opened his eyes. "Yes, of course. But what about you? Owein said you had a rough time of it."

Clara laughed. "I fear Neill's birth was far more difficult on his father than on me. Mared assured me my son came quickly, though during my labor I confess I didn't think he would ever arrive. But once I held him in my arms, I forgot all about the pain."

Marcus forced a smile. "Rhiannon will want to see him, of course. Her own babe will come in a few short months."

"Owein and I will make the journey as soon as I'm able." She gave a sigh of anticipation. "I cannot wait. I've been dreaming of a real bathhouse, Marcus. As soon as I get to the farm, I'm going to sink into the *calidarium* up to my neck and stay there half the day. Here on Avalon, I'm lucky if I get a whole bucket of hot water to myself."

"I'll be sure I have a good supply of charcoal waiting for you," Marcus said. Then he frowned. "But I don't see why things should be so primitive here. The flow from the spring is very good. It would be a relatively simple thing to divert some of the water to a cistern, and build a simple hypocaust and bathhouse nearby."

Clara laughed. "Surely you jest."

"No. I'm serious. Has no one ever considered it?"

She shook her head. "I don't believe that they have."

"I don't understand these Celts," Marcus muttered. "It's as if they *want* to be uncomfortable."

"They are simple people, Marcus. Farmers and former slaves. And the settlement is so small. There is no one here with the knowledge and experience needed to build a bathhouse." She sent him a pointed look. "Except you, of course."

He started. "You think I should build a bathhouse for Avalon?"

"Yes. And stay afterward."

"Stay?"

Clara stroked her baby's cheek. The skin looked so fragile. The babe sighed and released her breast, milk trickling from the corner of its rosebud mouth. Clara shifted him to her other breast and rearranged her blankets.

She looked up at Marcus. "Yes, my thick-skulled friend, *stay*. You don't have to leave Avalon. You could make your home here. With Gwen."

Marcus stood and ran a hand over his head. "But—I am Roman."

"So am I."

"It's not the same. You're a Daughter of the Lady. I have no magic." Other than his mental connection to Gwen, which she would not acknowledge.

"You found the sacred isle through the mist. You followed Gwen from Isca despite the spells she'd laid on her trail. You forged a magic sword and used it to fight Cyric's and Strabo's Deep Magic. You reached Gwen when she was all but lost in her wolf form—more than once. Are you sure you have no magic, Marcus? Because it seems to me that the talent of thwarting magic is as powerful as the talent of calling it."

Magic that thwarted magic? Marcus tried to wrap his mind around the notion. "How could that be? I come from mundane parents."

"That's another thing I'm not so sure about. Gwen tells me Breena's power is vast—even greater than Gwen's own. How can that be, if magic only flows on one side of her parentage?"

"You think my *father* has magic? That is absurd."

"Not Lucius himself, perhaps. But his family line? Yes, I think it's very likely there is magic there."

The thought was stunning. "Perhaps there is something to what you suggest, but, Clara, it hardly changes things. How can I stay here? I'm needed at home. My father and Rhiannon—"

"They would understand, Marcus. That much I know without a doubt."

"But . . . live *here?* On an island in the swamps? In a dirt-floored hut? Choking on peat smoke? Cut off from civilization?"

"It's not so bad. I've found that love more than makes up for a lack of luxuries. Though I confess, I have a selfish reason for wanting you to stay."

Marcus gave her a blank look. "What is that?"

Clara laughed. "That *bathhouse,* Marcus. If you stay, you can build it."

Live here, on Avalon?

Marcus surveyed a Druid roundhouse with a critical eye, mentally mapping the changes he would make before he even considered living in such a structure. A stone floor to replace the dirt, at the very least. A sleeping chamber separate from the living area. A flue, so he wouldn't spend the winter choking on smoke. More comfortable furniture.

A bathhouse near the spring. That was a certainty. And a building that housed a proper kitchen. And perhaps a small forge . . .

Excitement kicked in. It could work. He would *make* it work. He would live here, with Gwen, loving her day and night, watching her grow round with his children. And when Breena finally came to Avalon—and he'd come to believe it was inevitable that she would—he would be here to watch over her. Perhaps he would even build her a library.

He spotted Owein. "Have you seen Gwen?"

The big warrior raised his brows at the smile on Marcus's face. "By the Grail spring, I think. On the far side of the island."

He hurried in the direction Owein had indicated. Clara had told him of the red-tinged spring that flowed from the spot where she and Owein had lost the Lady's Grail the year before. It was a place of power now, where the Druids often gathered to pray, either in groups or singly.

He almost shouted out when he caught a glimpse of Gwen's white-blond hair. The greeting died in his throat. She was not alone.

Trevor was with her.

The Caledonian's large body was supported by a stout walking stick. His burned arm was bandaged with strips of wool. He and Gwen were deep in conversation; neither heard Marcus's approach.

Marcus cleared his throat. Gwen's head jerked up. Something like pain crossed her expression. Trevor, as always, was impassive. He greeted Marcus with supreme calm.

"Well met, Marcus. I am glad to have the chance to speak with ye before ye depart. I didna yet thank ye for your aid. All of Avalon is in your debt."

A polite and deferential speech. Why did Marcus have the urge to smash his fist into the man's face?

"I would speak with Gwen alone," was all he said.

Trevor nodded and left without another word. Marcus scowled at the Caledonian's retreating back. "That man is far too tranquil. It's not natural."

Gwen sighed. "Aye. But he is a good man."

"So I've heard," Marcus muttered. He eyed Gwen, but she kept her gaze averted, watching the place where Trevor had stood a moment before as if he were still there.

Marcus moved into her line of vision. "Is it so hard to look at me?"

She raised her gaze. Her gray eyes were carefully devoid of emotion. "I thought ye would be gone by now."

"And so you were making wedding plans with Trevor?"

"Nay!" The flash of deep hurt he saw in her eyes abruptly deflated his jealousy. "Nay. We were but talking. I promised ye Marcus, that I would never lie with another man. And I will not. Even if I never see ye past this day."

"What of the Daughter you are expected to bear for Avalon? And who will be Guardian after you, if not your child?"

"Clara and Rhys will have to see to those duties, for I will not."

He moved behind her and placed his hands on her shoulders. "You can. I'll be happy to give you any number of children."

She stiffened under his touch. "Oh, Marcus, do not jest with me. Not now. I cannot bear it."

He smoothed her braid to one side and placed a kiss on her neck, just below her ear. Her breath caught and a shiver ran through her body. When she spoke, he heard the tears in her voice. "Marcus . . ."

"I love you, Gwen. I love you and I want to be with you."

"You know that is impossible. I cannot be a wife to ye. My duty is here, on Avalon."

He wrapped his arms around her, pulling her tight against his body, her back to his chest. "Then I'll stay here with you."

He felt her astonishment. Her disbelief. She tried to turn to face him; he did not let her.

"Ye cannot be serious."

He smiled against her hair. "Why not?"

"Ye are Roman! Roman men do not run after their women. They expect their wives to—"

"To what? Abandon their people? Warm their beds? Use their hands and mouth to—" He dipped his head and whispered in her ear.

She nearly choked on a cross between a sob and a laugh. "Marcus, what are ye telling me?"

"That you are mine. But that shouldn't be such a surprise. I told you that before, more than once. I seem to remember that you agreed."

"Of course I did."

She tried to turn; he still wouldn't let her. His hands rose to cup her breasts as he caught her earlobe between his teeth.

"Say it, then." He swirled his tongue into her ear.

She bit back a moan. "I am yours, Marcus."

"Now tell me that you'll be my wife."

"Marcus," she whispered. "I can hardly believe ye mean it."

He let her turn in his arms. "I do."

She linked her hands behind his neck as he smiled down at her. Her expression was slightly dazed. "It is really true? Ye mean to stay?"

"Yes."

"But—how can that be? Ye cannot be blind to how primitive the village is."

"You're here, and that's enough for me. Besides," he added with a shrug, "Avalon is only primitive because no one has improved it. I can remedy that. Sturdier homes, better cooking facilities, a bathhouse . . ."

Gwen could only shake her head. "But . . . what of Rhiannon and Lucius? They need you in Isca—"

He silenced her with a long, deep kiss. "They will understand," he said quietly when he at last allowed her to catch her breath. "And Isca is not so far away. I can visit often enough, and if Rhys agrees to hold the mist from time to time, you can as well. Or they can come here. Breena certainly will, for I've come to accept she needs you and Avalon to help her understand her power. And now I'll be here to watch over her."

"But the wolf—"

"I told you before, the wolf will never harm me. Nor will it take you away from me."

"When ye say that, Marcus, I begin to believe it." Tears gathered in Gwen's eyes. "Ye would do this . . . change your entire life . . . for *me?*"

"Gwen. I'd *die* for you. Changing my life—living here on Avalon—that is no hardship." He kissed her again. "And so I'll ask you again. And again. Until you run out of protests. Will you have me? Will you be my wife?"

She started crying in earnest then, but she was

laughing through her tears. "Oh aye, Marcus Aquila, I will have you. Forever."

"Good," he said. "Because I intend to love you at least that long."

Epilogue

Laughter and merriment drifted down the hill to Avalon's dock, where Rhys sat alone in the dark. With Cyric gone these three moons, Gwen had asked her twin to bless her handfasting with Marcus. Rhys had agreed, of course. But it had been hard—harder than he had imagined—to give his sister to his best friend.

Gwen had been a beautiful bride. The smile she'd given Rhys when he'd bound her left hand to Marcus's right had gone straight to his heart. It was still there, transformed into an ache that would not go away. He could no longer hear Gwen in his mind. Even though they hadn't used the link very much as adults, Rhys hadn't realized how much it still meant to him. Its loss cut him deeply.

Gwen was Marcus's now. She would remain on Avalon and bear a Daughter, as Cyric had wanted. She was truly happy for the first time in her life. And Rhys was very glad for that. But he could not help feeling sorry for himself. A weakness in his character, he supposed.

His self-pity had not been helped by the sight of Owein's arms around Clara, who held little Neill in her arms. Nor the presence of Lucius and Rhiannon and their healthy, squalling infant son, who had arrived some weeks early but did not seem the worse for it. Breena had stood at her mother's side, dressed in a flowing green tunic with gold sleeve pins, flowers entwined in her brilliant red hair. She had not spoken to him—had barely glanced at him—since she'd arrived on Avalon. When she'd smiled up at young Penn, and laughed at something the lad whispered in her ear, Rhys felt as though someone had punched him in the gut. Penn was just a summer or two older than Breena. They made a fine pair, and had struck up an immediate, easy friendship. Which was all to the good, because when Rhiannon and Lucius returned to Isca, Breena would stay on Avalon. If she formed an attachment with Penn . . .

He did not want to think on it.

As the marriage feast progressed, Rhys's awkwardness only increased. How was it that he did not know how to act with the very people he'd brought to Avalon from all over Britain? They were a clan now. The children he'd rescued from squalor and neglect were growing tall and happy. The men and women were strengthening in Light every day. They loved him, he knew. But he did not feel as though he were a part of them.

After the feast, he'd played his harp, sung his songs, and watched the others pair off for dancing. When he was finally able to escape, he breathed a sigh of relief.

Perhaps he was not meant to belong.

He stared out over the swamp. The Roman mining camp was gone. Gwen's renewed protections on the

Druid mine had convinced Tribune Valgus that the silver he'd hoped to find was a myth. Once Strabo's body had been found, and news of his drowning had circulated among the soldiers, Valgus had ordered his men to dismantle the camp and return to Isca.

Black water disappeared into silver mist. Exchalybur lay somewhere beneath the ripples the night wind painted on the water's surface. Like the Grail, its power was veiled, but not gone. He could feel the sword's Deep Magic—tempered by its Light—bolstering Gwen's mist. The sword indeed protected Avalon, as she had envisioned. And as long as it remained hidden, no Druids would succumb to the temptation to take its Deep Magic for their own glory.

And so Rhys would not have to worry about those he loved while he was gone. Summer was waning; he meant to leave at dawn. Another day watching Breena flit about like a butterfly newly emerged from its chrysalis would surely kill him.

Picking up his harp, he plucked one of the strings. The note floated over the water, its plaintive tone spreading until it was too thin to hear. Was he to be like that note? Spread thin across Britain until he lost his own voice, his own desires? His own soul?

He meant to travel north again, perhaps even beyond the Great Wall and into Caledonia. Or across the water to the green isle of Hibernia. The journey would occupy him until next spring. Perhaps his melancholy would disappear by then.

The singing and laughter in the village subsided. No doubt the newly wedded couple, their hands still bound, had sought their bed. Rhys would do well to seek his own rest. He stood slowly, reluctant to retrace his steps to the village.

A light on the water's surface caught his attention.

A traveler, approaching Avalon through the mist? That just could not be. Frowning, Rhys paced to the water's edge and peered out into the night. There seemed to be a boat of some sort on the water. A woman was seated in the craft, surrounded by a nimbus of Light. Rhys strained his eyes, but he could not make out her features.

A Druid? Or a vision of the Lady? Rhys held himself still as the craft glided to a halt. The woman stretched her hand over the water, then her head lifted and she looked directly at Rhys.

There was something familiar about her, but Rhys could not grasp what it was. He lifted a hand and prepared to shout a greeting. The words died on his lips.

The boat and the woman had vanished.

But perhaps . . . not completely. The touch of her Light lingered in his heart; the dark melancholy of moments before had evaporated. Aye, he would leave his home once again, but his journey would someday bring him back.

To love.

He was sure of it.

Author's Note

I hope you've enjoyed *Deep Magic*, my small contribution to the vast amount of literature concerning the magical sword Excalibur. As is true of most Arthurian tales, I've woven a tapestry of historical fact and legend, combined with my own imagination.

The sacred isle of the Druids of Avalon is modern-day Glastonbury, England, believed by many to be the Avalon of legend. Today the Tor of Glastonbury rises above flat, fertile farmland, but in ancient times the sea level was higher, and the area surrounding the distinctive hill was swampland. Remains of ancient Celt settlements have been found nearby. Though no evidence of extensive settlement has been excavated on Avalon itself, I'm hopeful the evidence lies buried below the ruins of an early Christian monastery. The area was definitely a place of power for Celtic peoples. The red-tinted waters of the spring known as the Chalice Well were originally revered by worshipers of the Celtic mother goddess, a devotion that has been renewed in modern times.

A druid learning center much larger than the one I've envisioned for Avalon existed on the island of Anglesey (known in ancient times as Mona), off the north coast of Wales. It is true, as Marcus stated, that Celt resistance to Roman occupation, supported by the Celt priests known as druids, resulted in druidry being declared illegal by the Roman authorities around 60 CE. Druid learning centers, most famously the one on Mona, were brutally destroyed by the Roman army. If there had been a similar settlement on Avalon at the time, I'm sure it would have met the same terrible fate.

The Roman city of Isca Silurum, one of the three largest fortress cities in Roman Britain, is now the town of Caerleon, Wales. Extensive remains of the Roman fortress and amphitheater can be seen there. The fortress was the home base of the Second Legion for many years; however, Titus Strabo is my own invention.

Chalybs is the Latin word for steel, named after an Anatolian tribe famous for its ironwork. Though Roman swords containing some percentages of steel have been discovered, steel was never manufactured on a large scale by the Romans. The high temperatures needed were too difficult to sustain for long periods of time. At least by mundane methods! With magic, of course, anything is possible.

In the first book in the Druids of Avalon series, *The Grail King*, Owein and Clara form an uneasy alliance during the search for a Druid grail bound to dangerous Deep Magic. A "prequel" to the series, *Celtic Fire*, tells Lucius and Rhiannon's story. Both books are available and can be ordered through your favorite bookstores. The next Druids of Avalon book, *Silver Silence*, belongs to Rhys and Breena. Breena will finally learn the meaning of her terrifying visions and fight to win the man she's loved all her life.

Check my Web site, www.joynash.com, for updates and special features, such as character interviews and free short stories set in the Druids of Avalon world.

And, as always, thank you for reading!

Joy Nash

ENCHANTING THE LADY

In a world where magic ruled everything, Felicity Seymour couldn't perform even the simplest spell. If she didn't pass her testing, she'd lose her duchy—and any hope of marriage. But one man didn't seem to mind her lack of dowry: a darkly delicious baronet who had managed to scare away the rest of London's Society misses.

❦

Sir Terence Blackwell knew the enchanting woman before him wasn't entirely without magic. Not only could she completely disarm him with her gorgeous lavender eyes and frank candor, but his were-lion senses could smell a dark power on her—the same kind of relic-magic that had killed his brother. Was she using it herself, or was it being used against her?

❦

One needed a husband, and the other needed answers. But only together could they find the strongest magic of all: true

KATHRYNE KENNEDY

ISBN 13: 978-0-505-52750-9

JENNIFER ASHLEY

Egan MacDonald was the one person Princess Zarabeth couldn't read. Yet even without being able hear his thoughts, she knew he was the most honorable, infuriating, and deliciously handsome man she'd ever met. And now her life was in his hands. Chased out of her native country by bitter betrayal and a bevy of assassins, Zarabeth found refuge at the remote MacDonald castle and a haven in Egan's embrace. She also found an ancient curse, a matchmaking nephew, a pair of debutants eager to drag her protector to the altar, and dark secrets in Egan's past. But even amid all the danger raged a desire too powerful to be denied....

Highlander Ever After

AVAILABLE APRIL 2008!

ISBN 13: 978-0-8439-6004-4